Award-winning author **Jennifer Faye** pens fun, heart-warming, contemporary romances, filled with rugged cowboys, sexy billionaires and enchanting royalty. Internationally published, with books translated into nine languages, she is a two-time winner of the *RT Book Reviews* Reviewers' Choice Award. She has also won the *CataRomance* Reviewers' Choice Award, been named a TOP PICK author, and has been nominated for numerous other awards.

Christy Jeffries graduated from the University of California, Irvine, with a degree in criminology, and received her Juris Doctor from California Western School of Law. But drafting court documents and working in law enforcement was merely an apprenticeship for her current career in the dynamic field of mummyhood and romance writing. She lives in Southern California with her patient husband, two energetic sons and one sassy grandmother. Follow her online at christyjeffries.com.

Also by Jennifer Faye

Once Upon a Fairytale miniseries
Beauty and Her Boss
Miss White and the Seventh Heir

Also by Christy Jeffries

A Proposal for the Officer
A Family Under the Stars
The Makeover Prescription
The Matchmaking Twins
From Dare to Due Date
Waking Up Wed
A Marine for His Mom
The Maverick's Bridal Bargain

Discover more at millsandboon.co.uk

HEIRESS'S ROYAL BABY BOMBSHELL

JENNIFER FAYE

THE MAVERICK'S CHRISTMAS TO REMEMBER

CHRISTY JEFFRIES

MILLS & BOON

First Published in Great Britain 2018
by Mills & Boon, an imprint of HarperCollinsPublishers,
1 London Bridge Street, London, SE1 9GF

Heiress's Royal Baby Bombshell © 2018 Harlequin Books S.A.
The Maverick's Christmas to Remember © 2018 Harlequin Books S.A.

Special thanks and acknowledgement are given to Jennifer Faye for her contribution to the *The Cattaneos' Christmas Miracles* series.

Special thanks and acknowledgement are given to
Christy Jeffries for her contribution to the *Montana Mavericks: The Lonelyhearts Ranch* continuity.

ISBN: 978-0-263-26540-8

1118

MIX
Paper from
responsible sources
FSC™ C007454

HEIRESS'S ROYAL
BABY BOMBSHELL

JENNIFER FAYE

PROLOGUE

Mid-August, Milan, Italy

A CASUAL PARTY full of joy and hope for the future was just what she needed.

It was her chance to forget that her opinions were unwanted and disregarded. That acknowledgment sliced deep into her heart. But she refused to become a silent shadow in her own family.

Noemi Cattaneo, heiress to the Cattaneo Jewels dynasty, welcomed the loud music and the sound of laughter. After yet another argument with her older brother, Sebastian, she needed space. She took a drink from her second glass of pink champagne. When was he ever going to treat her like an adult instead of his kid sister and realize that her opinions had merit?

She took another sip of bubbly, hoping to cool off her rising temper. Every time she recalled her brother saying that being a *silent partner* suited her, frustration bubbled within her. How dare he tell her to stick to modeling! There was more to her than her looks—a lot more. And she refused to spend the evening worrying about her brother.

Someone bumped into her. The champagne sloshed over the edge of the glass and onto Noemi's new white dress. She glanced down at the pink stain starting at her chest and streaking down to her midsection.

She might need to cool off, but this wasn't how she'd intended to do it. Noemi's gaze lifted as she looked around for the klutz who'd bumped into her, but she couldn't pinpoint the culprit. They hadn't hung around to express their regret. Maybe coming to this engagement party hadn't been such a good idea.

She searched the crowd for Stephania, her friend who'd convinced her to come to the party. As Noemi's gaze scanned the room, it strayed across a man with mysterious hazel eyes. He was standing across the room surrounded by a half dozen eager, smiling women. Even though each woman appeared to be vying for his attention, he was staring at Noemi. Her pulse quickened. This wasn't the first time that she'd noticed him staring her way.

"Hey, Noemi," Stephania said. "What are you doing standing over here all alone?"

"Apparently getting champagne spilled on me."

Stephania gasped when she saw the stain. "I'm sure they have some club soda around here."

Noemi shook her head. "I'll just go home."

"But you can't leave yet. We just got here. Besides, if you go home, you'll just mope around."

And think about how her brother refused to give her any respect. Noemi hated to admit it but Stephania was right. Her gaze strayed to the tall sexy stranger. His eyes caught and held hers. Her pulse quickened. Perhaps there was a reason to stay.

Twenty or so minutes later, with the help of club soda, paper towels and a hair dryer, Noemi's dress was once again presentable. By then, she'd talked some sense into herself about the attractive man whose gaze seemed to follow her around the room. He was probably the type who enjoyed the chase—not the capture.

However, there was something slightly familiar about him. Not one to keep up with gossip or who to know, Noemi couldn't place him. But if he was at this exclusive gathering, he must be someone important.

She glanced around the room but didn't see any sign of

him. Disappointment assailed her. This wasn't like her. She could take guys or leave them. She thought of asking Stephania if she knew the man's name but shrugged off the idea. Her life had enough complications. She didn't need more.

But just the same, her mood had dimmed. Her problems once again started to crowd in around the edges of her mind. Needing some fresh air, she stepped out onto the terrace. There was just enough of the evening sun for her to admire the distant mountain range as a gentle breeze caressed her skin.

"Beautiful."

The deep rich voice had her turning her head. And there stood the intriguing stranger with the mesmerizing eyes. His voice held a slight accent. She couldn't place it, but it was extremely sexy—just like the rest of him.

"I'm sorry. Am I disturbing you?" She glanced around for his harem of women, but he appeared to at last be alone—with her.

"Not at all. Please join me." He motioned for her to join him at the edge of the terrace.

She stepped closer but not quite the whole way. "You were admiring the mountains, too?"

He sent her a puzzled look.

"When I stepped out here, you said beautiful. I assumed you were referring to the view."

He smiled and shook his head. "No. I was talking about you. You are beautiful."

She'd been complimented many times over the years. Being the face of Cattaneo Jewels, compliments came with the job. But the man looked at her as though he wanted to take her in his very capable arms and devour her with hungry kisses. The heat of a blush engulfed her cheeks.

"Thank you."

The warm August evening was no help in cooling her down. She knew it was polite to make small conversation, but for once, her mind was a blank. This man didn't seem to know who she was, and for the moment, she found that to be a welcome relief. She didn't want him to treat her differently. For tonight, she wanted to be just a face in the crowd.

But when she turned her head and gazed into this man's eyes, her heart began to race. For a moment, she glanced at his mouth. If she were someone else tonight, would it be wrong to give in to her desires—to live in the moment?

But then she realized if she wanted people to take her seriously, she couldn't give in to her whims. No matter how delicious they may be.

"We should probably get back inside before people start to wonder where we've gone," she said, though there wasn't any part of her that wanted to return to the party. She was quite content to stay right here with him.

He leaned in close. "Let them wonder. I like it much better out here, especially now that you are here."

She cocked her head to the side and looked at him. "I'm starting to understand."

His brows drew together. "Understand?"

"Yes. I understand why all the women surround you. If you flatter them like this, they simply can't help themselves."

The worry lines on his face smoothed and a devastatingly sexy smile lifted his lips. "Trust me. I have done nothing to encourage those women. But when it comes to you, it's different. What brings you to such an exclusive party alone?"

She wanted to believe him when he said she was different. His words were like a soothing balm on her bruised ego. Her parents and her brother might think she should remain nothing more than a silent partner, but this man wanted to hear what she had to say. A smile lifted her lips.

"I'm not alone." The smile immediately slipped from his face. Then realizing how her response must have sounded, she was quick to supply, "I came here with a friend."

"And your friend doesn't mind that you're out here instead of inside with them celebrating the engagement?"

Noemi couldn't help but notice his strange wording. "Do you even know the engaged couple?"

"As a matter of fact, I don't."

Noemi's mouth gaped. Only the very famous or the very rich who knew the couple had been invited. The newly engaged couple didn't want the paparazzi to know the details. They wanted a chance to celebrate and enjoy the moment. And he was a party crasher.

She tilted her chin upward, taking in the man's handsome face. He didn't strike her as the type to intrude upon a stranger's good time. His chiseled jawline gave his face a distinctive look. But it was his mesmerizing eyes that held her gaze captive. The breath caught in her throat.

And then the urge once again came over her to kiss this stranger. But she didn't even know him. She glanced away. She was letting his good looks and sexy smile get to her.

Maybe if she got to know him a little better. There was something about him that made her curious to know more about him. "So if you don't know the engaged couple, why are you here?"

He shrugged. "The host of the party invited me."

She took in the man's straight nose and fresh-shaven jaw. "Do you live in Milan?"

He shook his head. "I'm just passing through."

"On your way to where?"

He shrugged. "I haven't decided yet."

The fact he didn't live in Milan—that he was moving on—appealed to her. The last thing she wanted at this juncture in her life was a relationship. She had her modeling career to focus on—even though it was rapidly losing its appeal.

But an evening of fun—an evening with no strings—what would be the harm? Tomorrow she could decide if she wanted to continue to fight for a more significant place in the family business or look elsewhere. Just then, the French doors burst open and a couple wrapped in each other's arms stumbled onto the veranda. When they bumped into Mr. Tall and Sexy, they straightened up.

"Sorry about that," Matteo DeLuca, an award-winning actor, said. "We didn't know anyone was out here."

The young woman in his arms burst out in a giggle. Her eyes were glazed and as Matteo led her away, she tripped over her own feet. Upon their exit, they forgot to close the doors. The loud music and cacophony of voices came spilling forth.

Noemi's companion closed the doors and then turned back to her. "How would you feel about going someplace quieter?"

"But I don't even know your name."

His brows rose ever so briefly. She couldn't help wondering if his reaction was due to the fact that he expected her to know him. Or whether he was surprised that she'd resisted jumping at his offer. Because right at that moment, she couldn't think of anything she'd like better than spending the evening with this intriguing man.

She took a moment to study him. His dark designer suit definitely didn't come off a rack. As he took a drink of what appeared to be bourbon, she noticed his watch. A Rolex no less. This man looked right at home at this party.

He smiled and his eyes lit up. This man, he was... Well, he was confident. It was in the way he stood with his broad shoulders pulled back and his chin held high. But he wasn't unapproachable either. He seemed to have a sense of humor. But most of all, he came across as the type to go after what he wanted. And right now, he appeared to want her.

"My name is Max."

"Max, huh?" She tried the name on for size. It wasn't as imposing as Zeus or Hercules but it'd do—it'd do just fine.

"You don't like my name?"

"It's not that." It's that it was such a simple name for such a complicated man. And yes, she sensed there were many facets to this man in the ten or so minutes that they'd been talking.

"Then what is it?"

She shrugged. "I just wasn't expecting such a common name."

He smiled and it made her stomach shiver with nerves. "I won't tell my mother you said that."

"Please don't." They were acting like one day soon she would meet the woman. That was never going to happen. But it was fun to play along with him.

"And what's yours?" His voice interrupted her troubled thoughts.

"My what?"

Amusement twinkled in his eyes. "Your name?"

"Oh." Heat rushed up from her chest and settled in her cheeks. "It's Noemi."

"Noemi. That's a beautiful name for a very beautiful woman." He took a step closer to her, leaving little distance between them. She searched his face for any sign of recognition of who she was. There was nothing in his expression to suggest that he recognized her as an heiress to the infamous Cattaneo Jewels worn by the rich and famous worldwide. But there was something else reflected in his eyes.

Desire.

Their gazes locked. This gorgeous hunk of a man, who could have his pick of the eligible women and some not quite so eligible at this party, desired her. Her heart raced. It'd been such a long time since a man had turned her head. But there was something special about Max.

The *thump thump* of her heart was so loud that she could barely hear her own thoughts. And then he reached out to her. His thumb ever so gently traced down her jaw before his finger brushed over her bottom lip. It was such a simple gesture but it sent a bolt of heat ricocheting from her mouth down to her very core.

Before she could figure out how to react to these unexpected sensations, his gaze lowered to her lips. He was going to kiss her?

Her heart lodged in her throat. She should... She should do something. But her body betrayed her. Her feet refused to move and her chin lifted ever so slightly.

As though that was all the invitation he needed, Max lowered his head. Her eyes fluttered closed. She shouldn't want this—want him. But she did, more than she thought possible.

His lips were smooth and warm. And a kiss had never felt so good. She didn't make a habit of going around kissing strangers, but in the short time she'd spent with Max, she had this uncanny feeling that she could trust him.

She slipped her arms up over his muscled shoulders. As the kiss deepened, her hands wrapped around the back of his neck. She'd never been kissed quite so intently and with such unrestrained passion. She wasn't even sure her feet were still on the ground.

Suddenly Max pulled back. It happened so quickly she had to wonder if she'd imagined it. But her lips still tingled where his mouth had touched hers. And he sent her a dazzling smile that promised more of the same.

If she were wise, she would end things right here, but her body hummed with unquenched desire. For once, she wanted to throw caution to the wind and enjoy herself. After all, her brother accused her of being impulsive. Why not live up to the accusation…just this once?

Max pulled his cell phone from his jacket pocket.

"What are you doing?" The words slipped from her lips.

"I'm calling my driver." And then he spoke into his phone. Seconds later, the conversation ended. He turned back to her. "The car will be waiting for us downstairs in a couple of minutes. Shall we?"

But she'd never said she would go anywhere with him. Was it that obvious in the way she looked at him? More than likely he was taking his cues from that kiss they'd shared. That short but arousing kiss.

"What are you thinking?" His eyes searched hers.

"I was thinking…um…that it would be nice to go somewhere a little quieter."

He smiled again. "My thoughts exactly."

He held his arm out to her. It took her a moment to figure out what he was doing. Did men even do that anymore? Wasn't it just something she saw in the old black-and-white movies that her mother collected?

But Noemi found the gentlemanly gesture endearing, even

if it was a little dated. There was something about this man that was so different from anyone she'd ever known and that appealed to her. She had a feeling this evening was going to be totally unforgettable.

CHAPTER ONE

Three months later
Mont Coeur ski resort, the Swiss Alps

WHAT WAS SHE going to do?

Noemi paced back and forth in her luxurious bedroom in her family's palatial chalet. A gentle fire flickered in the fireplace, keeping her suite cozy. She couldn't sit still.

So much had happened in the last few months that it made her head spin. First, the pregnancy test had turned up positive. As she'd struggled to come to terms with what this meant to her future, she'd stumbled across the fact that she had a long-lost brother. The realization had jarred her entire world. How could her parents have kept Leo a secret all her life?

An ensuing row between her and her parents had her shouting out hurtful words—words she didn't mean. And yet now she couldn't take them back. She couldn't tell her parents she was sorry and that she loved them.

They were dead.

The reading of their will had succeeded in driving home the fact that her parents wouldn't be here at the chalet as was their Christmas tradition. But the three siblings intended to spend the holiday together.

It had been strange to meet her brother Leo for the first time, even stranger to hear the contents of her parents' will. She never would have imagined that the terms of the will would be the way they were. Clearly Sebastian hadn't either, because when he'd discovered that his parents had given Leo controlling shares in Cattaneo Jewels for six months, he'd been furious. And although Leo had been clearly reluctant, the terms stated that should Leo refuse, Cattaneo Jewels would cease trading and be liquidated. And none of them had wanted that.

But tempers and emotions had risen, and it was all Noemi had been able to do to convince her brothers to think on it and to return here to the chalet in Mont Coeur just before Christmas for the final decision.

Even now, she could only guess at what her parents had been thinking when they'd written the will and its unusual terms. She missed them dearly—most especially her mother. She needed her now more than ever.

Noemi swiped at her eyes as she thought of her mother. And though their last conversation had been heated and hurtful, Noemi didn't doubt her parents had loved her—even if she had made mistakes along the way. But all the wishing in the world wasn't going to erase the last angry words that they'd exchanged, nor would it bring them back to her.

Noemi moved to the French doors in her room and stared out at the cloudy afternoon sky as big lazy snowflakes drifted ever so slowly to the ground. It was a light snow. The kind that melted as soon as it touched the roads. And any other time she'd be caught up in the peaceful relaxing view. But not today.

She was running out of time to keep her secret to herself. Her hand pressed to her slightly rounded abdomen. No amount of baggy clothes was going to hide her pregnancy much longer.

And what was she supposed to say to people when they asked who the father was? *His name is Max? He has the dreamiest eyes that appear to change colors to suit his mood? And his body is like a sculpture of defined muscles? Or when he laughs it is deep and rich?* Even now, his memory brought a smile to her face.

After the most magical night, he'd insisted that it would be best not to exchange full names or phone numbers. She'd hesitantly agreed. Neither of them had been looking for a lasting relationship. And now that she really needed to speak to him, she didn't know how to reach him. She'd even asked Stephania about him, but she didn't know him—

Noemi's cell phone buzzed. She moved to the bed and picked it up. She wasn't in the mood to speak to anyone, but when she saw that it was Maria, her sister-in-law and close friend, she answered.

"How are you doing?" Maria asked.

"Okay. I guess." Noemi sighed.

"Really? I'd hate to hear you if something was wrong."

"What's that supposed to mean?"

"You're usually bubbly but lately you've been really down. Is it your parents?"

"No. I mean, I miss them a lot."

"So something else is bothering you?"

Maria had always been good at reading her. And she was the closest thing Noemi had to a big sister. If she didn't talk to someone soon, she was going to burst.

Noemi worried her bottom lip. "Can I tell you something?"

"Sure. You know you can always talk to me. Is it about the reading of your parents' will?"

Noemi shook her head and then realized Maria couldn't see her. "It's not that. But if I tell you this, you have to promise not to say a word to Sebastian."

There was a slight pause on the other end of the phone.

"Never mind," Noemi said. "I never should have asked you to keep anything from my brother."

"It's okay. You need someone to confide in and I promise your brother won't hear a thing from me. Sometimes he can be a bit overprotective where you're concerned."

"And when he hears about this, he's going to hit the roof. He'll be just like Papa—" She stopped, recalling how poorly her parents had taken the news of her pregnancy.

Even though her parents had had a child in their teens and had given him up for adoption, they'd still been disappointed with her unplanned pregnancy. What was up with that? It wasn't like she'd set out to wreck her life. She'd thought that out of all the people in the world, they would have been the ones to understand. They hadn't. And it had hurt Noemi deeply. Worse yet, they'd died before she could ever put things to right.

"Relax." Maria's voice drew Noemi out of her thoughts. "We'll figure out how to deal with him."

"Thanks. But I'll deal with him."

"Whatever you want. But you still haven't told me your problem. Maybe I can help. Perhaps it isn't as big as you're imagining."

"No. It's bigger." Noemi's insides quivered with nerves. By saying the words out loud, it was going to make this pregnancy real. Just like the reading of the will had made her parents' deaths startling real. Once she told Maria about the baby, there would be no more pretending. In less than six months, she was going to give birth.

"Noemi…"

"I'm pregnant."

Silence. Utter and complete silence.

Noemi's heart raced. Her hands grew clammy. And her stomach churned. What was Maria thinking? Was she disappointed in her, too, just like her parents had been?

"Are you sure?"

Noemi nodded. "I took three home pregnancy tests and then I went to see the doctor. It's official."

"I don't know what to say." There was a pause as though Maria was searching for the right words. "How do you feel about it?"

"I knew I wanted kids someday, but not yet—not now. I'm only twenty-six."

"And the father, how does he feel?"

"I… I don't know."

"Noemi, you've told him, haven't you?"

She inhaled a deep breath, trying to calm her nauseous stomach. And then she launched into how she'd met Max and how stupid she'd been that night. She'd been hurting and not thinking straight. And she thought it would be a good time without any strings.

"Don't worry. Everything will be all right," Maria said, though her voice said otherwise.

"Even you don't believe it. What am I going to do? I'm not going to be able to hide my condition much longer. Most of my clothes don't fit."

"I know." Maria's voice rose as though she'd just discovered the answer to all Noemi's problems.

"What?" She was desperate for some good advice.

"You need some retail therapy."

Noemi's shoulders drooped. That was the very last thing she wanted to do. "Are you serious?"

"Yes. I'm very serious. What are you doing right now?"

"Maria..."

"Tell me what you're doing?"

"Pacing in my room."

"And that is helping you how?"

"I'm thinking."

"And so far it hasn't gotten you any answers. You need to get out of that chalet. The fresh air will do you good. Shopping is just what you need."

"Is that what you did when you and Sebastian separated?" And then realizing that she was touching on a very painful subject, she said, "Forget I said that. I'm just not myself today."

"Actually, it is what I did."

"Did it help?"

"Temporarily." Her voice filled with emotion. "Enough about me. I hope you know that if I could manage it, I'd be there with you, but trust me, after you buy some Christmas presents and new clothes for yourself that are comfortable, you'll feel much better. There's nothing worse than squeezing into clothes that don't fit."

Maria had given birth to Noemi's nephew, Frankie, nearly two years ago. She knew a lot more about pregnancy than Noemi. Maybe she was right. She glanced over at her discarded jeans on the bed. She'd barely gotten them buttoned, but she hadn't been able to pull up the zipper. And no matter how much she enjoyed her leggings, she couldn't stay in them forever.

"You'll do it, won't you?" Maria prompted.

"Yes, I'll go."

"Good. Call me later and let me know how it goes."

After the conversation ended, Noemi still wasn't certain that shopping was the right thing to do, but what else did she have to do considering she was at the chalet alone? Her gaze moved to the discarded jeans on her king-size bed. No way was she going to put those on again. Her black leggings would have to do.

She moved to the walk-in closet, hoping she could find something to wear besides her T-shirt. She sifted through the hangers until she strayed across a white long-sleeve V-neck knit tunic. It was loose but not too baggy and it'd go great with her leggings as well as her knee-high black boots.

With her wardrobe sorted, she was ready to head into the village. She would search for some roomier clothes and see what she could find for Christmas, which was only a few weeks away.

He didn't want to be here.

Not really.

Crown Prince Maximilian Steiner-Wolf, known to his friends as Max, sat in the back seat of his sports utility vehicle as one of his three bodyguards maneuvered it along the windy road in the Swiss Alps. His bodyguard and friend, Roc, sat in the passenger seat while Shaun, a bodyguard of similar stature and looks, sat next to him. He couldn't go anywhere without at least a small security detail.

Being the crown prince came with certain nonnegotiable restrictions. One of them was his safety. He may insist on traveling but the king demanded that his safety always be taken into consideration. It was a hassle but the guards were very good at becoming invisible unless their presence was required.

Max turned his head to the window and stared out at the snowy landscape of the mountainous region with some of the best slopes in all Europe. He was planning to spend a week or two skiing at Mont Coeur before returning to the palace in the European principality of Ostania.

He hadn't been home in months, but the approaching holidays were a big thing, not only at the palace but also throughout Ostania. And his mother had called, insisting he spend Christmas with them. After all, he was still the crown prince, even though he would never be king. However, the royal family was still keeping up appearances with the public.

Though Max was the firstborn and had been groomed from birth to take the throne of the small European country, no one had foreseen that he would be diagnosed with cancer in his teens. Although his treatment had been successful, doctors informed him that the cure had very likely rendered him sterile. Royal decree stated that the ruler of Ostania must produce an heir verified by a paternity test. From then on, Max knew it was impossible for him to take the throne.

So as not to cause the nation to panic over the future of Ostania, the palace had kept Max's infertility quiet while attentions turned to preparing his younger brother, Tobias, to become the future ruler of Ostania. No one outside of the court circle knew, and meanwhile, to the world, Max was still the crown prince.

While all of his parents' attention was showered on his little brother, Max roamed the world. He wasn't as much of a party animal as the press claimed him to be, but he did know how to have a good time. However, that was all about to change.

The truth was he was tiring of his partying ways. Moving from city to city, beach to beach and resort to resort was growing old or maybe he was getting old. In the beginning, it had been fun. The freedom had been intoxicating, but now he was starting to get a hangover from too much partying. He needed to do more with his life and to do that he had to go home—he had to officially step down from his position as crown prince in order to find his future.

That acknowledgment stabbed deep into his heart. He'd always been competitive. His parents had raised him that way. And stepping aside to let his younger brother take his place didn't come naturally to him. But it was more than that—it was knowing he was letting down his family—his country.

His stopover in Mont Coeur was to be his last. After he hit the slopes and cleared his head, he planned to return to Ostania to have a difficult talk with the king and queen. It had been put off long enough. Then he would lead a quieter, more productive life.

The SUV slowed as they entered the heart of the resort. Max instructed the driver to pull to a stop outside a ski supply shop. He'd lost his sunglasses at the end of last season and he needed a new pair of shades before hitting the slopes.

Not waiting for his security to get the door for him, he let himself out. He'd just stepped into the narrow road when someone with a camera pointed at him. Max inwardly groaned. It was going to be one of those trips where he was besieged for photos and autographs. Normally it didn't bother him, but right now he had a lot on his mind.

"It's the Prince of Ostania!" someone shouted.

Everyone on the sidewalk turned in his direction.

Quickly his security guards flanked him. None spoke. They didn't have to. The serious look on their faces said they meant business. Being recognized didn't happen all the time. However, it happened more than Max would like.

Security escorted him around the vehicle. He forced a smile as he passed the tourists and then dashed into the shop. He hoped the people wouldn't follow him.

Inside the shop, the walls were lined with snowboards and skies. In the background, "Let It Snow" played. Colorful twinkle lights were draped around the checkout where the workers wore red Santa hats with white pom-poms on the tips.

Figuring it might be easier to search for the sunglasses on his own, he bypassed the people at the checkout who were openly staring. He turned into the first aisle and nearly collided with a pretty young woman. She flashed him a big toothy smile. He intentionally didn't smile, not wanting to encourage her attention. He gave a brief nod and excused himself as he made his way around her.

Ever since he'd met Noemi, no other women had turned his head—not the way she had. And yet, he'd let her get away without even getting her number. He'd thought at the time that he would get over her quickly. That's the way it'd been with the other women who'd passed through his life. But there was something different about Noemi.

She acted tough, but inside where she didn't want anyone to see, there was a vulnerability to her. She'd let him get close enough to gain a glimpse of her tender side. Much too soon, she'd hidden behind a big smile and a teasing comment.

He could clearly recall her beautiful face. Her brown eyes had gold specks like jewels. And when he closed his eyes, he could feel the gentle touch of her lips pressed to his. With a mental shake, he chased those thoughts to the back of his mind.

It didn't take him long to find what he wanted and then he strode to the checkout where the pretty woman was standing, pretending to check out a display of lip balm while she stared at him.

He pretended not to notice as he paid the clerk. All he wanted now was to get to his private chalet and unwind. However, when he pushed open the front door and stepped onto the sidewalk, the crowd had multiplied. Flash after flash went off in his face.

CHAPTER TWO

MAYBE SHOPPING HADN'T been such a bad idea.

Noemi clutched the colorful shopping bags stuffed full of goodies and headed for the door. She'd purchased some jeans in a bigger size that had spandex in them, making them so much comfier. They fit her a lot like her leggings. She'd pulled on the waistband and was surprised by how roomy they were without being baggy.

She'd also found some loose blouses and sweaters that hung down to her hips. For a while, they would hide her growing baby bump. It wasn't the figure-flattering clothes she normally wore, but it was so much better than what she had before. And she just wasn't ready for maternity—not yet.

As Maria had suggested, Noemi had taken time to do some Christmas shopping, including purchasing two designer sweaters. One for her newfound brother, Leo, and one for Sebastian. She and Sebastian might disagree—heatedly at times—but she still loved him.

With big black sunglasses and a gray knit beanie pulled low, she stepped outside the store and started up the sidewalk toward her car. The snow clouds had passed and the sun shone once more. Up ahead a crowd of people swarmed the sidewalk and spilled out into the roadway. She glanced around, wondering what was going on.

She would love to turn and avoid the crowd, but they were standing between her and her vehicle. And her numerous bags weren't light. She kept moving toward them. Surely the crowd would part and let her through.

She was on the edge of the group when an excited buzz rushed through the crowd. Noemi paused and turned to a young woman who was holding up her cell phone as though to snap a picture.

"Do you know what all the fuss is about?" Noemi asked.

The young woman with dark hair pulled back in a ponytail smiled brightly. "It's the best thing. Crown Prince Maximilian Steiner-Wolf has just arrived."

Noemi had heard the name before, but she knew nothing of the man. It seemed as though she was in the minority as the crowd continued to grow.

Noemi glanced around, curious to see the prince.

The young woman pointed to the shop in front of them. "He's in that store. Right there. Can you believe it? But his bodyguards aren't letting people in."

Noemi felt sorry for the guy. As the face of Cattaneo Jewels, she'd had her fair share of exposure to publicity, but the crowd of people forming around the store was extreme even to her. "And everyone is just standing around waiting for him to come out?"

The young woman gave her a look like she'd just grown a second head. "Well, yeah. Of course."

Noemi nodded in understanding, even though she didn't. Her arms ached from the weight of the bags. She continued to make her way to her car.

"Excuse me," Noemi called out, finding it difficult to thread her way through the crowd.

A cheer rose in the crowd. Then the crowd rushed forward. At last, there was room to walk.

Thud!

Someone ploughed right into Noemi. She lurched forward. In an effort to keep herself upright, she lost her grip on the packages. They fell to the ground in a heap. Her arms waved to the side as she tried to steady herself. Suddenly there were strong hands reaching out, gripping her by the waist.

Once she'd regained her balance, she turned and found herself staring into intriguing hazel eyes. It was Max. Her heart lodged in her throat. What was he doing here? Waiting to see the prince?

"Noemi?" His eyes widened with surprise. And then a smile lifted his lips. "I'm sorry. I didn't see you."

He bent over and started to pick up all her bags. She hadn't realized until then just how many packages there were, but Christmas was her favorite holiday. She had to make sure she bought something for everyone. Maybe more than one thing for everyone—especially her young nephew. It was going to be a difficult Christmas without her parents. And she felt driven to do everything possible to make the holiday bearable.

But right now, her thoughts centered around the father of her baby. And here she'd been thinking she would never see him again. She averted her gaze from him as she knelt down next to him. She scrambled to gather her packages.

"What are you doing here?" she asked.

He scooped up most of the packages and straightened. "I was planning to go skiing."

When she straightened, she had to lift her chin in order to look him in the eyes. And that was a dangerous thing to do because every time she gazed into his eyes, she forgot what she was about to say.

Just then a flash went off. And then another. And another.

"What's going on?" She glanced around as everyone was looking at them. And then the lightbulb went on in her mind. "You." Her gaze met his again. "You are the prince?"

His jaw flexed as his body stiffened. "Yes. I am Prince Maximilian Steiner-Wolf."

Her mouth gaped. Realizing that everyone was watching them, she forced her mouth closed. How was this possible? Was she really that out of touch with reality that she'd missed the father of her baby was royalty?

She had so many questions for him, but they lodged in

her throat. This wasn't the time or the place to rehash the not-so-distant past.

"Come with me," he said.

Not waiting for an answer, he took her hand and led her to a waiting black SUV. With the help of two men, they reached the vehicle without people stepping in their way.

She wasn't sure it was wise being alone with him, not when he still filled her dreams, but it beat being in public where everyone was watching them and eavesdropping. Once inside, she turned to him. She needed answers. She needed to know why he'd kept his title from her. She needed to know so much.

"Not now," he said as though reading her mind. Turning to the driver, he said, "Go."

"My vehicle is back there," Noemi said.

"Don't worry. We'll come back for it. Later."

The driver, as though used to driving through crowds, safely maneuvered the SUV past the sprawling mass of people.

She turned to the window and stared blindly at the passing shops. This had to be some sort of dream. Perhaps she'd fallen back there and hit her head. Yes, she thought, grasping at straws. She'd hit her head and this was all a dream. Because there was no way that she was pregnant with a prince's baby.

"Noemi?" Max's voice cut through her thoughts.

She had absolutely no idea what he was asking her. She turned to him. "What?"

"I asked where you are staying."

"Um…" She thought about returning to her vehicle and decided that Max was right. Later would be better to pick it up. "Take a left at the next intersection."

His dark brows rose. "Those are private residences."

She nodded. Her neighbors were some of the most prominent actors and actresses, athletes and notable figures in the world. Since she'd been coming here all her life, she took it all for granted. But now, seeing it from a stranger's perspective, she realized that it might be impressive. But to a prince? Nah.

He was probably wondering why she lived in such an exclusive neighborhood. Apparently she wasn't the only one in the dark. He didn't recognize her even though her face had been plastered on every glamour magazine as well as television promos for a number of years.

She gave the driver directions to her family's chalet. When they reached the gate to the exclusive community, she put her window down and assured the guard that it was okay to let them through.

"I've never been to this part of Mont Coeur," Max said. "I've always preferred to have my accommodations close to the slopes."

As they passed the large and impressive chalets, she noticed that most displayed Christmas decorations. Some sported a door wreath while others had a bit more. Normally their chalet was the most festive of them all—but not this year. Her father had always taken care of the outside decorations. However, this year Noemi had done it by herself and the twinkling lights weren't quite as spectacular as prior years.

Her palms grew damp as her heart raced. She couldn't relax, not with Max next to her. She didn't know what made her more nervous—the fact that they'd spent the night together or the fact that the man she'd slept with was royalty. When Maria heard this, she was never going to believe it.

He longed to kiss her berry red lips.

The memory of their sweetness taunted him.

Max gave himself a mental jerk. Now that he'd found Noemi again, the last thing he wanted to do was scare her off. What were the chances of them running into each other again?

Slim.

Had she figured out his true identity and planned this reunion? Not possible. He hadn't decided on coming to Mont

Coeur until last night. Even then, he'd only told his trusted staff.

Max gazed over at Noemi. Her posture was stiff and she kept her face turned away. He wondered if the source of her discomfort was from their collision, the run-in with the fans, learning he was a prince or all of the above.

Normally learning that he was the crown prince had women falling all over him. But Noemi had pulled away. In fact, if she sat any closer to her door, she'd fall out. Most interesting. He'd thought they'd both enjoyed their time together.

But it wasn't too late. He still had a chance to find out if there was truly a spark between them.

When the SUV pulled to a stop in front of a luxurious chalet, Noemi said a quick thank-you followed by goodbye. It'd be so easy to just let her go. He'd still have his good memories, but he'd never know what had been real and what had been part of his wishful imagination.

As he watched her head for the front steps, he told his security team to wait for him. He hopped out into the snowy driveway and followed her.

"Noemi, wait."

For a moment, he didn't think she was going to stop. Her hand reached for the doorknob, but then she hesitated. She turned to him but didn't say anything. Her gaze didn't quite meet his. She stood there waiting for him to have his say.

"You didn't even tell me your last name. I don't want to make the same mistake twice." When she sent him a puzzled look, he added, "Letting you get away without knowing your name."

"Oh. It's Noemi Cattaneo."

"Your name. It sounds familiar."

"You've probably heard of our family business. Cattaneo Jewels."

Of course, he'd heard of them. Who hadn't?

"Your family's business has the distinction of handling some of the world's finest and rarest jewels."

"Have you done business with us?"

"Not me personally, but my family has." He was getting off point. "Anyway, I wanted to say…" his Adam's apple bobbed "… I'm sorry. I've handled this all wrong."

"It's not your fault that people recognized you."

"No." He shook his head. "Not that. I'm sorry for before, when I insisted that we keep things casual and not exchange phone numbers." He stepped closer to her. "I've been thinking of you—"

"Don't." She shook her head. "I don't need your pity."

"It's not pity. I—I just handled things poorly before. And I want to apologize."

Her gaze momentarily widened but then she glanced away. "We did the right thing. Our lives are too diverse. I mean you…you have a country to run. And I am… I mean, I have things to do."

He'd never witnessed Noemi nervous before, not that they'd spent a lot of time together. But in the time he'd known her, she'd come across as confident and fun. The Noemi standing before him was different and he wanted to know what had changed her. Why did she avoid looking at him directly?

He is a prince?

How is that possible?

Noemi had so many conflicting emotions flooding her body that she didn't know what to say to him. Part of her longed to fall into his arms and pick up where they'd left off before. But logic told her to tread carefully. Max was a very powerful man. There was no way she was going to blurt out that she was pregnant with his baby. Finding out that he was royalty changed everything. She needed time to think.

"Have dinner with me?" His voice stirred her from her thoughts.

She shook her head. "I don't think that's a good idea."

The hopeful look on his face faded. "Was our time together that forgettable?"

"It definitely wasn't forgettable." The words were out her mouth before she realized she was revealing too much. She'd barely been able to think of anything else these past few weeks since learning she was pregnant.

That wasn't exactly true. She'd thought a lot about him ever since they parted—even before she'd learned she was pregnant. She would wonder what he was doing and who he was doing it with. And she wondered if he ever stopped to think about her.

"That's good to hear," he said. "So we'll do dinner."

She recalled the mass of people waiting for him outside the ski shop. She couldn't even imagine the spectacle they'd make by having dinner in public. It would be an utter zoo.

Though it pained her to say, she uttered, "We can't."

"Sure we can." He smiled like he had all the answers to their problems.

Again, she shook her head. "Everyone knows you're here at the resort. They'll all be on the lookout for you."

"And you don't want to be photographed with a prince?"

She glanced away and shrugged. The ramifications of the photo would be catastrophic once her pregnancy became known. Until she had a plan for this baby, she didn't want to make any more mistakes, especially where the public was concerned.

He laughed. "Do you know how refreshing you are?"

He was amused? Her lips pressed together into a firm line. She didn't know what there was to be smiling about, but then again, he didn't know about the baby.

She lifted her chin. "I don't care to be laughed at."

"I'm not laughing at you." His amusement faded. "I think you're amazing." As though her lack of response went unnoticed, he said, "Most women I've met would fall over themselves to have dinner with me. But not you. Which makes me that much more determined to see you again. In fact, I'm not leaving here until you agree to have dinner—no strings attached."

"Not tonight." She wanted to clear her head—and do an internet search.

He arched a dark brow. "I have the feeling if I let you get away tonight that there won't be another chance for us to get together. You'll always have an excuse. And I can't stay here forever—no matter how tempting that may be."

"I promise we'll do it another time."

"Must I beg, *ma chérie*?"

"You speak French?"

He nodded. "French and Italian as well as English. Ostania is situated near France, Italy and Switzerland. We speak French but it's heavily influenced by the surrounding countries. I could tell you more about my country over dinner."

It wasn't his country that she was interested in learning more about. And they did have much to discuss. Her hand instinctively moved in the direction of her tiny baby bump, but she caught herself in time and lowered her arm to her side.

"If you're worried about privacy, we can have dinner at my condo." A hopeful look reflected in his eyes.

"You're serious, aren't you?"

He nodded. "I've never been more serious in my life."

She didn't miss the part of a wealthy, devastatingly handsome prince begging her to have dinner with him. But as much as she wanted to spend more time with him, there was another part of her that worried about what would happen when he learned of the baby. Would he reject her? Would he reject his own flesh and blood? Or would he try to take the baby from her? The thought of it sent a chill through her.

Proceed with caution.

The only way she would find the answer to any of these questions was if she were to do as he asked and dine with him. Not sure if it was the right decision or not, she said, "Okay. I'll have dinner with you."

He didn't hesitate. "I'll send a car for you at seven."

She shook her head. "I can drive." And then she recalled that she'd left her car back in the village. "Except my car is still in the village."

"I'll send my car. And if you give me your keys, I'll make sure your car is picked up and waiting for you at my condo."

That would be convenient, but it would also make her an easy target for the paparazzi. And she wasn't ready to be a headline on every gossip site.

She checked the time on her phone. "You may send your car for me at…seven fifteen." That should give her just enough time to sort through her purchases to find something appropriate to wear and do an internet search. "Does that work for you?"

Both his brows rose. She wasn't sure if he was surprised that she hadn't fallen all over herself to do as he wanted. If that's what he expected of her, he was in for a surprise. With a baby on the way, she had to stand firm and speak up when necessary.

Max gave a curt nod. "I'll see you then." He turned for his vehicle. A few steps later, he paused and turned back. "Is there anything specific you would like for dinner? Perhaps something you've been craving?"

Craving? Did he know about her pregnancy? She sucked in her stomach. As he continued to stare at her with an expectant look on his face with no hint of suspicion, she realized he'd meant nothing by his choice of word.

She shook her head. "Anything is fine. I'm not a picky eater."

That response rewarded her with another surprised look on his face. Apparently the prince wasn't used to women who weren't picky. She wondered just what sort of women he normally dated, but she resisted the urge to ask.

"I'll pick something special." He turned and walked away.

The desire to run in the house and head straight to her computer was overwhelming, but she restrained herself. She waited until he was inside his vehicle before she let herself in the chalet. With the door shut, her movements became rushed. She threw off her hat and coat before kicking off her snowy boots. And then she took the steps two at a time.

She grabbed her laptop from the desk and threw herself

down on the bed. Her fingertips moved rapidly over the keyboard. Maybe it wasn't right snooping on the internet, but now that she knew her baby's daddy was a famous royal, she had to learn more. From her own dealings with the paparazzi, she knew most of the articles would be fiction or wildly exaggerated. But that didn't stop her from looking—

Noemi's breath caught in her throat as she caught sight of headlines splashed across the screen that were worse than she'd allowed herself to imagine. In fact, with photos to back up the headlines, she wondered if she'd been wrong about Max.

"Twin Blonde Bombshells for the Prince!"

"Prince Maximilian with Woman Number Five in as Many Evenings!"

"The Playboy Prince Strikes Again!"

"Prince Max and His Harem!"

Disheartened, Noemi closed her laptop. She'd thought the night their baby was conceived that they'd shared something special. She never imagined that she was just one more notch on his bedpost. The thought hurt—a lot.

She placed her hand upon her midsection. "What have I gotten us into?"

CHAPTER THREE

MAYBE HE SHOULDN'T have pushed. After all, he wasn't a man to beg for a woman's company—until now. What was it about Noemi that had him acting out of character? Was it her dazzling smile? Her bewitching eyes? Or her sweet, sweet kiss?

As Max sat at the desk in his bedroom suite, he gave himself a mental shake and tried to concentrate on the plethora of emails awaiting his attention. He checked the clock for what must be the hundredth time. It still wasn't even close to when Noemi was due to arrive. He sighed.

He may not be at the palace, but that didn't mean his responsibilities ceased to exist. In fact, he was beginning to think his parents gave him more than his fair share of work to make sure he didn't stray too far from the business of governing Ostania.

He still had two hundred and seventy-nine unopened emails. He groaned. How was that possible? He'd checked his email last night because he knew he'd be traveling most of today. He'd had it semi under control, but not any longer.

He wished his email was like other people's and full of spam that he could readily dismiss. However, his email was directed through the palace, where it went through stringent screenings. That meant all two hundred and seventy-nine emails would need to be dealt with personally or would require forwarding to someone else with directions.

He worked his way through the emails in chronological order. And then his gaze strayed across an email from his mother—the queen. She didn't email him often as she was a bit exasperated with him. She thought he should be at the palace acting the part of proper crown prince. She had no idea how hard it was for him to act his part because the royal court knew that when the time came, he would not be crowned king.

That role would go to his younger brother, Tobias, who at this moment was being meticulously groomed to step up and assume Max's birthright. He didn't blame his brother. If anything, he felt indebted to Tobias. His brother was the one sacrificing his youthful adventures in order to learn the rules of governing and the etiquette for dealing with foreign dignitaries.

And yet his brother had stepped up to do what was expected of him without complaint. Max would do no less. He checked the time once again and found that he still had close to an hour and a half before Noemi showed up. It was plenty of time to work through some of these emails.

He opened the email from his mother. He didn't know what he expected, but it wasn't the very cold businesslike email telling him the schedule of Christmas events and how he was expected to take on a prominent role in the festivities. He hated pretending to the whole nation that he was something he wasn't—the heir to the throne.

He closed his mother's email without responding because there wasn't anything for him to respond to. There hadn't been one personal word in the whole email. In fact, he would have thought that his mother's personal secretary had written and sent the email except for the fact it had come from his mother's private email that not even her secretary could access.

So the cold, impersonal email from his mother indicated that she thought he'd been gone too long. Or worse yet, she'd been reading the paparazzi headlines—which he might add were wildly exaggerated or utter works of fiction.

He opened an email from his own secretary, Enzo, who stayed on top of everything for him. It sorted his duties into priorities, escalating and FYI items. The only problem was the priorities were now taking up more room than the other two categories. It was definitely time to go home.

Max typed up his response to his secretary, letting the man know how to handle things until he returned to Ostania. And then he moved on to the next official email...

Knock. Knock.

Max granted access just as he pressed Send on another response and deleted the original email.

"Sir, Miss Cattaneo has arrived."

"She has?" How could that be? He'd just checked the time, hadn't he? His gaze moved to the clock at the bottom of the laptop monitor. A lot of time had passed totally unnoticed. "Please offer her a drink and tell her I'll be right there."

He closed his laptop and moved to the adjoining bathroom. He'd meant to clean up before her arrival. He jumped in the shower, not even waiting for the water to warm up.

Five minutes later, with his hair still damp, Max strode into the living room. Noemi was still there. He breathed a sigh of relief.

"I'm sorry about that. Time got away from me." He smiled at her. "Do you need more to drink?" He gestured to her empty glass on the coffee table.

"Actually, yes. That would be nice."

He moved forward and accepted her glass. "What were you drinking?"

"Water."

Water? He didn't know why that struck him as strange. Perhaps he'd become accustomed to serving wine on a date. This was just one more example of how Noemi was different from the other women who'd passed through his life.

He quickly poured water from a glass pitcher. "Here you go."

When he handed over the now full glass, their fingers brushed and, in that moment, he recalled the silkiness of her skin, the warmth of her touch and the heat of her kiss. With a mental jerk, he brought his thoughts back to the present.

His mouth grew dry and he decided to pour himself some cold water. He took a drink and then sat on the couch opposite hers.

He smiled. "It's really good to see you again. I just never expected to run into you here."

She arched a fine brow. "Why? Is skiing only for men these days?"

He inwardly groaned. She just wasn't going to give him an inch. She was angry about the way they'd left things. And that was his fault.

"Noemi, about our time in Milan, I handled things poorly. Is there any chance you will forgive me? And perhaps we can start over?"

"I told you I'm fine." Her lips said one thing but her eyes said something quite different.

"The frostiness in this room is making me think I should go get my ski jacket and gloves."

Her beautiful brown eyes momentarily widened. "It's not that bad."

"Maybe not on your side of the room, but standing over here, it's downright nippy."

A little smile pulled at her lips. It wasn't much but it was something.

"That's better," he said.

She tilted her head to the side. "Why?"

"Why what?"

"Why are you trying so hard when you could have any women you want?" Her gaze searched his as if she could read the truth in his eyes.

"I've thought a lot about you since that night. I've wondered what it might have been like if we'd have had more time together."

"Really?" There was a tone of doubt in her voice.

"Do you find that so hard to believe?"

Her eyes narrowed. "It's the way you wanted it—no strings attached."

"As I recall, you agreed." He wasn't going to take all the blame for the circumstances of their parting.

The frown lines on her face smoothed. "You're right."

At last, they seemed to be getting somewhere. Perhaps they could build on this and get back to where they'd once been—happy and comfortable with each other.

He took another drink of water and then set the glass aside. His gaze rose and caught hers. "Noemi, is it possible for us to start over?"

A noticeable silence filled the room. He knew it was too much to hope that they'd recapture the magic of that special night, but he had to try. With each passing second, his hopes declined.

"Yes, we can try."

Her words caught him off guard—that seemed to be a common occurrence where Noemi was concerned. He would need to tread carefully around her in the future.

"Would you like to eat?" he asked.

Her eyes lit up. "I would."

"Good. I hope you like the menu."

He stepped into the kitchen to let the cook know. Then he escorted Noemi to a table that had been set next to the wall of windows where the twinkling lights of the resort illuminated ski slopes trailing down the mountainside beneath the night sky.

He'd had the cook prepare something basic because he had absolutely no idea what Noemi liked to eat, other than pizza. That's what they'd had in Milan when neither of them felt like dressing and going out for a proper dinner. Since then he'd never been able to eat pizza without thinking of her.

And so, after a Caesar salad, they were served a heaping plate of pasta with Bolognese sauce topped with grated Parmigiano-Reggiano. He didn't have to ask if Noemi approved of it. He tried not to smile as she made quick work of the pasta. It was a quiet dinner as he didn't push conversation, wanting to give Noemi a chance to relax.

When they finished, he noticed there was still a small pile of pasta on her plate. "I take it you had enough."

She patted her stomach. Then just as quickly she removed her hand and a rosy hue came over her cheeks. To say she was beautiful normally was an understatement, but she was even more of a knockout with the rush of color lighting up her face.

"It was amazing. Thank you." She got to her feet. "It was good seeing you again. But I should be going."

He couldn't let her go. Not yet. "Stay. We haven't even had dessert."

"Dessert? I don't have any room left. Not after that delicious meal."

"Come join me." He moved to the couch in front of the fireplace with a fire gently crackling within it. When she didn't make a move to follow him, he said, "Please, give me a chance to explain—about the way we left things."

A spark of interest reflected in her eyes. She moved to the couch. When they sat down, she left a large space between them. He hoped by the time they finished talking that the space would shrink considerably.

"The night we met," he said, "I was captivated by your beauty."

A small smile played on her lips. A good sign. Still, she remained quiet as though giving him room to explain where things had gone wrong.

"The thing was I wasn't looking to meet someone—certainly no one like you. You were like a warm spring breeze on an icy cold night. And the next morning, I received bad news from home."

He hadn't wanted to burden Noemi with the news of his father's collapse. It wasn't like they were in a committed relationship. It had been his burden to carry on his own.

Perhaps he had that in common with his father. Because when his mother had called to tell him of this father's declining health, Max had made plans to fly home immediately.

He had been at the airport when his father called and told him that his mother had overreacted.

His father had insisted he was fine and told Max in no uncertain terms that he would not be welcome at the palace for a pity visit. His father had been so animated on the phone that Max had been inclined to think his mother had gone a little overboard with worry. But that didn't mean his father's lifelong battle with diabetes wasn't taking its toll on him.

Instead of flying home, his father rerouted Max to Spain. It was a diplomatic mission to encourage increased trade between their countries—something Ostania needed.

"Listen, you don't have to explain," Noemi said quickly. "You didn't mean for it to be more than a fling. And that's fine." But the tone in her voice said that it wasn't fine with her.

In that moment, he decided to tell her the whole truth. She deserved that much. "It was about my father. He was ill and my mother was very concerned about his health."

Noemi studied him for a moment. "That's why you were so different in the morning? It was the worry about your father and not regret over spending the night together?"

"Maybe it was a bit of both." When the look of hope faded from her face, he rushed on to say, "I regretted rushing things. I lost my head that night."

She arched a brow. "Do you mean that? You're not saying all this nice stuff just because you don't want to hurt my feelings?"

He shook his head. "I didn't handle the news well. My mother—well, she can be a bit dramatic when it suits her purposes—she made it sound like my father wouldn't last through the day."

Noemi moved to his side. Her gaze met his. "I'm sorry. How is he?"

Within her eyes, he saw caring and understanding. He cleared his throat. "Much better. And quite stubborn."

"I'm glad to hear that—about him feeling better. But why

couldn't you have told me? I would have understood you having to leave immediately."

"I didn't want you to know. I didn't want anyone to know. Telling someone would have made the whole situation real and at the time, I wasn't ready to deal with it."

"And now?"

"Now, I regret how I reacted. I shouldn't have dismissed what we had so readily. I would have liked if we'd been able to keep in contact." He continued to stare at her, wondering if she felt the same way about him.

"That would have been nice." Softly she added, "I thought of contacting you, too."

At last, he could breathe easier. She was slowly letting her guard down with him. He could finally see a glimmer of that amazing woman who'd caught his attention from across the room at the party. He was glad he hadn't given up. He knew if he kept trying that he'd find her.

He resisted the urge to reach out and touch her. He couldn't rush things. He didn't want to scare her off. "I'm going to be here at the resort for the next week before returning to Ostania. I'd like it if we could spend some more time together."

Noemi looked as though she was going to agree, but what came out of her lips was quite different. "I don't think that's a good idea, especially with the press watching your every move."

"I'll take care of the paparazzi. They won't bother us."

"But how?"

"Trust me. I have a lot of experience evading them. So are we good?"

She shook her head. "It's more than that."

He'd come too far to let it fall apart now. "Speak to me. Whatever it is, I'll fix it."

"You can't." She stood and walked to the wall of windows.

He followed her as though drawn in by her magnetic force. He stopped just behind her. Again, he resisted the urge to reach out to her. "Noemi, I know we haven't know each other long, but I'd like to think you look upon me as a friend—someone you can lean on."

She turned to him. "I do—think of you as a friend."

"Then tell me what's bothering you. Surely it can't be as bad as the worry reflected on your face."

"No. It's worse." Her gaze lowered to the floor. "I'm pregnant."

He surely hadn't heard her correctly. "You're what?"

"Pregnant with your baby."

The words knocked the air from his lungs.

He never thought anyone would say those words to him. And now he couldn't believe it was true. At the same time, he wanted it to be real. Torn by conflicting emotions, his body stiffened. What was she hoping to accomplish with such a wildly improbable claim?

CHAPTER FOUR

She shouldn't have just blurted it out.

And now that it was out there, she couldn't take it back.

This was not how Noemi had envisioned telling Max about the baby. The truth was she hadn't figured out how to tell him this life-changing news. It certainly wasn't something you blurted out, like she'd done. The fact she was pregnant was still something she was trying to cope with. By the paleness of Max's face, he'd been completely caught off guard.

"No." He adamantly shook his head. Then his eyes narrowed on her. "It's a lie."

She refused to squirm under his intense stare. Her mouth pressed into a firm line as she started to count to ten. Her mother had taught her to do this after Noemi had shot her mouth off one too many times in school. Noemi had imagined a lot of reactions but being called a liar hadn't been one.

She made it to the number six when she straightened her shoulders and lifted her chin. "I am not a liar. I'm pregnant and you're the father—"

"Impossible." His voice was adamant as he started to pace.

"Actually, it's quite possible. You're going to be a father in about six or so months."

He stopped and his disbelieving gaze met hers. "Have you gone to a doctor?"

"I have. It has been verified by an official pregnancy test." She could see that he was still in denial. Perhaps she should give him some idea of the changes this pregnancy had brought to her life. "I've started to grow out of my clothes. And I have morning sickness. The doctor says I should start to feel better in my second trimester."

Max shook his head again. "It must be someone else's—"

"It's not." How dare he? What did he think of her? That she got around so much that she wouldn't be able to name the father? "This baby is yours. It doesn't matter how many times you claim it isn't, it won't change the facts."

"You're mistaken."

She crossed her arms and glared at him. "You might be a prince and all, but that doesn't give you the right to talk to me this way. This pregnancy is nothing either of us planned, but now that it's happening, we've both got to figure out how to deal with it."

He stepped closer to her. There was torment in his eyes. "You aren't listening me. I'm not this baby's father. It's an impossibility."

What was he saying? He wasn't making any sense. She hadn't expected him to take this news well, but this was far worse than she'd been imagining.

She forced her voice to remain calm. "I don't know how many ways I can say this to get you to believe that you and I are having a baby."

He turned his back to her. "You need to go. Now."

"You're dismissing me?"

"Yes, I am."

Her hands clenched at her sides. Her lips pursed as she struggled to control her emotions. "Fine."

Her face warmed as anger pumped through her veins. Did he think it had been easy for her to come here? She quickly gathered her things. Did he really think she would make something like this up?

She strode to the door with her chin lifted. She refused to slink off into the night. She paused at the door and glanced back. Max's back was still turned her way and his posture was rigid.

She tried to think of something to say—some parting shot—but her pride kept her from speaking. And so without a word, she let herself out the door.

Once she was outside, tears of frustration and anger rushed to her eyes, blurring her vision. She blinked them away. She refused to cry over such a stubborn, infuriating man.

She had to be lying.

That was the only possible answer.

Max sent his staff away that evening—even his security. It may have taken a raised voice and an empty threat or two to clear the condo, but he'd succeeded. He needed to be alone.

One hour faded into another as he sat alone in the dark. Noemi's words played on his insecurities and inadequacies—things he'd thought he'd put behind him. He'd only deluded himself into thinking that he'd made peace with losing his rightful place as heir to the throne and the knowledge that he would never be able to father a family of his own. Noemi couldn't have wounded him more if she'd been trying.

Sleep eluded him that night. By the next afternoon, he'd made a decision. Without giving himself a chance to talk himself out of it, he drove to Noemi's chalet and knocked on the door.

When Noemi opened the door, he didn't give her a chance to speak. "Are you ready to admit it?"

She frowned at him. "I already admitted that I'm pregnant. I don't know what else you expect me to say."

He needed to hear her say that she'd made up the whole thing about her pregnancy. He searched her eyes for the truth. He was pretty good at reading people. And he saw nothing but honesty reflected in them. Either she'd talked herself into believing her lies…or she was telling him the truth. But that wasn't possible. Right?

He raked his fingers through his hair. Maybe he needed to come at this from a different angle.

He exhaled an unsteady breath. "Can we talk?"

For a moment, she didn't move nor did she say a word, as though weighing her options.

He couldn't walk away until he made her understand what she was claiming was absolutely impossible. "Please," he said. "It won't take long and it's important. I've been up all night thinking about what you told me."

He was beginning to think she'd refuse to let him inside when she suddenly swung the door wide open and stepped aside. "Hurry before someone sees you."

He ventured inside. After slipping off his snow-covered boots and coat, he moved toward the great room. Not sure what to do with himself, he stood in front of the darkened fireplace beside the large Christmas tree.

Noemi perched on the edge of the couch. "I know this is hard for you to believe. It was for me, too."

He turned to her. "It's not hard. It's impossible."

"Why do you keep saying that?"

He ran a hand over his unshaven jaw. The stubble felt like sandpaper over his palm. He'd come here to settle this once and for all. He couldn't stop now.

"Come sit down." She patted the cushion next to her.

He joined her on the couch, leaning his head back against the cushion, and closed his eyes. "Some of what I'm going to tell you, no one outside my family and trusted members of the court know." He opened his eyes and gazed at her. "Can I trust you?"

"I won't tell anyone."

"You already know that I'm a prince, but you might not know that I am the firstborn—the crown prince. Ever since I took my first breath, I've been groomed to take the throne of Ostania. It is a small country, but it is prosperous. However, when I was thirteen, I was diagnosed with Hodgkin's lymphoma."

Noemi let out a soft gasp.

He cleared his throat. "At that moment, my entire world stopped. Everything became about my health. I never knew it was possible to become so sick of being sick. Of course, this was all kept hush-hush. With me being the crown prince, it was decided that it was best that the citizens of Ostania not know about my cancer diagnosis."

Sympathy reflected in her eyes. "That must have been scary for you to go through."

The cancer had been more than scary, it had changed the way he looked at himself. From the time he was little, he'd known exactly who he was, what was expected of him and what his future would entail. The cancer robbed him of that identity.

After the cancer, he'd gone out into the world searching for himself—searching for a new identity. He'd done crazy daredevil stuff, from parachuting to cliff diving to bungee jumping to more responsible endeavors, such as being a diplomatic liaison for his country. Through it all, it still felt as though something was missing from his life.

"I was young. At the beginning, I was certain I could survive anything. And it helped that everyone around me was so positive. But the more aggressive treatments left me extremely sick and my positivity faltered. At one point, I gave up. I didn't think I would live to see my next birthday."

She reached out, placing her hand in his. "I can't even imagine."

"I didn't tell you that to gain your sympathy. I wanted you to realize the intensity of my treatments. I was told it was quite likely I'd never be able to father any children."

He stopped there. He didn't tell her that royal decree stated the ruler of Ostania must produce an heir. That wasn't her problem.

Nor was it her problem that after his treatments were over and the doctors had declared him in remission that the nightmare hadn't ended. The doctors had said he was likely sterile. The palace attentions had turned to preparing his younger brother, Tobias, to become the future ruler of Ostania. Max had to take a step back as his brother replaced him.

"Well, obviously they were wrong." Noemi sent him a

wavering smile. "Because I am pregnant and you are most definitely the father."

He wanted to believe her. But he knew the doctors had been the best in their field. They hadn't told Max and his parents their dire warning lightly. If he was the father, it was truly a miracle. But he didn't believe in miracles.

"I just don't think this can be true," he said. "The doctors said—"

"Stop. I'm telling you it's true."

He stared deeply into her eyes. He wanted so desperately to believe her. But he was hesitant. "I need time."

"I understand."

"We'll talk again." He got to his feet and left. He needed to walk. He needed to think. He needed space.

The stakes were so high. If Noemi was telling the truth, then he would be eligible to inherit the throne of Ostania. He'd be able to assume his birthright. At last, he'd once again feel whole.

The breath hitched in his throat. He hadn't allowed himself to consider it for years. This would change his entire life—his brother's life—if it was true.

CHAPTER FIVE

A RESTLESS NIGHT left Noemi yawning the next morning.

Her first thought was of Max. By the time he'd left, he'd at least been willing to consider that the baby was his. She knew it was going to take time for him to come to terms with the news, especially after being convinced he could never father children.

After a round of morning sickness had passed, she showered. Dressed in the new clothes she'd bought while out shopping the other day, she felt much more comfortable and more confident. Whatever happened next, she could deal with it. After all, she was going to become a mother. Dealing with the unknown came with the job.

Knock. Knock.

Who in the world could that be?

She checked the time, finding it wasn't even eight o'clock in the morning. Perhaps it was Sebastian. But that didn't make sense. He wouldn't knock as he had his own key. Maybe it was Leo. They hadn't had a chance to make him a key. Maybe he'd returned early for the holidays.

Noemi liked the thought of seeing her new big brother again. She'd immediately hit it off with Leo. She rushed to the door and swung it open to find a disheveled Max standing with his hair astray, dark shadows under his eyes and heavy stubble trailing down his jaw.

"Max?"

"I've done nothing but think about what you told me. And I'd like to talk some more."

A gust of wind rushed past him and swept past her, sending a wave of goose bumps down her arms. "Come in."

When he didn't move, she reached out and grabbed his black leather jacket. She gave him a yank toward her. Once he was inside, she swung the big wooden door shut against the gusty wind. She glanced out the window to see if he'd been followed by the paparazzi.

"What are you looking for?"

Max's voice came from much closer than she'd been expecting. When she turned, she almost bumped into him. She tried to put some space between them but her back pressed against the door. She swallowed hard. Being so close to him made her heart palpitate.

"I... I was checking to see if you were followed." She sidestepped around him and moved across the foyer. From that distance, she could at last take a full breath.

"You don't have to worry," he said. "No one followed me."

"How can you be so sure? What if they saw you come here yesterday?"

"After I was spotted in the village, I activated my backup plan."

"Backup plan? What's that?"

"One of my bodyguards is a body double from a distance. The morning after the paparazzi spotted me, he departed Mont Coeur and flew back to Ostania. I and my remaining staff have since switched vehicles and residences."

Noemi arched a fine brow. "Has anyone ever told you that you're devious?"

"I don't know. Is that good? Or bad?"

"In this case, it's a good thing. And here I figured you for the cautious type."

"Cautious, huh? I did pursue you at the party. I don't think anyone would classify that night as cautious."

She turned her head to the side, but not soon enough. She

knew he saw the smile pulling at her lips. "We aren't discussing that night."

"We aren't?"

She shook her head. "No, we aren't." They had a lot more pressing matters to discuss—matters that had apparently kept him awake most of the night. Perhaps the shock was starting to wear off and reality was taking hold.

His bloodshot eyes met hers. "I shouldn't have bothered you so early. I just didn't know who else to talk to."

"It's fine. I didn't sleep well last night so I was up early." She held out her hands for his jacket. "Let me hang that up for you."

After his jacket and boots had been tended to, she led him into the spacious living room. She started a fire while he quietly took a seat on the couch. For a man who wanted to talk, he certainly wasn't saying much.

She left a respectable space between them when she sat on the couch. Even in his disheveled appearance, she couldn't deny that he was devastatingly handsome. And when he lifted his head and stared at her with that lost look in his eyes, her heart dipped.

"How can you look so calm?" he asked.

She shrugged. "I've had time to adjust to the news."

"If we hadn't run into each other, were you ever going to tell me?" His gaze searched hers.

"I wanted to, but remember, I didn't have your last name or your cell number. I didn't have any idea how to reach you."

He rubbed the back of his neck. "That's my fault."

"But it all worked out. It was as if fate made sure our paths would cross again." She paused as her stomach took a nauseous lurch.

Please not in front of Max. Her mouth grew moist and she swallowed, willing herself not to get sick—again.

"What's wrong?" A look of concern came over his face.

Great. So much for hiding it. "It's nothing."

He studied her. "It sure looks like something. You're pale. Is it the baby?"

"In a way." Her stomach lurched again. "I'll be back."

She dashed from the room, leaving Max to come to his own conclusions. She didn't have time to explain.

Was it something he'd said?

He wouldn't know. He'd never been around a pregnant woman. Sure, his mother had been pregnant with his younger brother but Max had only been a kid back then.

Max paced around the living room. Was this really happening? Was he really going to be a father? And if so, how would his family take it?

For years now, Tobias had been learning to be Ostania's new ruler. How would he feel when Max pushed him aside to resume his birthright? Would Tobias be disappointed? Or would he be thankful to have his life back again?

Max honestly didn't know how this news would impact his brother. The truth was that ever since Max's illness and the attention had started shining on his brother, they'd grown apart.

"Sorry about that." Noemi's voice interrupted his thoughts.

He glanced at her. She was still pale, but there was perhaps a bit more color in her face. "Are you feeling better?"

She nodded. "It's just morning sickness. The doctor and books say that it is common and nothing to worry about."

He couldn't see how being sick could be nothing to worry about. "Which way to the kitchen?"

She pointed toward the back of the chalet. "Why?"

"Stay here. I'll be back." He headed for the door off to the side of the large fireplace.

The kitchen was spacious. He glanced at all the white cabinets. Maybe he should have asked a few more questions—like where to find things. But it couldn't be that hard to locate what he needed.

He moved to the cabinet closest to him. He yanked open the doors. He knew what he was looking for and if it wasn't here, he'd go to the store in the village—even if it meant dealing with the crowd of onlookers.

Cabinet after cabinet, he searched. Three quarters of the way through, he opened a door and found exactly what he was searching for—peppermint tea. He set to work filling a kettle and placing it on the stove to heat up.

While it warmed, he searched a little more and located a box of crackers. He placed a few on a plate and turned to set it on the island when he noticed Noemi sitting on a kitchen stool staring at him.

"How long have you been there?" he asked.

"A while."

"You don't trust me?"

"It wasn't a matter of trust but rather curiosity." She eyed the crackers and the now boiling kettle. "Are you hungry?"

"This isn't for me."

"Oh. Well, thank you. But I don't usually drink tea."

"I think you'll like this tea. It should help settle your stomach."

The teakettle whistled. Max set to work steeping the tea. Once everything was ready, he turned to Noemi. "Why don't we take this to the living room where you'll be more comfortable?"

In silence, she led the way and he followed with a loaded tray. He glanced around at the spacious chalet, something he hadn't taken time to do the day before. Nothing had been skimped on in its construction. It had some of the finest details.

"This is a really big place for one person," he said, trying to keep the conversation going.

"It's not mine. It belongs to my parents—well, our family."

"Are your parents here?" He glanced around.

Here he was spilling his guts to her and he didn't even think to ask if they were alone. He wondered how her parents felt about the pregnancy. And then he wondered if Noemi had told them.

"No one is here." Noemi's face once again grew pale as she sat down on the couch.

"What's bothering you?" He sat next to her. "Is it my mention of your parents? If you want me to talk to them—"

"You can't." Her gaze lowered. "They, um…" Her voice grew faint. "They died."

He hadn't seen that coming. "You mean, since we met?"

She nodded as her eyes shimmered with unshed tears. In that moment, he didn't think about right or wrong, he just acted. He moved next to her, wrapped his arm around her and drew her head to his shoulder.

He leaned his cheek against the top of her head. "I can't even begin to tell you how sorry I am."

He didn't know how long they sat there with their bodies leaning on each other. His hand smoothed down over her silky hair. And when he pressed a kiss to the top of her head, he inhaled the berry fragrance of her shampoo.

When she finally pulled back, she swiped at her cheeks. "I'm sorry. I'm not normally so emotional."

"It's okay. You don't have to explain. In fact, you don't have to talk about it." He'd do or say anything to get her to stop crying because he was not good with tears. They left him uncomfortable and not sure what to say.

"Thank you for your shoulder."

"Anytime." He just hoped the next time would come with happier circumstances. "Do you have siblings?" After the words were out, he wondered if it was a safe subject.

She nodded. "An older brother—actually make that two older brothers."

That was an unusual thing to get wrong. He had a feeling there was a story there, but he was pretty certain he'd delved far enough into her life for one day.

For a moment, they sat quietly while Noemi sipped the tea and nibbled on a cracker. Then she turned on the television, letting a morning talk show fill in the awkward silence.

A half hour later during the break in a morning news show, Max asked, "Are you feeling better now?"

"I am. Thank you. How did you know about the tea and crackers?"

He glanced away. "This is what they gave me after my cancer treatments."

"And it worked?"

"Sometimes. If it didn't work, nothing did. I just had to wait it out." He looked at her, noticing the color was already coming back to her face. "Is there anything I can do for you?"

She shook her head.

"Does this just happen in the morning?"

She nodded. "I read that some women get it at any time of the day." Noemi visibly shuddered. "Sounds absolutely horrid."

"Maybe I should go now. I really shouldn't have bothered you so early."

"It's fine. I'm sure you have a lot of questions."

"I really just have one."

She leveled her shoulders and met his stare straight on. "What is it?"

"I wanted to know if you had plans for tomorrow."

Where had that come from? He hadn't come here intending to ask her out, but he could see the benefits. Getting her out of the house, doing something together might smooth out some of the tension coursing between them.

She didn't say anything at first but then she shook her head. "I don't."

"Would you like to do something with me?"

"Are you sure? You probably have other more important things that require your attention."

"There's nothing more important than us getting to know each other better," he said, meaning every word. He couldn't think about anything but Noemi and the baby.

"You don't have to do that—"

"I know. But I want to."

Her eyes flared with surprise.

In the end, they made plans for the following morning to go snow tubing. It was short run meant for kids and adults alike. But right now, he needed to get some work done and then he'd get some much-needed sleep.

"What do you mean, she's pregnant?"

"Shh…" That evening, Max gripped the phone tighter. "I don't need anyone overhearing you."

He was speaking to Enzo, his private secretary and his confidant. He had to tell someone. He couldn't keep this huge—this amazing news to himself. He was going to be a father. His world was about to change.

Enzo's normally monotone voice took on a higher pitch. "But you can't have children—the doctors said—"

"I know what they said, that the possibility was very unlikely. Not impossible."

"Your Royal Highness, do not get your hopes up. This woman is not the first to lie in order to become included in the royal family. Remember—"

"I remember." He'd tried to forget Abree. She'd portrayed herself as everything he could ever want. They'd been happy for three months and then she'd claimed to be pregnant.

When the paternity test was done, he was not the father. The extent of her lies had been devastating for him. But in the process, he'd learned she wasn't the woman she'd portrayed to him. She was nothing like he thought. Thankfully his family never found out how deep her lies had gone.

It was why he'd insisted on keeping his relationships casual since then. Until Noemi. She was different. She didn't seem to care what he thought or what he expected. She did what she wanted. And so far, she wanted nothing from him. There's no way she was lying to him. Right?

Enzo's voice sliced through Max's thoughts. "What is this woman's name? I'll run a background check on her."

Enzo didn't say it, but Max could hear the wheels in the man's mind spin. He wanted to see if Noemi was a liar, a cheat, a scam. He wanted to find every little thing she'd done wrong in her life and prove to Max that she was unsuitable for him. Because Enzo, like his parents, had very definite ideas of how a royal should act and exactly who they should marry.

"I'm not telling you," Max said with finality.

"But, Your Highness—"

"Leave it alone, Enzo."

There was a distinct pause. "Yes, sir."

In time, Max would learn everything he needed to know about Noemi, but it would all come from her. He didn't need a private investigator or a credit report. He was going with his gut on this one. And his gut said he could trust her.

To help alleviate Enzo's worry, Max said, "I will take care of the situation."

"Did you tell her about the necessity for a paternity test?"

Max resisted the urge to sigh. "Not yet."

"What are you waiting for?"

Max didn't say anything. The truth was he didn't know why he was hesitating. He hadn't hesitated when it came to Abree. He'd known from the start that she was lying. He'd insisted on the test as soon as it was safe for the mother and baby.

"Your Highness?"

"I wish you'd just call me Max." He'd never been one for royal protocol. That was his mother's thing—not his.

"That is not possible. You are the crown prince. As such, you deserve the respect due your station."

"And we grew up together. You know me. We played polo together."

"That was a long time ago, sir. And I know that when you don't want to talk about something, you change the subject."

"Don't worry. I'll take care of this."

He didn't want to. He didn't want to do anything to ruin his time with Noemi, but Enzo had a point. He couldn't stand to be played again. And his family deserved to know that their lives were about to be disrupted, once again. This time, though, the disruption would be a good one.

He would talk to Noemi in the morning about the test. Surely she'd understand. Right?

CHAPTER SIX

THE NEXT MORNING, Max decided they should talk first and play in the snow later. The stakes were high and he had to make sure Noemi understood how high.

"Max, what's wrong?" The smile had slipped from Noemi's face. "If you have to cancel our plans, it's okay. I understand."

He shook his head. "It's not that." Max leaned forward, resting his elbows on his knees. "We need to talk."

"I thought that's what we were doing."

"I'm serious, Noemi."

She sighed. "I know."

"We need to talk about the baby and the future."

"If you're about to tell me that you don't want anything to do with the baby, I can deal with it."

"What? No. That isn't what I was going to say."

She gave him a weak smile. "That's good."

"Our child will know me." Max stated it with conviction.

"Okay. Was there something else you wanted to discuss?"

He cleared his throat. "My country dictates that we must provide proof of the baby's legitimacy."

She moved back. "What are you saying?"

Surely she would want her child to be legitimate. Wouldn't she? He'd never imagined that she wouldn't want her child to be a part of the royal family—to be heir to the throne.

"You must have a paternity test done as soon as possible."

"I got that part but why?"

"So we may become a family and the baby will be heir to the throne."

She shook her head. "No."

"What do you mean no?" He got to his feet. Now she was being totally unreasonable. His child had a right—a duty to assume the throne of Ostania.

She got to her feet, straightened her shoulders and lifted her chin until their eyes met. "I know with being a prince and all that you aren't used to hearing the word no, but I'm saying it now and to you. No."

In that moment, his heart sank. He wasn't sure if it was the thought of losing the prospect of being a father and all it entailed, or if it was the realization that once again he'd been lied to by a woman. And not any small lie—but one that was so close to his heart.

It took him a moment to muster up the strength to vocalize the words. He swallowed hard. "Are you saying you lied about the paternity?"

"What?" The expression in her eyes was unreadable. "Is that what you're hoping?"

"No. But if you're refusing the paternity test, there has to be a reason. And the only one that I can think of is you lied to me."

"Or the fact that you totally misunderstood my answer."

He sighed and rubbed the back of his neck. He never knew talking with a woman could be this complicated, but then again, he'd never let his relationships get serious. All his conversations since Abree had been flirting and casual talk about his travels. His whole future had never been on the line.

"Does that mean you agree to the test? It's the only way we can become a family and put the child in line for the throne."

"It means that no matter what is revealed by the test, we are *not* getting married. And I'm not becoming a princess."

He processed what she told him, but he wanted to make sure they were on the same page. "So you're agreeing to the test?"

She nodded.

"But you don't want to be my wife."

"Exactly."

"And the child? How do you expect that to work out? Because if it is my child, I will not turn my back on it."

"I… I don't know how things will work out. I haven't had much time to consider it."

"But you're sure you don't want to be a part of the royal family?"

She nodded. "I already have a complicated family. I don't need another. If I marry, it will be for love and nothing less. And you do not love me."

He wanted to argue with her. But he couldn't lie to her. Sure they'd spent some wonderful time together, but he wasn't ready to put his heart on the line.

He'd been raised to do what was expected of him—to put the needs of the royal family ahead of his own. And he was told from a young age that marriage was a business contract and it had nothing to do with romantic fantasies.

However, Max learned from his time on his own that many people held tight to their dreams of love and happily-ever-after. He didn't know why when so many people ended up with a broken heart. There really wasn't such a thing as love. There was respect. There was friendship. That had to be enough.

His gaze moved to Noemi. A glint of determination reflected in her eyes. He knew there was no arguing with her. He needed to show her that they could have a good life together—even if they didn't love each other.

"It's okay," she said. "Why don't we give it some more time to think through our situation? And then we can figure out what makes the most sense."

At last, they could agree on something. "I think that's a good idea. In the meantime, spend the rest of the week with me."

"I… I don't know."

"I don't know how the future will play out, you know,

with the baby and all, but I think we should take advantage of our relative privacy here at the resort in order to get to know each other better. Because at the very least, I'm going to be the father of your child."

Noemi silently stared at him as though weighing his words. And then she nodded. "You're right. We should know each other better since we'll be linked for life. But I have one condition."

"And that would be?"

"As long as you don't pressure me about the baby and marriage."

He held up his hand as though he were about to take the oath to the throne. "I swear."

Marry a prince…

Wasn't that every girl's dream?

Noemi longed to talk to her mother. What would her mother tell her? To hold out for love? Or be practical and give the baby a mother and father living under one roof—even if they didn't love each other?

She was torn. Both options had their positives and negatives. But what was best for all of them?

At least Max had heard her and was giving them time to figure this thing out. He had no idea how much it meant to her that he valued her opinion.

Noemi tied her hair back in a short ponytail and pulled a white knit cap down over it. She selected her biggest sunglasses and headed for the door. It'd been a long time since she'd gone tubing and she was looking forward to it.

And it was just as she'd remembered. The sun beaming on her face. The cold air filling her lungs. And her racing to the bottom of the hill. The first trip down, Max had won. The second time down, she'd won.

Noemi walked through the fluffy white snow, feeling like a kid again. No responsibilities. No messy family stuff.

It helped that Max hadn't mentioned the M-word again that day. In fact, he'd kept everything light and casual.

She couldn't remember smiling so much.

But she wasn't a child and neither was Max. He was all man—tall and muscled. His eyes said he'd experienced more in life than most people his age, and yet he was able to have fun with her.

"You have to stop this," Noemi said.

The smile immediately fled his face. "What's wrong? Is it the baby?"

She continued to smile as she shook her head. "The baby is fine. It's my cheeks that are having the problem."

"I don't understand."

"My cheeks are sore from smiling so much." She glanced at him. "Speaking of cheeks, are you ever going to shave again?"

He ran a hand over his thickening stubble. "You don't like it?"

She pursed her lips and studied him. "I don't know."

"I'm keeping it temporarily. It's part of my disguise."

With things going so well between them, she had an idea. She didn't know what Max would think of it, but it was something she wanted to share with him.

"Hey, I have a doctor's appointment next week and I was wondering if you'd want to go with me?"

His eyes widened. "You mean for the baby?" When she nodded, he asked, "Is anything wrong?"

"No, it's a regular checkup. They're going to do a sonogram and we'll be able to hear the baby's heartbeat."

"Already?" When she smiled and nodded again, he said, "I'd love it. Thank you for asking me."

She never thought she could be this happy. She told herself this feeling wasn't going to last, but a voice in her head said to enjoy this moment as long as it lasted. When it was over, she'd have the memories to cherish.

And then there was Max, Crown Prince Maximilian Steiner-Wolf, who made her stomach dip every time he smiled at her. Not only did they have fun together, but he'd also been there to comfort her through the morning sickness.

He was so sweet to insist on making her tea. This prince was something extra special.

"Let's go again." She trudged toward the lift.

"Aren't you hungry?"

She shook her head. Okay. Maybe she was a little hungry, but she wanted to go down the hill one more time. And then she had something special in mind for after lunch.

"Please," she begged. "It'll be a tiebreaker."

He sighed. "How can I say no to that pouty look on your face?"

"Yay!" She grabbed his hand without thinking and pulled him toward the line for the tube lift.

Was it possible she could feel the heat of his body emanating through their gloves? Or was it just a bit of wishful thinking? She should let go of him. But it was so much easier to live in the moment and not think about what the future would bring them.

She tightened her hold on him as they slowly moved closer to the lift. "Isn't this the most beautiful day?"

Max looked at her and then glanced up at the sky. "Are we looking at the same sky? It's cloudy."

She breathed in deeply. "I can smell snow."

"You can't smell snow."

She nodded. "Can too. It smells fresh and crisp." She inhaled deeply. "It smells like snow."

He smiled and shook his head. "If you say so."

When his gaze connected with hers, her stomach dipped again. "I do."

"Next," the attendant said. He waved her forward.

With great reluctance, she let go of Max's hand. She didn't know why that connection should mean so much to her. It wasn't like they were in love or anything.

They were friends. Nothing more. Well, not quite. They were going to be parents to a little, innocent baby. That was a connection unlike any other. They had to continue to get along for the child. That was the most important part. She didn't want her child growing up in a stressful environment where the parents always argued.

At the top of the small hill, she waited for him to join her. Once they were side by side in their respective tubes, she turned to him. "First one to the bottom gets to pick what we do this afternoon."

"You think you're really going to beat me?"

"I know I am." She took off down the hill.

"Hey…" His voice got lost in the breeze as the first few snowflakes started to fall.

She laughed as the tube glided down over the dips. This was one of the best days of her life. And for the first time since learning she was pregnant, she felt everything was going to work out. She didn't quite know how, but she believed it would work out for the best and her baby would be happy.

She reminded herself not to get too wrapped up in the prince. They were just friends. There were no strings attached. But the harder she tried to resist his charms, the more she fell for the sexy prince.

She tempered her excitement with the knowledge that the people she loved eventually let her down. Max would eventually let her down, too—whether he meant to or not.

CHAPTER SEVEN

"YOU CHEAT."

Max didn't mind losing the race to Noemi—not at all. But he liked teasing her and keeping the smile on her face. She had the most beautiful smile with her rosy lips and it lit up her brown eyes.

"I do not," she said emphatically. "I can't help that you're slow."

"I am not."

There had been nothing slow about his attraction to her at the party that now seemed a lifetime ago. There was nothing slow about the rush of desire that came over him every time she was close by. And there was nothing slow about his yearning to care for her and their unborn child.

They'd just finished lunch in the ski lodge in a private room away from any curious eyes. He worried his beard wouldn't be enough to keep him from being recognized. And he knew he'd stand out if he wore a hat and sunglasses throughout their meal.

And now it was time for him to ante up for losing the tubing race. "So what do you have in mind for the afternoon? Please tell me it isn't skiing."

Her eyes twinkled with mischief. "Well, now that you mention it, skiing doesn't sound so bad—"

"Noemi, you really should be careful—"

"I never would have guessed you'd be a worrier."

"I don't worry. I'm just being cautious. There's a difference."

She shook her head. "Anyway, I've decided to give it up until the baby is born. Better safe than sorry."

"Thank you. So, what did you have in mind for this afternoon?"

She wiped the corners of her mouth with the white linen napkin and pushed aside her empty plate. "I was wondering if you would want to do some shopping with me."

"Shopping?" It was definitely not something he would have suggested. And it was not something he would enjoy. In fact, it was one of the last things he wanted to do. A dentist appointment sounded more appealing.

Noemi frowned. "I can see you don't like the idea."

He'd have to work harder in the future to keep his thoughts from reflecting on his face. "Not at all." He forced a smile. He knew how to be a good loser. "What are we shopping for?"

"I thought we could look at some baby stuff."

Baby stuff? He had absolutely no idea what that would entail. "Where do we have to go?"

"It's right up the road from here. What do you think?" The hopeful look on her face was too much for him to turn down.

"I think we should go. I'll call my driver."

Once the bill was paid, they were out the door. Max's car and two bodyguards were waiting for them. They were quickly ushered into the village, where upscale shops carried most anything you could think of to buy. And there in the heart of the village was a baby boutique.

The boutique was small but that didn't detract from its appeal. Pink, blue and white checked nursery bunting adorned the window, while in the center sat a bassinet, some stuffed animals and itty-bitty clothes. Noemi grinned with excitement. Maybe this surprise baby thing wasn't all so bad. And then her gaze slipped to Max, who opened the shop door for her. No, definitely not so bad at all.

Inside, the shop was brightly lit and filled with pastel colors of every shade. In the background, children's music played. A saleswoman approached them with a smile and offered to assist them, but they waved her off, saying they were just there to look around.

After the woman returned to the checkout, Max turned to Noemi. "We are just looking around, aren't we?"

Noemi shrugged. "It would be so hard not to buy something. It's all so cute. Don't you think?"

It was Max's turn to shrug. She could tell he was trying hard not to be moved by what this shopping trip meant to their future. In less than six months, they were going to have this tiny baby in their arms. He or she would be relying on them for everything. The enormity of the responsibility didn't escape her—in fact, it downright scared her. She'd never been responsible for another human. What if she messed up?

When she'd first learned she was pregnant, she'd considered adoption. She'd quickly dismissed the idea. That's what her parents had been forced to do with Leo and they'd regretted it ever since. She didn't want to be separated from her child. Her hand instinctively moved to the ever-so-slight bump in her midsection. She was already in love.

As she perused a pink, yellow and white dress that looked like it was made for a fine china doll, she couldn't help but feel people staring at them. When she lifted her head, she noticed a young woman had joined the older saleslady at the checkout. She was staring at them. Noemi slipped her sunglasses on and pulled her cap down so it covered all her hair.

"Maybe coming here wasn't such a good idea," Noemi whispered.

"It's fine. My security is by the door. Nothing will happen."

"I think we should go." She worried her bottom lip, but as she looked around this time, she didn't notice anyone staring at them.

"Just keep shopping. Everything is fine."

Perhaps he was right. After all, he was far more familiar with fame than she was. Once off the runway and with her heavy makeup removed, she wasn't easily recognized as the face of Cattaneo Jewels. That used to bother her. Once upon a time, she'd longed for fame.

She used to wear her runway makeup and finest fashions every time she went out. She'd wanted the attention that she failed to get at home. Where her family was concerned, everything had been about Cattaneo Jewels while her opinions were disregarded—while she, as a person, was disregarded.

But ever since she'd learned she was pregnant, her parents had died and Leo had entered her life, being recognized and asked for her autograph had lost its appeal to her. She was learning that there were far more important things in life.

Noemi fingered through the selection of baby clothes. The outfits were all so tiny and adorable. But at this point, she didn't know if she was having a boy or a girl. That would make buying things difficult. But that didn't stop Noemi from leisurely strolling up and down the aisles, feeling the ruffles and placing a pair of booties on her fingertips.

She glanced at Max. "Do you want to know if it's a boy or girl? You know, at the sonogram?"

"Can they tell this soon?"

"I don't know but we can ask." She had a baby book back at the chalet. Maybe it would tell her.

He glanced at the booties dangling from her fingertips. "Can you believe they'll be small enough to wear those?"

"I hope so. Or else I'm in really big trouble." She smiled back at him before turning back to the itty-bitty clothes.

"You're going to be a fantastic mother."

She turned to him and lifted her chin in order to look him in the eyes. "Do you really think so?"

"I do." There was no hesitation in his voice and his gaze did not waver.

"At least one of us thinks so."

His voice lowered. "Trust me."

His gaze lowered to her lips and lingered there. The heat

of excitement swirled in her chest before rushing up her neck and warming her cheeks. He was considering kissing her. And even though they'd already spent the night together, everything had changed since then.

His desire for her, was it real? Or was it fleeting? She didn't know. And to be honest, she didn't know what she wanted it to be. She stepped back.

"Oh, look." She rushed over to an entire display of stuffed animals. There were yellow ducks, green frogs, purple hippos, brown monkeys, polka-dotted inchworms and a whole assortment of other creatures. "Aren't they adorable?"

"Why don't you pick one out?"

She shook her head. "I don't think so."

"Why not?"

"Because I couldn't pick just one. They are all so cute."

"Then I will buy them all for you."

She turned to him, hoping he was joking. He wasn't. "Max, you can't."

"Sure, I can. Watch me."

As he went to make his way to the checkout, Noemi reached out and grabbed his arm. "Wait. You're not being reasonable."

"Of course I am. You like them all. Your smile lit up the whole room. I like when you smile like that. I'll buy the stuffed animals so you'll keep smiling."

When he went to pull away from her hold, her fingers tightened on his black wool coat. "Seriously, you can't. What would I do with all of them?"

He paused as though giving her question some serious thought. "Decorate the nursery?"

"There wouldn't be any room left for the crib or changing table."

"I hadn't thought of that. Maybe the baby will have two rooms. One for the practical stuff and one for the fun stuff."

Noemi's smile broadened. "Something tells me you'd actually do that."

"Sure, I would."

"How about, for now at least, we pick out just one stuffed animal for the baby?"

"One?"

She nodded and then turned back to the display that spanned the whole length of the back wall. "What do you think? A puppy? A kitty? A turtle?"

He shook his head. "I shouldn't pick it out. You're the one who fell in love with them."

"So you're making me do the hard job?"

"Just this once."

She didn't argue. It was a tough job, but she was up to the challenge. Then her eyes scanned the top shelf. Each plush creation called out to her. This definitely wasn't going to be easy.

But she was thoroughly excited to pick out their baby's first stuffed animal. It would be a keepsake. A stuffed animal that hopefully her child would still have when they were all grown up. Something to measure the time of her child's life—when they looked at it, they would remember their earliest childhood memories. Her eyes grew misty. She blinked repeatedly.

Oh, boy, were the mommy hormones kicking in full gear. She'd never been this sentimental in her life. But everything was different now. She was different, but she didn't feel as though she was done changing yet.

The purple snake she skipped over. That was an easy decision. She also crossed off anything pink or blue. Knowing her luck, she'd pick the wrong color.

She didn't know how much time had passed when she heard Max ask, "Do you need some help?"

She shook her head. "I've got this."

She had it narrowed down to a teddy bear, a lion or an elephant. She was tempted to take all three. But then how would she decide which was her child's first stuffed animal? She had to wonder that if something this simple was giving her such great pains to decide, how would she ever make the bigger decisions concerning her child?

Her stomach tightened as she realized the lifetime of responsibilities facing her. And with her parents gone, she wouldn't have anyone to turn to with her questions and doubts. But then she looked over at Max, who was trying so hard not to look bored. At least she wouldn't be all alone with this parenthood thing. Something told her Max would always be available for his child.

She glanced back at the three stuffed animals in her arms. And she knew right away which one to pick.

"Close your eyes," she said.

"But why?"

"Just do it. Please."

Max sighed. "Okay."

She waited until he'd done it and then she stuffed the other animals back on the shelf. She turned back to Max and said, "Okay. Hold out your hands."

A little smile pulled at his lips as he did what she asked.

She placed the animal in his hands. "Okay. You can open them now."

He opened his eyes and lifted his hands closer to his face. "You picked out a purple lion."

She nodded and smiled.

"And how did you decide on him?"

"I wanted our child's first animal to be something special. The lion will remind them of their father. A lion is king of the jungle, just as you are king of a great nation. The lion is also strong and protective of those he cares about."

"And that's how you see me?" His gaze studied her.

"That's how I see you as a father. Or rather a father-to-be."

She'd dodged that question. Her heart sped up when she thought of herself belonging to him—of him belonging to her. Realizing her thoughts were gravitating toward dangerous territory, she shoved them to the back of her mind.

Max studied the lion as though pondering her words.

"Shall we go?" she asked.

He glanced up at her with a puzzled look. Had he been so deep in thought that he hadn't heard her? Could her words really have affected him so deeply? Not wanting to make a big deal of it. She repeated her question.

"Sure," he said.

When she reached out for the lion, she noticed the booties in her hand. She wasn't sure what to do with them. She should probably put them back. After all, she could pick out all that stuff once the sex of the baby was determined—

"Get them." Max's voice cut through her mental debate.

She glanced down at them. They were so cute. "Okay."

Noemi followed Max through the narrow aisles to the checkout. All the while, Noemi was admiring her finds. It wasn't until they were at the register and the items were on the counter that flashes lit up the room.

Max turned his back to the store window and pulled her to his chest, shielding her from the probing cameras. What were they going to do if they came inside?

"Oh, my," the older saleslady said.

"Isn't this great?" the younger woman said, all the while her fingers moved rapidly over her phone.

If Noemi was a betting person, she'd hazard a guess that the young woman had alerted the paparazzi to the prince's presence in the shop. And then reality started to settle in— they were in a baby boutique. The whole world was about to know that she was baby shopping with the Prince of Ostania. She inwardly groaned.

"I'm sorry about this," the prince said softly. Over his shoulder, he said to the salesclerk, "Is there a back way out of here?"

The older woman gestured to the back of the shop.

"Come on." With the stuffed animal and booties left behind, Max took Noemi's hand and rushed her out the back while his bodyguard led the way.

But where was the other security guy? There had been two of them. She glanced around but didn't see him anywhere. How strange.

As they ducked out the back door into a single-lane alley, she realized the other man had gone off to get their vehicle.

They scrambled into the black SUV with tinted windows and set off down the alley just as the photographers rounded the corner. More flashes went off, but it was all right. The back windows were so heavily tinted that it was doubtful they would get a usable photo.

It wasn't until they were away from the press that her muscles began to relax. She leaned her head back against the leather seat. What had just happened?

CHAPTER EIGHT

"I'M SORRY."

Max kept repeating those words the next morning at Noemi's chalet. It was earlier than they'd intended to meet up, but he knew she was already up because she'd texted him, canceling today's plans to go snowmobiling.

He didn't need anyone to tell him the reason for the cancellation. The paparazzi had once again messed with his life. Before it hadn't mattered so much, but now it was jeopardizing his future.

His phone had been ringing since last night, but he had yet to speak with his mother or Enzo. Apparently they'd been apprised of the headlines. He needed time to make a plan before he spoke with either of them.

Noemi turned away from him, hugging her arms across her chest as she sat on the couch in her gray pajama pants and a silky pink robe. Her hair was yanked back in a ponytail holder and her face was pale. "You really shouldn't have come over. I know you have plans."

"Those plans included you. And I needed to check on you." He also had some more bad news to share with her, but he wasn't quite ready to spring it on her just yet.

"I'm fine." Her complexion said otherwise.

"I should have thought more about going into the village." The truth was that he hadn't been thinking about much of anything yesterday except for making Noemi happy. "With our ability to avoid the paparazzi on the ski slopes, I'd hoped they'd grown bored and moved on to another story—another town."

Noemi lifted her gaze to meet his. "Did you really think that would happen?"

"I guess I've grown accustomed to them being on the fringes of my life. Perhaps I got too careless. And I'm sorry you got caught up in the middle of all of it."

There was a definite pause. "It's not your fault."

"You might not feel that way when I show you this." He pulled his phone from his pocket.

"What is it?" Worry lines marred her beautiful face.

It killed him to be the one to cause her such distress. "I'll let you see for yourself."

He pulled up the headline and photo before handing it over to Noemi.

"Crown Prince to Daddy!"

Beneath the headline was a photo of him in the baby boutique. And standing just behind him was Noemi. But her head was turned and the view of her face was partially obstructed by his shoulder. Her ski cap and sunglasses also added to her anonymity.

Below the picture, the caption read, *But who's the baby's mama?*

Max hadn't been surprised to find it in the headlines today. The only thing to surprise him was the fact that Noemi's identity was still a mystery. And that's the way he wanted it to remain.

With great reluctance, he handed over his phone. Immediately Noemi gasped. Her face grew pale. An awkward silence ensued as she read the article summarizing his life and his eventual ascension to the throne.

Over the years, the paparazzi had written many false stories about him, from him eloping to him abdicating his crown to him joining a professional rock band. None of them had even been close to true. But this story, it hit too close to home for his family to ignore. It would change so much for everyone. And so he needed to return to Ostania immediately.

He didn't want to do that without Noemi. But would she go with him?

She handed his phone back to him. If her face was pale before, now it was a pasty gray. And then without a word, she darted out of the room. He didn't have to ask; he knew the morning sickness had returned.

His body tensed as frustration swept through him. He had to do better in the future. It was his job to protect his family and see to their well-being. If he couldn't care for the mother of his child, how was he ever to look after an entire nation?

It was then that he decided no matter what it took, Noemi would go back to Ostania with him. In that way he could see to her well-being. And while they were there, they could make plans for the future—their future. Because somehow—someway—he intended to marry Noemi.

This couldn't be happening.

Noemi's heart pounded. Ever since the run-in at the boutique, she'd realized the fantasy of her and Max living an ordinary life had been nothing but a dream. They weren't ordinary. She was an heiress and he was a crown prince. It meant that neither of them would have any privacy—now or ever.

Right now, she needed her stomach to settle. She sat on the cold tile floor of the bathroom and leaned her pounding head against the wall. She thought the morning sickness was behind her, but the stress gave her a headache that started her stomach churning.

There was a tap on the door. "Noemi, are you all right?"

She supposed she had been gone for a while. Usually her morning sickness wasn't this bad. She must look quite a sight, but she knew Max wouldn't leave until he was certain she was all right.

"You can come in."

The door slowly opened. Max stood there with a worried frown. "You don't look so good."

"Thank you. That's what all women want to hear."

"I'm sorry. I just meant—"

"I know what you meant. I was just giving you a hard time."

He moved to the sink, where some fresh towels were laid out. The next thing she knew, he sat down next to her and gently pressed a cold washcloth to her forehead.

"Maybe that will help."

The coldness was comforting—so was having Max by her side. She didn't say it, though. It wasn't good to encourage this relationship unless she was ready to share her life with the world. Yesterday proved that. She didn't want her baby to be fodder for headlines.

And then a worrisome thought came to her. "Did the press follow you here?"

He shook his head. "Do you think I would intentionally do that to you?"

"No. But that doesn't mean it couldn't happen accidentally."

"They've been camping outside the gates of the community where I am staying. Thankfully it has guards. One paparazzo did sneak onto the grounds, but he was quickly dealt with. I was able to sneak out in the back of a neighbor's car covered with a blanket. They didn't even notice me. They were intent on watching my SUV."

She breathed a little easier. "Thank you." Feeling a bit better, she removed the cloth from her forehead. She got to her feet. "Sorry about that."

"You don't have to apologize. I can't even imagine all the changes your body is going through right now. And then this thing with the paparazzi doesn't help matters."

"At least they don't know who I am."

"Yet."

"You mean they aren't going to give up until they find out what you were doing in the boutique?"

He nodded. "They can be like a dog with a bone. Relentless."

"How do you live like that?" She thought she'd had it bad,

but her notoriety was miniscule compared to his. For the most part, she could pick and choose when to engage with the press, but Max didn't have that choice.

He cleared his throat. "Some would say it is something you are born into—something that comes along with the job of being royal. Others would say it's a privilege to have access to the world. I don't know what I'd say. Right now, it is a curse. But I also know from watching my father over the years that the press can be used for good things. I'm just sorry that you're caught up in the middle of all this."

"And that's why I want out." She'd wrestled with this decision a large part of the night. She hadn't realized that she'd made the decision until the words popped out of her mouth.

Max didn't say anything at first. It was as though he wasn't sure he'd heard her correctly. But then his eyes grew darker, like that of a stormy sky.

"You want out of what? Having our baby?"

"No." She crossed her arms. "How could you think that?"

He rubbed the back of his neck. "What am I supposed to think?"

"I want out of this." She waved her hand between the two of them. "I want you to walk away. There's nothing tying you to this baby. No paper trail. I haven't told anyone."

"But you forget the one very important tie—I am the baby's father." His mouth pressed closed in a firm line as the muscle in his jaw twitched.

She turned away from him and pressed her hands against the cool granite of the sink counter. "But if you don't tell anyone, no one will know. We can each go our separate way."

Even though she had turned her back on him, his image was there in the mirror. She couldn't tell what he was thinking, only that he wasn't happy. Well, neither was she. This was not the way she wanted things to work out for herself or her child. But they had to be realistic.

Creating a scandal wouldn't be good for their baby either. She didn't want people pointing their fingers at their child and whispering. She didn't want paparazzi hiding behind bushes and springing out, scaring their son or daughter. She didn't want her life to be any more of a three-ring circus than it already was—even if it meant sacrifices had to be made.

"I'll let you finish up in here." His tone was even with no hint of emotion.

She knew he wasn't that calm—that detached. But he strove to hide it well. It must be something about being born a royal. Her family was not that restrained—that in control.

When the bathroom door shut, Noemi pressed a hand to her stomach. "Well, little one, it looks like I've really made a mess of things now."

CHAPTER NINE

SHE WANTS OUT.

Max knew what she was really saying was that she wanted away from him—away from all the baggage that came with being the crown prince. But what she seemed to fail to realize was that was impossible. That little baby within her was the heir to Ostania. But more than that, Max couldn't walk away from his responsibility to the baby—to Noemi.

They were in this together whether they liked it or not.

He moved to the kitchen, where he grabbed some crackers and brewed some tea. He took the food back to the living room to wait for Noemi. He had to return to Ostania right away and he was still determined to take Noemi with him. He wasn't going to leave her alone to deal with the press by herself. But how was he going to convince her that going with him was for the best?

A few minutes later, Noemi returned to the living room. Her eyes widened when they met his. It appeared she hadn't expected him to hang around. The other men in her life must not have been as determined to keep Noemi in their lives. It was their loss and his gain.

"I got you some crackers. Maybe they will help." He gestured to the plate and cup on the large coffee table.

"You really didn't have to—"

"I wanted to."

She sat down and sipped the tea. "I'm surprised you're still here."

"Did you really think I would leave without straightening things out between us?"

"I thought that's what we'd done." Her gaze met his. "It's best for everyone if we just part ways now."

He didn't believe her. "Is that what you really think?"

Her gaze lowered. "It is."

Why was she being so stubborn? Surely she didn't believe what she was saying. She was scared. The paparazzi could be intimidating. And he supposed she might be intimidated by his position—though most women had the opposite reaction.

Still, he had to get through to her. He had to jar her out of this fantasy that she could just erase him from her life. It wasn't going to happen. He wouldn't let it.

"Noemi, I'm not going anywhere. We're in this together."

She shook her head. "I'll be fine on my own."

"But will our baby be fine without a father?"

Her gaze was still lowered. "Lots of children are raised by a single parent."

"And most don't have a choice. But you do. Our child can have two invested parents."

"But at what cost?" Her gaze at last met his. "My pregnancy will become a front-page scandal. It'll be all over the television and internet. And they'll call it our love child. Your illegitimate heir. Or worse."

"Do people still say illegitimate?" he asked in all honesty. "I don't think it will be the scandal that you imagine."

She shook her head. "You aren't going to change my mind."

Oh, yes, he was. Somehow. Some way.

He had one last plan to bring her to her senses. It was with tremendous trepidation that he said, "Are you better off having lost your parents?"

Immediately the pain reflected in her eyes. "That's not the same thing."

"How so? Don't you think our son or daughter will wonder why their friends have both a mother and a father, but they don't? You don't think it will hurt them? You don't think they will grow up with questions?"

For an extended moment, silence filled the room.

Perhaps he'd been too tough on her. But he just couldn't let Noemi delude herself into thinking that exiling him from her life was for the best. It wouldn't be good for any of them. Least of all their child.

"All right," she said, "you've made your point. But I don't see how this is going to work out."

It was time to get to the reason for his visit. "I have to leave today for Ostania."

"Because of the article about us at the baby boutique?"

"Partly." He had a lot of explaining to do with his family—especially his brother.

"Then there's no rush to figure this out." The worry lines on her face eased a bit.

"I want you to come with me."

"To Ostania?"

He nodded. "Have you ever been there?"

She shook her head as she reached for the crackers. "I've always wanted to visit. It looks like such a beautiful country, but I've just never had the opportunity."

"So this is your chance. Let me show you my world. It will be better than sitting here while the paparazzi scour the area for the mysterious woman in the photograph."

She didn't say anything at first. He took that as a positive sign. The longer she was quiet, the more confident he became that she would accompany him to Ostania.

Just then, her phone chimed. She frowned as she read the text message. She responded. Once she set her phone aside, she glanced at Max. There was still a hint of worry written on her face.

"Is everything all right?"

She sighed. "It was my brother Leo. He was letting me know that he has flown back to New York."

"So it's just you in Mont Coeur?"

She nodded. "Until Christmas."

"Then there's no reason for you to stay here alone." Feeling that she might need a little more encouragement, he said, "You can do as much sightseeing or as little as you like. You can consider it a vacation. And we'll be able to get to know each other better."

"But won't you be busy with your duties?"

He would be. He wouldn't lie to her about it. This baby would mean so many things would change. He would be taking on a lot of responsibility that previously had been given to his brother. He had many things to learn about governing a nation.

"I will be busy. It's unavoidable. But I promise you'll have plenty to do. Every amenity is at the palace. And there will be a car at your disposal should you want to go anywhere."

She finished the last cracker. "You make it sound like a relaxing trip to a five-star spa."

"It can be if that's what you'd like."

A look came over her face as though she'd just recalled something. "I can't go. I have a doctor's appointment."

The one where he was supposed to hear his son or daughter's heartbeat and see their image. A pang of regret hit him with the force of a sledgehammer.

"You can't miss that."

A look of relief came over her. "I agree."

"But you could see the doctor in Ostania." When she started to shake her head, he said, "Sure you can."

"It's not that easy. I can't just go strolling into a new doctor's office."

"I can put the doctors in touch with each other. Or I can fly in your doctor."

"You know how to exaggerate a house call."

"I'm a prince. There's a lot I can do. Trust me."

She fidgeted with the hem of her shirt. "You aren't going to let this go, are you?"

He shook his head. "If you stay here, so do I."

"But your family—"

"Will have to wait. This is more important."

"I'm not ready to face your family and discuss the baby. We…" she waved her hand between them "…need to figure things out before we tell people."

"I agree." By the widening of her eyes, he could see that his response surprised her. "For the moment, we'll keep the fact that the baby is mine between us."

They sat there quietly staring at each other. If she was trying to find another reason not to go on this trip, he would continue to find ways to allay her worries. He would do whatever it took to ensure the safety of the mother of his baby.

Noemi expelled a sigh and pressed her hands to her hips. "If I do this—if I go with you—I have to return to Mont Coeur for Christmas as my family has some matters to sort out."

"Understood." It sounded like she'd just agreed to travel to Ostania with him, but he wanted to be absolutely certain. "So you'll accompany me?"

She nodded. "I just need to get packed."

"Do you need help?"

She shook her head.

"I'll wait here." He sat down and pulled out his phone. "Just let me know if you need anything. And don't lift the suitcase. I'll get it."

She didn't say anything else as she turned for her room. He couldn't tell if she was angry or just resigned. He hoped with a little time and some rest that she would see this arrangement was for the best.

Had she made the right decision?

Noemi smothered a yawn. It was too late to change her mind as the private jet soared above the puffy white clouds. Part of her said that she should have stayed back at the chalet and hibernated until the press gave up their search for the mysterious woman in the photo. But another part of her wasn't ready to let go of Max—of the dream that their baby could be part of both of their lives.

There was something special about him. It was there when

he smiled at her and made her stomach dip. And there was the way he looked at her that made her feel like she was the only woman in the world. And then there was his gentleness and kindness.

Not that she was falling for him or anything. She refused to let herself do that. She'd agreed to fly to Ostania because it was best for the baby to have parents who were good friends—who could work together to raise a happy and healthy child. Nothing more.

Noemi continued to stare out the window as the plane descended, preparing to land at the private airstrip somewhere near the Ostania palace—at least that's what Max had said when he'd told her to fasten her seat belt. Even though the sun was sinking low in the sky, she was able to make out the palace. The sight captured her full attention. This was where Max lived? *Wow!*

Even from this height, it looked impressive with its blue turrets and white walls. She couldn't even imagine calling this place home. It looked like an entire village could fit within its walls and still have some extra room for visitors.

With so much space, it made her wonder why Max had felt the need to leave here for so long. What had he been running from? Was it his parents? Were they overbearing? She hoped not. Second thoughts about this trip started to niggle at her.

Nestled in the jagged snow-covered mountains, she had no idea where they were going to land. But the plane kept descending and soon a small clearing came into view with a runway. All around the cleared airstrip was snow. It certainly wasn't large enough for a commercial jet. In fact, it seemed rather short—

The wheels touched down with a jolt. Her fingers tightened on the armrests. She closed her eyes and waited. They would stop in time. Wouldn't they?

"Are you okay?" Max asked, drawing her from her thoughts.

As the plane rolled to a stop, she expelled a pent-up breath. "Yes. Um…why?"

"It's just that you've been quiet the entire flight."

She shrugged. "I just have a lot on my mind."

"I understand."

Did he? Did he know how hard this was going to be for all of them? And what was his family going to say when they heard about the baby? But then again, they probably already heard the rumors that had been in the newspaper.

"What about your family?" she asked.

"What about them?"

"They must have heard the gossip. Are you going to confirm their suspicions that the baby is yours?"

He shook his head. "Not until you're ready. They know after my cancer treatments that children are unlikely. They'll easily dismiss the story as nothing but fiction."

She hoped he was right because this pregnancy was becoming more complicated with each passing day.

They were ushered into a waiting black sedan with the flags of Ostania waving on each front fender. She received surprised looks from everyone she met, but none of them vocalized their thoughts. It would appear Prince Max didn't make it a practice of bringing women home with him. She took comfort in the knowledge.

The car moved slowly over the snow-covered road. Noemi told herself the poor road conditions were the reason her stomach was tied up in knots. It had nothing to do with wondering if Max's family would like her or not.

Max reached out, placing his hand over hers. "Relax. My family is going to love you."

She turned a surprised look at him. How had he known what she was thinking?

"I don't know. I'm not royal. In fact, I don't have a clue how to address your mother and father."

"Don't make a big deal of it."

She sat up a bit straighter. As the car drew closer to civilization, she grew more nervous. "I'm serious. What do I do? Curtsy?"

Max laughed. It was a deep warm sound and it helped calm her rising nerves. "I don't think that will be necessary."

"But I need to do something."

"How about a slight bow and a nod of your head?"

"Really? Because I don't want to do anything to offend them."

Surprised reflected in Max's eyes. "You really care that much?"

"Shouldn't I?" Even if they weren't Max's parents and the grandparents of her baby, she'd want to make a good impression. After all, they were king and queen. Wait until she told Stephania and Maria about all this.

Their car approached a small village that was nestled in a valley while the palace sat partway up the mountain in the background. The palace glowed like a jewel as floodlights illuminated it in the darkening evening.

But down here in the village, rooftops were covered with snow. And in the center of the village was an enormous Christmas tree. It soared up at least two stories. And it was lit with white twinkle lights. The branches were dusted with snow. It was simple and yet at the same time, it was stunning.

Noemi longed to stay here in the village. There was nothing intimidating about it, unlike the palce. As the car slowly passed through the center of the village, all the pedestrians turned. Men removed their hats and covered their hearts while the women waved. With the tinted windows, they couldn't make out who was in the back seat but they waved nonetheless. Noemi resisted the urge to wave back.

"Do they always do that?" she asked, curious about Ostania and its people.

"Yes. And under different circumstances, I'd stop and greet them."

And then Noemi felt bad. "You won't stop because of me."

"Correct." He didn't elaborate.

He didn't have to. She already knew her condition was changing their lives. What would his family do when he told them about the baby? Would they demand they marry?

Her body stiffened at the idea of a marriage of convenience. If she ever married, it would be for love and nothing less.

But she was pregnant with the prince's child. A royal baby could change things. Would they try to force her?

No. Of course not. It wasn't like she was a citizen of Ostania. They had no power over her. She glanced over at Max as he stared out the window. He wouldn't let his parents force them into anything that they didn't want. She trusted him.

That acknowledgment startled her. She'd never really thought about it before, but she did trust him. That was the first step in a strong friendship, right?

Max turned to her. "Did you say something?"

"Um, no."

"If you have any questions, feel free to ask. I'll try to answer them or I'll find the answers."

She had a feeling he wasn't talking about their unique relationship but rather her magnificent surroundings and the history of the palace. "Thanks. I'll keep that in mind."

As the palace drew closer, she practically pressed her face to the window as she tried to take in the enormity of the structure. She gazed up at one of the towers and couldn't help but think of Rapunzel. Her hair would have been so long to reach the ground.

She smiled at the memory of the fairy tale. But she couldn't help it. She felt as though a book had been opened and she was about to step into the pages of a real-life fairy tale. And she had absolutely no idea how it was going to end. Her stomach shivered with nerves again.

"Relax. My parents aren't that bad."

"That bad?" Her voice rose a little. "You really know how to put a person at ease."

Max sent her a guilty smile as he took her hand in his. "You know what I mean."

"Uh-huh. Sure. They are going to hate me."

Max squeezed her hand. "It will be fine. I'll be right next to you the whole time."

Her stomach grew uneasy. *Oh, no. Not now.* She reached for her purse and pulled out a packet of crackers.

Max frowned. "Maybe this wasn't such a good idea. I thought I'd be rescuing you from the stress of the press, but it appears the thought of my family is just as bad."

She quickly munched on a couple of crackers.

"Is it helping?" Max gave her long hard look. When she nodded, he said, "Maybe I should have some."

"You're nervous?"

"Let's just say my father might be king of the nation but my mother runs the family. She has definite ideas of how things should work and this thing between us won't fit neatly into her expectations."

Noemi reached for another cracker. "I knew it. She's going to hate me."

"Would you quit saying that? It's just going to take a bit of adjusting on everyone's part."

"Especially when you tell her that we're not getting married."

This time Max didn't say a word. Not one syllable. He turned his head away as the car pulled to a stop in front of the palace.

With great reluctance, Noemi stuffed the remaining crackers back in her purse. Then she ran a finger around the outside her lips, checking for crumbs. The last thing she needed was to meet the king and queen looking a mess. But she had a feeling they'd be more interested in her relationship with Max than her appearance. And then a thought came to her.

"You did tell them you were bringing me, didn't you?"

CHAPTER TEN

ONCE AGAIN, MAX didn't say a word. He continued to stare blindly out the window. He hadn't told anyone about Noemi accompanying him home. Not his mother. Not even Enzo.

Telling them about Noemi would involve questions—questions he wasn't ready to answer. So maybe he'd failed to disclose a couple of things to his parents about his return—a couple of big things. But who could blame him under the circumstances?

It was such a tangled mess. And in the end, his family would insist on an immediate paternity test followed by a wedding, and that last part was a sticking point with Noemi. He had to handle this very carefully or she would bolt. And he couldn't let that happen.

"Max, you did tell them, didn't you?"

Before he could answer, both of their car doors swung open. He let go of her hand as he stepped out of the car. When he turned toward the palace, Enzo was standing there, and next to him was the queen. *Oh, boy!* She didn't normally greet him at the door.

Max straightened his shoulders and moved to Noemi's side. He presented his arm to her, in proper royal fashion, and escorted her up the few steps to the sweeping landing.

"Your Highness." He nodded in recognition of his mother's station—etiquette was something his parents had instilled in both him and his brother from a young age.

"Maximilian." The queen continued to frown at him. "It's about time you came home."

She was the only one to call him by his formal name. Not even his father, the king, called him that. But his mother was all about pomp and circumstance. He rarely ever saw his mother with her hair down, literally or figuratively. When he became ruler, things would change—they would be less rigid. But all that hinged on Noemi...

Not only did he have to sire an heir, but that heir must reside within the palace and be groomed from birth to take over the reins of the Ostania. There was no room for a modern arrangement of partial custody or holiday visitation. His child must remain here in Ostania with him. And he already knew Noemi would balk at the idea.

His mother's frown deepened. "What is that mess on your face?"

He smiled, knowing his mother abhorred beards. "I thought I'd try something different."

"Well, you're home now. Please shave." The queen turned to Noemi. "And who is this?"

Oh, yes, where were his manners? It was just that being home again after being gone since last Christmas had him a bit off-kilter. His relationship with his mother had always been a bit strained. He got along with his father so much better.

"Mother, I would like to introduce you to Noemi Cattaneo of Cattaneo Jewels." He turned to Noemi. "And this is my mother, Queen Marguerite."

He noticed the surprise reflected in Noemi's eyes when he mentioned her family's business, but that's how things were done within the palace. People weren't just recognized for who they were but what they represented. And Max knew his mother had commissioned a few special pieces from Cattaneo Jewels.

The frown lines etching his mother's ivory complexion eased a bit. "You are related to the owners?"

Noemi nodded. "My parents…started the business. And now, erm, my brothers and I run the business."

The queen's eyes widened. "How truly interesting. I'd like to hear more later." Then his mother turned back to him. "You did not mention you'd be bringing a guest."

"I didn't?" He knew how to play his mother's games as well as she. "I thought I had."

"No. You didn't." She turned to Enzo. "Did he?"

"Not that I recall, ma'am. But the phone connection wasn't the best. Perhaps I missed it."

Max couldn't help but smile at Enzo's attempt to play the impartial party. The man practically had it down to a fine science. When Enzo's gaze caught the slight smile on Max's face, the man refused to react. However, Max would be hearing more about this later.

"Mother, it's cold out. Shouldn't we go inside?"

The queen hesitated for a moment. Max knew his mother didn't like to be pushed around or have something pulled over on her. She liked to know things before everyone else.

And when she found out what was afoot, he honestly didn't know if she'd be overjoyed with the prospect of a grandchild that no one ever thought was possible or if she'd be outraged that his wild lifestyle had led to a child out of wedlock, to a commoner no less. With his mother, anything was possible. But when the time was right, the first person he had to tell was his brother—Tobias's life was about to be turned upside down.

At last, his mother nodded and turned for the door. It was then that Max glanced over at Noemi. Her face was pale and drawn as she wore a plastered-on smile. He thought the first meeting with his mother had gone rather well considering. But perhaps he should have taken time to warn Noemi that his mother wasn't the warm and fuzzy type. The queen loved her sons. He never doubted it. But she kept her feelings under wraps.

He clearly recalled awakening after his cancer surgery. The room had been dim and he had been a bit disoriented at first. He hadn't moved while gaining his bearings. And then he'd heard the soft cry of someone.

He recalled how his mother been leaning near him. Her head had been resting on his bed with her face turned away. And then she'd said a prayer for him. He'd never been more touched in his life—well, that was until he heard Noemi tell him that he was going to be a father. Those were the two most stunning moments in his life.

He understood that his mother had been raised to keep an outward cool indifference. But he wanted more for his life—for his child's life. He needed his child to never question his fierce love for them.

This had to be some sort of dream.

This just couldn't be real.

The grandmother of her baby was a queen. Noemi's stomach quivered yet again. And from all Noemi could gather, the woman didn't like her and they didn't even know each other yet. Panic set in. Noemi didn't even want to think about what the woman would say when she learned of the baby. Maybe it was best that she never did.

That was it. Noemi would leave right away. She just had to get Max alone. Surely he had to see that coming here was a mistake. She didn't know one thing about royalty. Sure, she'd done an internet search when she'd been alone at night, but she hadn't found much insight. Certainly nothing to prepare her for this.

Once inside the palace, Noemi stopped in the grand foyer. The breath caught in her throat as she took in the magnificent surroundings. The tiled floor glimmered as the lights from the enormous crystal chandelier reflected off it. The tiles were laid in a diamond pattern of sky blue and black tile.

To either side of the very spacious room were twin staircases with elaborate wrought-iron bannisters with gold handrails. Her attention was drawn back to the center of the room where the chandelier hung prominently. It must have been at least four meters wide with a thousand individual crystals. And straight ahead were four white columns with gold trim. In the center was a large window and between the side columns were archways leading to other parts of the palace.

Off to the side stood a stately Christmas tree. Noemi craned her neck as she looked up at the star at the tippy top. She'd guess the thing stood at least thirty feet tall. *Wow!* And she'd thought the twelve-foot trees that her father used to get for the chalet were tall. They were nothing compared to this tree.

The royal Christmas tree was adorned with white twinkle lights. And the decorations were of white porcelain. All looked to be painstakingly positioned on the tree. They no doubt had professional decorators take care of all the details.

At the chalet, the decorations on the tree had been collected over the years. Some were handmade by her and Sebastian. Other ornaments were from vacations or represented special moments in their lives. Each of her family's ornaments held a meaning whereas this palace tree, though magnificent, didn't seem to bear the weight of the memories and sentiments of Max's family.

For some reason, that made her sad. Surely there had to be another tree somewhere in the palace where they hung their treasured ornaments. Right?

"Noemi?" Max sent her a strange look, jarring her back to the present.

"Yes. Sorry." Heat rushed to her cheeks as she realized she hadn't been paying attention to what Max was saying.

"This is my father, King Alexandre."

The king? She swallowed hard. What was she supposed to do? Bow? Curtsy? Her stomach took that moment to become queasy once again. She wished she could reach in her purse and pull out the remaining crackers, but that would have to wait.

Not sure what to do, she bowed. "Your Majesty."

She hoped she'd got it right. When she straightened, the king drew closer. He was smiling, unlike his wife, who kept a serious look on her face.

The king held out his hand. He was going to shake her hand? She didn't know that kings did such a thing.

He continued to smile at her. "It's so nice to meet one of my son's friends."

"It…it's nice to meet you, too."

He released her hand. "A friend of Max's is a friend of mine."

"Thank you." Was that the right response? Honestly she'd met a lot of rich and famous people, but none of them had ruled their own country. And none of them had been Max's parents. And like it or not, she wanted to make a good impression. So far she hadn't impressed the queen, but she was doing much better with the king. That was at least a step in the right direction. Maybe she wouldn't rush back to Mont Coeur…just yet.

"Have you known my son long?"

"We met a few months ago," Max said.

His father glanced at him and Max grew silent.

Noemi wasn't sure how his father would take to hearing his son was partying it up so she said, "We met via some mutual friends. And we immediately hit it off."

"Immediately?" Max asked.

She turned to Max, not sure what to say.

"As I recall," Max continued, "you weren't so easily swayed to give me a chance."

"I, uh…" What was he doing? Was he trying to give his father a bad impression of her?

"Relax," Max said, "my parents can respect your selectiveness. And since you didn't recognize me, I was just one of your many admirers."

Heat rushed to her face. She felt as though her face were on fire. If Max was trying to smooth things over with his father, he wasn't doing a good job. She wished he would stop speaking.

"He's not serious," Noemi said, clarifying things. "We started to talk and soon we became friends."

"Friends?" Max wore an amused look. When she turned

a pointed look at him, he said, "Yes, friends. We've been enjoying the snow. And I thought Noemi would enjoy seeing where I lived."

His father was still smiling, but she could see the wheels in his mind turning. He was wondering what exactly was going on between them. Were they just a casual thing? Or was it something more serious?

She didn't have any answers for him because she didn't have any answers for herself. Only time would tell how things would play out for them and the baby.

"Well, we are glad you've come for a visit," the king said. "Isn't that right, Josephine?"

There was a pause before the queen spoke. "Yes, it is. And someone will show you to your suite so you can settle in while we speak privately with our son."

"Thank you for having me," Noemi said, realizing that she'd been dismissed.

As she glanced to the left, she noticed a staff member waiting for her at the bottom of the steps. She turned back to find the king and queen walking away.

"Don't worry," Max leaned over and whispered in her ear. "Everything is going to work out. I'll catch up with you in a bit."

Noemi hoped he was right. So far she was pretty certain coming here was a mistake, even if his father had been very nice to her. And what were they doing now? Talking about the scandalous headlines? Discussing her pregnancy?

She wondered if she should insist on being a part of the conversation if it was going to be about her. When she paused and glanced over her shoulder, they were gone now—down some long hallway or behind some closed door. Maybe it was for the best that she hadn't caught up with them.

She continued up the steps. The thought of lying down for a bit sounded so appealing. She had never been this tired in her life. Usually she was a bundle of energy. But not lately. This pregnancy was taking a lot out of her.

And then there was her uneasy stomach. Her hand reached

for her purse, anxious to retrieve the crackers, but then she returned her hand to her side. There was no way she was going to trail cracker crumbs through the palace. She'd waited this long, a little longer wouldn't matter.

All the while, she wondered what Max's parents were saying. She knew she needed to trust Max, but being here in this palace, it changed things. It drove home the power and wealth of Max and his family.

He should tell them.

He wanted to. Max couldn't wait to shout it from the towers that he was going to be a father. But he knew Noemi wasn't ready for the pressure or expectations that would bring to her life. For now, he had to protect her.

His country was steeped in archaic traditions, as were his parents. Max didn't agree with most of those traditions, but he wasn't in a position to change them—not yet. For now, he had to go along with what was expected of him, producing an heir and providing a paternity test. When he became king—when his authority could not be disputed—then he could implement changes.

Max stepped into the library and stopped, finding that it wasn't just his parents that wanted to speak to him. There were the two highest members of the royal cabinet as well as Enzo and their public representative. This felt more like the beginning of an inquisition than a homecoming.

From the doorway, he took a moment to really look at his parents. His mother looked much the same. She still had a trim figure, and she had no gray hairs but he had a feeling she had them discreetly covered up. His father, on the other hand, looked older and frailer. His face looked weathered and his eyes were dull. He was sicker than he was willing to admit.

The king stepped forward. "This is the woman, isn't it?"

Max sent him a confused look. It was like he'd stepped into the middle of a conversation and everyone expected him to know what had been said. He refused to be put on the defensive. He'd been in that awkward position too many times in recent years.

"The woman?" he asked.

"Don't do this." His mother stepped up next to his father. "I know we've given you a lot of freedom after your... your illness. Perhaps in hindsight it was too much freedom. It wasn't like we turned a blind eye to your activities. But honestly, the headlines have been getting worse and worse. And now you bring home this girl—"

"She's not a girl. She's a woman. And her name is Noemi."

The queen crossed her arms over her proper navy-and-white linen dress. "I suppose she's the one who claims to be pregnant?"

"Since when did you start believing the headlines? You know what the doctor said. I can't father any children."

The angry look on his mother's face deflated. "So it's not true? There's no baby?"

"Whatever they printed in the paper is nothing but make-believe. There's nothing serious between Noemi and me. We're...friends. She's really nice. I wish you would give her a chance."

The queen eyed him carefully. "She's important to you?"

He had to be careful here. "She's a good friend. And she's been through a lot lately. I want this visit to go well for her."

His statement only increased his mother's curiosity. "Been through what?"

"Darling, leave Max alone." The king spoke in a congenial tone. "He is home just like you wanted. Let's not rush him back out the door."

His mother hated it when they ganged up on her. "Am I not allowed to be curious about my son and his friends?"

"Of course," the king said. "But you don't have to make it sound like the inquisition."

His mother's eyes lit up as she glared at his father. "Fine. You deal with this. And when it blows up in our faces, it'll be on you." And then she turned back to Max. "Make sure you shave before dinner."

And with that his mother turned and left the room along with the other dignitaries. The door made a resounding thud.

His father shook his head before turning back to Max. "Your mother, she means well. She missed you. I wish you wouldn't stay away for such extended periods."

"I'm sorry, Father. It's just—"

"Easier. I know."

Max nodded. That's what he loved most about his father—his way of understanding him. Whereas his mother was fierce in her love and need to protect the family, his father was the opposite and let his love flow freely and without restriction. For being two opposite types, Max was impressed by the way his parents were able to make their marriage work and last.

"However, I agree with your mother. This woman, she is more than a friend." When Max went to dispute the claim, his father raised his hand to stop him. "Perhaps you don't even see it yourself. But you will. Trust me. It's in the way you look at her and the way you speak of her. However, I'm not so sure she feels the same way as you. So please be careful."

It was no wonder his father was the king. He could see straight through a situation to the heart of the problem—just as he had done now with Max and Noemi.

When his father was called away on urgent business, Max headed for the steps leading upstairs. He wanted to make sure Noemi was comfortably situated. As he walked, his father's words kept rolling around in his mind. Was it that obvious that Noemi wasn't into him?

And if that was the case, what did he do about it? Separate the mother from the child? The thought turned his stomach. There had to be a better way. Pay her to stay here with him and the child until their son or daughter was grown? Again, he didn't like the idea. What did that leave him? To make her fall in love with him?

Max paused outside her door. He swallowed down his thoughts. He didn't want her to sense his inner turmoil. He had to keep it all inside until he figured the best course of action for all concerned—especially their baby.

Knock. Knock.

"Come in." Noemi's voice was faint.

He opened the door and found Noemi sitting up on the bed. Her face was pale and she didn't meet his gaze. He pushed the door closed and rushed to her side. He knelt down in front of her. "Are you all right?"

She nodded. "I felt a little wiped out and I closed my eyes for a few minutes. I guess I fell asleep."

"I didn't mean to wake you."

"It's okay. I don't want to sleep the evening away or else I won't sleep tonight."

"Dinner will be at seven. Will you be up for it?"

She mustered a smile, but it didn't quite reach her eyes. "I'll be fine. By tomorrow, I'll be good as new."

Somehow he didn't quite believe her. The stress of the press compounded by his mother's cold welcome couldn't have helped Noemi's pregnancy. He was going to have to do better. He wanted Noemi to enjoy this visit. He wanted her to fall in love with his country—their child's birthright.

"What would you like to do this evening?" he asked. If it was within his power, he would give her whatever she wanted.

"Would you mind if we didn't do anything?"

That didn't sound like much fun, but he understood that she was tired after their earlier travels. "Not a problem." And then he had an idea. He checked the time and then turned back to her. "We have a little time before dinner, how about I give you a tour of the palace?"

She perked up a bit. "That would be nice."

"Would you like to change now or after the tour?"

"Change?" She sent him a puzzled look.

"For dinner." His mother insisted on formalities, even when it was just the family…and a very special friend.

Worry reflected in her eyes. "Exactly how dressed up do I need to be?"

"Don't worry. If you didn't bring anything to wear for dinner, it'll be fine."

"Of course I brought dressier clothes." She frowned at him. "I do know my way around society, you know."

That was true. She was a Cattaneo. He had worried for nothing. He nodded in understanding. "The men will be wearing suits. So a dress, if you have one, will work."

"I do. I'll change first. That way if the tour takes longer than imagined, I won't hold dinner up while I'm changing."

"Great idea. I'll go and change, too." He ran a hand over his beard. "I guess I'll shave, too. Kind of a shame. It was starting to get past the itchy phase." And with that he was out the door.

Was his father right? Noemi didn't act like the other women who had passed through his life. They were all too eager to be near him, to kiss him, to touch him.

Noemi wasn't that way. She was reserved. And though in part that should be a relief to him, there was another part that worried that she truly wasn't into him—that all they'd ever have was that one night. And that just wasn't enough for him.

CHAPTER ELEVEN

ACTING ALOOF WAS hard work.

Noemi assured herself that playing it cool was the best way to go. Being here at the palace and after meeting the queen, Noemi was certain she and Max didn't belong together. They came from totally different worlds.

And then she had the worst thought. The queen already seemed not to care for her. When the queen learned of the baby, what if she decided, with them being unmarried, that it would be best to have the baby sent away—put up for adoption—like her parents had been forced to do with Leo?

Noemi's imagination had a way of getting away from her. It was only when she reined it in that she realized an adoption would never happen. She and Max were in a totally different position from her parents. Noemi and Max weren't kids. They didn't rely on their parents for food and shelter. They could make up their own minds.

It was just her nervousness from being here. She glanced around the room. It was large with high ceilings and gold trim work. The landscape paintings on the walls were stunning. She moved closer to them. Each painting contained bright-colored wildflowers. In one painting, the wildflowers were part of a big field with blue skies and puffy white clouds overhead. In another painting, the flowers were next to a pond with a white swan. And the last painting was of the wildflowers with the palace in the distance.

Her initial thought was to move to the window next to her

bed to look out and search for the beautiful wildflowers, but in the next instance, she recalled that it was Christmastime and the ground was covered with snow. It would be many months before the wildflowers were to bloom again. And by the time they did, Noemi would have given birth to her baby and she would not be welcome at the palace.

Still, she couldn't resist glancing out the window. As she peered out the window, her mouth gaped. Max had his very own ice skating rink.

"Wow."

This place was just mind-blowing. It was more a private resort than a home. As she stared down at the ice, it beckoned to her. She'd been skating since she was a kid and she loved it. She wondered if Max knew how to skate.

Realizing that she was losing track of time, Noemi turned from the window. Her gaze scanned the room searching for her luggage. The suitcases weren't sitting on the floor. In fact, they were nowhere to be seen. How could that be?

Perhaps they were in the bathroom. She moved to the adjoining bath. The room was practically the same size as her bedroom. And on one wall was a line of cabinets. Was it possible they were in there?

She opened the first door and found it empty, but the second door she opened revealed her clothes. Someone had taken the time and trouble to hang her things up. That was so nice of them. She would have to remember to thank them.

She examined each of her dresses, trying to decide which one the queen might approve of. By the time she'd gone through them all twice, she was no closer to a decision. In the end, she picked a little black dress. It wasn't too flashy. And it wasn't too casual. And most of all, it wasn't too tight around her rapidly expanding midsection.

Not too bad. She glanced at her image in the mirror. *But not too great either.*

She couldn't help but notice the paleness of her face. And were those dark circles under her eyes? She sighed and turned back to the bed, where she'd scattered her things while searching for some concealer.

She'd learned long ago how to make herself presentable in a rush. When she was rushing from the stage to an after-party, there wasn't much time to waste. And when photos were being taken at the parties to distribute to the press, she had to look her best. After all, she was the face of Cattaneo Jewels. It was important to her to do her duty for the family business. She took her responsibility seriously. But perhaps she'd rushed too much today because she couldn't find her elusive makeup.

She didn't know why she was a ball of nerves. It wasn't like her. She was normally confident about her appearance. But that extra two or three inches on her waistline was knocking her confidence. At least that's what she kept telling herself. It had nothing to do with the fact that Max had been keeping a respectable distance from her.

His only interest appeared to be in the baby she was carrying. She tried telling herself that was a good thing. A baby was enough of a complication in her life. She didn't need a prince to mix up her world further. But it didn't keep her from wanting more.

By the time Max rapped his knuckles on her door, Noemi was dressed, her hair was straightened into a smooth bob and she'd at last located her makeup. It wasn't until she looked in the mirror that she realized she'd forgotten her jewelry, which she found ironic as she was now an owner of an international jewel company.

She yanked open the door. "Did you know there's a great big ice skating rink out there?"

Max laughed. "Yeah, I knew. If I'd have known you would get so excited about it, I would have brought you here much sooner."

"It's just that we never got to ice skate back at Mont Coeur." And then realizing that if they didn't hurry they'd be late for dinner, Noemi added, "I hope this dress is all right."

"All right?" His gaze skimmed down over her, warming her skin. "You look amazing."

The heat moved to her face. "Thank you."

She couldn't help but notice his clean-shaven face. Was it possible he looked more princely now? The black suit that spanned over his broad shoulders and cloaked his sculpted biceps looked quite dashing on him. A black tie and white shirt obscured her view of his chest with the smattering of curls that she so fondly remembered.

Realizing that she was letting her thoughts get away from her, she jerked her gaze back up to meet his. "And you're looking rather amazing, too." And then another thought came to her. "Does your family dress formally for every meal or is it just dinner?"

"For breakfast and lunch, it's casual. But my mother insists people dress for dinner. I take it your family isn't so formal?"

She shook her head. "My parents were casual at home. They…" Her voice caught in the back of her throat. She missed them so much. "They were more concerned about getting the family together than anything else."

"It sounds like your family is very close."

Her thoughts turned to her brothers. One was growing more distant by the day and the other one she was hoping to get to know. Not quite the definition of closeness.

She noticed Max watching her as though waiting for an answer. She swallowed down the lump of emotion. "We used to be—at least I thought we were."

But was that truly the case? Had she only seen what she wanted to? After all, her parents had lied to her all her life. The acknowledgment stabbed at her heart. That was not the definition of a close family.

Her thoughts turned to her baby. She would do better by it. She wouldn't lie to it. Never about the big stuff. And she'd listen to him or her—really listen.

"Noemi?"

She blinked. And then she glanced up at Max. Deciding

to turn their conversation back to a safer subject, she said, "Perhaps after this evening, I could eat in my room."

Max's brows drew together. "Why would you do that? Is it my mother? If so, I'll have a word with her. She can come on a bit strong."

Noemi shook her head. "It isn't her." Although his mother's disapproving stare did make her uncomfortable, Noemi wasn't one to back down. "If you must know, I don't fit in most of my dresses any longer. They don't hide my expanding baby bump."

A slow smile pulled at Max's tempting lips. "Is that all?" When she nodded, he said, "Then tomorrow we shall take you dress shopping and you can pick up anything else that you need…or want."

"But do you think that's wise?" When he sent her a puzzled look, she added, "You know, after the paparazzi spotted us at the baby boutique in Mont Coeur."

"Let me worry about the paparazzi."

Who was she to argue? She already had her share of worries. "I just don't want to be a bother."

"That's an impossibility." He smiled at her—a genuine smile, the kind that lit up his whole face including his eyes.

Oh, boy, is he handsome.

Her stomach dipped. No man had ever made her feel that way with just a smile. She'd have to be careful around him or she'd end up leaving her heart in Ostania and that wouldn't be good for either her or the baby.

Max checked the time. "Shall we go? We have just enough time to visit a couple of rooms before we are expected in the great dining hall."

"So this isn't going to be a small intimate dinner in the kitchen?" Somehow facing the queen in a more relaxed setting seemed so much more appealing.

Max shook his head. "I'm not even sure my mother has ever been in the kitchen. I know my father has as I would run into him when I was a kid in the middle of the night searching for a snack."

Noemi smiled. She liked the fact that the king was so

much more approachable. Now if only she could find a way to win over the queen. She wondered if that was even possible.

Max once again presented his arm to her. She really liked his old-world charm. Whoever said that manners were outdated hadn't met Max. He made everything relevant.

Her gaze moved from his clean-shaven face to his extended arm and then back again. Without a word, she slipped her hand in the crook of his arm.

She couldn't deny the thrill she got from being so close to him—from feeling the heat of his body emanating through the dark material. Her heart picked up its pace. It'd be so easy to get caught up in this fairy tale… A snowy palace and she the damsel on the crown prince's arm as they set off on an adventure.

"Where shall we start?" she asked Max.

"I thought we'd start with the public rooms."

"Public rooms?"

"Yes, those are the rooms where the royal family entertains."

"I'm intrigued. Lead the way."

She pushed aside thoughts of dining with his mother. At least, she tried to push the worries aside. Still, it was difficult. She'd never had anyone instantly dislike her. She tried hard to get along with everyone. Maybe she hadn't tried hard enough with his mother. Yes, that was it. She would try harder.

"Is something bothering you?" Max's voice jarred her from her thoughts as they descended the grand staircase.

"Why?"

"You're quieter than normal."

"Sorry." She glanced around the grand foyer. It was spacious enough to have a formal ball right here. "I can't believe this place is so big."

"It's great for playing hide-and-seek."

"Really?" She turned to him, finding a serious look on his face. "You really played in here."

He nodded. "When we were young, my brother and I could spend hours playing hide-and-seek. Why do you seem so surprised?"

"Because this is a palace." She glanced over at the oriental vase beneath a large mirror. "Everything in here is breakable and must cost a fortune. It's more like a museum than a playground."

He smiled. "Maybe to you. To my brother and me, it was home."

"Was home?"

Max shrugged. "I guess I've been away from here longer than I thought." He pointed to the left. "Shall we go this way?"

She gazed up at the priceless artwork on the walls. "Sounds good to me. This place is absolutely amazing."

Max chuckled. "My mother would approve."

So she needed to compliment his mother. Noemi tucked away this nugget of information. They toured a lot of the rooms on the main floor, including a red room with portraits of Max's ancestors. Some of the paintings were very old. The outfits they wore were quite elaborate, both for the men and the women.

And then Noemi came across a portrait of a baby in a christening gown. It was the eyes that drew her in. They looked so familiar. "Is that you?"

"Yes. One day it will be replaced by a formal portrait after the coronation with my crown, scepter and cape."

It drove home his importance and how Max was so not like any of the other men that she'd ever dated. One day he would rule Ostania. She couldn't even imagine what it would be like to carry such an enormous responsibility. And here she was struggling with the demands of caring for one baby whereas he would be responsible for millions of lives.

As she continued to stare at Max's baby picture, she wondered if that was how their baby would look. Would it be a boy and the image of his father? Or would it be a girl?

Noemi glanced around the room to make sure they were

alone and then lowered her voice. "Do you want a son? Or a daughter?"

Max's eyes momentarily widened. When he spoke, it was in a hushed tone. "To be honest, I hadn't given that much thought. Just finding out that I'm going to be a father has been quite a shock."

"But if you had to choose, would you want a son or a daughter?"

Max looked as though he were giving the question some serious thought. "Would you be upset if I say I don't care as long as it's healthy?"

She smiled. "No. I like that answer. I feel the same. I will love this baby no matter what."

"Me, too."

"The thing worrying me is that I don't have a clue what I'm doing. So I bought some baby books. They tell me what to expect at the different stages."

"Maybe you should loan me those books when you're done."

Her gaze met his. "You'd really read them?"

"Of course I would. I keep telling you, we're in this together."

"You don't know how much I want to believe you." And then she realized she'd vocalized her thoughts.

His head lowered to hers. Ever so softly, he said, "Then believe this."

He pressed his lips to hers. In that moment, she knew how deeply she'd missed his touch. As his lips moved over hers, she couldn't remember the reason she'd been holding him at arm's length. She was certain it must have made sense at one point but not any longer.

Her hands rested against his chest—his very firm, very muscular chest. His kiss teased and tempted her. As a moan built in the back of her throat, she slipped her arms over his shoulders and leaned her body into his.

Knock. Knock.

And then someone cleared their throat.

Noemi jumped out of Max's arms. Heat scorched her cheeks. *Please don't let it be the queen.*

"Yes, Sloan," Max said.

"Your Highness, I was sent to let you know that dinner will be served in fifteen minutes."

"Thank you."

And with that the butler turned and disappeared down the hallway.

Noemi wasn't sure how to react. When she turned back to Max, he was quietly chuckling. She frowned. "I don't know what you find so amusing."

He sobered up. "Absolutely nothing." His eyes still twinkled with amusement. "Shall we continue the tour?"

"Are there more rooms on this floor to see?"

Max nodded. He led her down the hallway to the throne room with two massive chairs with carved wood backs and red cushions. Behind the chairs was the family's coat of arms. And then there was a library, but not just any library. The room was enormous. The bookcases soared so high on the wall that there was a ladder to reach the upper shelves.

"Do you think your family would mind if I borrowed a book or two while I'm here?" She liked to read at night. It relaxed her and was something she looked forward to in the evenings. "I was in such a rush to get packed that I didn't think to grab any of mine."

"Help yourself. This room doesn't get utilized as much as it should." He glanced at the gold clock on the console behind one of the couches. "Shall we head into dinner? I can show you the rest of palace later or perhaps tomorrow."

"Yes, let's go." The last thing she wanted was to upset his mother by being late for dinner.

"That hungry?"

"Something like that." Right now, food was the last thing on her mind.

Max stepped in front of her. "Before we go, I want to reassure you that I have not forgotten about your doctor's appointment. In the morning, we can make some phone calls and if worst comes to worst, I'll fly you back to Mont Coeur for the day."

"You really would, wouldn't you?"

"I'd do anything for my family."

Before she could say a word, he kissed her. It was just a brief kiss but enough to make her heart skip a beat.

As Max took her arm to lead her into the dining room, he leaned in close to her ear. "Don't worry. Once my mother gets to know you, she's going to really like you."

"I hope you're right." Though Noemi doubted it, that didn't mean she wouldn't try to make a good impression.

His parents and brother were already at the other end of the long narrow room. The dining table was bigger than any she'd ever seen. It could easily seat two dozen people.

Noemi leaned close to Max, catching a whiff of his spicy cologne. For a moment, she forgot what she was about to say. All she could think about was Max and how easy it would be to turn into his arms and kiss him again.

"Noemi?" Max sent her a puzzled look. "Are you all right?"

"Um, yes."

He guided her across the room. The family stopped talking and turned to them. Noemi's stomach shivered with nerves. Her gaze met the king's. He sent her a warm smile. The queen didn't smile but she didn't frown either. Noemi chose to count that as a positive sign.

"So you're my brother's girlfriend?" Tobias asked.

Noemi's gaze moved to Max's younger brother. He had blondish-brown hair like his brother. Tobias was an inch or so shorter than Max. But he wasn't as reserved as Max. In fact, he was free with a smile that made his eyes twinkle. He wasn't as handsome as Max but he'd be a close second.

He took her hand in his and kissed the back with a fluttery kiss. She was so caught off guard that she didn't have time to react. It took a moment for her to realize her mouth was slightly agape. She quickly pressed her lips together.

"It's so nice to meet you, Prince Tobias." And then because she wasn't sure how to greet him, she did a slight curtsy and dipped her head.

When she straightened, Prince Tobias shook his head. "Relax. It's only us here. Please tell me my brother doesn't make you curtsy to him."

Max cleared his throat. "That's enough, Tobias."

"That's right, Tobias," the queen spoke up. "Please remember your manners."

Noemi wasn't sure if the queen was coming to her defense or if the queen didn't like the lack of proper etiquette.

The queen turned to her. "I hope you found your room adequate."

"It's quite lovely." *Lovely? Really? That's the best you can do.* "Thank you so much for having me. Max—erm, the prince has shown me around the palace and it is breathtaking. I especially love the library."

The queen's eyes widened. "You read?"

Noemi smiled and nodded. She was at last making some headway with the queen. "I read every chance I get." Not wanting to let go of this first legitimate connection with the queen, Noemi said, "I find biographies fascinating. And I enjoy historical accounts."

Before the queen could say more, dinner was announced and everyone moved to the table. Noemi was relieved to see that they were all seated at one end of the table. She didn't want to have to shout the entire length of the table in order to make dinner conversation.

Max hadn't warned her that dinner would be quite so lengthy. It had six courses and it was not rushed. The family for the most part was like any other with each person catching the others up on what was going on in their lives. However, they were more reserved than her family as there was no joking, teasing or laughing. Still, the meal was more relaxed than she'd been expecting.

And so she made her way through the whole evening without any problems with the queen. Maybe the need to rush back to Mont Coeur wasn't necessary after all. She really was curious to learn more about Max's home.

Noemi turned her attention to Max as he discussed the possibility of purchasing a new horse with the king. And her other reason for wanting to stay might have to do with those kisses he'd laid on her. What did they mean? And where would they lead them?

CHAPTER TWELVE

PERHAPS HE'D BEEN hoping for too much—too soon.

The next morning, Max had been summoned to a cabinet meeting to bring him up to speed on everything he'd missed during his time away. The only problem was his mind kept straying to Noemi.

Though dinner the prior evening had gone without a hitch, it had still been reserved with Noemi left out of most of the conversation. He hadn't realized until then just how important his family's acceptance of Noemi was to him. But what was even more important was Noemi feeling comfortable around not only him but also his family. How else would she consider raising their child as an Ostanian?

All was not lost yet. He still had a chance to win her over. And if she felt up to it, he planned to show her some of the charms of Ostania.

"I have to go," he told his mother and father, as well as the royal advisors. He'd promised Noemi that they'd sort out her doctor's appointment.

"Go? Go where?" his father asked.

"This is important," his mother chimed in. "You can't just disregard your royal duties. I know that we've given you a lot a leeway—"

"Perhaps more than we should have," his father finished his mother's sentence. "It is time you quit chasing women and partying. It's time you take your position in this family seriously. You may not end up as king, but that doesn't mean you won't have an important role to fill."

Max noticed his father didn't look quite right. His complexion was paler than at dinner the prior evening and there were dark circles under his eyes. Max couldn't help wondering how long his father had looked this way. Things had definitely changed in the time he'd been away. It appeared that he'd been gone too long.

"I understand," Max said. "I will do more. But right now, I have a guest."

"Right now, you have work to do," the queen insisted. "Your guest can wait."

His mother was right. He needed to do more to alleviate some of the burden from his father's shoulders. And to be honest, Noemi with her morning sickness wasn't up for much until her stomach settled. He checked the time. He had at least another hour before she'd want to go out. They could arrange for the doctor's appointment before they left the palace.

"Just let me make a phone call." Then on second thought, he didn't want his family to overhear his conversation. He settled for jotting out a note and sending it with one of the staff. He didn't want Noemi to think he'd forgotten her.

Noemi smiled.

For the first time in a while, she didn't feel like utter rubbish. Now that she was settling into her second trimester, the doctor said the morning sickness should start to abate. Apparently her doctor had been correct. *Thank goodness.*

She'd actually slept well and had some energy. She couldn't wait to go explore Ostania. So when there was a knock at the door, she rushed over and opened it with a smile. The smile slipped from her face when she realized it wasn't Max.

A man in a dark uniform handed her a white folded paper. "This is from His Royal Highness Prince Maximilian."

She accepted the paper. "Thank you."

With a curt nod, the man took a step back. He turned and headed down the hall. She wondered why Max was sending her a note instead of showing up in person. She hoped that nothing was wrong.

Apologies.
    Unavoidably delayed. Will catch up with you ASAP.
Feel free to make use of the library.
Max

She was disappointed he couldn't join her. She realized she'd been missing him more than she probably should. In fact, he'd been on her mind since the prior evening when he'd escorted her back to her room after his family had coffee. She'd been hoping for another kiss but it hadn't happened.

She wondered if all the royal dinners took close to two hours. Or was it something special because she was there? Then she realized it was more than likely due to Max's return.

Either way, it had gone far better than she ever imagined that it would. Max was charming. His brother was entertaining, almost comical at times. His mother, though still reserved, was more cordial and even gave her some reading suggestions regarding the history of Ostania. And though the king was far quieter at dinner than he had been when she'd first met him, all in all it had been a good evening. Maybe the royals weren't all that different after all.

Max's invitation to explore the library more fully was an invitation that she couldn't pass up. Bundled in a bulky sweater—without being situated near a roaring fire, the palace was a bit on the chilly side—Noemi made her way to the library without getting lost. But even if she had, there was so much staff around that someone would have pointed her in the right direction.

When she reached the library, the sun was poking through the stained-glass windows, sending a kaleidoscope of colors throughout the room. She didn't know the room with its floor-to-ceiling shelves could look any more appealing, but the touch of color made it seem…well, magical.

She moved to the closest shelf and started reading the titles. When she found one that intrigued her, she pulled it out to examine more closely. It wasn't until she strayed across a book the queen had recommended that she was hooked. Noemi knew the book wouldn't include Max but it would be about his ancestors and her baby's ancestors. She wanted to know as much as she could.

She carried the book back to her room to read while waiting for Max. She moved to a couch near one of the windows and settled in. The more she learned of Max and his life here in Ostania, the more she wanted to know about the country. She opened the leather-bound book and started to read. However, every couple of minutes her gaze moved to the doorway. How much longer would he be?

As chapter one turned to chapter two, then three, she had to wonder what was keeping him. He hadn't hinted about the cause of his delay in the note. Had something happened? Had he changed his mind about spending the day with her? Had he realized that she didn't fit in here?

As though he sensed her worries, Max appeared in the doorway. She immediately closed the book and got to her feet. She smiled but he didn't return the gesture.

She approached him. "What's wrong?"

"Why should there be something wrong?"

She shrugged. "I…um…it's just that you look like you have something on your mind. If it's me—"

"It's not. Don't ever think that." He paused as though gathering his thoughts. "I'm just sorry for being late. I hope you didn't get bored."

"Actually, I found this very informative book about the history of Ostania. Do you think anyone would mind if I keep it here until I finish reading it?"

He shook his head. "Please borrow whatever books appeal to you."

She placed the book on her nightstand. "I think just this one for now."

"To make up for being late, I have a surprise for you."

It was then that she noticed he was holding his arms behind his back. "Did I tell you that I love surprises? I always hoped my parents would throw me a surprise party with all my friends from school."

"I take it they didn't?"

She shook her head. "They were always too busy with the company."

"Would you like me to throw you a party?"

She studied him for a moment. "You're serious, aren't you?"

"Is there any reason I shouldn't be?"

She smiled at him and shook her head. "I'm past the age of longing for a surprise party, but I think I'll do one for our son or daughter. What do you think?"

"As long as you include cake, balloons and a pony, they'll love it."

Her smile broadened as they talked of their child's future. "I think the only thing that will capture their attention will be the pony."

"You might be right." A serious look came over his face. "Will you continue to work after the baby's born?"

"I'd like to." She'd been rolling this around in her mind for some time. "But I plan to step down as the face of Cattaneo Jewels."

"Really?" His eyes reflected his surprise.

She nodded. "I've been thinking about this for a while."

"What will you do? Take another role within your family's business?"

She shook her head. "I don't want to work with my brother. He…he doesn't take my opinions seriously."

"You have plenty of other career choices."

"I'd like it to be something meaningful like…like head up a foundation…or champion a worthy cause."

"I'm sure whatever you settle on will definitely benefit from your attention."

"I hope you're right." Her gaze moved to his arm that was still behind his back. "So what's my surprise?"

"Are you sure you still want it?" He sent her a teasing smile. "Are you sure you're not too old for a surprise?"

"I'll never be that old." She reached for his arm, but he stepped back out of her reach. "Show me."

He was still smiling. "After this big buildup, I hope you aren't disappointed with them—"

"There's more than one?"

He nodded and then he held out the purple lion and the white booties.

"You got them?" She accepted the gifts. "But how?"

"I have my ways. And I knew how important they were to you."

In that moment, Max left a definite impression on her. No one had ever done something so thoughtful for her. Her eyes grew misty. *Stupid hormones.*

"Thank you."

"You're welcome." He closed her bedroom door. "Are you ready to make some very important phone calls?"

The doctor's appointment. "Yes, I am."

She talked to her doctor in Mont Coeur and then Max spoke with a local doctor he said could be trusted. In the end, the sonogram would be done in Ostania two days from now. It was arranged for after office hours to aid their privacy.

"Now that that is all settled, would you like to go visit the village?"

"I would." Already dressed in a bulky sweater and her black tights, she was ready to go exploring.

Lucky for her, she'd remembered her black knee-high boots along with her long-sleeve black hooded coat with gray faux fur trim. And so a few minutes later, she was settled in the passenger seat while Max sat behind the steering wheel.

"I didn't know you knew how to drive," she said, surprised to find him so at ease behind the wheel.

"The security staff doesn't like when I drive, but I don't like being escorted everywhere I go."

She glanced in the side mirror. "Isn't that your body-guards behind us?"

"Yes, but at least I have a little distance from them. I can talk on the phone without being overheard or I can turn up the stereo as loud as I want without them frowning."

"So you aren't a perfect prince after all?"

"Perfect prince?" He laughed. "You do remember how we met, don't you?"

"Oh, I remember." She lightly patted her belly. "I'll never forget it."

For a while they road in a comfortable silence. She hadn't seen this playful side of Max since they'd arrived in Ostania. He always looked as though he was carrying around a great weight. She didn't realize until that moment how much she'd missed this part of him—the dreamy smile on his face— the way his eyes sparkled when he teased her. Maybe today would be more entertaining than she ever imagined.

"What are you thinking?" Max asked.

"What makes you think I have something on my mind?"

"Because you have that devilish look in your eyes."

"Devilish look? No one has ever accused me of that be-fore." She leaned her head back on the seat as a smile played on her lips. This was the best she'd felt in a very long time. "Why, Prince Max, is this your attempt to flirt with me?"

Max maneuvered the small car into a street-side parking spot. He cut the engine and then turned to her. He rested an arm over the top of her seat. "I don't know. Is it working?"

With his face so close, her heart started to pound. "Do you remember what happened the last time you flirted with me?"

"I do." His face was so close now that his breath tickled her cheek. "In fact, I can't forget it. You've ruined me for any other woman."

She knew he was just having fun with her, but it didn't stop her from lowering her gaze to his lips. The truth was she hadn't been able to forget about their night together either or her desire for a repeat. It filled her dreams at night and tantalizing images swooped in during the day, stealing her train of thought. The way he kissed her made her feel like she was the only woman in the world. And when his fingers stroked her cheek, as they were doing now, her heart skipped a beat.

She leaned toward him as he gravitated toward her. They met in the middle. There was no hesitation. Both kissed as though they needed the connection as much as they needed oxygen.

His lips pressed hard against hers. She opened her mouth to him and their tongues met. Her pulse quickened. Her hand reached out to him, wrapping around the back of his neck and stroking up through his thick hair.

Mm… Each kiss was better than the last. She released the seat belt, wanting to get closer to him. If only they weren't in a car—

Tap. Tap.

Noemi jerked back. Her eyes opened and glanced around, finding the men in dark suits on either side of Max's car.

"Sorry they startled you." Max settled back in his seat. "It's their protocol when we're in public. They were letting me know that the vicinity is safe for me to exit the car."

"Oh. I felt like a teenager getting busted making out in the car."

He smiled playfully. "So you were that kind of girl?"

"Hey." She lightly smacked him on the shoulder. "I didn't say I did it. I said… Oh, never mind. I shouldn't have said anything."

"Yes, you should. I like learning these things about you."

"Really?" Somehow it just struck her as surprising that a royal prince would be interested in her rather boring life.

He nodded. "Why wouldn't I be? I find you fascinating."

"You're the fascinating one. A prince who escapes the confines of the palace to live a wild partying lifestyle."

"Maybe. Maybe not."

"Maybe not?" He'd piqued her curiosity. "What aren't you telling me?"

Max hesitated. "Never mind. We should go explore the Christmas market."

And with that he alighted from the car. She joined him on the side of the road. Without a word, he reached for her hand. With the sun out, it warmed the air ever so slightly, making it unnecessary for gloves. His fingers wrapped around hers.

She knew she should pull away, but she didn't want to. It felt right to have her fingers entwined with his. The more time they spent together, the more it seemed as though this was how they were meant to be—together.

She glanced up at him. "Aren't you worried about the press?"

He shrugged. "This is Ostania. And more so this is Vallée Verte. These people have known me all my life. They are, shall we say, protective. So when the press comes sniffing around, they make sure they are not welcome. As a result, the press doesn't come here much."

She could see why the townspeople would feel an allegiance to Max. He was kind and thoughtful to everyone, even those he didn't know.

And so they strolled through the village and had a leisurely lunch at a bistro with a hot cup of soup and a warm sandwich. Noemi's appetite kept growing and so did her waistline. It was one of the reasons for the sonogram a few weeks early.

After lunch, they strolled to the Christmas market. Noemi found something to buy for each of her family members. This Christmas was so important. It was the first without their parents and it was the first with Leo. She desperately wanted her brothers to come together, but she feared control of the family business would drive a permanent wedge between them. And she would never have a close family—like she used to know.

Her gaze moved to Max as he checked out some Christmas ornaments. Technically he would be her family, too.

The baby would form a lifetime connection between them. But what would that look like?

In that moment, a little girl bumped into her.

"Hi there," Noemi said.

The girl must have been about four or five. She peered up at Noemi with tears in her eyes. Noemi looked around for the girl's parents but no one appeared to be with her.

The girl started to move away.

Noemi ran after her. She stepped in the girl's path. "Where is your mommy?"

The girl's gaze frantically searched the market. "I... I don't know."

Noemi felt bad for her. She glanced around for Max, but he was some ways away with his back to them. She couldn't just let the little girl run off alone—not even in Vallée Verte.

Noemi knelt down. "Can I help you find your parents?"

The little girl shrugged. Tears in her big brown eyes splashed onto her chubby cheeks.

"My name's Noemi. What's yours?"

"Gemma."

"Well, Gemma, it's nice to meet you." She didn't have much experience with children. She supposed she'd better learn quickly, seeing as in just a handful of months, she'd be a mother. "Come with me." She held out her hand.

The little girl hesitated.

She couldn't blame her. She didn't know Noemi at all. "I promise I won't hurt you. I just want to help you find your parents."

The little girl slipped her cold hand in hers.

"Do you have gloves?"

Gemma shrugged.

Noemi spied a bit of white sticking out of the pockets of the little girl's bright red jacket. "There they are."

She helped Gemma put on her gloves.

"I'm hungry," the little girl whined. And by the looks of her, probably tired, too.

"Okay." Noemi glanced around. There were a lot of food

booths in the Christmas market. "We'll get you some food first and then find your parents. They have to be around here."

As Noemi made her way toward Max, she asked the vendors if they knew the girl. None of them did. The parents had to be frantic. But where were they? If this was her baby, she'd be standing on a table, yelling so everyone could hear her.

"Noemi?" Max's gaze moved from her to the little girl. "Who is this?"

"Max, meet Gemma. She is lost. We're trying to find her parents." Noemi noticed that he had some food in his hand. "Are you going to eat that?"

He glanced down at the pastry. "You can have it."

Though it did look tempting, she said, "It's for Gemma. She's hungry."

Max knelt down. "Would you like this?"

The girl hesitated but eventually accepted the pastry. She took a bite. Then another.

While Gemma enjoyed the food, Max turned to Noemi. "We'll give her to one of my security men. They'll make sure the authorities find her family."

Gemma tightened her hold on Noemi's leg. The girl looked up at her with pleading eyes.

Noemi's protective instinct kicked in. "Can't she stay with us? You know, until we find her parents?"

Max's brows furrowed together. "Noemi, how do you expect to find them?"

She'd been giving this some thought. Her gaze met Max's. "I have an idea but I'll need your help."

"What do you want me to do?"

"Can you lift Gemma onto your shoulders?" When he nodded, Noemi knelt down next to Gemma. "The prince is going to pick you up so you can look over the crowd for your parents. Is that all right?"

Gemma cupped a hand to her mouth. "He's the prince?"

Noemi smiled and nodded. "He is. Can he pick you up?"

The girl sent Max a hesitant stare and then shook her head.

The girl clutched Noemi's leg. Noemi's heart went out to her. She couldn't imagine how scared the girl must be.

Noemi smoothed a hand over the girl's head. "It's okay. We're just trying to help you."

Gemma glanced at Max again, but she didn't release Noemi's leg.

Noemi mouthed to Max, *Say something.*

Max sent her was puzzled look. He mouthed, *What?*

She mouthed back, *Anything.*

Max cleared his throat. Who would have guessed Max would be nervous around a child? She wondered if he would be that nervous with their baby.

Max knelt down next to the girl. "Hi. My name's Max. Would you like to be friends?"

Gemma shrugged, keeping a firm hold on Noemi's leg.

Noemi intervened. "Gemma, he's a really good friend of mine. You can trust him. I promise." When Gemma didn't lessen her hold, Noemi continued, "And I'll be right here with you the whole time. He'll just pick you up for a moment to look for your parents. And then he'll put you back down." She paused a moment to give the little girl a chance to think about it. "You do want to find your parents, don't you?"

Gemma slowly nodded.

With Max kneeling, he held out his arms to Gemma. The girl let him lift her.

This interaction made Noemi eager to meet her own child. She wondered if it would be a girl or boy. Should she find out soon? Her gaze moved back to Max, trying to imagine him with their child.

"Do you see them?" Max asked.

Gemma shook her head and then she reached her arms out to Noemi. The girl was so sweet. The parents must be so worried. Noemi took the girl in her arms.

Max leaned over to Noemi. "Don't worry. We'll make sure she gets back to her parents."

It was then that Noemi noticed the policeman approaching them. He must have been patrolling the area when one of Max's guards flagged him down. She wasn't the only one to notice the man's approach. The girl's arms tightened around Noemi's neck.

"It's okay," she said to Gemma. Then she turned to Max. "I can't hand her over. She's already scared enough."

"They are better equipped to handle this." Max pleaded with his eyes. "Noemi, this is for the best."

Max turned to speak with the officer, explaining the situation. The officer assured Max that he would return the child to her family. The officer moved to Noemi and reached for Gemma.

"No…" Gemma tightened her grip to the point where it was uncomfortable for Noemi.

"Stop." Noemi stared at the officer. There had to be a better way to do this. Then her gaze strayed across the concerned look on Max's face. "Just give me a moment."

"Noemi…" Max frowned at her.

"Just wait." She rapidly searched her mind for the best way to reunite this little girl with her parents.

The policeman stepped away and spoke into his radio.

Noemi's gaze searched the market. There were a number of people in this part of the market, but none appeared to be looking for a lost little girl. A band playing folksy music was situated in the center while food vendors and artists had tents along the edges of the market area where they displayed their goods.

Noemi got another idea and took off.

"Noemi, where are you going?"

She waved at Max to follow her. She rushed over to the band that was on a little stand. When the band members noticed the prince approaching, they stopped mid-piece. With a flustered look, they got to their feet and bowed their heads at the prince.

Max greeted them and told them what a marvelous job they were doing. And then Noemi asked them for a favor. The four older men were more than happy to accommodate her.

With Max and Gemma next to her, Noemi stepped up to the microphone. "Excuse me."

Most of the crowd wasn't paying attention. Noemi placed her fingers between her lips and blew. The high-pitched whistle brought silence over the marketplace. Everyone turned her way.

"I'm sorry to disturb your afternoon but we have a bit of a situation. This little girl has been separated from her parents, are they here?" She scanned the crowd, searching for frantic parents to come rushing toward the stage.

There was no movement. No frantic parents.

And then she had another thought. "Please help me reunite the little girl with her parents. Everyone who has a cell phone, please pull it out. If you all start texting on your social media accounts, hopefully word will make it to Gemma's parents. Use #HelpGemma. Thank you."

When no one moved, Noemi turned to Max. She whispered, "You do have cell phones in Ostania, don't you?"

Max laughed, a deep rich sound that warmed her insides. "Yes, *ma chérie*. We have cell phones and the internet."

Noemi sighed. "Thank goodness." She glanced at the people who were still motionless and staring at them. "Why aren't they doing anything?"

Max looked at her. "Excuse me." When she stepped aside, he moved to the microphone. "Please, help."

All it took was two words from Max in order to spur people into motion. She glanced at him and sent him a small smile—a hopeful smile. This was going to work. It had to work—for Gemma's sake.

Max moved away from the microphone. "Now what?"

"We wait. We'll browse the Christmas market and maybe get some more to eat." She turned to Gemma. "Would you like that?"

Gemma nodded.

And then Noemi added, "Your parents will find us. Just wait and see."

Max sent her a reassuring smile.

She set Gemma on the ground and took her small hand in her own. Then Noemi turned to Max. "Why do you keep looking at me like that?"

"Because I've never seen this side of you."

"What side?"

"The assertive, take-charge mode. You are quite impressive. And you think fast on your toes. You would make a good leader."

"Leader?" She couldn't help but smile. Not letting his words go to her head, she said, "I'm helping a lost child. Nothing more."

"I think you're capable of far more than you give yourself credit for."

She didn't even know if she would make a good mother. She had so much to learn and no parents to turn to for advice. A rush of pregnancy hormones hit her. Doubts about her ability to be a good mother assailed her. What if she messed up her kid? What if she was the worst mother ever?

"Hey, relax." A concerned look came over Max's face. Apparently, her worries were reflected on her face. Max placed a reassuring hand on her shoulder. "I didn't mean to upset you. I was just trying to help."

Noemi shook her head. "It's not you."

"Then what is it?"

She shook her head. "Nothing."

But inside she was a ball of nerves. She didn't even know what she was going to do for a job if she walked away from modeling. Sebastian had made it clear she wasn't welcome in the family business except as a silent partner. She recalled how her parents were hard on him while growing up and how he'd done his best to shield her.

Noemi wondered if that's what he thought he was still doing—protecting her. Sometimes habits were hard to break. And now with Leo joining the company, she would definitely be in the way.

Her whole future was one big question mark.

CHAPTER THIRTEEN

MAX GLANCED OVER at Noemi with her hand wrapped around Gemma's. They'd stopped at a stand where handmade toys were displayed. He was captivated with the way Noemi's face lit up as she talked to the little girl.

He could so easily imagine her with their own child. And after witnessing her strong protective instincts today and her caring way with Gemma, he had no doubt Noemi would make a remarkable mother.

"Shall we eat?" Max asked. He'd spotted a stand where they offered a variety of food that didn't involve sugar.

Gemma turned to Noemi as though trying to decide if she should agree or not. When Noemi agreed, Gemma smiled and nodded her head.

It was remarkable how the little girl had taken to Noemi so quickly. But then again, he'd been drawn to Noemi from across the room without having spoken one word to her. And it went beyond her outward beauty. There was something in her smile and a genuine kindness in the way she dealt with people. Everyone around her seemed to enjoy her company. Even his mother was beginning to thaw around Noemi. And that was saying a lot.

After the food had been presented, the vendor refused to take Max's money. This wasn't the first time something like this had happened. And though Max was touched by the offer, he knew these people couldn't afford to freely give away their goods—nor should they be expected to. And so he mentioned to his bodyguard to make a note of their names and then they would be generously compensated later.

As the three of them ate their selection of croissants and meats while sitting on a bench off to the side of the market, Max noticed that Noemi was busy on her phone. He wondered what had her so preoccupied that she'd barely eaten any of her food. But then he noticed she was following the hashtag for Gemma.

"Relax. We'll find her parents."

Noemi slipped the phone back in her purse. "Don't make promises you can't keep."

"This is one promise I intend to keep."

The urge to lean over and give Noemi a reassuring kiss came over him. It was so strong that he started in her direction before he caught himself. This wasn't the place for a public display of affection. Suddenly he was anxious to head back to the privacy of the palace.

"I'm sorry," Noemi said.

Lost in his thoughts, he wasn't sure what she was referring to. "Sorry for what?"

"I'm sure you have more important things to do than sit here with us."

The truth was that he did have a meeting with the royal cabinet. They wanted to discuss options to pump up a sluggish economy. At first, the subject hadn't interested him. It had sounded dry and boring. But after spending this time in the village with the very kind and generous residents, he was anxious to do what he could to improve their lives.

However, he wouldn't just leave Noemi to deal with Gemma. He could already sense the strong bond forming between the two. If the police tried to remove the child before the parents were found, he knew there would be a scene. And he didn't want that for Noemi or Gemma.

"I have nothing more important than being here with you." Did that sound as strange to her as it did to him? He never talked that way.

Noemi rewarded him with a smile. "Thank you. I'm certain Gemma's parents will turn up soon."

And then there was a commotion off to the side of market. Both of Max's bodyguards and the police officers stood between him and the commotion. The excited voices were getting louder as though approaching them. Max's body stiffened.

Once as a child, his family had come under attack from an angry and disillusioned person. They had blamed the king for all their personal problems and had tried to harm the royal family. Since then, loud commotions in public spots put Max on guard.

He got to his feet and motioned for Noemi and Gemma to remain where they were. When he spoke to his guard, the man said he didn't know what was going on.

Max was about to call in additional security for Noemi when a man and woman appeared in front of the police. The woman had tears in her eyes and the man was speaking so quickly that it was hard to catch what he was saying.

And then Gemma rushed forward. "Mama! Mama!"

That was all the confirmation Max needed to move aside and let the girl by. Gemma rushed into her mother's arms.

In the end, it came to light that Gemma had been anxious to see the Christmas market, but her parents had some shopping to do first at the local shops on the other side of the village. Gemma had slipped away to visit the market, but then couldn't remember how to get back to her parents. Gemma had learned a valuable lesson and had promised her parents never to do something like that again.

"Thank you so much," Gemma's father said to Prince Max.

"It's not me you should thank." Max turned to Noemi. "She was the one that thought of using social media to locate you and reunite you with your daughter."

With a watery smile, the mother profusely thanked Noemi. And though Noemi looked uncomfortable with all the attention, she accepted the kind words graciously.

And then out of nowhere Gemma pulled away from her mother and gave Noemi a big hug. Noemi asked if they could have their picture taken together. When Gemma and her parents agreed, Max pulled out his phone. He noticed that he had three missed calls on his phone. His absence had not gone unnoticed. This trip into the village had taken much longer than he'd imagined. He dismissed his thoughts of what would face him back at the palace and used his cell phone to snap a picture, promising to forward it to Noemi.

Max's bodyguard, Roc, stepped up next to him and spoke softly near his ear. "You are needed at the palace right away. It's an emergency."

That word was never thrown around lightly. The hairs on the back of his neck raised. Max nodded and then waited until there was a pause in the conversation between Noemi and Gemma's parents.

"Noemi, I must go back to the palace."

Noemi's smile faded. "We were just going to finish touring the remaining shops."

He felt bad that their day had been interrupted. He lifted his phone and checked his missed phone calls. To his surprise, only one was from the royal cabinet and the other two were from his mother. His mother didn't make a phone call unless it was important. The emergency must be personal. His father?

None of this concerned Noemi and she wouldn't have anything to do back at the palace while he was dealing with his mother. He wanted this trip to be enjoyable for her. And so far, it hadn't gone quite as he'd planned.

"Why don't you stay here and finish touring the village?" he said to Noemi before he leaned over to his bodyguards and instructed one of them to stay with her.

"Really? You don't mind?" Noemi looked unsure about the idea.

"Not at all." Liar. He did mind. He longed to spend more time with her. "I'll meet you later for dinner."

"It's a date."

He liked the sound of a date. It gave him something good to look forward to. "Roc will be staying with you and escorting you back to the palace."

"But that's not necessary—"

"It's nonnegotiable." The lift of her brows told him he'd misspoken. He'd never felt so protective of another person. The rush of emotion had him coming across too strongly, "I just want to make sure you don't get lost or anything."

Her face took on a neutral tone. The smile on her face returned. "I don't think that will happen. It's a little hard to miss the palace on the hill. It kind of stands out."

He smiled, too. "I guess you have a point, but this way you'll have a ride back whenever you're ready to go. It's a long walk. Trust me. I know from experience."

"Thank you. That would be nice."

He definitely had to make sure to take a lighter approach when the protective instinct came over him. "You're welcome."

She had no idea how much he wanted to stay there with her. He didn't care what they toured, he just wanted to be around her and bask in the glow of her smile and listen to the musical sound of her laughter. He was hooked on Noemi. And it was a dangerous place to be should she decide life in Ostania wasn't for her—he couldn't leave now or ever again. He had to prepare to rule a nation.

Back at the palace, the bright cheery decorations seemed to mock him.

Max was torn between duty to family and duty to nation. On top of it, he was greatly concerned about this emergency. The butler instructed him to go upstairs. It was his father and the doctor had been called.

Max rushed to his father's bedchamber. He'd stayed away for too long. He'd made his father carry the brunt of the weight of caring for a nation all on his own and it had been too much for him.

His mother stopped him in the hallway. "Maximilian, slow down."

"But Father...how is he?"

"The doctor is in with him." His mother didn't say it but she was very worried.

"What happened?"

His mother gazed up at him. In that moment, it was as though she'd aged twenty years. "It's your father's diabetes, there've been complications. His kidneys—they aren't functioning well."

Max raked his fingers through his hair. He knew about his father's diabetes. His father had had it most of his life, but it had always been under control—until recent years. But Max had no idea it was this bad. "Why is this the first I'm hearing of it?"

His mother frowned at him. "Because your father refused to let anyone tell you. He said you needed time to recover from those years of dealing with...with your illness." His mother never could bring herself to say the word cancer. "Your father said everything would be all right and there was no reason to worry you or your brother. But over time, it's getting worse."

"So Tobias doesn't know either?"

With tears shimmering in his mother's eyes, she shook her head.

The door to the bedroom opened and the doctor exited. Max stepped up next to his mother. He had so many questions. He needed to know just how serious this situation was and what he could do to make it better.

The doctor held up a hand to him. "The king just wants the queen right now. Please wait here."

In this instance, the doctor trumped royalty. His mother disappeared into the room and the door closed. Max was left alone—on the outside, looking in. His head started to pound as question after question came to him. How did he let himself become this disconnected with his family?

He had to do better. How was he ever going to make a

good father when he couldn't even stay on top of the family members he already had?

He turned around to start pacing when he noticed his brother sitting at the far end of the hallway. Tobias was sitting with his head in his hands.

Max approached him. He took a seat and searched for something comforting to say. It wasn't easy when he was as worried as his brother looked. "Hey, it's going to be okay."

Tobias shook his head. "No, it isn't."

"Do you know something I don't?" Considering Max didn't know much at this point, it was quite possible.

Tobias ran his forearm over his face. "They've been talking about Father stepping down."

"From the throne?" Max never imagined his father would ever agree to such a thing.

Tobias nodded. "I… I can't do it."

"Sure you can."

Tobias's eyes were wide with worry. "No, I can't. This should be you. You should be taking over."

Max searched for the right words to comfort his brother. "You're just worried. Everything will seem clearer tomorrow."

Tobias shook his head. "I don't know why they make such a big deal of having an heir. Look at you. You're calm. You can handle this stuff."

Max raked his fingers through his hair. "They've been working with you. You know how to run the country."

Tobias got to his feet. "I don't want to!"

Max stood. He placed his hands on his brother's shoulders. "Okay. Calm down."

"How am I supposed to do that? Our father is sick. Very sick. I'm too young for all of this. I… I'm not the right person."

Max knew how to comfort his brother. But was it the right time to mention the baby? Things with Noemi were still unsettled.

But he never imagined his father's health would have

declined this drastically. Max's gaze searched his brother's bloodshot eyes. He'd never seen his brother so scared. Not since Max had cancer. It was so wrong for his brother to be this upset when he could help alleviate some of his worry.

"Tobias, you can stop worrying about shouldering Papa's responsibilities."

"What?" Tobias's gaze searched his. "Of course I can't. You know this. I'm the spare heir."

"Tobias, listen to me." Max glanced around to make sure they were alone. Then he turned back to his brother. "I have something I need to tell you."

Tobias turned to him. "If it's bad, now isn't the time."

The thought of his baby brought a smile to Max's face. "It's not bad. In fact, it's good news. Really, really good news."

"Well, don't just stand there. Share."

"You can't tell anyone this. Okay?"

His brother nodded.

Max lowered his voice. "Noemi is pregnant. I'm going to be a father."

"You are?" Confusion flickered in his brother's eyes. "But how? The doctors said that isn't possible."

"I know. But it's true. She's pregnant." A smile pulled at Max's lips. "Miracles do happen."

"Why haven't you told anyone?"

"It's complicated. Noemi and I are still getting used to the idea."

"Are you sure it's yours?"

Max nodded. "Definitely. But as you can imagine, it wasn't planned." He pleaded with his eyes. "Please don't say anything to anyone. The situation is delicate. Noemi and I haven't decided how to handle this. I told you this so you wouldn't worry so much. This will all work out."

"I hope you're right."

So did he. There were still so many unknowns about his father's health, the state of the country and what Noemi planned to do next. But right now Max surprised himself by stepping up to the plate to help—could it be that preparing for fatherhood was preparing him for taking over the responsibility and care of his country?

CHAPTER FOURTEEN

It just wasn't the same.

Not without Max.

Though Gemma and her family were the nicest people, Noemi missed Max. She assured herself it was because they were becoming good friends. Nothing more.

Noemi returned to the palace to find another note in her room from Max. Excitement coursed through her body when she read his handwritten note telling her to meet him in the blue room at six thirty. She glanced at the clock on the mantel. That wasn't far from now.

Her gaze returned to the note. The blue room? She didn't remember visiting it on her tour of the palace. She wondered if this dinner would go better with his mother. She'd been a bit friendlier at their last meeting. Noemi hoped their relationship would continue to improve since they would play some sort of role in other's lives once the baby was born.

Noemi rushed to the wardrobe and flung open the doors. She shouldn't have stayed in the village for so long, but for the first time since her parents had passed away, she had that sense of family—of belonging. The residents of Ostania were so friendly and welcoming.

Her gaze scanned over the selection of dresses she'd bought in the village. Red—too daring. Black—already wore the color. Green—too short. Silver—too casual. Why had they all looked so good when she'd picked them out?

A bit of blue lace called to her. She pulled out the dress.

Long lace sleeves led to a modest neckline. But the blue chiffon skirt was short. Too short? But she was out of options.

She wore her hair loose and swept off to the side. She took extra care in applying her makeup, not putting on too much. She looked in the mirror and knew she wouldn't fit in this conservative household. If Max was hoping she'd change, he was in for a reality check. Max would have to accept her the way she was. Not that she needed his acceptance or that of his family's. She wasn't princess material.

With a second and then a third glance in the mirror, she assured herself that she hadn't forgotten anything. Then she let herself out the door. It was time to go find the blue room. She didn't want to be late.

In the hallway, she glanced around for someone to ask directions. She looked up and down the hallway, but there wasn't anyone around. How could that be? There were always people going here and there with their arms full of cleaning supplies or fresh linens, but when she needed them, none were about.

She recalled Max saying that all the public rooms were on the first floor and so that's where she would start. Although in a palace this size, it would take her all evening to search the rooms.

At the bottom of the steps, she peeked in the first room. There was no one in it. The next was vacant and the walls were red. And so she continued down the hallway, checking each room.

When she stepped into a room with cream walls, she found it wasn't vacant. An older woman, with her white hair up in a bun and wearing a black uniform, looked over from where she was drawing the curtains.

The woman turned to her and gave her appearance a quick once-over. "May I help you, ma'am?"

"I was looking for the blue room."

The woman's brows momentarily lifted. "Ma'am, the blue room is in the west tower on the second floor."

The woman went on to explain how to get there and

Noemi appreciated it because she never would have found it any other way. There were so many hallways and doorways that a person could easily get lost in here. Noemi resisted the urge to ask the woman for a map.

When Noemi reached what she hoped was the right tower, she poked her head inside the doorway. It was then that she noticed a candlelit table near the windows. She took a step into the room. "Max?"

"Over here." He was standing in front of the windows wearing a dark suit and tie. He looked like he'd just walked off the pages of some glamor magazine. And the way he looked at her made her knees turn jelly soft. It was all she could do to stand up.

"I… I had a little trouble finding you. I hope I'm not late." She glanced around, looking for the rest of his family.

"You're right on time. And sorry. I totally forgot to put directions in the note. I was distracted."

"Where is everyone else?"

"Everyone else?"

"Yes." When he sent her a puzzle look, she added, "You know, your family."

"They aren't coming. This is a dinner for two."

It was then that her gaze moved to the table set for two. There were candles and flowers. "What is all this?"

"Just an apology."

"Apology? For what?" She couldn't think of anything he'd done wrong. In fact, he'd been quite charming.

"For abandoning you today. I wouldn't have left if I didn't have to. I hope you know that."

She nodded. "Did everything work out for you?"

He didn't say anything at first. "It went as well as could be expected."

She approached him. "That doesn't sound so good." She stopped when she was in front of him and lifted her chin until their gazes met. She could see storm clouds of emotions reflected in his eyes. The meeting must have been much worse than he was anticipating.

"What is it?" she asked. "You can talk to me."

"You'd really be interested in hearing about state business?"

She nodded, wanting to be included.

And so Max started to fill her in on how the country's economy was being jeopardized by their insistence on following tradition. Ostania mainly exported agriculture goods such as vegetables, trees and seeds. They had some of the most exotic seeds in the world. But their insistence on relying on one form of export was making the global reach limited and in some cases it was shrinking.

Noemi looked at him thoughtfully for a moment. "So what you need is to broaden your country's expertise?"

He nodded. "But you seem to be the only one to really get this concept. The cabinet is insisting that this is merely an economic hiccup—a blip in the economy."

"But you think it's much more?"

"I do."

She took a sip of ice water as she considered his problem. "Have you considered retraining your people?"

"This country and its people are steeped in archaic traditions—whether they make sense or not. Most people won't consider changing the way things have always been done."

"Then start with the young people. These are the ones that strain against tradition."

"I've thought of that but once the progressives leave Ostania for higher education, they don't return."

"And that's where you're losing your country's most valuable resource. Have you considered opening your own university?"

A light of interest shone in his eyes. "And then we could gear the curriculum toward the future of Ostania."

"Something like that."

"You are brilliant. I will start plans for a university as soon as I am king. No." He shook his head. "It can't wait. This must be started immediately."

She loved being able to contribute to a solution that would

help the country. And she loved it even more that Max took what she had to say seriously.

He smiled at her, but he didn't say anything.

Feeling a bit conspicuous, she asked, "Why are you smiling?"

"It's nice to have someone who gets what I'm saying."

She relaxed and smiled back at him. "And it's nice to have someone listen to me and take what I have to say seriously."

A look of concern came over his face. "Who doesn't take you seriously?"

"My family. Sometimes it's like I'm not even there. They talk right past me."

"I understand."

"You do?" He was probably just saying that to be nice. "But you're a prince, everyone must listen to you."

He shook his head. "After my infertility diagnosis, I became invisible as they rushed to groom my brother to assume the crown. It got so bad that I felt I... I just couldn't stand feeling so inadequate."

Her gaze met his. "You really do understand. I'm just so sorry for all you've gone through. And here I am complaining and what I've endured is nothing compared to you—"

"Don't do that. Your pain is no less important."

His words meant so much to her. "I became the face of Cattaneo Jewels by default. My family didn't know what else to do with me."

"I thought you were the face of the line because your beauty is absolutely stunning. Men can't help but stare at you. And women wish they were you. And by wearing Cattaneo Jewels, it's the closest they'll ever get to your amazing looks."

Noemi's mouth gaped. He surely hadn't meant all that. She forced her lips together. Had he? Because no other man had ever swept her off her feet with merely his words.

As though he could read her thoughts, he said, "Don't look at me like that. You have to know it's true. But there's so much more to you to admire, such as your generous heart and your smarts." He reached out, covering her hand with his. "I think we could make a great team."

She didn't know if he meant romantically or professionally, but either way, her heart beat faster as she gazed into his eyes. What would it be like to be his partner? The thought appealed to her on every level.

Just then a server entered the room carrying a tray of food. Noemi and Max pulled apart and her hand became noticeably cold where he'd once been touching her. The server placed the food on the table and quietly left.

Max pulled out a chair for Noemi. "I hope you don't mind that I chose dinner."

"I'm sure whatever you picked will be good."

They started with onion soup topped with sourdough bread and gruyere cheese. She had to admit that it was the best she'd ever had. The soup dishes were cleared and a plate of hardy greens with a lemon and garlic vinaigrette was placed before them.

Once Noemi finished her salad, she said, "I'm going to be too full for the main course."

"You're going to need all the energy you can get for what I have planned this evening."

Was he hitting on her? Suddenly her mind filled with images of them upstairs putting her king-size bed to good use. His lips pressed to hers. His hands touching her… She jerked her runaway thoughts to a halt. The heat of embarrassment rushed up her neck and set her cheeks ablaze.

"Noemi, are you okay?"

Not able to find her voice, she nodded.

And then a smile eased the worry lines on Max's face. "Did you think I was planning to have my way with you?"

"Are you?"

He laughed. That wasn't the reaction she was expecting. Was the thought of making love to her again that preposterous? A rush of emotions had her eyes growing misty. Before the baby, she wasn't the wishy-washy type. She blinked repeatedly, refusing to give in to her pregnancy hormones.

Suddenly a look of dawning came over Max's face. "Hey, I didn't mean anything by that thoughtless comment. You already know how much I enjoy making love to you. I thought I made that quite clear. But if you'd like me to remind you—"

"No." The response came too fast and too loudly. They both knew she was lying. She stared into his eyes, seeing that he was being perfectly honest. "I... I'm just feeling a little emotional right now."

"I've read that about pregnant women."

"You've been reading about my pregnancy?"

He nodded. "You had a good idea about learning as much as we can before that little guy—"

"Or little girl."

He smiled. "Or little girl gets here. Anyway, I will try to watch what I say in the future. Are we okay?"

She nodded. "But you never said what you had in mind for this evening."

"That's right. I didn't."

"Well..."

"It's a surprise."

The server returned with the main course, *pot-au-feu*. Noemi inhaled the inviting aroma of the beef and vegetable stew. It was perfect for a cold winter evening. She gave it her best effort but she couldn't finish all of it.

She pushed the plate back. "I'm sorry. I am so full."

"Does that mean you don't want some bubbly and dessert?"

"First, I can't have bubbly—"

"You can if it's sparkling grape juice."

She smiled at his thoughtfulness. "Do you think of everything?"

"No. But I try. I want you to enjoy your visit to Ostania."

"It's really important to you, isn't it?"

He nodded. "So dessert can wait." He got to his feet and held his hand out to her. "Shall we go?"

She placed her hand in his and stood. "Go where?"

His eyes twinkled. "You'll see."

She followed his lead as they made their way toward the rear of the palace. By the back door, he stopped. On a chair near the door sat a white box. Max picked it up and held it out to her.

"What's this?" She loved presents. Her parents always made sure there were plenty of presents under the Christmas tree. "An early Christmas present?"

"If you want it to be."

While he continued to hold the box, she removed the gold tie and lifted the lid. Inside were a pair of white ice skates. Her gaze moved from the present to Max. "You got me skates?"

He nodded. "Do you like them?"

"Yes. But I didn't get you anything." She had no idea he was planning to give her anything. "It's not Christmas yet."

"I wanted to get a jump start on the holiday."

And then she noticed her coat resting on the back of the chair. "What are you up to?"

"Put on your coat and you'll find out." He paused and his forehead creased as his gaze skimmed over her short dress. "On second thought, would you like to change? It's cold outside."

She glanced down at her exposed legs. "I'll be right back."

Noemi took off for her room, all the while trying to remember her way back to this spot. When she reached her room, her cell phone rang. She considered ignoring it as she was anxious to get back to Max. But then she checked the caller ID. It was Leo.

"Hey, Leo. Is something wrong?"

"No. I'm just checking in. Are you still in Mont Coeur?"

"After you left, I decided to take a little trip, but I will be back for Christmas. You're still planning to be there, right?" When the only response was silence, she said, "Please, Leo. This is really important to me. I want to get to know you. We're family and we should spend our first Christmas together."

"Okay. If it means that much to you—"

"It does."

They chatted a few more minutes while she located her leggings and then shimmied into them. With a promise to see each other next week, they ended the call.

Noemi dashed out the door and down the hallway, hoping she didn't get lost. And then she came upon Max texting on his phone while he waited for her. He lifted his head and smiled. Her stomach felt as though a swarm of butterflies had taken flight within it.

They both put on their coats and headed outside. It was then that she noticed the ice skating rink had been lit up with thousands of white twinkle lights. She hadn't recalled noticing the lights before. Was this another detail Max had seen to? The lights reflected off the ice and made the snow on the sides look like a million sparkling diamonds.

She turned to him. "You did all this?"

"The ice skating rink was already set up. It's part of our tradition."

"But the lights. I don't remember seeing them the other day. It looks…" She paused taking it all in. "It looks magical."

It looks romantic. Just like the dinner.

"I have to admit that I did have the lights put up. I noticed in Mont Coeur that you like Christmas lights."

"I do. I love them."

They moved to the edge of the skate rink and laced up their skates. Max knelt in front of her and made sure her skates were tied properly. When he stood, he held his hand out to her. She placed her hand in his and let him help her to her feet.

"Come on. I'll show you how to skate." Max stepped onto the ice.

How did he get the idea that she couldn't skate? She thought of saying something but resisted. She decided to let him take the lead. She enjoyed the touch of his hands and the nearness of his body.

"Don't worry," he said. "I've got you. I won't let you fall."

Maybe she should fess up about her ability to skate. "You don't have to do this—"

"But I want to. There's so much I want to share with you."

She was pretty certain they were no longer talking about skating. As she continued to stare deep into his eyes, she said, "I'd like that."

"Do you feel steady on the skates?"

She nodded. "You really want to show me, don't you?"

"Yes. We'll take it slow. Take a step. Another step. And then glide."

She did exactly as he said. She could so clearly imagine him being a good parent and patient teacher with their child. They continued around the rink slowly. After the second pass, Max picked up the pace a little.

"You're doing great." He smiled at her. "Instead of being a prince, perhaps I should become a skate instructor."

"You're looking for a career change?" She knew he wasn't serious, but part of her wondered if he was just an ordinary citizen whether their lives would mesh.

"Maybe." His voice cut through her meandering thoughts. "What do you think? Want to give me an endorsement?"

"I don't know how much help I would be. Anybody would be excited to skate with a prince."

"I'm not so sure about that."

She gazed up at him, noticing the smile had fled his face. "I am. You're an amazing man. You're thoughtful, sweet and strong. This country is lucky to have you."

His gaze probed hers. "And how about you? Do you feel lucky to have me in your life?

Back when they'd collided on the sidewalk in Mont Coeur with the crush of fans, her answer might have been different. But since then she'd learned the tabloid headlines were not accurate. Max was nothing like the sensational gossip.

"Yes, I'm lucky. And so is our baby." She meant every word.

On the fourth loop, Max said, "Would you like to try it on your own?"

"Do you think I should?"

"Go ahead. I'll be right here." And then he let go of her hands.

The cold seeped in where he'd once been holding her. She took a step, getting her bearings without his steady grasp. It had been a few years since she'd been skating, but as she took one step after the next, it all came back to her like riding a bike.

She moved past Max. The cool air swished over her face and combed through her hair. She picked up pace and soon she was gliding over the ice.

When she looped back around, she found Max standing there staring at her. She did a spin and came to a stop in front of him. A look of surprise came over Max's face. She couldn't tell if that was a good or bad sign.

"You know how to skate?"

She nodded. "I've been skating since I was a little girl."

"But I didn't think you did."

"You didn't ask. And you were so sweet about it. I… I didn't want to ruin the moment. I hope you're not mad."

He shook his head as he moved closer to her. "What else don't I know about you?"

"My parents loved the holidays. They loved skiing, but they would indulge my passion for ice skating." Talking about her parents filled her with deep sorrow and regret.

Max skated in front of her and took her hands in his. "What's wrong?"

Noemi pulled away from him. She clasped her hands together. The mention of her parents brought back a barrage of memories—some of them good but then there was their final conversation.

"Noemi, what's wrong?" The concern rang out in Max's voice. "If I said or did anything wrong—"

"No. It's not you. It's me." She skated to the edge of the ice.

He followed her. "I don't understand." He took her hand

and led her to a nearby bench. "I hope you know that you can talk to me about anything."

She gazed up at the twinkle lights. "When I found out I was pregnant and I didn't know how to contact you, I visited the Cattaneo Jewels headquarters in Milan. Not having anyone to turn to, I told my parents I was pregnant. They didn't take it well. They made me feel like…like I'd let them down. It was terrible."

"I'm sorry. I should have been there. I never should have walked away from you that morning without knowing your full name and your phone number. If I could go back in time and change things, please believe me I would."

"I would change that, too."

Max's head dipped and his lips caught hers. It was a quick kiss but it said so much. His touch was a balm upon her heart.

Noemi pulled back. She needed to get this all out. "While I was at my parents' offices, I was handed a piece of mail. I didn't know it at the time but it wasn't meant for me—it was intended for my mother. We share the same initials. Anyway, I opened it and found a letter from my brother Leo. At the time, though, I didn't know I had another brother. He was writing to my mother to agree to meet his biological parents."

Max reached out and placed his hand on hers. "That must have been quite a shock."

She took comfort in his touch. "It was devastating. I hate to admit it, but I didn't take it very well. I just didn't understand how my parents could keep such an important secret from Sebastian and me."

"Noemi, you don't have to tell me this if it's too painful."

She shook her head as she attempted to get her emotions under control. She swallowed past the lump in her throat. "Sebastian and I never had a really close relationship. With him being older and not sharing the same interests, he never had time for me. And then to learn that I had another brother—a brother that my parents kept a secret—it hurt. A lot."

"I can't even imagine what that must have been like."

"When I took the letter to my parents and confronted them about Leo, we argued. I couldn't understand how they could have been so hard on me when they'd also had an unplanned pregnancy. I…" Her voice faltered.

"Noemi?"

"I told them I never wanted to speak to them again." She swiped at a tear as it slipped down her cheek. "And…and a few days later, they died in a helicopter crash on their way to meet Leo." One tear followed another. Her voice cracked with emotion. "Now I can never take back those words. I can never tell them that I'm sorry. That I love them."

"Shh…" He pulled her to him and held her until her emotions were under control. "Your parents knew you didn't mean it. They loved you. They wanted to find their other son because the bond with a child is stronger than anything, and they died united in their love for one another and for their family. And that's what I want—I want to unite our family."

And then without another word, Max lowered his head and caught her lips with his. Her heart fluttered in her chest. There, beneath the starry sky and twinkling lights, a prince was kissing her. This had to be a fairy tale.

His arm slipped over her shoulders, pulling her to his side. She willingly followed his lead. As his mouth moved over hers, deepening the kiss, she let go of the reasons this wouldn't work between them. For this moment—this night, nothing seemed impossible.

When he pulled back, he ran his fingers over her cheek. "You're cold. We should go inside."

She hadn't noticed the cold. Snuggled to him, she was quite warm. But she was in absolutely no mood to argue. "If you think that would be best."

"I do."

He made quick work of switching back into his shoes. He told her to wait and he'd be right back. He disappeared into the palace. She had no idea what he was up to. It was a night of surprises.

Noemi finished switching shoes and was just about to step

inside the palace when Max swung the door open. He had nothing in his hands, but he wore an expression that said he had something planned.

"What did you do?" She stepped inside.

Max shrugged his shoulders and feigned a totally innocent expression as they headed toward her suite of rooms. "Nothing."

Just the way he said it told her that he was most definitely up to something.

"Max?" She couldn't help but smile. Being with him made her happy and she didn't want it to end. "Just tell me."

"Why do you think I did something?"

"Because this night, it has been amazing. And…" She stopped on the landing and turned to him. "I don't want the evening to end."

This time she lifted up on her tiptoes and pressed her lips to his. The kiss was brief, but there was a promise of more—oh, so much more.

When she pulled back, she took his hand and continued up the steps. His thumb rubbed over the back of her hand, sending the most delicious sensations throughout her body. Was it just a prelude to something more?

'Thank you for tonight," she said, as they headed down the long, quiet hallway. "It was the most amazing evening."

When he spoke, his voice took on a deep timbre. "And it's not over yet."

A shiver of excitement raced over her skin. "What do you have in mind?"

"We haven't had dessert yet."

That wasn't what she'd been thinking of, but she was curious as to what he had planned. "What is dessert?"

"You'll see." He swung her bedroom door open.

Max gestured for her to go first. The lights were dimmed. Inside was a table with two tapered candles, whose flames flickered. She moved to the table. There was a bowl full of plump strawberries and a bowl of whipped cream. Off to the side was an ice bucket with a bottle of sparkling grape juice and two flutes.

When she turned to Max, he closed the door and approached her. "I hope you like berries."

"I love them." She loved everything. Most of all, she loved that he'd gone to so much trouble for her. "But how did you get them in the winter?"

He smiled. "Being a prince does have its advantages."

"It does, huh?" She turned, picked up a strawberry and dunked it in the whipped cream. She turned back to him and held out the berry.

He bit the berry. Then he did the same for her, only she moved at the wrong moment and some whipped cream ended up on the side of her mouth. When she moved to clean it, Max brushed her hand aside. He leaned forward and licked the whipped cream from the side of her mouth. Then his tongue traced around her lips.

A moan escaped her lips. The dessert was so very sweet. And she wasn't thinking about the berries and cream. This was going to be the best night of her life.

CHAPTER FIFTEEN

THE NEXT MORNING, Noemi woke up with a smile.

Her hand moved to the other side of the bed. The spot was empty and the pillow was cold. But Max's imprint was there. And when she rolled over, she could still smell Max's intoxicating scent on the linens.

When her gaze strayed across the time on the clock, she groaned. It was after nine. She'd slept in. No wonder Max wasn't around. She was being a total slacker and yet there was nowhere she had to be until lunch. That's the time she'd agreed to meet Gemma's mother. They were going to grab lunch in the village and then visit the local botanical gardens. She was told it was decorated for Christmas and quite a sight to behold.

She slipped out of bed and rushed through the shower. She was certain that she'd missed breakfast, but she hoped she could grab something to tide her over until lunch. Her stomach growled in agreement. This pregnancy stuff had certainly increased her appetite.

Wearing another pair of leggings and a long flowing top, she rushed back into the bedroom to find Max at the table with a covered dish sitting opposite him. He paused from flipping through a manila folder full of papers to give her his full attention.

"Good morning, beautiful. I wanted to make sure you got something to eat." He set the folder aside.

Heat rushed to her cheeks. "Why didn't you wake me up?"

"You were sleeping so soundly. I didn't want to disturb you."

"I would have gladly woken up." She leaned forward and pressed a quick kiss to his lips. When she pulled back, she noticed the worried look on his face. "What's wrong?"

Max forced a smile on his face but it didn't ease the worry lines. "I can't spend the day with you. I'm sorry."

"It's okay. But you'll still be able to make it to the doctor's appointment this evening, won't you?"

"Nothing could keep me away."

Noemi breathed a little easier. She was worried about the baby for no particular reason other than she'd just read a chapter about all the potential complications of pregnancy. Once she saw the baby and heard its heartbeat, she'd feel much better.

"Then stop feeling bad," she said. "You'll be there for the important part."

"Being with you is important, too. I asked you here so that we could spend more time together. And now I have to bail on you. Again."

"Stop. I'm not upset. See." Noemi pointed to the smile on her face. "I'm good. I'm great. In fact, I have plans for today."

"You do?"

She nodded. "I'm planning to meet up with Gemma and her mother. We're going to visit the botanical garden. There's a Christmas display."

He stood and took her in his arms. "I was planning to take you there. I think you'll be very impressed with the display."

"I understand about you not being able to go, but I will miss you."

"It won't be long until we're together again for your doctor's appointment. Just a few hours. I promise."

He leaned down and pressed his lips to hers. Her heart pounded just like it had when they'd kissed for the first time. Something told her that no matter how many times he kissed her, it would always be special—like the first time.

The day would have been a lot more fun having him along.

It was the first time that she acknowledged just how much she enjoyed Max's company. If his goal had been for them to grow closer, it was definitely working.

But what would happen when this fantasy vacation ended?

Max couldn't get the images of Noemi out of his mind.

Kissing her.

Holding her.

Their night together had been better than the first time. It had bridged the distance between them. It had Max even more determined to make her his princess.

And then there was Noemi's growing baby bump. Now, as they stood in the examination room of the doctor's office, Max was filled with this sense of awe over the baby followed by a wave of unconditional love. In that moment, it really drove home the fact that in just a few months he would become a father.

And what would happen when it came time for Noemi to return to Mont Coeur? Each day they were growing closer, but would it be enough to convince her to stay? How else could he convince her that they could make this work? That he would do whatever it took to make her happy—

"Max?" Noemi's voice jarred him out of his thoughts. When he sent her a puzzled look, she said, "The doctor wants to know if you have any questions before we begin the scan."

Max shook his head.

As Noemi leaned back on the exam table, she gave him another strange look. It was as though she wanted to probe further, but she thought better of it in front of the doctor. Dr. Roussel had been around a long time—long enough to deliver his brother and himself.

However, the man was one to stay on top of technology, which was why Max trusted him with caring for Noemi and their baby. The doctor was also known for his discretion.

After the doctor squeezed some gel on Noemi's expanding abdomen, he ran a wand over her skin. Max watched everything intently, making sure nothing went wrong. Somewhere along the way, Noemi's hand ended up in his as they watched the monitor.

"There is your baby." Dr. Roussel pointed to the screen.

The breath caught in the back of Max's throat. That little white smudge on the screen was his son or daughter. He would never again say he didn't believe in miracles.

Max smiled brightly and then looked at Noemi. "Are you crying?"

She looked at him. "You are, too."

With his free hand, he felt the dampness on his cheeks. And so he was. But they were tears of joy.

"This is the head." The doctor pointed it out. "And this is the spine. And…"

The doctor's voice faded away as he continued to study the monitor. Then he grew quiet as he moved the wand. For the longest time, the doctor didn't say anything. He studied the image this way and that way. And then he started to take measurements.

Max looked at Noemi, whose joy had ebbed away and was replaced by a frightened look. So he wasn't the only one?

"Is something wrong?" Noemi asked.

Max couldn't find his voice because he was too busy praying that his son or daughter was all right. He was even willing to make a deal with God for the baby to be healthy.

"Everything is all right." The doctor turned to Noemi and smiled. "Your baby is healthy. I'm just checking something that might explain your rapidly expanding waistline and increased appetite."

Max's gaze caught Noemi's. She looked hesitant to relax. The doctor was being cryptic and that was not reassuring.

"Doctor—"

Dr. Roussel waved him off. "I just about have it." He moved the wand a little bit. "Yes, it's just as I suspected."

"What is it?" Max asked, staring at the monitor, not sure what he was seeing.

"It's this right here." Dr. Roussel pointed to an image. "And this right here." He pointed to another image.

JENNIFER FAYE 159

"What is it?" Noemi's voice was a bit high-pitched.

Dr. Roussel turned with a reassuring smile. "Those, my dear, are your twins."

"Twins?" Max felt a bit light-headed. His legs felt rubbery. He was glad there was a stool beside him. He sank down on it.

"Yes," the doctor answered. "See here." He pointed to the monitor. "That is baby number one's heart beating. And that is baby number two's. I'll turn on the speaker."

They heard one heartbeat. It was a strong whoosh-whoosh sound. The other heartbeat was softer. The doctor assured them that was natural.

When Max looked at Noemi, her face was wet with tears. He leaned over to her and kissed her gently on the lips. "You are amazing."

"Twins." Noemi's voice was filled with awe. "Do you know if we're having boys or girls? Or one of each?"

As the doctor wiped the gel from her abdomen, he said, "I'm afraid it's too early for anything definitive, but they should be able to tell you at your next appointment."

Max felt as though this was part of some sort of dream. Twins. That seemed so unreal. Sure, there were twins on his mother's side of the family, but he never thought it was a possibility because he wasn't supposed to have children in the first place.

When they were ready to go, Dr. Roussel handed them some paperwork and photos. "Here are pictures from the scan. They are both the same. One for each of you." And then the doctor said to Max, "Your parents are going to be so happy. This is the kind of news they could use right now."

Noemi sent him a puzzled look as Max had yet to find a good time to tell her about his father's condition or the fact that the king had been put on the organ donor list. And there was a more selfish reason. Telling her would make it real. Everything in his life was changing at once and he was having problems keeping his footing.

He would tell her everything, very soon.

* * *

The following morning, Max found himself stuck in another cabinet meeting. All his plans for Noemi's visit were ruined. And yet he couldn't turn his back on his responsibilities. Maybe it was the worry over his father's condition or learning he was about to be a father of twins, but he wanted to pitch in.

"Your Highness?" A royal advisor peered at Max over the top of his spectacles.

Max had lost track of the conversation about the sudden dip in Ostania's economy—a problem that could have a devastating effect for everyone in the nation if it wasn't dealt with swiftly. The whole cabinet was in the meeting, including his brother, Tobias. The only empty chair was his father's.

"Why are you looking to me for the answers?" Max asked, feeling as though he was missing something. "You should be talking to my brother."

"With your father under the influence of medication, his heir needs to make the decision."

Max glanced around the room. "And we all know that is Tobias."

"Do we?" the elder advisor asked.

He knew. Max's gaze moved around the room from one person to the next. The whole cabinet knew Noemi was pregnant. Max's body tensed. This wasn't good—not at all. Noemi wasn't prepared for what was to come.

And there was only one way the cabinet could know about Noemi's pregnancy. Max turned an accusatory stare at his brother.

Tobias cleared his throat. "I need to speak with my brother in private. Can you give us the room?"

The elder advisor looked as though he was going to protest when Tobias gave him a very stern look, silencing the man's words.

Once all the people had moved to the hallway and closed the door, Tobias turned to Max. "You need to tell them."

"Tell them what?"

"About the baby. That you are the legitimate heir to the throne."

Max shook his head. "No."

"Max—"

"I said no. It isn't the right time."

"I don't understand. I would think you'd be shouting this from the palace towers for all the world to hear. You aren't having doubts about the baby, are you?"

"The baby happens to be twins—"

"Twins?" Tobias smiled brightly. "That's awesome. Twice the babies to spoil."

Tobias gave him a hug and clapped him on the back. Max longed to tell everyone the great news but he had to be patient and so did his brother.

"Wait until you tell Mother—"

"Slow down. Noemi isn't ready for all that. She's still getting used to the idea of us and now she has to adjust to the idea of twins."

"Well, I have something to admit." Tobias at least had the decency to look guilty. "The cabinet knows."

"I thought as much." Max frowned at his brother.

This couldn't be happening. He'd been waiting for the right time to make the announcement. This wasn't it. But if the news was out, he could help run the country. He could lift the burden from his father and brother. He would talk to Noemi later. He'd fix this...somehow.

CHAPTER SIXTEEN

SHE NEEDED TO find Max. She couldn't wait.

After checking with everyone she passed in the palace, Noemi finally got his whereabouts from the butler. She had big news; the babies had moved. It was the first time she'd been able to feel them. It was the most amazing experience. And she needed to share it with Max.

She rushed down the hallway, glancing in each room that she passed. Max was going to be so excited. The babies were getting bigger.

And she was growing closer to Max all the time. She could talk to him and he listened. Just like in the village when Gemma had been lost, he'd listened to her.

Max was everything she could want in a man. He was thoughtful and caring. Maybe they could be more than co-parents. Her heart fluttered at the thought of him taking a more prominent, more romantic role in her life.

As such, she wanted to invite him back to Mont Coeur for Christmas. She wanted him to meet her brothers. She knew it might not be the smoothest of holidays and she would feel so much better if Max was there next to her.

As she turned the corner, she found a group of men standing in the spacious hallway. The voices echoed in the hallway. And then someone said Max's name.

Noemi paused next to a large potted palm plant. Something just seemed off to her. Max was nowhere to be seen and yet they were talking about him. It was probably nothing, but still she stayed in place.

"Prince Maximilian told Prince Tobias that we'd have to wait a couple more weeks before they can do an in-utero test to confirm the parentage of the baby. Once it's legally confirmed, we can proceed with plans for Prince Maximilian to take over the throne. At last, it will be the way it was supposed to be all along."

"And the prince? Is he certain this is his baby?"

"He said he needs the test to be sure. The sooner, the better."

Noemi's heart sank the whole way down to her black heels. Her word hadn't been good enough for Max. She moved until her back was against the wall. She needed the support to keep her on her feet.

All this time he'd had doubts.

Once again, her words didn't carry any validity.

Her heart felt as though it was being torn in two. She'd never felt so devastated—so angry. Tears pricked the back of her eyes, but she blinked them away. Giving into her emotions would have to wait. She had things to do now. She wouldn't stay where her word meant nothing.

The sound of a door opening had her glancing up.

"Gentlemen, let's continue the meeting. My brother and I would like to discuss the best way to make this transfer of control once we have the test results."

It was Max's voice. And he'd just confirmed what the men had said. The breath caught in her throat. She didn't move. She just couldn't face him now. She was afraid she would say something that she couldn't take back. And no matter what she was feeling in this moment, she had to think of the babies.

The men were moving away from her. When at last the door snicked shut, Noemi blew out an uneven breath. It was as if she were waking up from a dream and reality was so harsh.

Her feet started to move, retracing her steps. She had to

get away. She had to make sense of all this. The kisses. The steamy looks. The dinners. Were they all just some ploy? Did he feel nothing for her?

Her head started to pound. Her steps came faster and faster. She forced herself to slow down. She didn't want anyone to think that something was wrong. She didn't want to explain that she'd made an utter fool of herself—falling for a prince with nothing but power on his mind.

Everything would work out.

Max rotated his shoulders, trying to ease the kink in his neck. The meeting with the cabinet had been long and at times contentious. But in the end, it was best that the news of the twins was out. He was able to lift a lot of stress off his younger brother and he was able to fill in for his father who had just started dialysis.

Now it was time he talked to Noemi. Everything they'd arranged in the meeting hinged on her agreeing to do a paternity test. Otherwise, the bulk of responsibility would be thrown back at his brother and that just wasn't fair—not when Max was in the position to do the right thing.

But first, he needed a hug and a long tantalizing kiss. Just the thought of holding Noemi in his arms again had him moving faster up the steps until he was taking them two at a time.

When he reached her bedroom door, he rapped his knuckles on it. Then he opened the door and stepped inside, expecting to find Noemi. She was nowhere to be seen.

He checked the time. It was going on seven in the evening. Would she be in the village this late? Maybe Gemma's family invited her to dinner. It wasn't like he expected her to sit around, waiting for him.

He was about to turn and leave when his gaze strayed across an envelope propped up on the nightstand table. Was that his name on it? He took a step closer. It was.

A smile lifted his lips. He imagined there was a love note inside. The idea appealed to him. He'd never had anyone write him a love letter before. Warmth filled his chest—a feeling he'd never known before Noemi. She'd brought so many amazing firsts to his life.

With his hopes up, he stuck his finger in the top of the envelope and ripped. He slipped out the piece of paper. He couldn't wait to see what it had to say.

> *Max,*
>
> *I've gone back to Mont Coeur. I know that you've told everyone about the twins and I'm not willing to go along with this. You only have your own interests at heart—not what's best for me or our babies. I refuse to be a "silent partner" in both my own and our twins' lives. Please don't follow me. I need time to think. I'll send you updates on the babies.*

Some of the words were smudged as though tears had smeared the ink.

How had this happened? How did she know when he'd just found out about his brother spreading the news? Had Tobias said something in front of the help? Even so, they were usually so discreet.

He gave himself a mental shake. It didn't matter how she found out. It only mattered how he got her back. If he could speak to her, she would understand. Wouldn't she?

CHAPTER SEVENTEEN

HOME SWEET HOME.

Although Noemi didn't feel the comfort that the luxury chalet normally gave her. In fact, she'd barely slept the night before. That morning, the sun shone brightly, reflecting off the snow, but it didn't cheer her up.

Noemi didn't bother turning on the Christmas lights. She wasn't in the mood to be jolly. She hadn't had morning sickness in quite a while, but right now her stomach was sour and her head pounded.

She couldn't believe she'd been so wrong about Max. She'd thought he was such a nice guy. She'd thought that the news sources had gotten him wrong. He wasn't out for himself—he cared about others. Boy, had she been wrong.

Knock. Knock.

She wasn't expecting anyone. When she'd arrived last night, neither of her brothers were here. Christmas wasn't until next week. Maybe Leo had arrived early. After all, this was now his home, too. And maybe it would be better not to rattle around this big place by herself.

She swung open the door and the words of greeting stuck to her tongue.

Max stood there with red roses in hand. Flowers weren't going to fix this problem.

"You shouldn't be here." Noemi attempted to close the door.

Max stuck his foot in the way. "I flew all this way. Won't you even hear me out?"

She let go of the door and walked into the living room. Maybe it was best to have it all out now. Behind her, she heard the door close followed by approaching footsteps. She moved to the other side of the room and turned. She leveled her shoulders and crossed her arms. And then she waited.

"I...uh...brought these for you." He held out the roses. When she didn't move to take them, he placed them on the wooden coffee table.

When he straightened, his gaze caught hers. She refused to turn away. She hadn't done anything wrong here.

"Aren't you going to say anything?" he asked.

"You're the one that flew here after I told you I needed time. It's up to you to talk."

Max slipped off his coat and then rubbed the back of his neck. "You shouldn't have just left. If you'd waited and talked to me, we could have worked it out."

She shook her head. "No, we couldn't."

"You're overreacting."

"No. I'm not. I know what I heard."

He held up his hands in surrender as he sank down on the couch. "I didn't come here to fight with you."

"Then why did you come?"

"To tell you that I want you—" He stopped himself, shook his head and then started again. "I came here to *ask* you to be by my side as I ascend to the throne."

Not I love you. Or I'm sorry.

Noemi shook her head. "I don't want our children to be used as some bargaining chip to give you an easy path to the crown."

Max sat straight up. "That's not what I'm doing. There's been a lot going on at the palace—things I haven't told you. It's important that the babies are tested as soon as it's safe and then I can assume my position as the heir to the throne."

"You aren't listening. This isn't all about you. There's also the babies and myself to consider. Or don't we count?"

"Of course you do. And if you would just hear me out, you would understand how important the test is."

He was so focused on the throne and that blasted test that he wasn't hearing her. He was acting the same way as her family—making her a silent partner in her own life. How had she missed seeing this before?

Her heart ached over the future they wouldn't have. She drew in a deep steadying breath. "Do you know what hurts the most?" She didn't wait for him to say anything. "It's that after the loss of my parents—the loss of my mother— I thought that I'd finally found someone that I could count on. Someone I could lean on. Someone who'd listen to me."

"You did. I'm here for you." His eyes pleaded with her.

She shook her head. "Not when your sole focus is becoming king. Now, please go."

Max got to his feet. He looked at her. His mouth opened but no words came out. And then he turned and walked out the door.

Noemi didn't know whether to be relieved that he'd left without a fight or hurt that he'd given up on them so easily.

CHAPTER EIGHTEEN

HE WASN'T GIVING UP. He was regrouping.

Max strode back and forth in the condo he'd rented for the night. On this trip, he'd broken with protocol and traveled alone. He needed privacy in order to fix what he'd broken.

He walked away the night before because they both needed to catch their breath. He hadn't expected such resistance to the idea of her coming back to Ostania and having the babies tested. He thought she liked it in Ostania. She had been making friends.

He continued to pace.

He was not giving up.

And that was something new for him. After his cancer diagnosis, he gave up. And yet he went into remission and since then he'd been deemed cured. And when he was told he couldn't have children—he couldn't live up to his birthright—he'd given up and left Ostania, left the palace life. This time when things weren't going his way, he refused to give up—to walk away.

He realized how much he wanted to stand up and take responsibility. He wanted to help his country. And at the same time, he wanted his family. He wanted Noemi.

He was being torn in two different directions. In that moment, he acknowledged that he couldn't live without Noemi and the twins. If he had to, he'd give up his claim to the throne.

He grabbed his coat and raced out the door. He had to tell Noemi that he chose her. He would always choose her.

The fresh snow from the night before slowed him down as he maneuvered his rented vehicle. Max stepped on the gas pedal harder than he should have and the back end fishtailed. He lifted his foot off the gas until the car straightened out. His back teeth ground together as he smothered a groan. He just wanted to get to Noemi as fast as possible. The longer this thing festered, the worse it would get.

Each second that passed felt like an hour. He wanted to tell Noemi that he chose her—that he loved her. It was the first time he'd been brave enough to admit it to himself. It was true. He loved Noemi and those babies with all his heart.

At last, he pulled to a stop in front of her chalet. He jumped out of the car and then realized he'd been in such a rush he'd forgotten to turn off the engine. Once he silenced the engine, he jogged to the front door.

Max pushed the doorbell once. Twice. Three times. "Noemi! Noemi!"

He paused and waited. Nothing.

She had to be here, didn't she? Surely she wouldn't have left. Would she?

His hand clenched and he pounded on the door. "Noemi, please. We need to talk."

Still nothing, but he sensed she was listening to him.

"Noemi, please open the door." He placed his palm against the door and lowered his head. "Noemi, I love you."

He heard the snick of the deadbolt. He lowered his hand and took a step back, not wanting to crowd her. And then the door swung open.

Noemi stood there. There were shadows under her eyes. And her face was devoid of makeup. Her hair was pulled back in a haphazard ponytail. And she was wearing a baggy T-shirt with some pink leggings. He wasn't the only one who'd had a bad night.

She stood there. Silent.

"Noemi, may I come in?"

"Do you really think that will change anything?" Her eyes said that she didn't think it would.

It was okay. He had enough faith for both of them. "Yes."

To his surprise, she stepped back and swung the door wide open. He brushed off the snow from his coat and hair and stepped inside. He deposited his coat on a chair in the foyer and then followed her to the living room. Noemi sat down and he did the same, leaving a respectable space between them.

He couldn't help but notice that once again all the Christmas lights were dark. He knew how much she loved the holiday. This told him that she wasn't all right with the current circumstances either.

Max turned to Noemi. She was staring down at her hands as she fidgeted with the hem of her shirt. This wasn't going to work. He needed her full attention.

He knelt down in front of her. "Noemi, I've made a mess of all this. And I'm sorry."

Her gaze lifted. "You are?"

He nodded. "And I want you to know that I didn't tell the royal cabinet about your pregnancy. But I did tell my brother. I know I shouldn't have. It's just that he was so upset and scared when he heard how sick our father is. I didn't think, I just reacted. Later, he went behind my back and told the cabinet."

"Wait. What's wrong with your father?"

Max drew in a deep breath and told her about his father's diabetes and the kidney damage as well as his father waiting for a new kidney on the organ donor list.

"So you told your brother because you were comforting him?" When Max nodded, she asked, "You didn't tell him because you wanted to reclaim your position as next in line for the throne?"

Max shook his head. "I wouldn't have done that."

"But it doesn't change the fact that the babies are the key to you having everything."

"I've done a lot of thinking—a lot of soul searching. And

I've come to a decision." He drew in a deep steadying breath. "I love you."

"You do?"

He nodded. "And I don't want to live without you. If I need to choose, I choose you. You and our babies."

"You'd walk away from your birthright—from the crown?"

"I would if that's the only way I could have you in my life."

CHAPTER NINETEEN

HER HEART HAMMERED.

He was saying all the right things.

Noemi struggled to find her voice. She couldn't hear her thoughts for the beating of her heart. He'd picked her. He wanted her. He loved her.

She swallowed hard. "I love you, too."

Noemi leaned forward and pressed her lips to his. Max moved to sit on the couch and pulled her onto his lap. They kissed some more. She wondered if he could feel the beating of her heart. It felt as though it was going to burst with love.

When she pulled back, she slipped onto the couch cushion next to him. She rested her head on his shoulder. She knew they couldn't leave things like this. She couldn't expect him to walk away from his heritage for her. In the end, they'd both be unhappy.

"Noemi, do you think your parents would have been pleased that you and I—that we are together?"

"You mean because you're a prince?"

"No. Because I love you so much. I didn't know it was possible to care this much for another person."

Noemi's chest filled with the warmth of love. "I think my parents would have approved of you. I wouldn't have given them a choice. I can't live without you either. I love you very much." Before he could say anything, she momentarily pressed a fingertip to his lips, causing his brows to rise. "And I could never ask you to give up your claim to the throne. You are a wonderful leader, caring, compassionate and determined. You will make an excellent king. But you have to know that I'm done being a silent partner. If we do this…" she gestured to him and her "…then I need your assurance that you won't take me for granted." When his lips parted, she held up a finger to once again silence him. "And I need to know that you'll hear me when I speak and you'll take my opinion into consideration."

She looked at him expectantly. He arched a questioning brow and she smiled. "Yes, you can speak now."

"See. I do know how to listen. And I promise we will be in this life's adventure together—as equals. What you say matters to me, whether it's to do with our relationship, our children or the running of the country."

Her heart swelled with love for this most amazing man. "How did I get so lucky?"

His thumb caressed her cheek. "I'm the one that's lucky."

Max moved away. She thought he was getting ready to kiss her, but instead, he got up from the couch. What was he doing? He moved to the foyer. Where was he going?

"Max?"

"Stay there. I'll be right back."

Seconds later, he rushed back into the room. He was smiling—a great big smile that lit up his eyes. He stopped in front of the Christmas tree and turned on the twinkle lights. "Come here."

Her pulse picked up its pace. "Max, what are you up to?"

"Just come here." He held one hand behind his back as he waved her over with his other hand.

Her heart pounded with a blend of excitement and anticipation. "If you have an early Christmas present, you have to wait. I don't have any presents wrapped for you."

"Just come here. Please." His eyes pleaded with her.

Without another word, she moved from the couch and joined him next to the tree. It was then that he dropped down on bended knee. Her eyes filled with tears of joy. Was this really happening?

He took her hand in his. "Noemi, I love you. I've loved you since that first night when I spotted you across the room. I never believed in love at first sight, but you've turned me into a believer. And I can't imagine my life without you in it."

She pressed a shaky hand to her gaping mouth.

He moved his hand from behind his back. And there, nestled in a black velvet box, was a stunning sapphire engagement ring. Noemi knew from her tour of the palace that the ring was in Ostania's royal colors.

"Noemi, will you please be my partner—because we'll decide everything together—be my lover—because I could never ever get enough of you—and be my wife—because I want to spend every single day of my life with you?"

After a lifetime of being relegated to a silent partner and not having her thoughts or feelings heard, Max had presented her with a proposal she couldn't turn down. Hand in hand, heart to heart, they would step into the future as equals.

She didn't hesitate. "Yes." Tears of joy raced down her face. "Yes. Yes."

Max stood up and pressed his lips to hers.

CHAPTER TWENTY

THE STAGE WAS SET.

The Christmas tree twinkled and carols played softly in the background.

Noemi glanced around the great room at Mont Coeur. Evening had settled on the resort and Max had started a fire. It crackled and popped in the large fireplace, casting the room in a warm glow.

She couldn't help but miss her parents. Her father had always taken charge of the fireplace and her mother had made sure there was something delicious to eat. Family gatherings had been a highlight for her parents. Family had been important to them. And now it fell to Noemi to pull her brothers together—she just wondered if that was even possible.

And what were they going to say when she revealed her news? Leo, well, she didn't think that he would feel one way or the other as they were still getting to know each other.

But Sebastian, he was a different story. Not so long ago she thought she knew how he'd react, but over the past year he had grown rather distant and then with their parents' deaths, he just wasn't acting like himself.

Max approached her. He placed his finger beneath her chin, lifting her head until their gazes met. "What's the matter?"

"Why does something have to be the matter?"

He lowered his hand. "Because I know you. And you're

worried. Are you afraid your brothers won't take the news of the baby well?"

She continued to stare into Max's eyes, finding strength in his gaze. "Sebastian and I haven't been getting along very well lately. I just… I don't know how he's going to take the news."

"Would it be easier if I wasn't here? You know, so you could talk to your brothers one-on-one."

She reached for his hand and squeezed it firmly. "I want you right here next to me." And then a thought came to her. "Unless you don't want to be here."

This time he squeezed her hand. "There's no place I'd rather be."

It was only then that she realized she'd been holding her breath, awaiting his answer. "Have I told you lately how much I love you?"

"Mm…it has been a while. Almost a half hour."

She grinned at him. "How could I be so remiss?"

"I was worried you might have grown bored of me."

"That will never happen." She lifted up on her tiptoes and said in a soft, sultry voice, "I'll show you how much I love you later."

"Can't wait."

She pressed her lips to his. Her heart picked up its pace. There was no way that she'd ever grow bored of him. He was her best friend and her lover. He was her first thought in the morning and her last thought at night. If someone had told her that she could be this happy, she never would have believed them.

Someone cleared their throat.

Noemi reluctantly pulled away. Max smiled at her, letting her know that this would all work out. She ran her finger around her lips, drew in a deep breath and turned.

Sebastian's dark gaze met hers. She couldn't read his thoughts. She supposed she should have given him a bit of a heads-up about Max.

"Sebastian, thanks for coming. I'd like you to meet Max."

She'd intentionally left out the part about Max being a crown prince. She didn't want to overwhelm her brother all at once.

After the men shook hands, Noemi realized that he was alone. "Where are Maria and Frankie?"

"I… I don't think they're going to make it."

Before she could delve further into Maria's absence, the doorbell rang. That must be Leo. She would have to make sure to tell him that this was his home as much as theirs and there was no need for him to ring the doorbell.

She rushed to the door and swung it open to find that her brother wasn't alone. Standing next to him was a beautiful blonde with a warm smile.

"Come in." She glanced at Leo. "You know you don't have to ring the doorbell. This is your home, too. I hope that one day it will feel like it."

"Um…thank you." Leo's gaze moved to Sebastian and the smile faded from his face.

Not ready to deal with the tension between her brothers, she helped them with their coats and then walked them into the great room. Noemi turned to the woman with Leo and held out her hand. "Hi. I'm Noemi. Leo's sister."

"Nice to meet you. I'm Anissa. Leo's, um, friend."

"Girlfriend," Leo corrected, placing his arm around her slender waist.

"Welcome. I hope we'll get to be really good friends."

Just then the doorbell rang again. Noemi cast a glance over her shoulder at Sebastian. He moved toward the door and Noemi turned back to the get-to-know-you conversation going on between Leo and Max.

A few seconds later, she glanced back at the front door to see Maria and Frankie had arrived. Noemi smiled as she'd missed Maria and her nephew dearly. But seeing as Sebastian and Maria were having a hushed conversation, she didn't want to intrude. She really hoped those two would be able to patch things up.

A couple of minutes later, Sebastian, Maria and little two-year-old Frankie joined them in the great room. Noemi couldn't hold back any longer. With a big smile pulling at her lips, she rushed over to them.

"Hi." She gave Maria a quick hug. Then she knelt down in front of Frankie. His eyes were big as he glanced around the large room at all the people he didn't know.

"Hey, Frankie," Noemi said, trying to gain his attention. When his gaze met hers, she said, "Can I have a hug?"

Frankie sent his mother a questioning look.

"It's okay," Maria said.

That was all it took for Frankie to release his mother's hand and let Noemi draw his little body to her. "I'm so happy you're here. I've missed you tons."

He pulled back and returned to his mother's side.

Noemi straightened. Her gaze moved to Maria, noticing the worry reflected in her eyes. "That goes for you, too."

Maria glanced in Max's direction. "I take it things are going well with you."

Noemi couldn't hold back an enormous smile. "Better than I could ever imagine."

"I'm so happy for you." The smile on Maria's lips didn't reach her eyes.

Noemi moved back to stand next to Max. He placed his arm over her shoulders. And then he leaned close. "Are you sure you want to do this now?"

She smiled up at him. He knew how nervous she was about her brothers' reactions—most especially Sebastian's. She nodded at him.

"Noemi," Sebastian said, "why did you call us all here? Is it the attorney? Does he have news for us?"

She shook her head. "This isn't about the will."

"Then what is it about?" Sebastian's gaze moved to Max and then back at her. "You know I don't like guessing games."

Maria elbowed him and he quieted down. But it was her brother's stormy look that he gave his wife that worried Noemi. Instead of things getting better for these two, they appeared to be getting worse. Maybe when her brother heard her good news, he'd relax some, knowing that she wouldn't be bothering him about the business any longer. She clung to that hope as her brother hadn't been himself in a while.

"Maybe we shouldn't be here," Leo said, meaning him and Anissa.

"Of course you should," Noemi said. "You are my brother as much as Sebastian is. Our separation as kids was a horrible mistake, but I hope going forward that there will be no distance. Because I'm going to need all of you." When her brothers got worried looks on their faces, she said, "It's nothing bad. I promise. I… I'm pregnant. You're going to be uncles." And then glancing at the women, she added, "And aunts."

For a moment, there was silence as everyone took in the news.

Noemi's heart pounded. "And we're having twins."

Sebastian was the first to approach her. He had a serious look on his face and she wasn't sure what he was going to say.

"Are you happy?" he asked, in the same manner that their father would have asked.

She smiled at him. "I've never been happier."

He studied her face for a moment as though to make sure she was telling him the truth. And then he put his hands on her shoulders. "Then I am happy for you, too. Congratulations."

He pulled her into his arms and gave her a tight hug—something he hadn't done since they learned of their parents' deaths. She was so thankful that this time it was good news that had brought them together.

When Sebastian released her and backed away, Leo stepped up to her. "You do know that I have no idea about children or how to be a cool uncle, right?"

She smiled and nodded. "I think you'll figure it out. In fact, I'll insist." She reached out and hugged him. At first, he didn't move. His body was stiff and she thought that he was going to resist, but then he hugged her back.

When they pulled apart, Noemi moved to Max's side. She

placed her hand in his, lacing her fingers with his. "Do you want to tell the rest?"

"You're doing fine."

Just the fact that he was standing there with her filled her with such happiness. All she needed was this right here—the people she loved. She needed to pinch herself to make sure this was all real, but she resisted the temptation.

"First, I should probably introduce Max by his proper name. I'd like you to meet Crown Prince Maximilian Steiner-Wolf. He is the heir to the throne of the European principality of Ostania."

Everyone's face filled with surprise. It felt so strange introducing him as a prince, as he was just Max to her. She really hoped his title and position wouldn't make a difference to her family.

Noemi drew in a deep breath and then slowly expelled it. "And he has asked me to marry him."

Maria said, "You'll be a princess."

"Wow," Anissa said in awe.

"Yes, she will," Max spoke up. "She will be the most beautiful and compassionate princess. And I couldn't be luckier. I promise you that I will do my best to make her happy."

Sebastian's gaze moved between her and Max. "So you're moving to Ostania?"

Noemi nodded.

Max spoke up again. "I'm afraid that my duties are increasing and after Christmas, I will need to spend the bulk of my time in Ostania. I'm sorry to take your sister away from you all, but you will always be welcome at our home."

"Don't you mean your palace?" Maria asked.

Max nodded. "Yes. And trust me when I say it has a lot of guest rooms."

"Guest rooms that I expect all of you to use regularly," Noemi said. "Wait until you see this place. It's so beautiful. And they have great skiing. But I wanted you all to know that we will be here for Christmas. It'll be a family Christmas just like Mama and Papa would have wanted."

It would take time, but slowly they were coming closer together—just as their parents always wanted.

EPILOGUE

Five months later
Ostania Palace

"IT'S A BOY."

Max exited his wife's birthing chamber to carry his new-born son to the library, where the king, queen and his brother waited. He couldn't stop smiling. He'd never been happier.

Everyone oohed and aahed over Prince Leonardo Sebastian, named after Noemi's brothers. And after the decreed paternity test had been done a month ago, his son was now third in line for the throne. And when his sibling was born, they would be fourth in line.

"He's absolutely perfect," the queen declared with a big smile. And, to Max's surprise, she began to speak in baby talk to his son. His mother really did surprise him at times.

His father was doing much better after his transplant surgery. In the end, Tobias had been a perfect match and had given their father one of his kidneys. Both had come through the surgeries with flying colors.

"How's Noemi?" the queen asked.

"She's exhausted and resting before baby number two arrives. She came through Seb's delivery like a real trouper."

"Your Majesty?" came a voice from the doorway.

Every head in the room turned.

"Yes?" the king said.

The nurse looked a bit flustered. "I need Prince Max."

She turned to Max. "The next baby is about to make its entrance into the world."

Max felt torn. His son was still in the queen's arms and she didn't look as though she planned to give him up any time soon.

"Go," the queen said. "I need a little time to get acquainted with my grandson." And then she turned back to the baby. "Your father acts like I've never been around a baby before."

Max didn't have time to argue with his mother. The baby should go back to the medical staff to be cared for before being passed around the room. Max turned to the nurse. "Will you take my son to the nursery?"

The older nurse smiled at him. "It would be my honor."

That's all Max needed to hear before he tore off down the hallway. He couldn't believe his blessing. Not that many years ago, he'd wondered if he'd live or die. And now he had the most loving wife and instead of being sterile, he'd fathered twins. It just proved that you never knew what was right around the next corner. You could never give up believing that there was something better—something amazing awaiting you if you just kept looking.

Max entered the chamber to find his wife groaning. He rushed to her side, taking her hand in his. He wished she didn't have to go through the pain. It didn't seem fair. But she didn't complain. She didn't yell at him like he'd read in some pregnancy blogs.

"You're doing amazingly," he whispered in her ear. "I love you." And then he kissed the top of her head.

In just a couple of minutes, the room filled with the loud cry of a baby.

The doctor held up the baby and smiled. "Your prince has a very healthy set of lungs."

"Yes, he does." Max smiled as his vision blurred with tears of joy. And then he turned back to his wife, who also had happy tears in her eyes. "You make beautiful babies."

"We make beautiful babies," she corrected.

"Yes, we do." He leaned down and kissed her lips.

Once again, Max cut the umbilical cord. The baby was cleaned up, wrapped in a blue blanket and handed over to his mother. Prince Alexandre, named after his grandfather, grew quiet as he gazed up at his parents.

Max's heart grew two times larger that day. He didn't know it was possible to love this much, but Noemi showed him each day that miracles really did come true.

* * * * *

THE MAVERICK'S CHRISTMAS TO REMEMBER

CHRISTY JEFFRIES

To Kate Gove Campbell,
one of my favorite people on earth and a member
of my Golden Girls. You are always the first to order
my books, the first to respond to my texts and
posts and the first to laugh at my dumb jokes. Even
from across the country, your support is always
constant. Not only do you give the best and tightest
hugs, you have taught me how to be a better friend
and you make the world a warmer and happier
place. You are the Rose to my Dorothy, and
I can't wait to share a lanai with you...

Chapter One

Caroline Ruth loved romance and happily-ever-after stories and all sorts of things that her academic-minded mother considered nonsense. That was how she knew with absolute conviction that this career as an assistant wedding planner in Rust Creek Falls, Montana, was tailor-made for her. And so did her boss, who was currently on her honeymoon and had left their newest client in Caroline's more-than-capable hands.

Josselyn Weaver sat across the desk from her, poring over bridal gown catalogs as they both waited for the groom to arrive to the couple's initial consultation. Picking a gown always seemed to hold the most excitement for the brides, but Caroline knew that booking a venue was the foundation of building a successful event.

After all, the guest list and decorations and theme usually depended on the location.

Caroline's stomach growled and she wished she had stopped for a breakfast croissant at Daisy's Donuts on her way to work this morning. But she'd been so eager to get to the office and prepare for this meeting that she'd barely allowed herself time for a couple of bites of a disgusting protein bar she'd found smashed in the bottom of her giant tote bag.

"So when we met a couple of months ago, you were pretty adamant that you wouldn't be getting married anytime soon," she finally said when Josselyn looked up from a glossy magazine spread. Not that she wanted to rush the bride, but Caroline had too much energy for long periods of silence, no matter how comfortable they were. Besides, the more she could learn about the couple she was working with the better. "I'm glad to see you changed your mind."

"I know. I remember you telling me that you'd be planning my wedding soon and I thought it was the craziest thing I'd ever heard." Josselyn's eyes were bright with humor, and Caroline smiled since she was well accustomed to people not really taking her instincts seriously. The bride continued, "I'd just moved to Rust Creek Falls to take the school librarian job and wasn't even looking for a date, let alone a relationship. I know people say that love finds you when you're not looking for it, but if someone had told me that I'd be engaged by Christmas, I never would have believed it."

Caroline gulped as a shiver made its way down her back.

Engaged by Christmas.

The words brought back the memory of Winona Cobbs's prediction that Caroline would be engaged before she turned twenty-four. That was a bit more than a month away, which meant that if the old psychic was correct, the right man would need to come along soon.

Shaking off the tingling vibration along her skin, Caroline glanced down at the wastebasket by her feet and wondered if she'd been a little too quick to throw out the half-eaten protein bar. She was suddenly feeling a bit light-headed and needed to keep this meeting moving along.

"So tell me about your fiancé," she suggested. She was almost as new to the small town as Josselyn was, and despite the fact that she'd already assisted with a few weddings out at Sunshine Farm, Caroline hadn't met the groom yet.

"Drew is an obstetrician at the Rust Creek Falls Clinic. His first wife died in a car accident several years ago, and since this is his second wedding, I want to make sure that I'm being respectful to her memory."

"Of course." Caroline nodded sympathetically. "And if I remember correctly, he also has an adorable son that introduced you two, right? I'm guessing you'd like him to be involved in the wedding somehow."

"That would be wonderful," Josselyn replied as her cell phone vibrated. She looked at her screen. "Drew just texted. Apparently, he ran into his brother at Daisy's, but the good news is that he's bringing donuts to apologize for running late."

"No problem." Caroline waved a hand in dismissal as

her stomach clenched in anticipation of a sugary treat. Josselyn picked up another bridal gown magazine, and Caroline decided to steer her toward the more important decisions. "Have you guys talked about the size of the wedding or whether you want it to be indoors or outdoors?"

"Well, he's originally from Thunder Canyon, so we were kind of thinking something in Kalispell might be a bit more accommodating for everyone traveling. I'm not really sure how many people we're inviting, but his family is huge. And I was hoping we could set the date within the next couple of months, so we would probably need an indoor venue since Montana winters can be pretty unpredictable."

"I know the perfect place!" Caroline jumped up so quickly she hit her knee on the corner of the desk drawer. "Hold on, I have more information on it in one of these binders."

Their current office building used to be an old train depot at Sawmill Station, and when her boss, Vivienne, converted it for her wedding planning business, her husband had built her a wall of bookshelves. Cole had promised to install a rolling ladder when they returned from their honeymoon, but until then, Caroline had to drag a piece of furniture over and climb up on it every time she needed to reach something on the top shelf.

To take her mind off the fact that she was balancing on an antique wooden chair in a pair of high heels, Caroline kept talking, hoping her enthusiasm disguised her nervous energy. "There's a historical brick building in Kalispell that is currently an art museum, but the back opens up into this huge open space. And get this. It used to be a Carnegie library before the city relocated the library to their current location. But the historical society rents it out for events and, well, if I wasn't so short I could reach the brochure and just show you."

"Can I help?" Josselyn asked, coming to stand nearby.

"Nope, I almost have it." It wasn't very ladylike—especially in an above-the-knee ruffled skirt—but Caroline put one foot onto a shelf to shimmy up just a little higher and stretched her arm as far as it would go until her fingers could grasp the bottom of the binder. As luck would have it, that was the exact moment when the front door opened.

"Drew…!" Josselyn said, her voice trailing off as she obviously walked away from the bookshelves and toward the entrance. Caroline would've stayed focused on what she was doing, but then the bride added, "I didn't know you were bringing Ben and Craig with you."

Caroline turned in surprise at the mention of unexpected people and brought her foot off the shelf a little too quickly. There were three men standing in the entryway. However, she only had eyes for the one carrying the pink bakery box. He was wearing a tan Stetson with a red plaid shirt, but that kind of standard cowboy attire was a dime a dozen around this town. What made her dizzy with excitement was the hook-shaped scar on the right side of his neck…just like the man Winona Cobbs had predicted.

Biting her lip, Caroline blinked in wonder at the new arrival. This was it. He was here. She just knew it.

Overwhelmed, underfed and perhaps a bit too eager, Caroline rocked the chair as she tried to climb down. Unfortunately, her high heel hooked onto one of the narrow armrests and she went down fast. The last thought to go through her mind was *Engaged by Christmas*.

Craig Clifton saw the woman fall as if it was happening in slow motion. Dropping the box of donuts, he sprinted toward her just as he heard the deafening *thunk* of her forehead bouncing off one of the wooden shelves. Still a couple of feet away, Craig dived at her in a last-ditch effort to brace her landing. But the odd angle and the impact of her deadweight knocked them both to the ground.

Luckily, he was able to pivot his torso at the last minute, and the back of the lady's head, as well as her shoulders, landed on his abdomen instead of the hardwood floor. Craig had absorbed most of the impact, but they were now sprawled out in the shape of a T and his childhood friend was yelling at them to stay still.

"Don't move her," Drew ordered as he knelt by Craig's hip. Catching his breath, which had been knocked out of him when they'd collided, Craig sucked in a gulp of air and saw the woman's long brown hair rise and fall with his chest.

"I can barely move myself," Craig replied, lifting a hand to the bump rising along the back of his scalp, not surprised to find his Stetson missing. His brothers referred to it as his "going to town hat" since he tended to wear it whenever he left the ranch. Craig wiggled his toes inside his boots and relaxed when he was confident that all his appendages were in working order.

"She's unconscious," Drew continued as he touched the lady's neck, probably checking for a pulse or a broken bone or whatever else it was that doctors checked for. Then Drew looked over to his brother, who was also a physician and currently crouched down with his hands on his knees, staring at the unresponsive woman instead of asking how his best friend's spine was. "Ben, I left my bag in my car back at Daisy's. Do you have yours in the truck?"

"I'm on my way," Ben replied.

"Should we call an ambulance for her?" Josselyn asked as she stood over all of them, concern etched on her forehead.

"It would probably take too long for one to drive here from Kalispell," Drew replied. "Her heartbeat and breathing seem to be stable and I'm not feeling anything broken. But judging by how hard she hit that shelf on the way down, I wouldn't be surprised if she has a concussion."

"That was my first thought," Ben said as he returned with his doctor bag. "We could take her to the clinic in town, but she's going to need a CT scan and would have to go to the hospital in Kalispell for that anyway. If we're going to drive her anywhere, it should be there."

"Wouldn't it be dangerous to move her?" Josselyn asked her fiancé, and Craig found himself thinking the same thing.

"Well, we can't leave her on top of Craig forever, as much as he might enjoy that." Ben smirked, then must've noticed the concern on his soon-to-be sister-in-law's face. "I promise she'll be fine."

Craig had grown up with the Stricklands and knew that if Ben could make jokes during a time like this, the situation couldn't be entirely dire. He forced his muscles to relax and wondered how he'd gotten roped into accompanying two of his best friends over here for a wedding planning appointment of all things.

One minute he'd been in line at Daisy's Donuts with Ben, discussing leasing fees for bulls, and the next, Drew was taking them both over to the new ranch at Sawmill Station to get a look at the latest herd of longhorns the Daltons were selling. Apparently, it just so happened that the wedding planner's office was located on the same property.

"I'm fine, by the way," Craig said, since nobody seemed to be concerned about his health after he'd taken a dive like that. He looked across the floor to where the pink bakery box had opened and spilled out its contents all over the wooden planks. "But since I'm stuck down here, can someone hand me a donut?"

"If you're healthy enough to complain, you're healthy enough to wait your turn." Drew's eyes flickered briefly over Craig before he slipped a Velcro cuff onto the arm of the unconscious woman, whose head was still propped up just below Craig's chest. "Besides, I've seen you take worse falls off a bucking horse back in the day. Now, hold still while I get her blood pressure."

"But he's not a young buck anymore," Ben said, wiggling his eyebrows with humor and making Craig feel every one of his thirty-five years. The hard floor underneath him and the odd angle of his body weren't helping the uncomfortable stiffness settling over him.

"I could still outride you," Craig challenged. "Unless you're getting in a lot of saddle time in between shifts at that fancy hospital of yours in Billings."

"Possibly," Ben said, passing him a glazed twist that had landed halfway on top of a piece of wax paper. "I haven't seen you move that fast since Brown Fury slammed you up against the pen in the midstate finals."

"That bull was one mean son of a—"

"Should I call someone?" Josselyn asked, interrupting Craig's reminiscing about his rodeo days. But it was either talk about something else to get his mind off the injured woman currently on top of him or lie here thinking about the last time he'd been powerless to help a different injured woman.

"She's stable," Drew responded. "But we should get her to the hospital in Kalispell to have some tests run."

Having grown up on his family's ranch in Thunder Canyon, Craig was no stranger to small towns and medical emergencies. The people there were used to taking care of their own. Not that this particular lady was his own. Hell, he didn't even know this woman resting so peacefully against him, the porcelain-white skin of her cheek relaxed against the red plaid checks in his shirt. But if the doctors said they could drive her from Rust Creek Falls into Kalispell, then that was what they would do.

As Drew and Ben gently lifted her off him, Craig left his uneaten donut on the floor and rose to his feet, tamping down his impulse to scoop the woman into his arms and carry her himself. After all, he was the one who'd saved her from a second blow to her head when he'd landed underneath her. That kind of bond made a man feel a certain responsibility. But Ben already had her off the ground, with Drew stabilizing her head as they walked toward the door. Which was probably for the best considering they were both trained in moving patients, whereas Craig was better trained to haul her around like a bale of hay.

"I'll grab her purse," Josselyn said as everyone seemed to spring into action.

Craig had barely enough time to scoop up his fallen hat and make it outside to open the back door of his crew cab truck. He quickly hopped up and slid across the seat to help gently maneuver the unconscious woman inside. He found himself with her head resting on him again, but at least this time it was on his lap as he sat upright on the bench seat. If he'd wanted to badly enough, he probably could've switched spots and let Drew sit back here with her. However, Craig had already taken on the rescue role inside the office and he didn't feel right about abandoning the poor lady now.

He had to shift his hips carefully in order to fish the truck keys out of his front pocket and pass them to Josselyn, who volunteered to drive so that Drew could be available to check the woman's vitals during the twenty-five-minute drive. Ben, realizing that there wasn't enough room in the truck, decided to drive Josselyn's car back to Sunshine Farm.

"Who should I notify?" Ben asked, and all eyes turned to Josselyn.

"Um, she works for Vivienne Shuster, but Viv and Cole Dalton are in Fiji on their honeymoon. Like me, she's new to Rust Creek Falls, so I'm not really sure who she'd want me to call locally. I think her parents are college professors or something but I don't know where they live."

It seemed so intimate to be talking about the personal details of a woman he'd never met. A woman whose brown hair fell in soft waves against the denim of his jeans. Craig cleared his throat. "What's her name?"

"Caroline Ruth," Josselyn said, then put the truck into gear.

Caroline.

Her body was slender and petite, but she had curves in all the right places. A rush of shame filled him as he realized he was blatantly staring at an unconscious lady. An unconscious and vulnerable lady with a body encased in delicate, clingy feminine fabric that would never suit life on a ranch. Not that Caroline looked like the type to spend much time working in the outdoors. He narrowed his gaze toward her high-heeled sandals and the bright pink polish on her toes. She never would've fallen off that chair if she'd been wearing sturdy boots and functional jeans. But she was a wedding planner, so what did she know about physical labor?

Josselyn took a bend in the two-lane highway a bit too sharply and Craig instinctively wrapped his hand around Caroline's waist to make sure she didn't accidentally tumble off the seat. The touch sent an electric vibration up his arm, making him feel like even more of a creep, so he yanked his hand away quickly, but didn't know where to put it. Lifting his elbow to the top of the backrest, Craig studied her face for signs of pain or discomfort. Fortunately, she appeared to be completely relaxed in her unconscious state, almost as though she were blissfully at peace.

Caroline Ruth was definitely an attractive woman, he'd give her that. Still. He was in no position to be noticing such things, and she was clearly in no position to be receiving his unwanted attention. Craig shifted guiltily in his seat and Caroline's eyes suddenly shot open.

"Hey there," Craig offered weakly. What else was he supposed to say to a complete stranger with her head in his lap? Caroline smiled dreamily at him before her lids fluttered closed and she was out cold again.

Chapter Two

Caroline heard steady beeping before feeling something squeeze around her upper arm. It took considerable effort to raise her eyelids, and when she finally got them to stay open, there were a few seconds of blurriness.

Where was she?

What had happened?

"She's awake," a woman said, and Caroline blinked several times until the light fixture in the middle of the white ceiling came into focus. She wiggled her toes as her hands flexed against something that felt like a starched sheet. Was she in a bed? She was definitely lying down.

"Caroline?" someone else asked and she turned toward the voice, her eyes narrowing on the person standing beside her. A woman with steel-gray curls and smooth skin the color of dark copper placed a calming hand on Caroline's shoulder. "Can you hear me?"

"Where am I?" Caroline asked.

"You're in the emergency room at Kalispell Regional. I'm Dr. Robinson. Do you remember what happened?"

Caroline shook her head and then flinched at the stabbing pain that shot through her forehead.

"Careful, now," the doctor continued. "From what I understand, you hit your head pretty hard. Your friends brought you in and we did an MRI while you were still unconscious. We think you have a concussion, but we'd like to get a CT scan of your brain to rule out anything more serious."

"My friends?" Caroline asked, then turned toward the other woman in the room. She sighed when she saw Josselyn Weaver on the other side of her bed.

"Hey, Caroline." Josselyn squeezed Caroline's hand, accidentally dislodging some little white wires and causing a shrill beep.

"Don't worry. It's just the oxygen reader," the doctor offered, putting the plastic device back over Caroline's pointer finger. "You up for answering some questions?"

"Sure," Caroline said as she tried to sit up. She was relieved that the rest of her body cooperated and that her head was the only thing hurting.

"Do you know your name?" Dr. Robinson asked.

"Caroline Ruth."

"And what day is it?"

She blinked a couple of times until it came back to her. "November 21."

"Good." The doctor's bright white smile was reassuring. "And what did you have for breakfast today?"

Caroline's stomach rumbled at the reminder. "Only a couple of bites of a protein bar. I should've gotten a breakfast sandwich at Daisy's this morning but I didn't want to be late for my appointment."

"Oh? What kind of appointment?"

"I'm a wedding planner."

The physician looked over to Josselyn, who nodded in agreement. The questions must be part of some kind of test and Caroline hoped she was passing.

Dr. Robinson lifted a finger in front of Caroline's nose. "Do you know where you live?"

Caroline's eyes followed the finger as she rattled off the address for the tiny guest house she'd rented in the heart of Rust Creek Falls several months ago. The sooner she answered everything and proved she was perfectly fine, the sooner she could get something to eat.

"What's the last thing you remember before coming to the hospital?"

"I was talking to Josselyn about her wedding and I climbed up on a chair to get the binder with a brochure for a venue when…" Caroline trailed off as she couldn't recall what had occurred after that. Lifting her fingers to stroke her forehead, she asked, "Is that how I fell?"

"Yes," Josselyn said, sighing as though she'd been holding her breath up until this point. "You went face-first into one of the shelves on your way down and were out cold. We didn't want to wait for an ambulance, so we brought you straight to the ER."

"We?" Caroline asked and looked around the room.

There was another man near the partitioned curtain of the exam room, but he'd been talking to a nurse outside and she'd assumed he was another doctor.

"That's—" Josselyn started, but Dr. Robinson cut her off.

"Do you know the name of this man?"

"No idea," Caroline replied, hoping her honesty wouldn't mean that she couldn't get a snack soon. When she'd been ten years old, her dad had to be rushed to the hospital near the faculty housing at Berkeley. He'd insisted that it was only heartburn and asked Caroline to go to the cafeteria and get him some vanilla soft serve to soothe the acid. Turned out it was a perforated gallbladder and because he'd eaten the ice cream, the anesthesiologist delayed the surgery until his stomach was empty. It had been a long ten hours of her dad doing his awful Oliver Twist impression by begging for more food and insisting he was starving.

"Technically, she hadn't met me prior to her fall." The man the doctor had just asked about stepped forward and placed an arm around Josselyn's waist. "I'm Drew Strickland, by the way. You're planning our wedding. We had just walked in the door and you'd turned to look at us. That's when you got your foot twisted in the chair and fell."

"We?" Caroline asked again, feeling like a parrot. Her eyelids were getting heavy again and all she wanted was a hot breakfast sandwich and a nap. "Who's we?"

"Me and—" Drew was cut off by Dr. Robinson holding up a hand like a stop sign.

"Do you remember them walking in the door before you fell?" the emergency room physician asked.

Caroline focused on a bright red electric outlet on the wall in an effort to concentrate, trying to form an image in her mind. But nothing was coming to her. She replayed the events of the morning over and over again, and the weight of the silence in the room suggested that everyone else knew what two plus two equaled and were desperately waiting for her to shout out, "Four!"

However, she was drawing a complete blank. In fact, she was positive that there wasn't anything else that happened after that. She was getting tired again, probably from concentrating so hard, and just wanted to fall asleep. Couldn't they simply tell her what had happened and let her take a nap?

"Sorry, I don't." Caroline shrugged, then yawned. "The last thing I remember was reaching for that binder on the top shelf."

It was then that a second man walked into the room and Caroline's breath caught as he took off his cowboy hat and ran a golden hand through his black, close-cropped hair.

Her entire body eased back onto the bed and she smiled in relief, everything finally making sense. "Oh, there you are."

"So you know him?" the doctor asked, jerking a thumb to the newcomer.

"Of course," Caroline said, then blinked slowly as the pillow cradled her head. "That's my fiancé."

Her fiancé?

Craig's head whipped around to the hallway behind him. But nobody else was there. He opened his mouth to tell the doctor that he'd never even met this woman, but nothing came out. The air had been sucked out of his lungs, and probably out of the entire room, judging by the equally confused expressions on everyone else's faces.

Caroline's head injury must be more serious than they'd originally thought if she was babbling incoherent randomness. Scratch that. Her statement had been clear and articulate, but it made absolutely no sense. Nor did the way she was looking at him, her doe-shaped brown eyes all dreamy and her wide lips parted in a hazy smile as though he was the only one in the room, or at least the only person who mattered. It was the same look Tina had given him before she'd died, and the comparison made his blood go cold.

Caroline looked nothing like his high school sweetheart, but Craig's memory had already been triggered, and that rush of helplessness filled his veins the same way it had all those years ago when they'd been trapped on the highway, waiting for the rescue workers to pry them out of the wreckage. He would've looked to Drew or Josselyn for an answer, but he couldn't tear his gaze away from Caroline.

Logically, he knew he wasn't reliving that awful night nearly fifteen years ago, but when Caroline's eyes finally drifted closed, Craig raced to her bedside and grabbed her hand as though he alone could will her back to consciousness.

"She'll be fine," the ER doctor told him with a gentle pat on the shoulder, a move likely designed to reassure loved ones. No doubt, it had worked for the doc countless times in the past. The only difference in this situation was that Craig didn't know the current patient, let alone love her.

"But I'm not—" Craig started and Dr. Robinson interrupted him.

"Let's step into the hallway where we can talk." The physician's reassuring pat turned into a firm nudge as she steered him toward the nurses' station.

Craig turned back toward his friends, who were slowly following them. Josselyn's mouth was slightly open and there were a few squiggly creases between her eyebrows while Drew simply stared in concern as though Craig had been the one to hit his head and get the sense knocked out of him.

Not that Craig could blame the guy. There might be plenty of reasons why Caroline accidentally called him her fiancé, but there was absolutely no explanation for his intense emotional reaction to someone who was a total stranger.

While it was already embarrassing that the others saw him respond like that, it would be even more confusing and downright mortifying to explain what prompted him to run to her side and clutch her hand as though she was dying.

Despite the couple approaching, Dr. Robinson faced Craig and directed most of the information his way. Something about a concussion and needing consent for a CT scan to rule out any long-term damage. "My recommendation is to run a few more tests and then have her stay overnight for observation. Does your fiancée have any other family members we should notify or can you authorize consent?"

"She's not my fiancée." The words finally tumbled out of Craig's mouth in a rush as he tugged on the collar of his work shirt. "In fact, I've never met her before."

"Well, she certainly lit up when you came in the room," Dr. Robinson replied, one hand on her hip as though she wasn't buying Craig's version of the situation. "I didn't even need to shine my light in her eyes when I was examining her because her pupils contracted and focused on you like you were the be-all and end-all."

"I promise I've never seen her before today. Right?" Craig shot a pleading look toward Drew for confirmation. "I have no idea why she would think we knew each other, let alone that we're engaged. Maybe I resemble her real fiancé and the concussion just has her brain rattled?"

"I'm pretty sure she's single." Josselyn finally spoke up and Craig felt the oxygen slowly return to his lungs. "We've only talked a handful of times, but she's never mentioned a significant other. Plus, she doesn't have an engagement ring."

At first Craig was filled with a sort of vindication from the proof that he wasn't her fiancé. However, that was soon replaced by utter bafflement. "Then why would she imagine herself being in a serious relationship at all?"

"Maybe she has amnesia?" Josselyn suggested.

"I suppose that's possible." Drew turned down one corner of his mouth, his expression suggesting that it wasn't possible at all. "However, she had full recollection of all the events leading up to her fall."

"It could be confabulation." Dr. Robinson now spoke to Drew, her voice lowered as she threw out phrases such as *memory production* and *cognitive distortion* and something else Craig couldn't quite make out.

"Hmm." Drew nodded. "I've read case studies, but have never seen it manifested in a patient."

Craig rolled his eyes. "Do you think you guys could use some layman terms for us nondoctors?"

"Confabulation is similar to amnesia in that it's a memory disturbance. It can happen when there is some type of damage to the brain. Caroline seems to remember almost everything leading up to her injury, but to fill in the gaps on what she doesn't know, her mind has invented a story to explain it."

Oh, boy. He should've stayed in Thunder Canyon this week. Pinching the bridge of his nose, Craig asked, "But why would she need to make up a lie about being engaged?"

"It's not a lie." Dr. Robinson shook her head. "To her, it's very real."

"Okay, so then we just tell her that she doesn't know me and that she doesn't have a fiancé and she's good to go." He slapped his palms together as though it were that simple. And it would've been if Craig had been speaking to the vet out on the ranch. Cows and horses never had issues like this.

Dr. Robinson shared another look with Drew before answering. "In theory, we would always recommend telling a patient the truth. But in this case, she hit her forehead, where the frontal lobe is encased, and that makes it hard for her to retrieve and evaluate memories. So in instances of confabulation, it doesn't matter what you say. Her brain is in a fragile state right now and will only be able to understand what her frontal lobe is telling her."

"How long does this last?" Craig folded his arms across his chest and looked longingly toward the ER exit doors. "I mean, do I actually have to pretend to be her fiancé?"

"I'm sure Dr. Robinson doesn't want you to pretend to be anything," Drew offered, looking at his watch.

"No, of course not. I'm simply recommending that we don't upset the patient until all the tests come back and we know more about what's going on."

"So when will that happen?"

"As soon as her fiancé gives us consent?"

"But I'm not—"

Dr. Robinson held up her palm. "I was kidding. When she wakes up again, we can get her verbal consent. But is there anybody else we should notify in the meantime? Anyone else who can give us a better medical history?"

All eyes turned toward Josselyn again. "I looked through her purse, but I couldn't find her cell phone. I heard back from Vivienne earlier, and she confirmed that Caroline's parents are out of the country right now on some sort of teaching sabbatical and she doesn't remember her mentioning any friends or family nearby. I would hate to leave her here all alone. What if she wakes up and is confused again?"

"Obviously, we can't leave her here alone," Craig said.

Drew looked at his watch a second time. "I have to get back to Rust Creek Falls before my son gets out of school."

"I'd stay, but I have to speak at the city council meeting this evening to ask for extra funding for the elementary school library. If I miss it, I'll have to wait another month to get my proposal approved."

"Maybe I'll call Ben and ask…" Drew started.

"No way," Craig said, shaking his head before his friend could even finish the thought. "I can stick around."

Chapter Three

The words had flown out of Craig's mouth before they'd had a chance to logically form in his brain. Not because his skin itched with jealousy at the mention of another man staying with Caroline when she was this vulnerable, but because Craig hadn't been able to shake this sense of responsibility for her since he'd seen her slipping off that chair. If he tried to explain this impulse, it wouldn't make sense to his friends. Hell, it didn't even make sense to him.

"I mean, if I'm her… I…uh…mean…if Caroline thinks I'm her fiancé, then obviously she'll be expecting me to be here when she wakes up. I wouldn't want to make things worse. And it's not like it's a big deal," Craig added, more for his own benefit than to convince his friends. "I'm not really doing anything else today."

It was true. The late fall season was the slowest time on his family's ranch because they'd already sent their latest herds to market and didn't plan to start breeding the new calves until after the new year. He was in Rust Creek Falls to visit two of his brothers and to check in with some of the other local ranchers for what his dad referred to as "old-fashioned market research."

Josselyn frowned. "I'm not sure if it would be in Caroline's best interest to let her continue thinking that you two are really engaged. After all, she'll get her memory back eventually, won't she?"

Dr. Robinson lifted her shoulders in a shrug. "Like I said, we'll know more after her tests. I'd feel better holding off on any treatment plan or official diagnosis just yet, but if it *is* confabulation strictly caused by a brain injury and not caused by a mental health issue or dementia, then this memory setback likely won't last too long. With all that being said, while I wouldn't advocate lying to a patient, I don't necessarily see any harm in letting them believe in whatever is going to give them a sense of peace for the time being. Our biggest goal right now is to keep Caroline as calm and relaxed as possible."

Drew looked at his watch again. "Are you sure you want to stay, Craig?"

"I don't *want* to," Craig clarified, more for himself than for anyone else listening. "But if it's the easiest solution and it will keep Caroline calm so that she can heal, then I'll do it."

There, that sounded plausible enough, even to his own ears. After several more rounds of "Are you sure?"

followed by Craig's growing insistence, he eventually found himself sitting on the miserable plastic chair beside her bed in the exam room, drinking cold coffee and scrolling on his smartphone for the latest feed and grain reports. It wasn't the same as getting out to the other ranches and talking directly to his fellow cattlemen, but he couldn't just blow off all his work duties to sit around playing nurse.

Normally, he rarely used the device except for making calls and often told his brothers that any cattleman worth his salt didn't rely on fancy gadgets that could easily get busted working on the ranch. If Craig was in the field and needed information off the internet, he usually just asked his brother Rob or waited until he could use the computer at the house. However, now that their father had been bitten with the technology bug and insisted on sending group texts with links to online articles, Craig found himself a reluctant user.

"Do you think I could have one of your Life Savers?" Caroline's soft voice was so unexpected that Craig dropped his phone, its reinforced hard-shell case preventing the screen from cracking on the tile floor.

"Huh?" Craig asked, then wanted to kick himself for sounding like such a dope.

"One of your Life Savers." Caroline pointed to the front pocket of his shirt, where he always stashed a roll of his favorite cherry-flavored candy.

His chin dropped toward the empty pocket. Okay, now that was weird. He'd had less than half a roll when he'd left his brother's house this morning and then had nervously plowed through the rest of them by the time

Caroline had undergone her MRI. Since she'd never been conscious during any of the times he'd popped one into his mouth, there was no way for her to be aware of his little sugar habit.

"How do you know about my Life Savers?" he asked, trying his best not to completely disregard the doctor's instructions about keeping Caroline calm.

"You always have them," she replied, her smile all dreamy again and his insides responding the same way they had the last time she'd woken up and grinned at him. "Plus, you smell like cherries."

Craig let out the breath he'd been holding, mildly relieved with the second part of her explanation. "Do you know who I am?"

Caroline's smooth forehead pinched into several lines as she studied him. Thinking that maybe she'd lost a pair of glasses in the fall and couldn't see his face clearly, Craig leaned closer as intense concentration took over her expression. She opened her pouty bow-shaped lips several times before defeat filled her eyes. "I don't know why I can't think of your name."

"It's Craig," he replied, wanting to pump his fist in celebration. Not that he should be basking in her confusion, but if she didn't know his name, then she'd finally realized that he was actually a complete stranger. That meant that her amnesia spell or confabulation—or whatever it was—had finally passed and she no longer needed him to take care of her. He extended his hand as he introduced himself. "I'm Craig Clifton."

Caroline inhaled deeply through her nose as she nodded. But instead of taking his proffered handshake, she laced her fingers through his. "Of course you are. I must've hit my head pretty hard to forget my own fiancé's name."

Poor Craig looked about as confused as Caroline felt. It must be difficult for him to see the woman he loved like this. But then again, at least he wasn't the one who'd completely forgotten most of the specifics about the person he was supposed to be marrying. Hopefully, it wasn't a bad omen for their relationship if she could perfectly recall every other detail of her life except for the one that was arguably the most important.

She squeezed her eyes closed as though it might help paint a more accurate picture of the man in her mind. Caroline remembered the hook-shaped scar on his neck, she remembered he liked cherry-flavored candy and… And that was where all the details stopped.

"Are you in pain?" Craig asked. "Should I call for a nurse?"

"Oh, no." Caroline's lids popped open. "I was just trying really hard to recall something more concrete about us, like how long we've been together or where we first met or where you live and work. But I'm drawing a complete blank, and to be honest, it's making me a little nervous."

"Don't be nervous," he said quickly, then rolled his lips inward, causing him look like a child who was trying to bite back a secret. The expression didn't exactly alleviate her fears. Her growing anxiety must have been obvious because he added, "The doctor said that when you hit your head, it might have caused a few problems with your memory."

Panic clawed at her throat, and she could feel the cold, dry air hitting her eyes as they grew wider than normal. "Like amnesia?"

"Not exactly." Craig rubbed the scarred area of his neck. "The doctor called it something else, but it's similar. She can probably explain it to you way better than I can."

Craig stood up, and his cowboy boots clicked against the floor as he strode over to the open curtain and waved down a hospital employee in surgical scrubs. Caroline couldn't hear what he was saying, but his thumb gestured her way and her gaze traveled from his hand down his tan, muscular forearms to where his red plaid work shirt was rolled to the elbows. Because of the way he was standing, Caroline could only study him from a side angle, but as she took in his well-rounded shoulders and flat abs and long, strong legs encased in faded denim, she couldn't help but wonder how in the world she could possibly have forgotten a perfect form like his.

When he pivoted to walk back toward Caroline, her tummy dropped and she got light-headed again. The view from the front was just as good as the one from the side. Heat flooded her cheeks and she asked, "Do you think I could possibly have a drink of water?"

"I asked the doctor about you being able to eat or drink when you woke up and she said only a sip of water until after your CT scan. She doesn't anticipate you needing any sort of surgery, but they haven't ruled it out yet."

The mention of surgery should've had her concerned. Instead, a sense of relief blossomed inside her chest. It was reassuring that her fiancé knew her well enough to understand that she'd be worried about eating and drinking and obviously had taken steps to provide answers for her. Maybe she'd even told him the story about her dad's gallbladder surgery and the soft-serve ice cream. It was crazy to think that this man beside her was probably privy to all of her secrets and all of her needs. Now if only she could recall some of *his* preferences—besides candy, obviously—then they'd be on equal footing.

Craig picked up a water bottle from the bedside tray table and unscrewed the plastic cap before gently holding it to her lips. "Not too much, now."

As she drank, she made the mistake of lifting her eyes to his face and was hit with such an intense attraction that she swallowed way too quickly and began coughing. Craig used the back of his hand to wipe the water that had dribbled down her chin. It was such an intimate gesture, not necessarily in a sexual way but in the way someone would take care of a loved one.

Something warm spread through Caroline's body. She was loved. By this man. While the feeling wasn't entirely familiar to her, it was certainly exciting. And very welcome. After all, Caroline had known that she wanted to be a wife and a mother since kindergarten, when she and five-year-old Scott Sullivan had staged a mock wedding during recess. Unfortunately, they'd barely gotten through the first-grade minister's line of "You may kiss the bride," before the teacher had put a stop to things and called Caroline's and Scott's parents to inform them that students needed to keep their hands—and their lips—to themselves at school. When her mother asked why she'd wanted to marry Scott Sullivan, Caroline had told her that he was the only boy who wasn't playing handball that day. After that, Rita Rodriguez, department chair for Women and Gender Studies at Wellesley College, had made her daughter promise that she would never settle for a man.

And Caroline never did again. In fact, she hadn't so much as had a boyfriend because every guy she'd ever gone out with hadn't felt like "the one."

So, while she couldn't remember a thing about the handsomely rugged cowboy before her, Caroline had every confidence that she belonged with him. Unlike her recess-length courtship with the first available kindergartner, there was a powerful emotional connection between Caroline and Craig. Because of her absent memory, she didn't understand it right that second but she felt it deep in her core. In twenty-three years, her instincts had never led her astray, and even her normally evidence-based mother had to admit that when Caroline felt something, she really felt it. In fact, after her college graduation, Caroline's father had given her a framed quote by Charles Dickens that read "A loving heart is the truest wisdom."

Her mother hated that quote.

Luckily, her parents were currently in India, her mom conducting research on the history and success of matriarchal tribes as her father compiled literary works by the lesser-known authors of the British colonies. Which meant they were too far away to question her every decision.

"How's everyone feeling in here?" Dr. Robinson asked, sliding back the partition.

Craig immediately stood up, because, of course, he would. As if Caroline would ever pick a guy who wasn't a complete gentleman at all times. However, his current white-knuckle grip on the bedside rail suggested his good manners were also helping to mask his discomfort and the nervous way his eyes were looking everywhere but at her.

"I'm still a little fuzzy on some things," Caroline replied before reaching out the hand not connected to the oxygen wires and placing it over Craig's. His fingers were warm, his skin slightly rough and very bronzed—probably from working outside or wherever it was that he worked. Caroline would worry about remembering those kinds of details later. She didn't want to make her fiancé feel awkward or unimportant. That was why her smile wasn't forced when she added, "But I'm content and comfortable for now."

Dr. Robinson nodded before looking away, lines scrunching across her otherwise smooth brow. Caroline followed the woman's gaze in time to see Craig give a brief shake of his head.

They were obviously referring to the fact that she hadn't fully regained her memory and Caroline wanted to kick her feet in frustration like a petulant child. But her legs were tucked in under a weight of blankets, reminding her of the utter lack of power she had over both her mind and body. "So when can I go home?"

"Well, the radiology tech is on his way now. After the CT scan, we'd like you to stay the night so we can keep an eye on your concussion. As long as all the tests come back negative, I don't see any reason why you couldn't go home tomorrow."

Caroline didn't even realize she was now clutching Craig's hand until his fingers slid through hers and squeezed with reassurance. "I've never stayed the night in a hospital before."

"Nothing to worry about." Dr. Robinson tsk-tsked, reminding Caroline of her Nan, who made that sound anytime she thought her granddaughter was too skinny and not eating enough. The physician nodded toward Craig. "And your man here said he plans to stay the night with you. So between him and all our nurses, you'll never be alone."

"You're going to stay?" Caroline smiled at Craig and his eyes seemed to turn a darker shade of blue.

He cleared his throat and focused on the blood pressure machine beeping behind her. "Um, if that would make you feel more comfortable. Sure."

If she had the full use of her faculties, Caroline would probably be able to better guess at what the man was thinking. However, she had absolutely no clue what her fiancé's normal response would be in a situation like this. Did he really want to stay? Or was he just being polite? Judging by the forced expression on his face, Caroline would assume the latter. But before she could let him off the hook, the tech showed up to take her for the CT scan.

As the hospital employee maneuvered her hospital

bed through the corridors, Craig walked beside Caroline, her bright pink tote bag looped over one of his broad shoulders. She recognized the purse as the one she'd picked out this morning to go with her new heels and had to swallow a giggle at how much it clashed with his red plaid shirt.

But when it got caught in the elevator door behind him, Caroline could no longer hold in her laughter. "Do you always carry my purse for me?"

He gave a slight grunt, then hefted it higher onto his shoulder. "It was either this or leave it behind in the exam room where anyone could walk by and steal it."

After the radiology tech helped her transfer off the bed and onto the cold platform for her scan, he asked her a series of questions, like whether she was wearing any jewelry or had any metal implants anywhere in her body. Then the tech asked the one question that really threw her. "Any possibility that you're pregnant?"

Caroline's lungs seized and her mouth froze into a circle, unsure of what the answer was. Surely she would remember something like that, wouldn't she? She was only twenty-three years old and had been waiting to have sex until she'd found "the one," which she'd obviously found. She turned pleading eyes to Craig, hating that she couldn't even recall if they'd had intercourse before, let alone whether they'd used any form of birth control. "Have we… I mean is there…?"

She couldn't finish the embarrassing question with the radiology guy looking on, his clipboard not even raised high enough to cover his curious smirk.

A rosy shade of pink stole along Craig's hardened

jawline and his eyes went wide, probably as he realized that he was the only person in the room who could possibly answer such an intimate thing.

"Uh…" His mouth opened and closed several times before he finally cleared his throat. "I think they did a blood test in the ER before the MRI. Maybe it says in her chart or something?"

"Let me take a look," the tech said before flipping a few pages. Caroline wanted to yell at the man for not bothering to check her file first. But she was too busy forcing her muscles to relax against the narrow sheet-covered table underneath her. "Nope, no baby on board. We're good to go."

Caroline almost sighed out loud as the air finally left her chest in a whoosh. Not because she didn't want to have a baby—she most definitely wanted to be a mother someday. She just wanted to fully remember the man who could possibly be the father of her child. Unfortunately, the more she tried to drag the information from her brain, the more her head pounded.

The tech raised and lowered the table and gave her some final instructions about remaining still. At some point, the room went darker, but Caroline's breathing remained ragged and her thoughts kept spinning.

While knowing that she wasn't pregnant gave her one less thing to worry about in the overall scheme of things, it didn't stop her from craving more details about the man she was planning to marry. And what their current physical relationship was like.

Watching Craig's retreating form as he exited the

room, she came to the pulse-elevating realization that just because she couldn't remember having sex with him didn't mean she couldn't vividly imagine it.

Chapter Four

Man, Craig had dodged a serious bullet back there in the radiology room when Caroline looked at him with those doe-shaped brown eyes and wanted to know if they'd ever had sex. How in the hell was he supposed to know the answer to that? Okay, so obviously he knew the actual answer, but he'd been clueless on how to phrase it out loud.

She'd fallen asleep again during the procedure, but Dr. Robinson assured him that it was pretty normal for a concussed patient to doze off occasionally and that resting could actually help her brain heal. As long as Caroline's pupils weren't dilated and she could hold a conversation when she was awake, she was supposedly fine.

By the time they finally got her admitted and assigned to a room, it was getting close to dinnertime and Craig was starving. When she'd confessed that she'd never stayed overnight in a hospital, she'd looked so scared, so frail.

The main goal was to keep her from getting stressed or putting any more strain on her traumatized brain. However, in order to keep his wits about him and do that, he also needed to eat something. Although, what kind of fake fiancé would he be if he sneaked off while she was sleeping to go down to the cafeteria to get some dinner?

Looking around for a pad of paper so he could leave a note, his eyes landed on her ridiculously huge purse sitting in the corner of the room. He had saddlebags smaller than that thing and never understood why some women insisted on hauling everything they owned all around town with them. If he were a betting man, he'd place odds that she had plenty of paper and at least several pens in the thing. The problem was, there was no way to look inside without feeling like he was invading her privacy.

Rubbing a hand through his close-cropped hair, he asked himself for the thousandth time today, "How in the hell did you get yourself into this situation?"

"What was that?" Caroline's sleepy voice was deep and husky, a stark contrast to her delicate and feminine looks. It was also as arousing as anything he'd ever heard before.

"I was just wondering where I could find a pen and paper."

Her sigh came from the back of her throat. "I always carry some in my purse."

"Yeah, I assumed as much but it didn't seem right snooping through your things when you're sound asleep."

"It wouldn't be considered snooping since I don't have any secrets from you." Clearly, her mind was way too fragile to grasp the magnitude of just how many secrets they actually had since they didn't know the first thing about each other. When he didn't respond, she continued, "Are you always this proper around me?"

"I...uh...I guess I'm just a proper type of guy." Or a guy who was simply way out of his element.

She studied him in the dim glow of the room, the sun fading outside the window. He rocked back on his boot heels and looked over his shoulder at the door. They should probably keep that open so nobody got the wrong idea about what was going on in this private room. And since when did hospitals have private rooms?

When Craig had surgery after his second clavicle fracture, he'd been stuck in traction next to an old man who used to confuse the emergency call button for the television remote. The volume on the evening news would go up every time the man didn't get his bedpan in time. If Caroline had a roommate like that, Craig wouldn't have to worry about that electric current charging through his body every time she turned those pretty eyes his way.

"Why did you need paper and a pen?" Caroline asked, and Craig turned back to her.

"Oh. I thought about grabbing a bite to eat downstairs and wanted to leave you a note in case you woke up and I wasn't here."

"So, you're both proper *and* thoughtful." Her full lips turned up at the corners, but her questioning gaze remained steadily fixed on him, as though she were awaiting more discoveries about him. "I'm starving."

"The doctor cleared you to eat after she got the radiology report and there was nothing to indicate you needed immediate surgery. They delivered a tray for you earlier," he said, wheeling the small table over to her bed. "I think it's meat loaf."

She lifted a plastic cover off the plate and crinkled her pert little nose at the cold gray lump underneath. "I'm missing part of my memory, not my taste buds. Since you're going to the cafeteria, would you mind bringing me something from there instead?"

"Sure." He replaced the lid and moved the offending plate out of the way. "What do you want?"

"Anything. Surprise me."

Crap. He'd walked right into that trap. Craig eyed her small frame and couldn't even begin to guess what kind of food she ate. Obviously, it wasn't his preferred meal of steak and potatoes because she looked like a strong wind would blow her away before the next winter storm. For all he knew, she was one of those women who constantly monitored every calorie in order to keep her waist so tiny.

"Maybe a salad?" he suggested because he got the impression that she didn't maintain her lithe shape by being a hearty eater.

"Ugh, no." Caroline stuck out her tongue and made

a gagging sound. "I hate vegetables. Except for french fries."

"I don't think french fries count as a vegetable."

"They're from potatoes, right?" Caroline's voice held a trace of laughter.

"Fine. I'll get you some french fries. How about a double bacon cheeseburger to go with that?" he offered, trying to match her playful tone but sounding more facetious.

"Mmm. That sounds perfect," she replied, and he did a double take at her flat stomach under the hospital gown. Where was she going to put all that food? "Oh, and if they have onion rings, I'll take a side of those, too. See, there's another vegetable I eat."

Apparently, her food preferences aligned more with a growing teenage boy than a consummate dieter. "Something to drink?"

"Strawberry milkshake, if they have it. If not, I'll just take a large orange soda. Oh, and a tapioca pudding. When I was ten, my dad had gallbladder surgery and I remember his hospital had the absolute best tapioca pudding in the world."

He tilted his head and wondered how she could remember a thing like the tapioca pudding she'd eaten when she was a kid, but not be able to remember that she'd never laid eyes on him before today.

When he didn't respond right away, her face turned a charming shade of pink and she pointed toward her purse. "Um, I have money in my wallet. I know it's kind of a big order and I'm not sure how we usually split costs—"

"I'm not taking your money," he interrupted loudly before she insulted him by implying that he'd let the woman he was marrying reimburse him for a meal. Not that he was actually marrying her. He ran a hand through his hair and lowered his voice. "I was just trying to figure out how to carry it all back to the room. Never mind. Don't worry about it. I'll hijack one of these tray tables or a wheelchair or something to push it on."

"Okay, then," she replied, not seeming to pick up on his sarcasm, or at least choosing to ignore it. "Can you hand me my cell phone before you leave? I should probably let my parents know what happened."

"Josselyn said she looked for your phone back at the office but only saw your purse."

"I don't suppose you have my parents' numbers in your contact list." She gnawed her lower lip, but Craig was saved from responding—as well as from staring at her sexy mouth—when she added, "Actually, they're probably out of cell range if my mom is still with the Khasi tribe. I'll just send them an email tomorrow."

"The Khasi tribe?"

"Yes. I'm sure she told you all about her latest research trip. Wait. You've met my parents, haven't you?"

"Uh, not in person. At least, not yet." There, that should be ambiguous enough. After all, Josselyn mentioned her folks were out of the country so it was plausible that he might've talked to them on the phone or via a video chat. Not that Craig knew the first thing about video chatting.

Caroline tilted her head at him. "What about you?"

"What about me?"

"I'm sure you probably need to call someone to let them know you're staying here overnight?"

He lifted a brow. "Like who?"

She shrugged, a deep V forming above her nose. "Do you live with anyone? Like roommates or your family or, um…me?"

His ribs squeezed with pity. It was bad enough that she couldn't remember the fact that they hadn't had sex. The poor thing really must be confused if she couldn't even recall whether they lived together.

It was on the tip of Craig's tongue to tell her that if they were sharing the same bed, he would've left a more lasting impression on her. Instead, he replied, "I live at my family's ranch in Thunder Canyon."

"Oh, good." She relaxed onto her pillows. "I was worried about who would take care of your cat while you're gone."

Craig took a couple steps forward and lowered his chin. "My cat?"

"Yeah, the one with only three legs!" Caroline exclaimed, her face brightening as though she'd just had a miraculous breakthrough in modern science. "I can't think of his name, but I'm sure it will come to me."

Disbelief and a slow-growing sense of alarm kept him from celebrating her achievement. How in the hell did this woman know about his pet? Not that it was completely inconceivable given the fact that most ranches had barns filled with various animals, but the three-legged part confounded him.

"Do you work there, too?" Caroline asked, seemingly

ignoring the fact that Craig was staring at her with his mouth hanging open in shock.

"Where?" Craig gave his head a slight shake to clear his thoughts.

"At your family's ranch," she said slowly, as though it was *his* brain that had been concussed recently.

"Uh, yeah. We raise cattle."

Caroline got that satisfied, faraway look in her eyes again. Every time she made that face, Craig's collar seemed to shrink around his neck and his skin got all tight. Her next question made his toes twitch inside his boots. "So I really am going to marry a cowboy?"

Craig didn't know about that. She certainly wasn't going to marry *this* particular cowboy. No woman was. But he kept his jaw clenched as his feet fought the urge to run right past the sign for the cafeteria and straight toward the exit.

After several more tests, including an EEG before bed, Caroline was surprised by how soundly she slept through the night. Of course, anytime a nurse came to check on her or take her vital signs, all Caroline had to do was look over to where Craig was partially reclined in a too-small chair, his cowboy hat pulled low over his eyes. Then a bubble of security would surround her, making her happily drift back to sleep.

She felt rested when her first visitor arrived.

"Is our patient allowed to have chocolate croissants this morning?" Josselyn asked as she carried in a cardboard tray of coffee drinks in one hand and a white bag in the other.

"She most definitely is," Caroline said, sitting up straighter and resisting the urge to clap excitedly by adjusting the blanket across her lap.

Craig just grunted, before standing up to stretch. Judging by the frown on his face, he either wasn't a morning person or he didn't particularly care for flaky breakfast treats. Caroline hoped it was just the croissants because she couldn't imagine a cowboy not being an early riser. Actually, she couldn't imagine someone not liking fresh-baked pastries, either.

A cracking sound echoed through the room as he twisted at the waist. "I'm getting too old not to sleep in a bed anymore."

Caroline took a quick gulp of coffee to keep from asking the question on the tip of her tongue. How old was he? It was another thing she should know about her fiancé, but couldn't remember. He certainly didn't look old, but there were a few more creases around his eyes than most men her age might have.

"Thanks for bringing breakfast," Caroline said to Josselyn.

"I also brought you a pair of comfy pajamas and some toiletries, not knowing how long you'd be here." Josselyn patted the small tote bag resting against her hip. "Since I didn't have a key to your apartment, you'll have to make do with things from the superstore in Kalispell."

"Anything is better than this hospital gown," Caroline replied, suddenly curious about where her own clothes were. The ones she'd been wearing right before she'd hit her head. She was about to ask, but Dr. Robinson entered the room.

As the physician examined her, Caroline saw Craig slip into the hallway and pull out his cell phone. It was difficult following the doctor's penlight with her eyes when her gaze kept returning to Craig and the way his jeans cupped his rear end as he casually leaned against the nurses' station and spoke into his phone.

"So all the tests suggest that there isn't any long-term damage," Dr. Robinson said just as Craig returned to the room. "Any changes with your memory?"

As much as Caroline sensed the connection with Craig, there was also an underlying nagging sensation in the pit of her stomach every time she smiled at him and he looked away. Had they had a fight recently? Or maybe it was just the fact that she couldn't remember any clear details about the guy and she was projecting her own sense of guilt onto him.

"I feel like things are slowly starting to come back to me." Caroline was trying to remain positive but it was impossible not to notice the way Craig, Josselyn and the physician all looked at each other.

Dr. Robinson finally nodded. "Good. Everything should resolve itself eventually as long as you give your brain time to heal and don't add any additional stress."

The older woman gave a pointed look toward Craig, who scrubbed at the lower half of his face, where dark stubble had blossomed overnight.

"So then I can go home this morning?" Caroline couldn't keep the hopefulness from her voice.

"As long as you're not left alone. With the concussion, I want to be sure someone is keeping an eye on you."

"I have to be at the school library during the day." Josselyn spoke up. "But you can come stay with me out at Sunshine Farm until you're feeling more like your old self."

"I *do* feel like my old self," Caroline insisted, hating the sympathetic looks directed her way. "The only thing that's off is my memory about Craig, which means I should probably stay with him to help jog my brain."

Josselyn sucked in her cheeks before looking at Craig, whose eyes had gone dark again. However, the man kept his lips pressed firmly together. In fact, nobody said anything and it made Caroline wonder what was really going on. What weren't they all telling her?

Finally, Josselyn spoke up. "Craig, you're staying at your brother's ranch while you're in town, right?"

"Right," Craig agreed a little too quickly for someone who'd just been so hesitant to say a word. "I'm bunking with Will and his wife, Jordyn."

"That might be a little cramped, huh?" Josselyn nodded the answer at them as though she were talking to her kindergarten reading circle. "But there's plenty of room out at Sunshine Farm."

"There's also plenty of room at my own house," Caroline said as her gaze narrowed at them in suspicion. "Unless you guys aren't telling me why my fiancé shouldn't be staying with me there…"

Like perhaps Craig was planning to call off the engagement. Caroline's throat constricted.

Josselyn looked up to the ceiling, then said, "Well, here's the thing—"

"It's okay, Josselyn," Craig interrupted. "Of course I don't mind taking care of Caroline."

Chapter Five

Craig felt the heat of Josselyn's eyes on his back as they followed the discharge nurse who was pushing Caroline's wheelchair toward the parking lot. He knew his friend's wife-to-be was staring at him like he was nuts, but all he could do was shrug.

"What about your own ranch, Craig?" A muscle ticked in Josselyn's jaw as she kept her voice too low for Caroline to hear. "Shouldn't you be getting back to Thunder Canyon soon?"

"We just sold the bulk of our herd in Helena and breeding season won't start until after Christmas." Craig fished in his pocket for his truck keys. "My dad and Rob can handle things during the slow season. Besides, the doctor said this was only temporary. I'll be back home before next week."

"You know that you can't stay with Caroline at her place, right? She lives in the center of town and Rust Creek Falls is a small place. People will talk."

"I'll mention that to her when we get in the truck and head in that direction. I'm sure I can convince her during the drive that staying at my brother and sister-in-law's house is for the best."

Unfortunately, when they got to Will and Jordyn's ranch house, Craig realized his sweet and agreeable fiancée wasn't as easy to convince. And if he kept insisting, she was likely to counter his argument and then they'd both be stressed out.

Caroline stood in the middle of the small living room, one arm wrapped across her waist as she stared in confusion at her surroundings. "None of this looks familiar. Have I been here before?"

"Um, I don't think so." Craig regretted not putting a little more confidence into his voice. He'd won the Professional Bull Riders World Championship two years in a row. When had he ever lacked confidence?

"Have I even met Will and Jordyn?" Caroline asked.

"I'm sure you have. Rust Creek Falls is a small town and chances are you've run into them before."

"You mean, you've never introduced us?" Caroline moved her hands to her hips and Craig suddenly wondered how he ever could've thought this petite woman was delicate or fragile. "Have you been keeping our engagement a secret from your family?"

When she turned her full glare at him, she looked eight inches taller than the five-foot-four height listed on her hospital admission paperwork. And a heck of a lot more intimidating than any bull he'd drawn during his time on the rodeo circuit. Craig knew this whole idea was crazy, and right now, he'd gladly welcome Josselyn's presence and her pointed looks of disbelief because that would at least take some of the attention off him. Or she'd at least help dig him out of this mess.

"It's not a secret. It just hasn't been that long since we became engaged." He flicked his eyes toward the clock on the wall. About twenty-four hours to be exact. Instead of keeping things closer to the truth, though, Craig added, "We were just waiting until the next family dinner to make our big announcement."

"And when exactly is the next family dinner?" One of Caroline's eyebrows shot up.

"Thanksgiving," he answered, then gave a silent prayer that Caroline would regain her memory by then.

Her lips parted as she blew out a puff of air, making her entire face soften. A shot of electricity zipped along his nerve endings. She really was a beautiful woman.

"Fine." She exhaled again. "I guess I can wait until next week to meet them all."

Wait. Next week? Damn, he hadn't realized how close the holiday was. That didn't give him much time to prove to Caroline that they really weren't engaged. Or for Caroline to regain her memory and figure it out for herself. For now, all Craig could do was offer a stiff smile and pray that he could untie himself from this lasso of deception that was twisting around him.

"Sorry for getting so snappy like that." She lowered her arms and clasped her hands behind her back and he tried not to notice the way her dainty sweater looked much snugger on her when her proud shoulders were thrown back like that.

"No problem," he said because he couldn't very well just stand here letting her get worked up thinking they had an actual problem. Other than the problem that there was no possible way he was going to take some stranger to Thanksgiving dinner and have his entire family think they'd *both* lost their minds. Not that it was Caroline's fault she'd lost hers temporarily. But Craig didn't have the excuse of a concussion to explain his recent bout with irrational decisions.

"You have been so patient with me through all of this and don't deserve to have me doubting our entire relationship like this." She held out a palm when he opened his mouth to protest that he wasn't the saint she was making him out be. "I mean, obviously I'm experiencing this connection between us, but it's just so frustrating not being able to remember all the details of our life together."

Imagine how he felt. He was standing in his brother's living room with a woman he didn't know, trying to keep her calm and relaxed as he pretended like he was her soon-to-be husband.

Hold on. He pushed the brim of his hat back on his forehead. "You're experiencing a *connection*?"

"Of course I am. I didn't hit my head that hard." Caroline rolled her eyes, then winced as she brought her fingers to her temples.

Craig was by her side in an instant. "Does it hurt?"

"Just when I move too quickly."

He put his hand on the small of her back and tried

to direct her toward the sofa. But her pointy high heels didn't budge. Maybe a strong wind wouldn't blow her over after all. "Why don't you lie down and rest?"

"Actually, Craig, I would really feel more comfortable if we just went back to my place."

"Honey, I can't very well stay the night at your place with you. You know how people love to gossip around small towns."

"Honey," she repeated before smiling wide. She took a step toward him and his knees went all rubbery, probably because he'd hardly slept a wink in that hospital chair. "That's what we call each other? I like it."

He rolled his lips inward to keep from admitting that it was the same term of endearment he used on all the young calves at the ranch when he was trying to herd them into a corral or lead them somewhere they didn't want to go. But she'd given him a lead and he didn't waste it. "Speaking of names people call each other, I would hate for anyone to say something unflattering about you if I were to spend the night at your house."

"Surely you know me well enough by now to realize that I don't care what people think about me." She waved a dismissive hand before resting her palm against his chest. A blast of heat lit underneath her fingertips and he stood there absolutely still, hoping the unfamiliar sensation passed. However, when she took another step closer to him and her eyelids lowered, the flame spread. "Plus, I'm sure it's not the first time we'll be staying the night together."

He gulped. "How do you figure?"

"How else would I know that you use two pillows?"

A jolt traveled down the back of Craig's neck as he wondered how she'd found out about his sleeping habits. Maybe that was just another good guess on her part. Plenty of people used more than one pillow.

"Anyway," she continued as her fingers made slow circles along the third button on his shirt, "I really think we would both be more comfortable at my place. Not to mention the fact that things are more likely to come back to me if I'm in my normal environment."

Craig searched her face, trying to control his breathing. The first problem was that if she continued touching him like this, there was no way he could remain in the same room with the woman, let alone the same house. At least, not unless he wanted to take their fake, temporary relationship to a real, permanent level. The second problem was that he had absolutely no idea where her house was, and he couldn't very well admit as much without further raising her suspicions.

While he may be willing to go along with this little delusion of hers to an extent, he wasn't about to have anyone believing that he didn't normally pick up his dates at their front doors like a gentleman.

When she was this close to him, it was impossible to concentrate on forming an acceptable excuse as to why he shouldn't stay with her. Only a weak-willed jerk would take advantage of a woman in this situation. And Craig had never been accused of being weak-willed.

"Please?" Her hands slipped up to his shoulders.

"Fine," Craig bit out, saying the only thing that would allow him to politely step out of her embrace and buy himself some more time. "Let me go get my gear and we'll head over to your place."

When he was in the spare bedroom packing up the duffel bag he'd brought to visit his brother, he shot off a text to Josselyn asking for Caroline's address. He shoved his toiletries in next, hoping that Joss wouldn't respond with a lecture on how he was making a massive mistake by taking Caroline home. Instead, the only thing she sent was an address to a smaller rental unit behind one of the historical houses in the heart of Rust Creek Falls.

"Ready to go?" he asked Caroline when he returned to the living room.

"Yes," she replied, setting down the picture frame she'd been studying. "Your family is huge."

He glanced at the photo of all his brothers and sisters and their spouses at his parents' anniversary party last year. "There used to be just eight of us kids, but our numbers keep growing."

"And you're the oldest in the family?" she asked.

"Yep," he replied as he walked toward the front door, hoping she'd follow. Something prickled at him. Why would she automatically assume he was the oldest? Did he look elderly next to his siblings? Because he was beginning to feel that way when he was with her. According to the hospital bracelet still on her wrist, Caroline was only twenty-three, and suddenly he wondered if she was aware of the twelve-year age difference between them.

She picked up another frame, this time a picture of all his brothers at Jonathan and Dawn's wedding, then set it down before walking past him to get to the front porch. "Do you always look so solemn in your pictures?"

First she'd accused him of being proper, and now she was calling him solemn. Perhaps her "oldest in the family" comment was simply an accurate observation. After his rodeo career ended, everyone had begun referring to him as the stuffy, serious big brother. "Well, someone has to be in charge and take care of the others. Besides, the photographer was taking forever to get the perfect groomsmen shot and all I wanted to do was get inside the reception and grab a beer."

"Speaking of photographers and receptions," Caroline said when Craig opened the truck door for her. "Have we started planning our wedding?"

He rubbed a hand on the side of his neck as he looked anywhere but at her face. Of course, she would've already been planning her wedding. It was what she did for a living. "I think you wanted to wait until after we told my family before we set a date."

"That makes sense." She nodded, and the ball of guilt that had slowly been building in Craig's gut got a little bigger.

He wanted to yell that none of it made any sense whatsoever. Instead, he climbed into the cab of his truck and steered toward Cedar Street, driving himself deeper into the next round of make-believe.

By the time he turned off Main Street, Craig had convinced himself that Caroline most likely had an actual fiancé or even a serious boyfriend who looked just like him. He was no brain surgeon, but it was truly the only way any of this could possibly make any sense. Josselyn had pointed out that Caroline wasn't wearing a ring, but that didn't mean anything nowadays.

When they got to her house, he was bound to see signs of whoever this mystery guy was. Of course, if there was in fact another man, Craig would need to figure out a way to explain why he'd gone along with the whole ruse.

He pulled into a long driveway of one of the large historical homes on Cedar Street and Caroline pointed toward the smaller cottage in the rear corner of the lot. "You can park in my space back here."

Her unit was a miniature version of the Craftsman-style house in front. There were well-tended flower bushes surrounding the green clapboard shingles, and a small cornucopia filled with mini pumpkins and color-ful gourds sat on a table next to a white wooden rocking chair that was way too big for the dinky porch.

As Caroline unlocked the dark walnut door, Craig realized that this might be his last chance to make a run for it. There were no other vehicles parked near the property, but what if her real fiancé was sitting inside? Even a framed picture of another man with Caroline could be waiting in there, on full display to counter every falsehood he'd allowed the poor woman to be-lieve about him.

Another unfamiliar pang of envy shot through him at the thought that this beautiful and optimistic woman might belong to someone else. Not that he should be jealous, he reminded himself as he cautiously followed her inside. If he didn't already know that Caroline was most definitely not his type, he would've been able to figure it out just by looking at her interior decorating choices.

There was an overstuffed white sofa in the middle of the living room and all Craig could think was how impractical the color was—it would be impossible to keep clean. Then there were the twenty or so throw pillows in varying floral and swirly prints piled on it, as well as the dollhouse-size chairs on either side of the full bookshelves that lined one entire wall. Okay, so maybe the chairs were a tad bigger than a doll, but he doubted they could hold all 190 pounds of him. Frilly yellow checkered curtains framed the windows, and expensive-looking paintings hung on the pale blue walls.

Craig had definitely been right about Caroline the first time he'd gotten a look at her silly high heels. A girlie girl like her would never last on the family ranch.

"I'm going to hop in the shower and wash the hospital smell off me," she said, setting her large tote bag down on the white kitchen table. "I think I have some deli meat in the fridge and I picked up a couple of bags of chips at the market a few days ago if you want to help yourself to a snack."

"I'm good," Craig said, trying not to think of what Caroline would look like naked, with the water sluicing off her.

Since the kitchen looked out into the living room, he guessed that the doorway she walked toward led to the bedroom. The only bedroom, judging by the look of things. That meant Craig would be bunking on the sofa tonight because there was no way he was going to sleep in a bed next to her, no matter how many pillows she thought he used.

He dropped his duffel bag near the sofa, and when he heard the water pipes hum to life, he began carefully examining the contents of the bookshelves. There were paperback novels shoved next to old-fashioned leather-bound volumes of those boring stories his high school English teacher referred to as "classics." There were ancient-looking artifacts and modern-looking sculptures. He recalled Josselyn mentioning something about Caroline's parents traveling quite a bit. She obviously had quite the collection of random souvenirs.

There were also plenty of framed photos of Caroline in all stages of her young life—from a pigtailed toddler to a college graduate—standing in between a proud man and woman who Craig assumed were her parents. He saw a handful of pictures of Caroline with other women her age, but there was nothing suggesting another man in her life.

His shoulders sagged in relief. Unfortunately, he didn't know if that relief was a good thing or a bad thing.

Chapter Six

Caroline wrapped her wet hair in a bun on top of her head and slipped on her favorite pair of cropped pink pajama pants. She debated putting on a bra, but her breasts were small enough that she could get away with a camisole-style tank. In the interest of modesty, she threw on her faded gray University of Montana sweat-shirt, the one with the women's tennis team logo on the front.

While it was still the middle of the afternoon and she should want to impress Craig with her more fashionable wardrobe, she was pretty exhausted and just wanted to be comfortable. As a wedding planner, she always felt the need to be well put-together with a professional hairstyle and a businesslike appearance that conveyed to her clients that she could handle any situation. But she wasn't going into the office today.

Before she walked out of the only bathroom in her one-bedroom house, she swiped on a layer of mascara and applied some strawberry-flavored lip balm so she would at least look somewhat healthy.

She wasn't sure if her fiancé had seen her in her most natural state before, but if they were going to eventually be living together, he might as well get used to it. As she walked out of the bedroom, she found him staring at one of the oil paintings on her living room wall.

"My dad painted that when we lived in Nice," she said, going for her most casual voice since there was a chance she'd already told him the story about the café near the Sophia Antipolis. It was one thing to allow the guy to see her in comfy clothes; it was quite another to bore him to death with repeated anecdotes from her family's travels.

"You know what," Craig said suddenly, taking a step back. "I'm going to go to the pharmacy and pick up your prescription."

"But I'm not having any pain right now. And I have some Tylenol in my medicine cabinet if I need it."

He couldn't seem to stop glancing toward the front door, and she wondered just how badly he was yearning to get away from her. Was it because of the plain way she looked? Or was something else going on with him? Not willing to be the source of his discomfort, she gave him an out. "Seriously, though, you really don't have to sit around here with me. I'm sure you have plenty of other things you could be doing on a Friday afternoon."

She couldn't tell if that was relief flashing across his face, but the short-lived expression was soon replaced with steely determination. "The doctor didn't want you to be left alone."

Caroline flicked her wrist. "But she didn't mean every single second. I'm sure you could leave and come back."

Despite the fact that *he'd* been the one who'd just suggested going to the pharmacy, he didn't appear convinced. So Caroline continued, "Actually, my phone and laptop are still at my office and if you could go and get those for me, I'd be able to get a little work done before tomorrow."

"What's tomorrow?"

"I'm meeting the organizers of the Presents for Patriots event. They're having a formal fund-raiser at Sawmill Station, and my company volunteered to host the event and coordinate the party planning."

Craig lowered his chin as he studied her. "I don't think you're supposed to be working yet."

"Well, my boss is out of town, so I'm the only one who can attend the meeting. Besides, most of the actual work is already done, but all the notes are on my laptop and I'd like to refresh myself with the details beforehand."

"Maybe I should call Josselyn and see if she can come over and watch you while I'm gone."

"Watch me? Like I need a babysitter?"

"Here we go again." Craig nodded at Caroline's arms, which were now crossed in front of her.

"What does that mean?" She narrowed her eyes at

him. "Has my work schedule been a problem for you in the past?"

"In the past?" He mumbled something else under his breath but she didn't quite catch it.

"Or currently?" Her bare toes dug into the plush rug under her feet as she prepared to stay rooted to the spot until she got some answers.

"Um…" Craig took a step back.

"Please tell me you're not one of those old-fashioned macho types who think their women need to be taking care of the farm and raising their babies?"

"I don't even have a farm." Craig was now backed up against the arm of the sofa. "It's a ranch. And no, I don't have a problem with what you do for a living. You can work wherever and whenever you want. I was just concerned about your injury."

"Then what did you mean by 'here we go again'?"

"I meant that when you get determined to do something, you go from a sweet, docile little thing to some sort of broncing—I mean, fierce warrior like that." He snapped his fingers.

Broncing? Caroline really hoped that the man hadn't been about to compare her to an angry rodeo animal. They were both pretty worn-out, though, so she decided to give Craig the benefit of the doubt.

"Well, if it's any consolation, I rarely bring out this so-called 'fierce warrior' unless absolutely necessary. At least not with most people." She tugged her lower lip between her teeth as she studied him. Then she asked, "Do we usually argue a lot?"

"What? No." One side of his mouth curled downward. "What would we have to argue about?"

"Sorry. Again." She felt her chest ease back, realizing she hadn't been aware she'd puffed it out in the first place. "I guess I'm just on edge because I'm pretty exhausted, even though it feels like I've been in a deep sleep for the majority of our engagement. Anyway, I was focusing on all the things I can't remember instead of being grateful for all the stuff that's clearly in front of me."

"In front of you?" Craig's skin seemed to lose some of its tan color.

"You." She rubbed his biceps in an effort to reassure him, but the physical contact only reminded her of how hard and well-shaped his muscles were under his shirt. She yanked her hand back a bit too quickly. "*You're* here in front of me. A wonderful man who was willing to spend the entire night in a miserable chair beside my hospital bed. A man who is willing to risk his proper reputation to spend the night with me at my house in order to nurse me back to health, even though I'm totally healthy, by the way."

He coughed. "Risking *my* reputation?"

Really, Craig was quite adorable when his eyebrow dipped into a squiggly line like that. Caroline had to wonder how often she confused the poor guy. Probably all the time if that was the cute face he made whenever she did.

"Thank you for being so good to me." She rose on her toes and kissed him on his cheek.

Craig didn't jump away from her in a desperate

panic, but he also didn't return her kiss. He just stood there, stiff as a granite statue, his eyes dark and full of caution.

So far, she got the impression that he was definitely the type of guy who would be overprotective. She hoped his lack of response was because he didn't want to unleash his passion and accidentally injure her. The alternative would be that he didn't feel any passion for her at all, and Caroline didn't want to think about that dismal possibility.

"I'm going to go take a nap," she finally said, because one of them needed to say or do something. His only reaction was a brief nod.

As she walked to her bedroom, she was too nervous to turn around to look at him. But she listened to him unzip his duffel bag as her head hit the pillow. She fell asleep before she could hear anything else. When she woke up an hour later, she found a note by her bed.

Went to pick up your stuff from your office. Craig.

There was nothing about when he'd be back. Or if he'd even be back at all.

Craig was trying another key off the same ring Caroline had used to open her front door when his cell phone rang. Still standing in front of her office, he scrambled to pull the vibrating thing out of his back pocket, thinking Caroline had woken up and needed him. But she didn't have her cell phone, and he hadn't seen a landline at her house. In fact, she didn't even have his number. Which might present quite a problem once she realized the man she thought she was going to marry wasn't listed in any of her contacts.

Looking at the name on the display, Craig sighed before sliding his finger across the screen and answering. "Hey, Rob."

"Oh, good, you finally found time to answer your phone, big brother." Rob's voice always had a teasing edge, but today it was downright buoyant, as though nothing was going to sink his good humor. "Mom wants to know if you'll be bringing your new lady friend home for Thanksgiving."

Craig squeezed his eyes shut and counted to three. "What new lady friend?"

"The one our baby sister, Celeste, heard you had in the front seat of your truck about an hour or ago."

"How could C.C. hear about that already?" Craig asked, using the youngest Clifton's nickname. "She's not even home from college yet."

"Some kid from her vet science class used to babysit for Will's neighbor, who saw you with the pretty gal that works for that wedding planning outfit over at Sawmill Station. Said you both went into Will and Jordyn's house and then little bit later, you left together. With your duffel bag."

That was how things went in a small town. A neighbor told a friend, who told a cousin, who told their former fourth-grade teacher, and before a person could blink, it was on the front page of the *Rust Creek Falls Gazette*. He knew it was bound to happen. He just hadn't expected word to get all the way to Thunder Canyon that fast.

Stupid him.

"It's a long story, but there is absolutely nothing going on between me and Caroline Ruth." Craig immediately looked around the wooden platform in front of the old-fashioned train depot, hoping none of the Daltons, who owned the land, overheard the blatant lie. Clearly, there was *something* going on between him and the beautiful woman who, brain injury aside, should've known better than to kiss him. Even if it was only on his cheek.

Those sweet lips of hers held a promise of something more. What that was, Craig didn't want to know. Finding out wouldn't be fair to either of them, but especially not to Caroline, who looked incredibly innocent and fresh standing in front of him in those pajama pants that were so thin they showed the outline of her rear end. He didn't even want to start thinking about that sweatshirt that fell off her shoulder, displaying a slinky spaghetti strap against her smooth, creamy skin.

"Caroline Ruth," Rob repeated, his smug tone latching onto the slightest revelation of new information. "Good thing our grandfather is coming for dinner this year. He eats so slow, you'll have plenty of time to tell your family all about this so-called 'long story.'"

"Nothing to tell."

"Want to know what I think?" Rob asked.

"Actually, no. I don't really care what you th—"

"I think that there's *plenty* to tell about this Caroline Ruth and that's why you're trying to keep everything under wraps."

"Speaking of wraps, have those new posts come in

yet for the southeast fence line?" Craig knew the best way to deal with his family was to redirect.

"Dad and I already took care of the fence," Rob replied, making Craig think that he'd successfully changed the subject. But his brother was like a mangy dog with a bone. "You know we're all going to find out about her anyway. Might as well come clean."

"Nothing much to tell." Craig scratched the scar tissue along his neck, thinking of ways to downplay the recent events that had completely bucked him like a greenhorn with his hand stuck in the bronc rein as he got dragged along for the ride. "Caroline is planning Drew and Josselyn's wedding. She took a pretty big fall in her office and smacked her head. When she came to, she thought she knew me, and the doctor said it was best not to correct her until she regained her memory."

"No way!" Rob whooped and Craig had to pull the phone away from his head before he ruptured an eardrum. "Like she's got amnesia? I didn't think that kind of thing happened in real life."

"It's not exactly amnesia," Craig started, before deciding it was probably best not to overexplain and get caught up in the details. "Anyway, that's why I said it was a long story. And I would appreciate it if you didn't tell anyone else what's going on. Caroline might not want strangers knowing her personal business."

"Right. So then how exactly did *you* get involved in her business?"

Craig sighed, but it came out as more of a growl. "Because her boss is out of town and her family's in another country and, with the concussion, the doctor didn't want her to be alone. So I gave her a ride home and I'm keeping an eye on things."

"Keeping an eye on things, huh?" Rob didn't bother to cover the mouthpiece on his end as he snorted.

"What's that supposed to mean?"

"You're my big brother. I know how you keep an eye on things. Growing up, you watched all of us like a hawk."

"I'm protective. So what?"

"*Protective* is an understatement, Craig. Remember the time we went to the county fair and Dad told you to watch us at the mutton busting competition? I was in third grade, but you told the judges I was only six because they made all the kids in that age bracket wear helmets."

"I'd like to point out that you were small for your age and the following year, they made everyone wear helmets. I was simply ahead of the times."

"Then," his brother continued, refusing to cede Craig's point, "you followed me into the pen and slipped the sheep I was riding a huge chunk of caramel apple. When the announcer blew the horn, instead of sprinting around the arena, the animal just stood there chewing its sticky cud."

"That sheep was nicknamed Wooly Widowmaker and I probably saved you from a broken arm and a lifetime of embarrassment. So, as much as I'd like to sit around and listen to you grovel out your eternal thanks, Rob, I actually need to get going."

"Anyway, back to the reason why I called. Are you

bringing your new lady friend for Thanksgiving or not?" his brother asked.

"It depends."

"On what?"

Craig looked at Caroline's key ring hanging limply in the office door. "On whether she remembers who the hell I am before then."

Chapter Seven

Caroline drenched the chicken pieces in flour as the oil sizzled in her cast-iron skillet. How could she remember the exact temperature for getting a perfect scorch on her fried chicken, yet not remember whether or not her fiancé even liked her cooking?

Glancing at the digital clock on the stove, Caroline realized that she was stressing about what to feed Craig when she should be worried about the fact that he might not be coming back at all.

No. Of course he would come back. Her gut knew it, even if her head was slow to see all the other signs. He'd sat with her in the hospital all night. If he was going to bail out on her, he would've done it long before now.

She'd spent the past hour walking around her house, looking in drawers and pulling out old family photo albums, gaining more comfort and confidence each time she'd come across another detail in her life that she recalled clear as day. If she had her laptop, she would get online and do some research on amnesia and concussions and anything else that could be wrong with her brain.

Not that anything else seemed to be wrong. As far as she could tell, Craig was the only person in her world that she didn't remember. Sure, it was disconcerting, but it would've been downright eerie if she didn't have that steady sensation that there was definitely something about the man that felt right.

Turning up the volume on the music channel on her television, Caroline sang along with the classic country station, taking further solace in the fact that she still knew all the words to every George Jones, Dolly Parton and Conway Twitty song by heart.

When Tammy Wynette came on and encouraged her to stand by her man, Caroline hiccuped a little giggle. Her mother had once caught her only child listening to that particular song and immediately put on her Helen Reddy CD and had her daughter memorize the lyrics to "I Am Woman" instead.

Caroline really needed to email her parents. She'd video chatted with them on Monday, but they never went more than four or five days without at least a text conversation. They were bound to get worried if they didn't hear from her soon. Not that Caroline would tell them about being in the hospital. Her dad had a writer's imagination and she didn't need him thinking the worst and flying back to the States early just to check on her.

A light knock sounded at the door and she padded out of the kitchen in her pink fuzzy slippers. Looking through the peephole, she felt a charge of excitement surge through her when she saw Craig standing on her porch.

"You didn't have to knock," she told him as she yanked the door open so quickly, it bumped against her shoulder. "I left it unlocked for you."

"I didn't want to just barge in and scare you, especially if you were still asleep."

"I'm awake." She smiled, then felt her lips falter as she realized she was standing there like an eager cocker spaniel, stating the obvious. Caroline stepped aside to let him into the house.

Craig handed her the laptop case and her smartphone with twenty-four missed calls and twice as many text alerts. He sniffed and asked, "Are you cooking something?"

Caroline was still leaning against the open door frame and the chilly air reminded her that she'd taken off her sweatshirt when she'd started working in the kitchen. Craig's eyes dropped to where her hardened nipples pressed against the soft cotton fabric of her tank top. However, instead of shivering from the cold, Caroline was filled with a rush of warmth from his intense stare.

If it had been any other person standing there, she would've clutched the laptop to her chest and blocked his view. But there was something slightly empowering about having this type of effect on her man. Overcome with a boldness she couldn't explain, Caroline pushed her shoulders back, making her small breasts thrust further out. She saw the muscles in his throat swallow and then she actually did shiver.

"Yes," she finally said, then spoke louder. "I'm making fried chicken and mashed potatoes. I wasn't sure what you liked to eat so I hope that's okay?"

Walking toward the kitchen, she set her laptop down on the dining table along the way. She heard Craig closing the front door and wondered if she should've also grabbed her sweatshirt off the back of the sofa and covered up. Even though they were engaged, she was completely alone in her house with the man. A man who looked at her as though she was the most attractive woman in the world and he was just now seeing her for the first time.

Of course that was silly on both accounts—she was by no means beautiful and, obviously, Craig had seen her before. But why did it suddenly feel as though she was now playing with fire?

Trying to ignore all these unfamiliar emotions battling inside her, Caroline flipped the chicken over in her trusty skillet, needing to ground herself in something she understood. Food.

A tingling crept up the back of her neck and she glanced over her shoulder, spotting Craig leaning one of his jean-clad hips against the counter.

"That's my favorite," he said, still staring at her, his nostrils slightly flared.

Caroline's mouth went dry. "What is?"

"Fried chicken." But his dark blue eyes weren't focused on the food in the pan. They were studying her and all that lovely heat was spreading through her body again. "You asked if it was okay."

"Oh." Caroline forced her own attention back to the stove.

"Do you need any help in here?" he asked.

She allowed her head to turn only slightly in his direction. "You know how to cook?"

"Of course. I'm the oldest of eight kids and I grew up on a ranch. My parents made all of us learn how to do every job around the place from wrestling steers to feeding baby calves to churning homemade butter."

"When I was a kid, I didn't even have baby dolls to take care of. I wish I had grown up with siblings. What was that like?"

"Trust me, my brothers and sisters were way more needy and annoying than baby dolls. But once in a while, they would come in handy when we had a lot of chores to do."

"Are ranches a lot of work?" she asked, wanting to keep the conversation off anything that would make her think about how close he was to her in this tiny kitchen.

"You have no idea." Craig made a weird huffy sound that came out as a chuckle. It was the same noise her college roommate had made when Caroline enrolled in the same linear algebra class as the serious math major. By the end of the semester, the roommate was coming to Caroline for tutoring.

There were few things in this world that Caroline actually found to be all that challenging once she set her mind to it. So when someone implied that she couldn't handle something, it only made her want to master that very thing. It didn't matter if it was ranching, advanced mathematics or mashing some potatoes while a sexy cowboy stood so close, her tummy felt like it was doing flips.

Oh, and she could also do flips, thanks to her years on two different junior high gymnastics teams.

She was tempted to say as much to Craig, but it was always easier to just show people what she could do. Although she had to admit that she'd been the first one to question *his* abilities when he'd offered to help her cook.

Instead, Caroline forced a smile and told her fiancé, "I've got things under control in here."

"Oh. Okay." He put his hands in his back pockets and she turned to the fridge to pull out more ingredients for the potatoes. She was reaching for a pint of half-and-half when he added, "Then would you mind if I used your shower?"

She turned around so quickly, the carton of butter she'd been holding slipped out of her grip, and one of the sticks popped out and landed near the toe of his cowboy boot. Before he could bend down to pick it up, she was already forming an image of a very naked Craig in her small, steamy bathroom.

"Unless you'd rather I stay here to help," he said, holding out the butter that was still wrapped in its wax paper, one corner completely dented. It was then that she noticed he was wearing the same clothes he'd had on at the hospital yesterday. No wonder he wanted to take them off. She stared at the buttons on his shirt, thinking how easy it would be to slip them through their little holes and... *Stop*, she commanded herself, then drew in a deep gulp of air and found her voice.

"No, I'm fine. I'll get you a towel as soon as I turn the heat down in here," she offered, then caught her breath at the double meaning. "The heat on the stove, I mean. Unless you already know where the towels are. Assuming you've taken a shower here before. Not that you would have, unless there was a time when you needed to. Although how would I know either way? It's not like I've been giving a lot of thought to you being in my shower. And now I'm just babbling and not making sense at all. I better just show you where the linen cabinet is."

Except he didn't seem the least bit confused by her rambling, awkward speech. In fact, his normally questioning eyebrow remained firmly in place as he lifted one side of his mouth and replied, "I think I can figure it out."

Caroline Ruth had almost as many bottles lined up on her tiled shower wall as she did on the narrow shelf above her pedestal sink. Although he'd never shared a bathroom with his sisters, Craig knew perfectly well that women tended to like a variety of beauty products, especially ones that smelled good. However, the amount of choices on display before him had to be some sort of record.

Craig sniffed at the open lid of the fancy shampoo. At least, he assumed it was fancy judging by the French label. He also assumed it was shampoo since he didn't speak French. But it wasn't like he was some young, inexperienced buck. He was thirty-five years old and had stayed the night at ladies' places before. But that was mostly when he'd been traveling on the pro circuit, and he usually did so only after a night out celebrating a good ride. Then he'd be back on the road, heading for the next city. He'd never really been all that invested in a relationship enough to pay much attention to what the women he dated stocked in their bathrooms.

Well, except for Tina. She'd been his neighbor and they'd practically grown up at each other's houses. Tina had been the type to use whatever soap was on sale at the local market. It was why she'd been the perfect partner for Craig. She didn't care about all these frilly, girlie things like—he squinted his eyes at the label across the white bottle he'd just knocked over—Paraben-Free Volumizing Conditioner with Added Boost. She cared about horses and working hard and merging her family's ranch with his. Unfortunately, Craig's dream of the perfect partnership and the perfect relationship had died along with Tina many years ago.

Pretending otherwise with Caroline wasn't fair to either of them.

Foregoing the shampoo bottle's posted recommendation of a five-minute wait time, Craig stuck his head under the nozzle to rinse off. Then he turned the water as hot as he could stand it, hoping the steam would drive away all the cravings the pretty wedding planner had recently brought back into his world.

His skin was red and stinging when he finally shut off the water. Maybe he should've taken a cold shower instead. He grabbed a fluffy lavender towel—because apparently there was nothing masculine in this house—and wrapped it around his waist. Wiping his hand across the fogged-up mirror above the sink, Craig stared at his reflection.

What was he doing here?

He needed to go out there and tell Caroline the truth. He needed to call Josselyn or Drew or Dr. Robinson and inform them that he couldn't do this. He couldn't keep lying to that poor, sweet girl.

No. She wasn't a girl, he reminded himself as he saw an edge of lace peeking out from behind the damp towel hanging off a hook on the back of the door. She was a woman. A woman who clearly wasn't wearing a bra right this second. And he'd boldly stared at her small, firm breasts as though he'd had a right to look. He'd stood there in her open doorway wondering what shade of pink her nipples would be as his palms had itched to slide up underneath her skimpy tank top.

Now that his body recalled the image, he had to re-fasten his towel over his growing arousal. Cursing, he dug into his duffel bag to pull out his shaving kit and ended up knocking the whole thing off the toilet. This bathroom was so tiny.

Hell, the whole house was tiny. It felt as if everything was shrinking in on him. How was he going to last the entire night with Caroline and not accidentally touch her? There had to be someone else who could stay here with her.

As though reading his exact thoughts, Craig's phone lit up with an incoming text from Drew. How's our patient?

She seems to be completely fine, Craig's big fingers tapped out awkwardly on the minuscule keyboard.

It was the truth. Caroline looked totally healthy. Almost too healthy, if one asked Craig's growing libido. He stared at his screen, hoping that his buddy would give him permission to abandon his caregiver duties.

Head injuries are like that. They can seem fine one minute, and the next minute… Drew didn't finish his sentence, letting three little dots at the end of his sentence imply all the potential risks to Caroline.

Those three dots were the reason Craig was here. Nobody knew what to expect.

When Craig didn't reply, another text bubble appeared from Drew. *Has she regained her memory yet?*

As far as I can tell, she knows everything else about her past except who I am. It's weird.

The brain is a weird and complex thing.

Thanks for the anatomy lesson, Dr. Drew. But what do I do in the meantime? I can't keep pretending that we're engaged.

What else do you have going on right now?

Craig pushed a lock of wet hair off his forehead before typing, *It's not a matter of my time.*

You want me to see if Ben can come stay with her?

Even with all the hot air surrounding him, Craig went cold at the thought. No, he typed and hit the send button.

It's me she wants, not Ben, he began typing, then immediately deleted the words. That would make him sound jealous when he clearly had nothing to be jealous of because none of this was real. Caroline didn't truly want him. She didn't even know him.

It's that none of this feels right. She's going to be so pissed when she finds out we have been tricking her, Craig wrote instead, purposely using the word *we* to remind Drew that he was in on this asinine plan.

There was no response for a while, so Craig set his phone down and lathered his face. He was halfway done shaving when Drew's next text came through. Just try to be as honest as possible without stressing her out. And remember, it's not YOU tricking her. It's her brain.

But why did her brain pick me? he replied. Not that he would've preferred it picking Ben.

This time, he didn't have to wait long for Drew's response. Buddy, I may be a doctor, but even someone as smart as me doesn't know why ANY woman's brain would pick you.

Haha, Craig texted, then added an emoji of a hand making a crude gesture. That was pretty much the extent of his technology skills.

He finished shaving and found a clean pair of jeans in his duffel bag. However, all the steam in the enclosed space made his skin damp and he had to wrestle the jeans over his legs. After he finally buttoned his fly, he decided he needed to let in some cool air before pulling on one of his T-shirts.

When he opened the bathroom door, Caroline stood on the other side, one arm raised as though she'd been about to knock. At first, her eyes were round with surprise, but then her lids lowered toward his bare chest. He resisted the urge to flex his pectoral muscles, but he also couldn't bring himself to break her concentration as she studied him, a slight hitch in her breathing. After all, it had been a while since his body was whole. Since a woman had been so obviously and physically responsive in her assessment of him.

They stared at each other for what felt like minutes before she finally squeaked, "Dinner's ready."

Caroline pivoted quickly and her slim legs practically ran toward the living room. When she was finally a safe distance away, Craig's only thought was that if they both kept looking at each other like that, they would never get through the night.

Chapter Eight

After accidentally confirming that every ounce of his upper torso was indeed made out of rippling muscle, Caroline decided that she couldn't face Craig across the dining table and carry on a conversation without thinking of his steamy tan skin underneath his T-shirt.

"Why don't we put something on TV while we eat?" she suggested, carrying their plates to the coffee table she'd found at a local antiques store and painted a soft shade of butter yellow.

"Wow, this looks great," he said when he sat next to her on the sofa, which was really more of a love seat. It was too late when she realized that being this close to him, sitting side by side, was almost as bad as making eye contact with him.

"What do you want to watch?" she asked when he had

a forkful of mashed potatoes and gravy in his mouth, then had to wait for him to finish chewing before he could answer.

"I don't care. What do you normally watch?"

"Whatever I programmed on the DVR the week before." She picked up the remote control and turned on the television and a list of her new recordings popped up on the screen.

He let out a little chuckle. "Looks like my choices are either all of last Saturday's college football games or else an assortment of movies from the Hallmark Channel."

"That'd be pretty much it," she said, scrolling down. "I'm guessing you don't want to watch this one about a big shot fashion designer returning to the small town where she grew up to attend her former prom date's wedding to another woman?"

"Pretty sure I already read the book," Craig said before biting into a crispy chicken thigh. His thick lashes actually fluttered closed as he moaned.

"So football, then?" Caroline said brightly, turning up the volume so the sportscasters drowned out Craig's sighs of satisfaction.

"Sure," Craig said as he wiped his hands on a napkin. "But I already watched the University of Montana game last Saturday."

"I know they lost, but they're still the top seed in the Big Sky Conference, and if they beat Portland State next week, they'll go to the FCS playoffs."

"Wait. You actually watch college football?" The squiggly eyebrow was back, but instead of looking surprised, his accompanying smirk made him appear doubtful.

"Craig, my parents have been guest lecturers at most of the top universities in the United States. So I've been to a football game at every Division 1 stadium and most of the Division 2 schools."

"Wow. I guess I didn't see that coming."

"Seems as if we're both still learning things about each other." She smiled as she picked up a piece of chicken.

"Why don't we see what's on live TV?" he suggested and then shoveled another forkful of potatoes into his mouth. "This gravy is almost as good as my grandma's."

"Almost?"

"Well, it's better, but don't tell my Meemaw."

"Will I be meeting your Meemaw at Thanksgiving?" Caroline tried to get her voice as neutral as possible. Now that the subject of his family had come up again, she didn't want to seem too eager or even pushy. But she was dying to know more about the rest of the Cliftons. It would give her more clues about the man she was planning to marry.

"Probably. Unless she and my grandpa get into one of their fights beforehand. Even then, she might still show up just to make him mad. If they *are* going at it, though, you have to be very careful not to pick sides."

"Please. I'm a wedding planner. Diplomacy during the heat of family disputes is my specialty." She pushed the live-TV button on the remote control and since it was already set to a sports channel, an announcer welcomed them to the North American Championship Rodeo. "How long have your grandparents been married?"

"Oh, they aren't married to each other. Meemaw is my grandma on my mom's side and Grandpac is my dad's dad."

"His name is Grand Pack? Two words?"

"No." Craig gave a slight grin and Caroline realized it was the first time she'd seen him not looking so blasted serious. Her knees would've gone all wobbly if she hadn't already been sitting down. "Grandpac. One word. When I was a kid in Wrangler Camp, we had to learn how to work with leather, and I decided to hand tool Grandpa Clifton's name onto the back of a belt. Unfortunately, as I started running out of room, my letters got squished closer together and I could only fit *Grandpa C*, which ended up looking more like *Grandpac*. My brother Jonathan had just learned to read, and when he sounded it out as one word, the name just kinda stuck."

"Aw." Caroline's rib cage felt all warm and liquidy, just like her gravy. "I bet your Grandpac was so proud to wear something you made especially for him."

"Oh, no, he couldn't actually wear it. My grandfather is a man of considerable stature." Craig extended his arms into a circle in front of his belly for emphasis. "And I'd used myself as the model and then added two inches because I had absolutely no concept of waist sizing. But he did put it in a display case and still brings it out every time Meemaw wears the feather-and-bead earrings I made her."

"That's sweet that your grandparents love showing off the gifts you made them."

He shook his head, but kept glancing at the television as he spoke. "It's not sweet, it's calculated. They've never gotten along and are always competing with each other to be the favorite grandparent. It usually means lots of great presents at Christmas and birthdays, but the rest of the year we all just try to get out of the room as soon as the bickering starts."

Craig shrugged before directing all of his attention at the bull rider on the screen and effectively ending any further discussion.

She finished eating and soon lost interest in whatever the commentator with the turquoise bolo tie was saying about the combined score in the short go-round. Plus, Caroline still needed to email her parents and look over her notes for tomorrow's meeting at work. Craig didn't seem to notice as she stood up and retrieved her laptop off the dining room table. When she settled back onto the couch, she powered on the computer and got to work.

At some point she'd brought her legs up into a criss-cross position and Craig's elbow ended up resting on her knee. Caroline enjoyed the discovery that they could spend a pleasant, ordinary evening side by side, in companionable silence. At least, they were enjoying it until the announcer said, "Our next rider is on pace to beat the record for consecutive rides, a record that was set six years ago by Craig Clifton before he retired from the pro circuit."

At the mention of her fiancé's name, Caroline lifted

her head in time to see an image of a younger Craig flash on the screen.

"That's you!" she said, pointing to the TV.

"Yep." His hand slipped between their bodies and Caroline held her breath, wondering if he was finally going to make some sort of move. Instead, he found the remote wedged into the cushions and hit the power button. "It's getting pretty late, huh?"

"I didn't know you rode in the rodeo," she said, pivoting her upper body toward him and resting an arm across the back of the sofa.

He wasn't rude enough to point out the obvious—that there were actually a lot of things she didn't know about him. But he also didn't seem particularly inclined to provide her with the details, either.

"Is that how you got your scar?" She had barely traced the hook shape when he pulled away.

"I'm going to do the dishes," he said, his hip knocking into her knee as he stood up quickly. Carrying their plates into the kitchen, he glanced back at her with a pointed look and added, "You should probably get to bed."

The guy had barely said two words for the past hour and now he only spoke when he wanted to boss her around. Caroline stood up and followed him, remaining on the opposite side of the kitchen counter that separated the sink from the rest of the living area. "What about you?"

"What about me?" he asked, not bothering to look up as he rinsed off their silverware.

"Are you coming to bed?"

"I'll go to sleep after I clean up the kitchen." Craig was proving to have quite the habit of carefully phrasing his answers.

Caroline angled her head, trying not to let the frustration settle onto her expression. "But where will you be sleeping?"

"I can bunk on the couch." He might have shrugged, but it was too difficult to tell since he was leaning sideways to load the dishwasher.

"It's more of a love seat," she replied, estimating that he had to be at least six feet tall. "I mean, it can fold out into a bed but the mattress is thin and the frame is kind of wonky with the support bar going right across the middle."

"I've slept on worse," he replied, his knuckles turning white as he tightly gripped the cast-iron skillet.

"Yeah, but don't you think you'd be more comfortable in my bed?" The words were out of her mouth before she could stop them. It wasn't exactly like she was eager to hop into bed with the man she was still trying to remember. But she also recalled his comment this morning about his back and she didn't want him spending another night in agony.

Besides, she was learning that she never got any answers out of Craig unless she pushed him.

"Here's the thing, Caroline." Craig glanced toward the bedroom, but when he faced her, he wouldn't meet her eyes. A pit settled into her stomach as she realized the answer before he said it. "We haven't slept together yet."

* * *

Craig hated the fact that he'd obviously brought that shocking pink color to her cheeks last night, but there had been absolutely no way he could've lain next to her in a bed all night and maintained his distance.

Hell, he was having a hard time maintaining his distance this morning as the scent of sizzling bacon woke him from his crooked sleep on the uncomfortable sofa bed. Caroline stood in front of the stove, stirring scrambled eggs in her cast-iron skillet, looking like one of those old-fashioned housewives from the *Leave It to Beaver* era.

A silky, flowery dress hugged her backside before flaring out above her knees, and she had another pair of high heels on her feet. Who dressed like that to cook breakfast?

When she turned around to pass him a mug of hot coffee, he noticed that a white apron with a cherry print covered the front of her dress. Her brown hair was clipped away from her face and fell in soft waves down her back. Craig didn't know what looked more appealing—her or the plate of perfectly crisped bacon she handed him next.

If he hadn't already seen how much food she could put away in her petite frame, he would've assumed that she was trying to impress him with her cooking skills. But since she divided the eggs into equal portions on their plates, it was obvious that she enjoyed food as much as he did.

"What time do you need to be at your office this morning?" he asked.

"I was hoping to go in around eight and get things set up for the meeting."

He glanced at the digital clock on the stove. "That was thirty minutes ago."

"I know, but I don't have my car and you were out cold on the sofa bed, so I didn't have the heart to wake you."

Craig rubbed his neck and tried not to think of the stiffness in his back that had kept him awake the first half of the night. Well, it was his aching muscles along with a side of guilt and a constant awareness of Caroline's physical proximity that had kept him from getting to sleep before two in the morning.

"Let me just grab a quick shower and I'll take you," he offered before carrying his coffee into the bathroom with him.

Fifteen minutes later, he was backing his truck out of the long driveway and she was handing him an English muffin filled with the eggs and bacon he hadn't wanted to take the time to eat.

When he pulled into the gravel parking lot at Sawmill Station, her little blue MINI Cooper was the only vehicle there. Just as it had been yesterday afternoon. Grabbing her laptop case out of his crew cab, Craig followed her inside the former one-room train depot that served as her office. The Daltons had bought the surrounding land last year for their ranching operation, but because the train depot and the larger freight house next door were historical landmarks, they couldn't tear them down. From what Craig understood, Vivienne, Cole Dalton's wife, had moved her wedding planning business to Rust Creek Falls and they now used the space to hold big parties.

Perfectly good waste of grazing land, if you asked Craig.

"You don't need to hang around," she said, flipping on the lights and setting a bright yellow tote bag— similar to the one she'd had yesterday—on an antique desk with fancy scrollwork.

"But there's no one else here," he said, dropping to his knees beside a modern wood-burning stove in the corner. It was freezing in this place.

"I know, but Brendan and Fiona will be here soon. Plus, it's not like I'm at risk of falling asleep or knocking myself out. Again."

"But the doctor said we shouldn't leave you alone," he reminded her.

"Did she say for how long?"

"Not exactly. Though I was under the impression that you needed someone with you until you got your memory back."

"But, Craig," she said as she smiled, "I *do* have my memory back. Or at least most of it."

So then why did she still think they were engaged? He wanted to ask her as much, but he didn't know how to without it sounding like some sort of test. Plus, he heard a car pull into the lot outside.

He got the fire going and rose up just as Brendan Tanner and his girlfriend, Fiona O'Reilly, walked inside. They greeted Caroline first, and when Fiona turned Craig's way, she did a double take.

"Hey there, Craig. I wasn't expecting to see you

here." Fiona's family owned a local ranch, and when Craig had been stuck in the hospital with Caroline and bored out of his mind, he'd read one of her online articles about the free-range grazing habits of Herefords. "Are you volunteering for the Presents for Patriots fundraiser, too?"

"Nope," Craig answered a bit too quickly and his single syllable response did nothing to wipe the curious expression from Fiona's face.

"My car got left here in the parking lot, so Craig had to give me a ride to work this morning." Caroline's explanation wasn't helping the matter, either. He held his breath as his supposed fiancée turned toward him. "You're more than welcome to stay, honey, but I'm sure you have other things you need to do today."

There was a slight gasp at her use of the endearment and he realized that it had come from his own mouth.

That settled it. There was no way Craig was sticking around and waiting for Brendan and Fiona's questions that would be sure to follow. He squared his shoulders and took Caroline up on her suggestion that he leave.

"Okay, then I'm going to head over to the Daltons' stable and talk to them about their new longhorn." It was his way of letting her know that he'd still be nearby if she needed him.

"We're supposed to be meeting Bailey Stockton here," Brendan called out to Craig, who paused as he made his way toward the exit. "So if you see a guy in the parking lot who looks like he's got a chip on his shoulder and would prefer to be out riding horses instead of inside talking to actual humans, go ahead and point him in this direction."

Craig knew some of the Stocktons from his past visits to Rust Creek Falls, but not Bailey. He was the most recent one to move to town, and Craig didn't blame the guy for wanting to get as far away from the wedding planner's office as possible. In fact, if Craig *did* run across the man, he'd probably invite him to hop in the truck with him so they could both get the hell out of Dodge.

Chapter Nine

No sooner had Caroline heard Brendan and Fiona pull away in their car than Craig swung the office door wide-open, bringing in the crisp late-afternoon autumn breeze. In fact, if she didn't know any better, she'd think he'd been purposely waiting for the others to leave before rushing back to her rescue.

It was on the tip of her tongue to remind him that she was more than capable of being by herself for a few minutes, but when she saw him standing before her in his dusty jeans and sweat-soaked T-shirt, her heart sent a little flutter along her nerves.

"Why are you all dirty?"

"The Daltons got a young bull this morning and he was pretty testy about there being a buffer field between the steer pasture and the heifers in the grazing pasture. Young buck busted through the first fence and was scratching his head against the second when I got there, totally oblivious to the thousands of jolts zapping him. I had to help get him back in the pen while they re-trenched the ground posts and ran the galvanized wires deeper underground to conduct a stronger current."

"I literally have no idea what you just said," Caroline said.

"Basically, one of their new bulls got loose and was trying to get to the female herd to get a jump start on the breeding season. We had to calm him down and then fix the electric fencing so that he wouldn't try it again."

"And here, I didn't need an electric fence at all," Caroline mumbled under her breath. Last night, Craig had made it clear that he didn't require any sort of buffer zone to stay well clear of her bedroom.

"What was that?" he asked, stepping inside and closing the door behind him.

She couldn't very well admit that she'd actually been comparing him to an overexcited farm animal. Or feeling jealous of whichever lucky cow had been on the receiving end of that bull's pent-up desire. "I just need to power off my computer and grab a couple of files and then I'll be ready to go," she said instead.

"No problem," he said. His boots paced over the wood floorboards as he walked toward the bookshelf. "I hope you didn't stand on any chairs today."

"Nope. Everything was on the lower shelves."

"Did you eat lunch?" he asked.

"Actually, we had a menu tasting with the caterer who is doing the fund-raiser. I saved you a portion of beef Wellington, but when you didn't come back by two o'clock, I assumed you were eating with the Daltons. Plus, Bailey Stockton was getting pretty antsy, so I gave him your food. But if you're hungry, we can stop at Buffalo Bart's on the way home and get some wings. Or if you're sick of chicken, I can whip up a lasagna for dinner."

"You say 'whip up a lasagna' like it's the easiest thing in the world to make."

Caroline shrugged as she took a step closer to him, wondering if he normally kissed her hello at the end of a workday. "I like cooking. It gives my hands something to focus on so that my brain can work on all the bigger things."

"Speaking of your brain, how's your head been feeling today?" He reached out to trace a finger across her forehead and she all but sighed and leaned into his hand. "Any headaches?"

"Nope," she replied, using his favorite word. She must've fallen in love with his protective and caring nature, because she certainly hadn't fallen in love with his quiet and aloof conversation style. Actually, he was not always reserved when he was speaking. If the topic involved ranches and cattle, he could go on for days.

But when he touched her tenderly like this, or studied her with those blue eyes dark with concern, he didn't need to use any sort of conversation. Her thighs trembled and she felt as if she could actually pass out. Again.

"You okay?" he asked, cupping her elbow. "I should've known putting in a full day at the office would be too much for you."

No, it was being too close to him—breathing in his musky fragrance of hard work and the outdoors—that was making Caroline suddenly grow weak. "Craig, I promise I'm perfectly healthy."

He took a step back, yet watched her carefully as she gathered her things—as though he wasn't the least bit convinced that she wasn't going to collapse at his feet at any minute.

Then, later that evening, when they were again sitting side by side watching television while they ate dinner, Craig kept his body practically glued to the opposite end of the sofa. It was almost as though he was worried that if he touched her, she would completely go to pieces.

Steeling her spine, she turned toward him to tell him as much. "I've been noticing that you've been keeping your distance from me lately."

"Lately?" he asked, but his tone wasn't incredulous as much as it was sarcastic, suggesting that the word was some sort of understatement.

"Ever since my accident, you back up every time I move closer to you," she said, then scooted across the cushion to prove her point. Since the armrest prevented him from moving any more to the left, he shot forward, knocking his knee into the coffee table. "See? Every time. That's exactly what you do."

"What am I doing?" he asked, standing up with their plates.

"You're trying to get as far away from me as you can."

He opened his mouth as though to deny it, but nothing came out. She also stood and took the plates from him and set them back onto the table. Then she swallowed the last bit of orange soda in her glass, wishing it was merlot for an extra boost of courage, before turning back to him and placing her palms on the fresh shirt he'd put on after his shower.

"You know, Craig, I won't break if you kiss me."

Craig had to fight every impulse and muscle in his legs to keep from stepping back and well out of kissing range. Not that Caroline was actively trying to plant her lips on his, but she was blinking those intoxicating eyes at him and pouting her pretty little mouth, the invitation clearly extended.

"I just think that maybe we should wait for…" For what? Why would an engaged couple wait to kiss each other? The problem was that they weren't the average engaged couple. Or even a couple at all. He seized on that logic. "I was just waiting until you regained your memory. I don't want it to feel like you're kissing a stranger."

As impossible as it was, the small living room got even smaller, and it felt as though a cinch belt was squeezing across Craig's chest, tethering him in place. There was no way Caroline was buying any of this.

"I know I don't remember you, but how could I ever think of you as a stranger? Even if I'd never laid eyes on you before I'd hit my head," she continued and he froze, wondering if she was aware of how close she was to the truth. But instead of going with that more accurate description of the relationship, she slid her palms up to his shoulders and countered, "We've spent the past forty-eight hours together."

He looked at the digital readout on the cable box. "More like sixty hours."

"My point is that a loving heart is the truest wisdom."

Huh? Were they talking about hearts or wisdom here? Because in Craig's mind, the two never seemed to work well together. "I'm not following you."

"It's a quote by Charles Dickens. He's my dad's favorite author and I was named after one of his books."

"Still doesn't make any of this clearer," Craig replied.

"What I'm trying to say is that your actions these past two days speak louder than anything else, and my heart already knows everything it needs to know about you based on how well you've cared for me." Her thumbs traced circles above his shoulder blades and she asked, "Why are your muscles so tight?"

"Because I'm trying really hard not to move right now." There was absolutely nothing stopping him from walking straight out her door, yet he'd never felt more trapped.

As much as he'd fought it, his attraction to Caroline was like that headstrong young bull trying to bust out of its corral today. Obviously, Craig didn't believe in any of that nonsense about her having a wise heart or his actions speaking loudly or whatever else it was she was suggesting. But there was some sort of unexplainable connection between them. Some sort of magical fencing that zapped at his senses if he so much as moved, so much as acted upon this attraction.

"Here," she said, sliding her hands down his arms

and pulling his wrists around her waist. "Let me help you."

Craig gulped. He certainly didn't need her help moving closer. Yet, she felt so damn good, her tiny waist warm under his loose grip. At this point, he might need a jolt of ten thousand electric volts just to keep him away.

When her fingers returned to his shoulders and traced underneath the opening of his collar, he offered one last warning. "What happens if you end up regretting this?"

"How will we know unless you kiss me?" she asked, her breath whispering against his lips.

Oh, hell. One little kiss wasn't going to hurt.

When he dipped his head to hers, pain was the last thing on his mind. In fact, finally kissing her felt like pulling into his driveway after months of being on the road. She opened her lips and her tongue tentatively reached out to his. Heat and urgency filled him and he drew her in closer and responded with his own tongue, more forceful and more exploratory.

Caroline pressed her small, lithe body against his and every alarm inside him went off. This was too much. She was too much. Craig couldn't let things go any further. Breaking his lips away from hers was the easy part. Maintaining the distance and getting his breathing under control was way more difficult.

Well, that and trying to ignore the way Caroline's chest pressed against his as her lungs expanded with each of her little breaths. Her fingers were twisted into his collar and his hands were still cupped under her backside and he slowly dragged them back up to her waist.

Her cheeks were flushed and her lids appeared to be heavy since they were halfway closed as she studied his mouth.

"Are you okay?" he asked, more for himself than for her. He'd kissed plenty of women before, but none as responsive as her. Craig didn't know if he would ever be okay again.

"I think I felt something," she whispered and he tried not to take the words personally. He'd just felt his entire world burst out of the chute and she thought that perhaps she might've felt *something*? "But just to be sure, maybe you should kiss me again."

Compelled to make her feel more than just something, Craig lowered his head to hers again, then pulled back right before their lips met.

"Just one more," he murmured, needing all of his energy to fight this inner battle of self-control. The inner battle he was clearly already in danger of losing. "We can't go any further."

When he kissed her the second time, it was even better than the first. Their lips already knew how to move over each other's. Her mouth already knew how wide it needed to open to accept his probing tongue, and her hips knew just where to press against his, cradling his stiff arousal.

Caroline's fingers slipped into the open neck of his shirt, working the buttons loose as she slid her palms down his chest. His own hands were busy squeezing and massaging her rounded rear end, the silk fabric of her dress gathering together and lifting higher with each caress. The hem rose enough that the material no longer served as a thin barricade to the heat of her warm skin underneath. His thumbs traced the lacy edge of her panties and Caroline threw back her head and moaned.

His lips followed along her exposed neck down to her collarbone and her breath came in soft little pants. It took every ounce of strength Craig possessed to drag his mouth away from her a second time. Again, he moved his hands back up to her waist, but only because he was worried that if he completely let go of her, she would melt against him. Or he would melt against her. At this point it, his blood was pumping too fast to figure out where her body started and where his ended.

Also, by holding her this close, he didn't have to look at her eyes, didn't have to face the damage he might've inflicted. He drew in a ragged breath, resting his chin on top of her head. "We really should stop, honey."

Again, he hadn't meant to use the endearment, but he wasn't sorry for acknowledging the tender and protective feelings she evoked in him. Not that there weren't plenty of other things he could be sorry for.

She nodded, and when she lowered her arms, Craig stepped back to allow his body the opportunity to cool down, but then he was forced to observe her upturned face.

Instead of that dreamy expression she often got when she was comfortable with him, the one where her eyes fluttered closed and her smile lit up the room, Caroline was staring at him like he'd just poisoned the herd's drinking water. Her eyes were huge and round and her mouth was frozen into a little O, as though she were in shock.

Oh, no. Had they gone too far? Had he pushed her too much? Was she completely disgusted by him? He hoped he wouldn't regret the answer, but he had to ask, "Caroline? Is everything okay?"

"Never better," she squeaked out in a hoarse voice before running to her bedroom and slamming the door closed.

Chapter Ten

Caroline had absolutely no idea who that man was out in her living room, but he most definitely was *not* her fiancé.

Lying on her bed and staring blankly at her ceiling, Caroline touched her swollen lips. There was no way she could ever have forgotten what *that* felt like. After their first kiss, she was sure that she'd never kissed Craig Clifton before in her life. But she'd begged him to continue the make-out session just to confirm it, and it was during their second kiss that all of it came back to her. When he'd pulled his lips from hers, everything flooded into her mind at once.

Yet, instead of confronting him about any of it, she'd run straight to her bedroom and slammed the door closed. Twenty minutes later, she was still struggling to get her breathing under control.

They weren't engaged. Craig wasn't even her boyfriend. She'd been thinking about the words of Winona Cobbs when she first laid eyes on him two days ago. The images from that morning came back with the kind of clarity that can only be seen by events being replayed in slow motion. All the pieces finally clicked into place—the way she'd been balancing on that stupid chair, seeing him come into her office wearing that sexy tan cowboy hat, spotting the hook-shaped scar on his neck and, finally, the way the pink donut box went flying in the air as he ran toward her.

Engaged by Christmas. That was what she'd been thinking before knocking herself out. Had the doctor specifically said Caroline had suffered from amnesia, or was there another word she'd used? Reaching for the smartphone on her nightstand, she did some research online and read about an amnesia-like condition called confabulation.

So I made it all up? Caroline thought, staring at her screen. She heard the television in the living room go off and the sound of something bumping into a piece of wood furniture, followed by Craig's muffled curse. No, the man was completely real and currently getting ready to fall asleep on the other side of the wall, oblivious to the fact that Caroline had just remembered the truth.

Which brought everything back full circle. Obviously, she hadn't imagined Craig, but for some reason, she'd imagined that they were engaged. Yet why *him*? Why not Drew Strickland or his brother, Ben, both of whom were strangers and also in the office when she'd injured her head? Because neither one of them was Craig. It was as simple and as complicated as that.

Before Caroline had moved to Rust Creek Falls, she and some of her friends from the dorms had driven to town on a lark. Their favorite reality show, *The Great Roundup*, was being filmed nearby and the other girls wanted to be close to the action. Caroline had been coming out of the Ace in the Hole bar for a breath of fresh air when an older woman passed along the sidewalk. There'd been something familiar about her and it wasn't until the woman got to the corner of Buckskin Road that Caroline realized she was Winona Cobbs, the psychic from that nationally syndicated show Rita Rodriguez didn't approve of her daughter watching.

Caroline had caught up to Winona, not because she wanted to ask for a free reading or an autograph, but because the woman was walking with a slow limp and approaching a dark intersection. Caroline had asked the little old lady if she needed help crossing the road and when Winona took the offered arm, a strange expression had crossed her weathered face. Her eyes had grown bright and stared right through Caroline, like Dr. Robinson's penlight, trying to search for answers.

Winona's voice was lower in person than it had been on her shows, but it was just as authoritative when, without warning, she'd predicted, "You'll find what your heart is looking for here."

"Here?" Caroline had asked. "In Rust Creek Falls?"

The old psychic had nodded, but didn't explain what

it was Caroline was looking for or how she would find it. "When?"

"Be patient, child," Winona had replied, patting her gnarled, freckled hand against Caroline's. "It'll happen before you turn twenty-four."

"What will happen?"

"Your engagement."

The pronouncement had taken Caroline aback, but she'd always wanted to get married and knew with absolute certainty that a wedding was the thing her heart was looking for. She hadn't been able to keep the eagerness out of her voice when she asked, "To whom?"

"To the one with the pocket full of Life Savers and the three-legged cat that sleeps on both his pillows. Just remember, your cowboy is scarred for a reason, so be careful not to let him go."

But before Caroline could ask for more details, the other patrons had spilled out of the bar and Winona Cobbs was caught up in the crowd, leaving Caroline standing on the street corner, full of hope and unanswered questions.

Until Craig had walked into her office over two years later.

Actually, seeing him hadn't really answered anything. But, according to one of the brain injury articles Caroline had just read online, her concussion had forced her mind to fill in the blanks with what she'd wanted to see—that Craig was the scarred cowboy from Winona's prediction. Everyone in that hospital room when she'd finally awakened must have thought that she was completely nuts. Even Caroline could see how absolutely crazy it sounded for her to think she was engaged to a total stranger. It certainly explained why Josselyn and Drew and Craig had all stared at her that day as though she'd lost her mind.

However, the only thing Caroline couldn't explain was why any of them would go along with the whole charade in the first place. Especially Craig.

Throwing off the comforter, Caroline stood and walked to her bedroom door, determined to wake him up and ask him exactly that. Her hand gripped the knob and it took two tries to twist it open because her palms were so damp. She'd barely opened the door a crack when she saw the mound under the blankets on her sofa bed move. Then she heard his soft sigh as he nestled deeper into the thin mattress and something pulled at her heart.

Standing there frozen, Caroline was flooded with another realization. If she went out there and admitted that she remembered they weren't truly engaged, there would no longer be a reason for Craig to stay and take care of her. Not that she really needed anyone looking out for her anymore, but if he left she would probably never see him again.

Not only had she made a complete fool of herself insisting that they were engaged, but then she'd doubled down on her belief by spouting all that stuff about a loving heart and the truest wisdom and trusting her instincts about a man who, in reality, was a total stranger.

In Caroline's defense, though, she'd suffered a head injury and had been relying on the very random mutters of an old psychic walking down the road late one night.

Not that believing in fortune-tellers made her appear to be any more rational, but when Winona Cobbs had spoken those words, Caroline had felt the premonition all the way down to her bones.

She'd believed it way before she'd met Craig, and now that she'd kissed him, she knew it with even more certainty. It wasn't scientific, but being with him just felt right. Besides, how else would she have known all those details about him? The pocket full of Life Savers, the three-legged cat, the sleeping with two pillows?

The scar?

The only part of Winona Cobbs's prediction that hadn't actually come true yet was Caroline being engaged by her twenty-fourth birthday—which was this Christmas.

Bracing her body between the small opening of the bedroom door and the frame, Caroline took several deep breaths as she contemplated her best course of action.

As much as she should admit the truth to Craig, she only had one more month to make him fall in love with her. Would it really be all that wrong to let him go on believing that they were engaged? Or that Caroline *thought* they were engaged?

She pressed her fingers to her pounding temples as she mentally sorted through all the confusion and her conflicting emotions. Caroline walked back to her bed, wishing she had someone to talk it over with. Someone who could make sense of it all.

Someone who could tell her how to keep the man she'd been destined to find.

* * *

The following morning, Craig was coming out of the shower when he heard Caroline talking in the kitchen.

"Oh, good, you're safe." Another female's voice echoed inside the small rental house and Craig froze in the doorway. He'd left his duffel bag in the living room and, having just slept in his boxers, the closest item of clothing he could shimmy into when Caroline came out of her room was a nearby pair of jeans, which was all he'd worn when he'd made a beeline for the bathroom earlier. If they had company, it would look pretty odd for Craig to walk out there bare-chested.

"It was just a concussion, Mom," Caroline replied and Craig eased away from his hiding spot behind the bathroom door. Her parents were out of the country, which meant they couldn't possibly be here at her house.

"We got your email, angel," a male baritone added to the conversation. "Who is this Craig fellow?"

She must have the speaker feature turned all the way up on her phone. His own father had once tried to show Craig how to do that so he wouldn't have to stop working anytime one of his brothers or sisters called, but he always hit the wrong button and ended up disconnecting the call.

"Oh. I forgot I mentioned him in the email," Caroline said as she walked to the edge of the kitchen, a mixing bowl cradled in one arm as she whisked some batter. She caught sight of Craig and gave him a tense smile before putting her forefinger to her lips in the universal sign to mean "Please keep quiet."

She didn't have to ask twice. The last headache Craig

needed was for her parents to find out some stranger was lying to their daughter and shacking up with her. Luckily, they weren't there in person. Craig's nose twitched at the scent of freshly brewed coffee and the promise of the maple-pecan waffles Caroline had said she was making when she'd woken him up this morning.

"Are you really engaged?" her mom asked as Craig practically tiptoed toward his duffel bag, unsure of how much sound her cell phone could pick up.

"We don't even know him," her dad added.

"You're not cooking for him, are you?" her mom asked. "Did you know that in the Aka society in Africa, the men do all the cooking? Many of the males even breastfeed the babies. Although, I suppose technically it would be suckling since they can't produce—"

"I like to cook, Mom," Caroline interrupted, thank goodness. Craig got to his duffel, only to discover that most of his clothes were missing.

Mrs. Ruth, or perhaps Dr. Ruth since she was a college professor, continued on about some pygmy tribe halfway across the globe and Craig tried to wave at Caroline to get her attention and ask where his shirts were. But her back was to him as she faced the stove.

Craig walked into the kitchen to whisper in her ear, and that was when he realized Caroline wasn't on speakerphone. Her laptop was propped on the counter and two very surprised people appeared on the screen facing him.

Oh, crap.

"He's real." Her dad was the first to speak.

"He's really *naked*," her mother replied, moving her reader glasses down her nose.

Craig looked behind him to judge the distance to the front door and tried to determine how cold it would be outside if he made a run for it. But Caroline shoved a cup of coffee into his hands before he could take off.

"Mom, you spent eight months in the Polynesian islands studying the history of ancient hula performances. You even made Dad dress in a loincloth."

"It wasn't a loincloth," her mother replied and Craig suddenly wished he would never have to hear the word *loincloth* again. "It was a ceremonial *malo* and it was a gift to your father from Professor Ka'ukai."

Caroline poured batter into the waffle iron on the opposite side of the stove as though making breakfast and video chatting with her parents about her half-naked fiancé was part of her normal Sunday morning routine. "My point is that you're well accustomed to seeing men without their shirts."

Too much information, Craig thought, resisting the urge to pull the cherry-printed apron off the sink and cover up.

"It's a pleasure to meet you, Dr. and Dr. Ruth," Craig offered weakly. Hopefully, nobody was appraising his chest for either breastfeeding suitability or hula-dancing capabilities.

"It's actually Dr. Ruth and Dr. Rodriguez," Caroline's father corrected with a wink. "We're not married."

Dr. Rodriguez then began a long lecture using phrases such as *female servitude* and *matrimonial bondage*, and

Craig whispered out one side of his mouth to Caroline, "Where are my clothes?"

"I needed to run a load of laundry," she said, her lips equally tight.

"Did you say *laundry*, Caroline?" Her mom's face moved closer to the screen, as though the woman could hear better by looking more closely into the little web-cam. "Please tell me that you're not already falling into the stereotypical gender roles that Western civilization has forced upon females as a means to exert the imbalance of power of a male-dominated society."

"I didn't ask her to do my laundry," Craig defended, one palm up as though he was being asked to swear on a stack of Bibles. "I normally do it myself."

"And he knows how to churn butter, too," Caroline added, making Craig glance at her sideways.

"Let them work out the distribution of domestic chores for themselves, Rita. It's still early in their engagement." Then the older man turned back to the screen. "And speaking of engagements, when our angel sent us an email mentioning some fiancé from out of the blue, we were a little worried, thinking we had our own Miss Havisham on our hands."

"Who's Miss Havisham?" Craig asked. There were a million ways this conversation should be steered, but he had no idea who was holding the reins. So he just tried to follow along.

"From *Great Expectations*?" her father said. "She's this old spinster woman who was jilted at the altar and goes around in her wedding gown—"

"Okay, Dad, I have to get to the office," Caroline in-

terrupted quickly. But her father continued his disser-
tation as Craig's phone suddenly rang. Relieved for the
excuse to get out of the kitchen, Craig quickly walked
toward the coffee table.

Trying to mute his phone, he accidently swiped on
the wrong button and his own mother's voice echoed
on the speaker. "Craig? Are you there?"

"Hey, Mom," he said, looking for the button to switch
off the speaker, but the entire display had gone black.
Really? The one time he didn't want the feature to work
was the one time he couldn't shut it down.

"I hear you're bringing a woman for Thanksgiving,"
Carol Clifton said, drawing Caroline's attention from
her own parental inquisition.

"Word travels fast," Craig muttered. He was trying
to push the circular home button on his phone, but it
wasn't recognizing his thumbprint. Probably because
his hands were so damn sweaty.

He heard more talking from the kitchen, where Dr.
Ruth and Dr. Rodriguez were still visible on the laptop.
Unfortunately, his mom heard the same thing.

"Oh, my gosh," his mother practically squealed. "Is
that your new fiancée?"

Fiancée? That was more serious than the "lady
friend" gossip Rob had mentioned. Craig glanced over
his shoulder to make sure Caroline hadn't heard and
then lowered his voice. "You know about that?"

"Oh, yeah. Ben Strickland told your brother Jonathan about it," his mom replied as though it was every
day that one of her sons managed to find himself in the
middle of a pretend engagement. "Put her on the phone."

"She's talking to her own parents right now," Craig replied, running his fingers over his scalp and wondering if it would be worth catching pneumonia to go outside with wet hair.

"You guys aren't going to her folks' for Thanksgiving, are you? It's the first year in a long time that I'm gonna have all my kids at the house together."

"No, we can come there, Mrs. Clifton," Caroline said from behind him, apparently disconnected now from her own conversation.

"Fantastic," his mom replied. "Dear, I can't wait to meet you. Craig, make sure you stop by Daisy's on your way out of town and bring a pie."

His free hand dropped from his damp head to his neck as he tried to massage some of the tension away. "But I thought Meemaw was baking the pies."

"She is. However, Grandpac is also coming now and unless you want your new girlfriend to see a repeat of the Pecan Pie Controversy of 2011, you'll bring an extra one."

"I'd be happy to make a pie, Mrs. Clifton," Caroline volunteered. Craig pivoted to face his pretend fiancée and shook his head at her before it was too late.

"That might work as long as Meemaw doesn't know you made it yourself, dear. And please call me Carol. Or even Mom?"

Okay, his mother's tone was a bit too hopeful and Caroline's smile was a bit too pleased. Taking her to his family's ranch for Thanksgiving would all but seal their fate. It was entirely too risky.

Luckily, Craig still had a couple of days to get out

of this mess. "Let's not finalize anything until later in the week, okay, Mom?"

"Sounds like a plan," his mom said and Craig wanted to reply that there was absolutely no plan. But the woman, who had raised eight children—and knew her way around the very best stall tactics—continued, "I'm guessing you two will be coming out on Wednesday? Everyone else is coming out on Wednesday."

"Probably Thursday morning, Mom," Craig sighed and Caroline smiled even wider.

"It's a long drive to Thunder Canyon from Rust Creek Falls, though. So don't be late."

Chapter Eleven

"Why couldn't I make the pie myself?" Caroline asked Thursday morning as she climbed into the passenger side of Craig's vehicle.

For the past three days, he'd insisted on driving her to and from work and he'd always held open the door.

"Remember I told you about making sure you don't take sides between Meemaw and Grandpac?" he asked, reaching across her legs to place the pink bakery box he'd picked up from Daisy's yesterday on the floorboard between them. It was the closest he'd gotten to her since the night they'd kissed.

Thousands of times this week, she'd been prepared to tell him that she'd regained her memory. But then he'd call her "honey," and her breath would bottle up in her lungs and all she could do was smile at him. Or he'd show up at her office, his boots and jeans all dusty from whichever local ranch he'd visited that day, and his concerned blue eyes and his sexy cowboy hat were a welcome sight after a long afternoon dealing with pushy vendors or mind-changing brides.

Then there was the morning when his brother had called him while they were in the truck. Craig's Bluetooth had automatically switched on and she heard Will ask if he and Caroline wanted to carpool to Thunder Canyon for Thanksgiving.

At that point, her curiosity became stronger than her guilt and she thought that meeting his family might give her some sort of insight about the man who'd established himself as her protector, while simultaneously keeping his distance from her. Maybe he wasn't as physically attracted to her as she was to him. This trip would give her the opportunity to find out.

Caroline reached for her seat belt. "And remember I told *you* that I can handle squabbling family members in my sleep? I do it at work all the time."

"That's the other reason I didn't want you to make the pie. You've been so busy at work and every night you come home and make me these fabulous home-cooked meals when you should be resting and taking it easy. Did you know that it can take weeks for a person to recover from a concussion?"

"I know." Caroline rolled her eyes and then sing-songed the same thing he'd been saying to her at least twice a day. "'Just because I can't see my injury doesn't mean it doesn't exist.'"

Normally, she would think it was sweet that he tried

so hard to take care of her, but she was running on limited time here. She needed to impress him with her domestic abilities and get him to fall in love with her so that he'd propose before Christmas. But Craig seemed to be thwarting her attempts at every turn.

While she'd been working at Mikayla Brown's post-birth baby shower at Sunshine Farm on Sunday afternoon, he'd finished the laundry and ironed every single article of her clothing, including her sports bras, her hand towels and her Egyptian cotton bedsheets. On Monday, he'd done the grocery shopping at Crawford's General Store while she'd been at the office, and on Tuesday, she'd come home to a spotlessly scrubbed bathroom.

Last night, he'd tried to grill rib eyes for her on her landlord's outdoor grill, but they'd run out of propane. And by the time he got back from the hardware store with a new tank, it was pouring rain and the wind was howling like crazy. She'd saved the meal by broiling the steaks and then wowing him with au gratin potatoes and her knowledge of useless college football stats.

If Craig needed a party thrown, Caroline had quite the résumé to show him. But Craig didn't seem to need anything. Or anyone. He certainly didn't need to kiss her again, she thought as he closed her door and climbed into the driver's side.

The sun was barely rising as they began the three-hundred-mile drive to Thunder Canyon. Since Craig didn't seem inclined to keep up any sort of conversation, Caroline turned on the radio. A blast of screaming

electric guitar shot through the speakers, and her first
instinct was to cover her ears.

But Craig raised the volume and then began singing
along with the heavy metal song. When he noticed her
staring at him in shock, his voice trailed off. "What?"

"You mean, you purposely have this station programmed on your radio?"

"What else would I listen to?" he asked.

"Um, maybe country music? You're a cowboy."

"Oh, really?" He winked at her and a shiver ran down
her spine. "I didn't get the memo."

They ended up compromising on a classic rock station and Caroline closed her eyes to prevent herself
from chattering on senselessly. The past few nights that
he'd stayed at her house, they'd settled into a routine of
comfortable silence when the television was on or there
was music playing, and she didn't want to do anything
now that might rock the boat.

Or to remind her that she really had no business tag-
ging along for a family holiday when they weren't really engaged. Yet.

That "yet" part was what gave Caroline an unprec-
edented bout of nausea. She would've liked to blame it
on motion sickness but she'd never been carsick before
in her life. It had to be her nerves telling her that this
was a bad idea. Sure, his mom had invited her, but did
his family really know the truth? That she and Craig
had really only known each other a few days? On the
other hand, if she didn't call him her fiancé or perpetu-
ate this myth that they were in a legitimate relationship,
then she wasn't technically deceiving anyone.

Plus, if she was being truly honest with herself, she really didn't want to spend Thanksgiving alone.

Halfway there, they pulled into a truck stop restaurant and gas station. Caroline used the restroom while Craig ordered them some breakfast sandwiches and coffee to go. The closer they got to Thunder Canyon, the more nervous Caroline's tummy became. Maybe meeting his parents and the rest of his family was a bad idea. After all, they'd been practically living together the last few days and not once had they socialized with any of his married siblings who lived nearby. Craig saw them while she was at work, but when he was with her, they didn't so much as go to the Gold Rush Diner to share a meal, let alone be seen anywhere out in public together.

Not that most of the people in Rust Creek Falls didn't already know there was something going on with them. But nobody seemed to know what that "something" was. In fact, a small group of ladies at the baby shower on Sunday had brought up his name with questions in their eyes, but Caroline had been in work mode and didn't think it would be professional to talk about her dating life. Or the fact that she and Craig had never truly gone on an actual date.

The irony was, the more nervous Caroline grew with each passing mile that brought her closer to lying directly to his family, the more relaxed Craig became. Okay, so maybe she wasn't exactly lying to his parents. Initially, she'd really thought she and Craig were engaged, and since he still hadn't corrected her, their engagement could be construed as a form of implied consent on his part. Perhaps he really *did* want to marry her.

Still, the fact remained that Craig had been quiet and tense during the first half of the drive. Yet now he began to speak more, pointing out landmarks and telling her a story about the creek where Grandpac had taken him and his brothers fishing when Craig had been in the sixth grade.

"Rob, my youngest brother, had been eager to catch the biggest trout and didn't bother looking behind him before casting his line. We hear this shout, followed by a slew of four-letter words, but it was too late. Rob had got his hook caught in Grandpac's ear, then felt so bad about it he yanked the pole to try and pull it out. He ended up ripping right through the cartilage."

"Your poor grandfather!" Caroline shuddered.

"More like poor Jonathan. He's the second oldest and was closest to the first-aid kit when it happened. Grandpac cussed up a blue streak when Jonathan tried to disinfect the wound and bandage it up. Between you and me, I think that's why my brother became a pediatrician instead of going into geriatric medicine."

"So one of your brothers is a doctor?" Caroline turned in her seat. She recalled that day coming home from the hospital, when Craig had admitted that she hadn't met any of his family yet. So it wasn't like she had to pretend that she didn't know anything about his siblings. "Tell me about the others."

"Jonathan is married to Dawn, who is a nurse. Next is Will. We went to his and Jordyn's house that day..." Craig didn't have to say which day that was. She remembered. It was the same day she'd insisted that he come stay with her at her house.

"Got it." She tried to sound casual. "Who's next?"

"My sister Catherine and her husband, Cody, then Rob, who is single and still lives on the ranch. Cecelia is after him—she's married to Nick—then Calista and her husband, Jake. My sister Celeste, everyone calls her C.C., is the baby. Maybe I should've written it all down for you ahead of time."

"Craig, it's my job to remember who's who. We once planned a wedding for a bride with thirteen bridesmaids. To this day, I can tell you their dress sizes and whether their dates requested the prime rib or the salmon." Then Caroline proceeded to list the names of his siblings in order, along with their spouses. "I got this."

When he smiled at her across the cab of his truck, her throat constricted. It occurred to Caroline that she had never seen Craig smile so broadly. She'd seen looks of concern, looks of curiosity, even looks of desire. She'd even seen several grins. But she had never seen him as truly happy as he looked at that exact moment.

Apparently, his family was everything to him. Caroline really hoped she didn't blow this.

When they'd passed the turnoff to Interstate 90, Craig's blood had run cold at the sight of the wooden white cross on the side of the road.

It was why he hadn't said much to Caroline during the first half of the road trip. No matter how many times he'd driven the stretch of highway from Rust Creek Falls to Thunder Canyon, seeing that small handcrafted monument to one of his biggest failures always haunted him.

He hadn't brought a woman home to meet his family

since Tina, and even then, he technically hadn't brought her home since she'd practically been there the whole time. In fact, it had been the opposite when she died. They'd been at a bar with some of her cousins outside Kalispell and returning to Thunder Canyon late at night. Craig had been sound asleep in the passenger side and Tina behind the wheel of her daddy's old Jeep, probably too exhausted to have even seen the stalled logging truck before it was too late.

After the crash, he'd been lost and hurt, his relationships with women more about filling a temporary physical need. But he could only ride bulls for so long before his body began reminding him that he was no longer in his prime. Eventually, Craig had been forced to go home to confront his past as well as the rest of life. The life he was now meant to have without Tina.

Craig liked to think that he'd made his peace with all of it. After all, he'd driven this exact same route hundreds of times before. But he'd never driven it with another woman. Fortunately, with each mile that separated him and that white cross, his guilt was slowly replaced with an eagerness to be home. To see his ranch and his family and his future.

By the time he and Caroline stopped for breakfast, Craig's muscles had lost most of their tension. And by the time they passed the sign welcoming them to Thunder Canyon, he was downright chatty. In fact, he felt like he'd been talking nonstop for the past twenty minutes while Caroline seemed to shrink against the passenger seat. His family was huge and overwhelming, and, of course, a city girl and an only child like Caroline—even if she could easily memorize and recite everyone's name—might be feeling out of her element.

He'd called his dad yesterday and spoken with all of his brothers, explaining Caroline's condition and urging them to just go along with the fake engagement. Craig knew better than to appeal directly to his mom and sisters. All of his female relatives would tell him that this was a horrible idea.

As if Craig wasn't already perfectly aware of that, thank you very much.

Still, what if someone in his family slipped and said something? Chances were that there was going to be a slew of people huddled on the front porch when they arrived, eager to meet her and bombard them both with questions. Perhaps he should gently prepare her for the fact that one of his relatives was likely to say something that might trigger her memory.

"So," he started, tapping his fingers against the steering wheel. "Your parents seemed a bit surprised that you were engaged."

Okay, so that wasn't exactly what he'd wanted to bring up. He was still trying to be cautious about not adding any undue stress on her, but he wanted her to understand that his family, too, might have a similar response. They might exhibit the same kind of curiosity to this unexpected engagement of theirs.

"They *did* seem surprised," Caroline replied, but didn't add any theories on why that might be.

"Are you feeling sick?" he asked and she followed his eyes to where her palms rested against her stomach.

She yanked her hands away quickly, then fiddled

with the strap on her seat belt. "I guess I'm just a little nervous."

"It's not too late to turn back," he offered even as he made a right onto the long driveway that would lead to his family's ranch house.

"No," she said, turning in her seat toward him, her brown eyes full of determination. "Don't turn back. I really do want to be here."

She also thought she wanted to marry him. And the longer he let her go on believing that, the more attached she would get. Even *he* was getting a little too comfortable in this alternate universe they'd inadvertently created. The problem was that when she finally remembered that he wasn't the man she thought he was, this carefully constructed bubble of theirs would burst. It was like chewing gum. The bigger the bubble got, the bigger the mess it would make when it finally exploded in his face.

But that didn't stop him from continuing down the gravel road toward his home.

Despite all the vehicles parked in the circular drive, Craig had been wrong about his prediction of everyone waiting on the front porch to greet them. In fact, when they got out of his truck, the only member of their welcoming committee was an old tomcat sunning himself on the front steps and watching their approach with equal parts mild interest and total disdain.

"You really do have a three-legged cat." Caroline shifted the pie box into the crook of her left arm and slowly approached the porch, holding out an open palm to the normally cantankerous feline. He was surprised the old grouch was allowing a stranger to pet him.

Craig reached out to scratch the tabby between the ears but was suitably rejected in favor of Caroline's ministrations. He stood back up, knowing the cat could only ignore him for so long.

"Yep, and he always punishes me like this whenever I've been away from the ranch. Don't you, Tiny Tim?"

The box wobbled against Caroline's hip and she set it down on the wooden step. "Wait, your cat's name is Tiny Tim?"

"Yeah, but he's obviously not very tiny, are you, boy?" The tabby finally purred at Craig before nudging its chin against his leg. "He also doesn't have the same sunny disposition as his namesake."

"His namesake?" she asked and Craig bent down to rub Tim's back when he realized Caroline's hand wasn't moving.

"I know what you're thinking, that it's not very politically correct to name a three-legged cat after the kid from that Scrooge movie. But my sister C.C. was the one who came up with it and since she was only seven at the time and already spoiled rotten, we never really corrected her."

"It's called *A Christmas Carol*," she offered, her eyes wide with disbelief.

"What is?"

"That Scrooge movie you're talking about. It's actually a book by Charles Dickens. I'm named after that story."

The hairs along the nape of his neck stood up and Craig's hand paused in midair above Tim's pointy ears.

Not wanting to acknowledge the coincidence, he replied casually, "That's right. I remember that night. You told me you were named after a Dickens book. But later on, your dad mentioned something about a Miss Havisham."

"No, that was just my dad's way of making a joke about my love for wedding dresses. Wait." She stood up straighter on the step above him. "Of all the things you remember from *that* night, me babbling on about my name is what stands out the most?"

"Not the most." He rose to his full height, unable to resist coming face-to-face with her and meeting her challenge. There was something about being on his own property, in his own element, that made Craig finally feel as if he was on solid footing. "I also remember every single sigh you made as you kissed me to within an inch of my control."

Color flooded Caroline's cheeks, but she didn't back away. Instead, she lifted her hands to the back of his neck and pulled him closer. "Maybe this time I can make you lose all your control."

Her lips had just met his when the unmistakable sound of his grandfather's truck horn blared through the yard.

Chapter Twelve

"You must be the little filly Craig plans on marrying," an older, heavyset gentleman said as he lumbered up the porch steps. Caroline's response was immediately muffled against the shoulder of the newcomer's tobacco-scented sheepskin coat as he swept her into a bear hug.

"Grandpac, you're gonna suffocate my fiancée before anyone else gets to meet her," Craig said from behind her.

"So you're sayin' I'm the first to welcome her to the family?" the man asked as he pumped a triumphant fist in the air, thereby loosening his grip while keeping one beefy arm planted around her shoulders. "So, when's the wedding?"

Caroline opened her mouth to explain they still had time to figure all of that out, but then she flashed back to her earlier vow to not say anything that might mislead his family. She aimed her tight-lipped smile at Craig so he could field this particular question.

"We haven't set a date yet," Craig replied vaguely, just as he'd done that day she'd been released from the hospital. And just like then, he looked at something off in the distance, probably so he wouldn't have to make eye contact with anyone. While Caroline was relieved to see that he seemed uncomfortable with playing fast and loose with the truth, her muscles also relaxed at his nonanswer. She didn't want to be complicit in any blatant lies.

"Well, as soon as it happens, I want to be the first to know." The older Clifton released his hold on Caroline so he could pull his grandson into an equally enthusiastic bear hug.

"The first to know what?" The front screen door slammed behind a woman with silver hair cut into a sleek bob. She was shorter than Caroline and wore a two-piece velvet tracksuit in a bright purple color that clashed with the turkey-printed dish towel cinched around her still-trim waist. There also appeared to be rhinestone letters spelling out something across the seat of her pants, but Caroline couldn't see the word from this angle.

"Happy Thanksgiving, Meemaw." Craig had to push against his grandfather's elbow to slip out of what looked to be a hearty and somewhat territorial embrace. He then gave his grandmother a hug and the smaller—and possibly stronger—woman didn't allow him to pull away either until he gasped, "I want to introduce you to Caroline."

"I already met her." Grandpac's barrel chest puffed out as Meemaw passed by him. "Before anyone else."

"You don't count, you ol' grizzly bear." The woman flicked her wrist at the older man before also pulling Caroline into a tight hug. Caroline's ribs threatened to snap in half. Yep, Meemaw was definitely the stronger of the two grandparents. Craig's grandmother whispered in Caroline's ear, "Just ignore him. I always do."

At least, she'd tried to whisper. Unfortunately, she didn't seem to realize how loud her voice was.

"I heard that," Grandpac called out. "Instead of wasting all that money on a new hearing aid that doesn't work, you should've invested in another one of your fancy cruises for single seniors. In fact, I'll pay for it myself if it means I can send you halfway around the world and get you outta my hair once and for all."

"What hair?" Meemaw rose onto her tiptoes as she knocked the sweat-stained cowboy hat off his forehead, exposing a shiny bald head. Then the older woman winked at Caroline as she sauntered toward the door. "Come on inside, you two. I'm gonna cut into my famous pecan pie so we can have a little dessert before dinner."

"The only thing that pie is famous for is a bad case of constipation," Grandpac muttered before bending down to retrieve his Stetson. But Caroline noticed the way the older man's sparkling blue eyes—the same color as Craig's—remained riveted on Meemaw's backside. When he rose, Grandpac slapped his hat against his thigh and stomped past them in full pursuit. He was barely stepping inside the house when he shouted, "And why in the hell does it say 'DIVA' across your rear end, woman?"

"So those are my grandparents," Craig said, hands planted on his hips as he rocked back on his boot heels.

"I think they're adorable." Caroline smiled.

"Well, everyone else thinks they're insufferable."

"Insufferable relatives are my specialty, remember?" She looped her arm through his and patted his muscular forearm, trying not to think of the way it had felt wrapped around her waist a few moments ago. "Don't worry. This isn't my first rodeo."

When it came time to eat the Thanksgiving meal, there was a brief skirmish between the grandparents as they fought over who got to sit next to Caroline. In the end, Craig's sister Catherine had to ask her husband, Cody, to scoot down a spot to accommodate Meemaw, and Caroline found herself sandwiched right in between the two bickering seniors.

Calista and Jake sat across from them, and poor Dawn, Jonathan's wife and a registered nurse, got stuck on the other side of Grandpac and was forced to endure endless questions about his new blood pressure medication, his elevated cholesterol levels and whether Meemaw's store-bought biscuits contained more saturated fat than Cecelia's crescent rolls.

"Whose biscuits are you calling store-bought, you ol' sourpuss?" Meemaw leaned forward, glaring over her crystal goblet.

"Is that your fifth or your sixth glass of wine, Doris?" he replied.

"You two need to knock it off," Carol Clifton called out from the head of the table. Caroline was relieved someone was trying to smooth the waters between the two feisty elders, because Craig was at the opposite end with Rob and C.C. and Will, pretending to be in a deep discussion about the vaccination schedules for calves. Fakers.

"Not that I would know where she gets her biscuits," Grandpac said under his breath to Caroline. "I wouldn't eat anything that woman put before me."

"Looks to me like you don't really discriminate about where your food comes from." Meemaw reached around Caroline and poked a finger right into Grandpac's generous belly.

"I know you normally have a hard time keeping your paws off me, lady, but you really need to control yourself in front of the kids." Grandpac swatted his napkin at the older woman's hand.

Meemaw's reflexes were too quick, though, and she snatched a corner of the orange linen cloth. Caroline plastered a smile on her face and stood up, using her body to break up their impromptu game of tug-of-war.

"Mr. Clifton, your sweet potato casserole is looking a bit cold. Why don't I go pop that in the microwave for you?"

Jordyn, Will's wife, had already reheated the man's plate when he'd complained that the gravy Meemaw made was coagulating. But when Caroline made the offer, several gasps sounded throughout the dining room and everyone's attention shifted to the chair Caroline had just vacated.

Nick, Cecelia's husband, appeared at her side and whispered, "Go. Save yourself. I'll slip into your seat and try to keep them separated for as long I can. The new in-law always gets Wall Duty at their first family dinner, and so far, you've lasted longer than any of us did our first go-rounds."

Luckily, Craig grabbed the empty bowl of mashed potatoes and followed her into the kitchen. It gave Caroline the opportunity to ask, "What is Wall Duty?"

"It's the person who ends up with the unfortunate task of being a literal barrier between my grandparents so they don't physically attack each other. They've never actually come to blows, so no need to look concerned. Although, it got real close that year when Grandpac allegedly fed Meemaw's secret recipe stuffing to her Yorkshire terrier."

"Allegedly?" Caroline asked, punching in the numbers on the microwave.

"Nobody actually saw him do it, but when Scruffins puked all over my dad's favorite recliner, Grandpac suggested it was proof that Meemaw's cooking wasn't fit for dogs, let alone human consumption." Craig used a wooden spoon to heap more potatoes into the serving dish. "Anyway, sorry you got put in the middle of the two of them. My family does it to all the new members as a sort of initiation, but let me know if it gets to be too much for you."

Something burst inside Caroline's chest as she followed Craig out of the kitchen, feeling about as warm and gooey as the yams and melted marshmallows on the plate she carried back to his grandfather.

She'd gotten Wall Duty. That meant his family had accepted her as one of its newest members.

"So tell me more about this amnesia of yours," Rob said to Caroline when Craig finally sneaked the remote control away from a sleeping Grandpac.

"Rob." Craig's voice issued a warning to his little brother. It was after dinner and several of his siblings had already left to return to Rust Creek Falls, but those were the ones who'd arrived the day before and hadn't already made a five-hour drive this morning. The thought of climbing back into his truck so soon for the return trip brought a throbbing ache to Craig's upper spine.

So far, most of his family had been pretty good about just going along with the flow and not asking Caroline any personal questions. Granted, it had helped to have his grandparents' constant quarreling as a diversion most of the day. But now that it was late in the afternoon and things were quieting down, some of his more daring siblings were getting a bit bolder in their curiosity.

"What do you want to know?" Caroline's smile was pleasant, but they were sitting so close to each other on the sofa, Craig could feel her muscles tense.

"Why don't I put on the football game?" he said, trying to distract everyone from the direction of the conversation. But his fingers were a bit too overeager and he pressed the wrong channel.

Goldie Hawn's face popped up on the screen instead.

"Oh, hey," his sister C.C. said, coming into the living room. "I love this movie."

"I don't think I've ever seen it," Caroline replied, leaning forward to hear whatever the actress was saying to Kurt Russell.

"It's about this rich lady that hires a guy to do some work on her yacht, but doesn't pay him. Then the woman falls overboard, knocking herself out and waking up in the local hospital with amnesia. The worker guy needs someone to watch his kids and clean his house and figures since she still owes him money, he should pretend to be her husband and..." C.C.'s eyes widened as she trailed off, then wrestled the remote out of Craig's grip. "Actually, isn't there a college bowl game on right now?"

But C.C.'s words hung in the air and Caroline apparently was no longer interested in football because Craig could feel her narrowed gaze studying him. Of all the movies that had to be playing, it had to be one about tricking someone who was suffering from amnesia.

Luckily, Meemaw chose that exact moment to walk into the room. "Who wants to play gin rummy?"

"Deal me in," Grandpac said, slapping his hands together. He'd been snoring, but at the sound of his nemesis's challenge to a card game, he suddenly rose from the recliner like a bifocal-wearing phoenix rising from the ashes to reclaim his glory.

"Okay." Meemaw scanned her remaining grandchildren as though she were a general choosing which soldiers to lead into battle. "Craig, you and Rob can be on the old fart's team. I'll take C.C. and Caroline."

"All right." Caroline began to stand up, but both

Craig and Rob grabbed onto an elbow and pulled her back down between them.

"Actually, I was going to take Caroline outside and show her around the ranch." Craig congratulated himself on the quick thinking even though he doubted someone like Caroline, with her impractical heels and her wispy dress, would want to go traipsing around the stables.

"At this hour?" Grandpac argued. "It's too dad-gum dark to see anything out there right now. You can show her around tomorrow."

"But we're going back to Rust Creek Falls tonight," Craig said.

"No, you're not," C.C. replied. For being the youngest of eight kids, his baby sister had no problem bossing everyone else around. "You're too tired and you've been rubbing your neck for the past hour."

"My neck's fine," Craig insisted, trying not to rotate it to stretch out the muscles.

"There's no way you're leaving me and C.C. alone to play cards with the grandparents." Rob leaned behind Caroline to whisper to Craig. Then his brother winked before raising his voice for everyone to hear. "I know senior citizens like you need their sleep, but stop being such an old fuddy-duddy, Craig."

"Fuddy-duddy?" Craig lifted an eyebrow.

"How old are you, Caroline?" Rob asked.

"Robert Clifton, you know better than to ask a lady her age." Meemaw flicked her dish towel against the back of his brother's head and Craig felt a brief moment of satisfaction.

Yet Rob pressed on. "All I'm saying is that if Craig is gonna go around robbing the cradle with a much younger—and much prettier—fiancée, then he should act like he isn't too old and broken down to actually fill a cradle when it comes time."

Meemaw smacked at Rob's head again and C.C. asked, "What do you mean 'fill a cradle'?"

"I believe they're talkin' about baby making," Grandpac volunteered, making the situation worse.

Caroline's cheeks blazed pink, and C.C., who was only a year younger than Craig's supposed fiancée, made gagging sounds. "Ew, gross."

"Making babies is a normal part of life," Meemaw told her youngest granddaughter. "Maybe if you went on one of those singles cruises with me you could find a nice gentleman to make babies with."

"Pish," Grandpac said with a shudder. "C.C., don't you dare go on a cruise with this man-hunting, she-devil grandmother of yours. She'll set you up with one of her wrinkly geriatric boyfriends. The kinda guy who'll buy you a cemetery plot right next to theirs for your wedding gift. Better to be a cradle robber like Craig than a grave robber like your Meemaw."

Craig wanted to draw Caroline to him and tuck her head against his shoulder so he could shield her from this humiliating conversation. And prevent her from hearing the repeated reminder of their age difference. But when he stretched his arm behind her, he realized she was shaking with silent laughter. Craig groaned. "Can everyone just stop talking about cradles and filling them?"

Meemaw pulled a deck of cards out of her purple velvet pocket. "I can as soon as you guys get your butts to the table and we start playing."

Chapter Thirteen

Carol's and Rudy Clifton's faces both jerked up from their newspapers when Caroline and the other five entered the recently cleared dining room.

"Oh, no," Carol muttered, her eyes darting to the playing cards in her mother's hand.

Laughter bubbled inside Caroline's chest as she realized why Craig and Rob had been so quick in their efforts to stop her from agreeing to this game. Apparently, everyone else in the house felt the same way. However, she'd never been a part of a big family game night and surely all the Cliftons were overreacting about the ferociousness of Meemaw and Grandpac's constant competetiveness.

"Guess those Black Friday deals aren't gonna shop themselves." Craig's dad stood up so quickly, his chair fell over backward. "Better head out to the stores now."

"Whoa." C.C. put out both of her palms. "You two have never been Black Friday shopping a day in your lives."

"So then we'll get a jump start on our Cyber Monday deals," Mr. Clifton replied.

Rob rolled his eyes. "It's still Thursday, Dad."

"Back in your seats," Craig commanded his mom and dad before using his thumb to gesture toward Meemaw and Grandpac. "They're *your* parents. If we have to play cards with them, then so do you."

When everyone moved to the opposite side of the table, Caroline decided to take matters into her own hands and suggested that they play with four teams and then orchestrated it so that the grandparents were paired together. Craig gaped at her like she was absolutely insane.

"Trust me," she whispered to him as his dad shuffled the cards. And when Meemaw and Grandpac won the first hand, everyone else relaxed and they were able to sit back and enjoy the game.

At least, it was relaxing until Rob had to leave to go check on the timer for the sprinklers in the south pasture and C.C. had to write a term paper and Mrs. Clifton told Craig that there was no way he was going to be driving back to Rust Creek Falls this late at night.

"I'll be fine." Craig stood, then held out his hand toward Caroline as though she needed his help to rise. Or maybe it was just his way of signaling to her that it was time to go.

"You of all people should know better than to risk it when you're this worn-out." His mom gave him a pointed look and even the grandparents disappeared. Quietly.

A pained expression crossed Craig's face and his jaw hardened to a rigidity Caroline had never seen on him before. Not that she knew him well enough to be an expert on his moods.

What she *did* know, though, was that even with his grandparents' perpetual squabbling—which she was pretty sure was mostly a ruse to gain attention from their grandchildren—she'd never had a better Thanksgiving. His huge family was loyal and hardworking and loving and everything she'd ever wanted to be a part of. However, if Craig was determined to leave, then she would stand by him.

"I can drive if you really want to go home tonight." Caroline placed her arm on his biceps, which was even more rigid than his jaw.

"Out of the question," Craig gritted out.

Caroline got the feeling that his determination didn't have anything to do with her head injury, yet, as an outsider, she wasn't sure what it was. Something wasn't right and she couldn't fix the problem unless she understood the source. And she wouldn't understand the source unless she got Craig to relax and tell her what was wrong.

All that muscle clenching was apparently taking its toll because Craig reached behind his neck and pressed three fingers to the base of his scalp. Since they were standing side by side, he must not have seen Caroline's hand lift up, causing him to give a slight jolt when she began to massage his neck. But at least he didn't move away. Taking that as a good sign, she stepped in front of him, forcing him to look at her.

"Honey," she started, smiling encouragingly at him until she had his undivided attention. "I'm fine with staying the night here."

"Don't you need to work tomorrow?" he asked, a muscle ticking along his upper jaw.

"I have the day off."

"But you didn't pack an overnight bag."

"She can borrow something from C.C.," his mom said from behind Caroline. "I'll go get some stuff now."

"See, I can borrow something from your sister," Caroline repeated, wanting Craig to understand that she was truly fine with staying the night. Rudy followed his wife out of the dining room, leaving Caroline and Craig alone.

Some of the tension eased from Craig's face and he lowered his voice to a whisper to ask Caroline, "But where will you sleep?"

Caroline thought she'd been in control until that point. Heat flooded her body and she licked her lips.

"She can sleep in your room," Meemaw said, coming out of the kitchen with the pink bakery box from Daisy's. "Anyone want more pie?"

Even though they were "engaged" and it was no secret that Craig had been shacking up with Caroline at her tiny rental house, Craig's mom knew the truth and insisted on her oldest son giving Caroline his room and sleeping in Jonathan and Will's old bedroom.

It was really for the best, Craig thought, staring

blankly at the shelf containing Will's 4-H trophies and
Jonathan's science fair award. Caroline fitted in so perfectly with his family and it had been all he could do
to keep his hands off her since that interrupted kiss
on the front porch this morning. But then Rob had
gone and made that joke about robbing the cradle and
Craig's pride—as well as his prior aches and pains—
had flared up, and suddenly, he'd never felt more like
an old man. An old man who was taking advantage of
a much younger, much more naive woman. A woman
who was under the mistaken belief that he planned to
marry her.

The truth was, Craig didn't plan to marry anyone.
He'd had his shot at the perfect partner with Tina, but
all of that had crashed around him. Literally.

Seeing Caroline at his family's ranch only served to
remind him that she was too young, too feminine, too
citified to ever suit this life. Working on a ranch required commitment and strength and hard work and…
and…proper footwear. Did the woman even own a pair
of boots?

Granted, she didn't buckle under the pressure of his
grandparents. However, Caroline was a tiny, dainty
thing with a closet full of high heels and a bathroom
full of beauty products. She had to be miserable being
stuck out on a ranch in the middle of nowhere. Not to
mention meeting his entire family must've been a total
overload for her recovering memory. He was supposed
to be keeping things calm for her so her head injury
could heal, not bringing more chaos into her life.

If she'd had her tiny little European car here, she

probably would've been gunning its four-cylinder engine down the driveway the second Rob had called him a fuddy-duddy. Actually, probably well before then—like when his elderly grandparents practically knocked each other over in their race to get the seat next to Caroline at the dinner table.

Craig scratched his head, wondering if he could actually use his boisterous and pushy family to his advantage. Perhaps the more time she spent here, the sooner Caroline would come to the conclusion that they were worlds apart. That they were never meant to be together.

Although, she *had* been so diplomatic and understanding with his ornery grandparents when she didn't have to be. Then she'd been helpful to his parents in the kitchen when she could've just sat back and been a guest. Caroline had also demonstrated complete ease with his siblings and their spouses, asking them questions about their jobs and their hobbies.

Another thought took root. As an experienced party planner, perhaps Caroline had simply switched into professional mode and spent the day dealing with his family as though it was some sort of pro bono requirement. It was hard to read someone else's thoughts when they didn't even know their own mind. Maybe she'd been miserable the entire time.

Regardless of whether it was all a performance on her part, the fact remained that Craig had invited her here. He was supposed to be acting as her host and he couldn't fall asleep if he kept pacing around his brothers' room all night, worried about her discomfort. Opening the door, he peeked out to see if everyone else had already gone to bed. Pulling off his boots, he hoped his socks muted his footsteps on the old squeaky floorboards as he sneaked down the hallway.

Craig lightly tapped on the door to his own bedroom and when Caroline opened it, he sucked in his breath. Not that she looked breathtakingly sexy with her hair pulled into a high ponytail and dressed in a borrowed pair of pajamas covered with dancing pugs in Santa hats. No, his lungs refused to work because she was giving him that wistful smile again, the one that looked so happy. So comfortable. So confident that he couldn't possibly stay away from her.

Instead of asking her how she was, he stepped over the threshold and placed his hands on either side of her face, leaning down to claim the kiss that had been interrupted this morning when they'd first arrived.

As his lips melded to hers, he felt her arm against his waist before hearing the lock behind him click into place. Craig had been so absorbed in the taste of her, he'd lost all foresight to keep this late-night meeting private. That was the thing about Caroline—she knew things about him and she knew what he wanted, without even asking him.

He finally pulled away, studying her face for any signs of discomfort. Her eyelids were heavy and her lips were full and swollen, a hint of a smile still playing at their corners. His pulse picked up tempo and he had to command his hands to keep her at an arm's distance until he could get his breathing under control.

"Before I went to bed," he started, then made the mistake of glancing over her shoulder and toward the foot of his own queen-size mattress. The hammering in his heart spread to his lower extremities, and he had to shake his head and clear his mind before he could continue what he was saying. "I just wanted to check and make sure you were comfortable in here. Is there anything you need?"

With her face turned up to his and her eyes focused on his mouth, she tugged her lower lip between her teeth, then released it. "Only you."

Craig groaned and pulled her against him. The next kiss was deeper than the first and in that loose pajama shirt, it was easy for his hands to slip underneath the hem.

Just for a second. He would only let his work-calloused palms stroke the intoxicating silkiness of her skin for a second. But it wasn't enough time.

Just another inch. He would only move his thumbs up another inch. But then the rest of his fingers followed suit and he was splaying his hands on either side of her rib cage.

Just hold still. He wouldn't go any further. In fact, now was the time he should stop this maddening kiss, as well. But Caroline dragged her head away first, breaking her lips apart from his long enough to pull the pajama top over her head.

Just make her yours already. It was his last thought before he totally consumed her. His mouth slanted over hers, coaxing her tongue deeper inside so that he could suckle it.

She wasn't wearing a bra and, while he hadn't been able to get a good view of her chest before she'd immediately plastered her body against his, her rounded breasts easily filled his hands and her nipples tightened into tiny buds against his palms.

Caroline's soft little moans increased and he felt her pulling against his belt buckle. Anticipation raced through him as she got the first button of his fly undone. When the backs of her warm fingers dusted the tip of his erection, an electric current shot through him.

Craig was trying to shrug out of his own shirt when a deep, scratchy meow sound stopped him cold. His head whipped up and he saw Tiny Tim using his sole front paw to claw, press and reshape the stacked pillows on his bed. "What's my cat doing in here?"

"Well, this is *his* room, isn't it?" Caroline looked over her shoulder at the overweight tabby, who was now pacing in circles around the comforter and scowling at them. "He looks pretty mad at us for waking him."

"Actually, he looks like that when he's happy, too. But I think you're right about his level of annoyance at this moment. He's not used to having a lot of late-night activity going on in his bedroom." Then Craig winced at his own implication. Only an old fuddy-duddy would admit to going to bed alone every night with his cat.

"Maybe we should move to your brothers' room and let Tiny Tim get his sleep." Caroline's thumbs were still hooked above the fly of his jeans, her breathing still shallow.

It took every last drop of strength he possessed to encircle her wrists and drag her hands away. "Honey, we can't."

"Do you not want to?" she asked, staring at him with

such a deep longing, Craig felt completely exposed. "Or is it that you don't want to right now?"

"I think you just felt how much I want to," he replied before buttoning his jeans back up so that the evidence of his desire wasn't further tempted. "But when I make love to you, I want you to know who I am."

"So you're saying that as soon as I remember, you'll finally make love to me?"

If you still want me to, he thought. But all he said was "Yes."

She sighed and backed away, but there was a promise glinting in her eyes. As he walked back to his brothers' room, he wondered if he'd just made a deal with the devil.

Because if Caroline Ruth finally learned the truth and she still wanted him, Craig would do much more than make love to her.

Chapter Fourteen

"I think I may be in way over my head," Caroline confided to the palomino in the stall before her. She'd already admitted as much a few hours ago to Tiny Tim—who'd ignored Craig's commands to follow him down the hall to a different room last night. The cat clearly regretted his choice in bedmates because after hours of Caroline's tossing and turning and talking out loud about what she should say to her pretend fiancé, Tim began scratching at the door, demanding to be let outside well before dawn.

But at least the cranky tabby had led her to the stables, where there were more pairs of triangle-shaped ears to listen to Caroline's venting. Obviously, she knew the animals couldn't really understand her, but growing up, she'd moved too often to keep a pet and she'd never had a sibling to use as a sounding board. She'd always been able to talk out her problems with her parents, then with her sorority sisters and, more recently, with her boss, Vivienne. But none of them were currently around, so these new four-legged friends—or three-legged in Tiny Tim's case—would have to do.

Caroline stroked the horse's silky blond muzzle as she went on. "I mean, how embarrassing and frustrating that he got me all worked up like that last night. And then he simply walked away, leaving me breathing all funny and wanting more."

The horse snorted in response.

"I know," Caroline continued. "You get it. You've probably had a stallion or two come sniffing around your stall. Maybe nipping you in the neck to get your attention. What I wouldn't have given for a good neck nip last night. Anyway, this might sound totally human of me, but this attraction I'm feeling for him? It's more than just the physical. I'm worried that if I lose him, I'll also lose all of this."

The mare's soulful brown eyes followed Caroline's arm as she gestured toward the rest of the ranch outside. She wanted Craig, but she also wanted the holiday dinners with all of the Cliftons and her own children carrying on their family's legacy. She didn't know it twenty-four hours ago, but his perfectly happy home out in Thunder Canyon, Montana, contained the entire life she'd always envisioned for herself and didn't know existed.

"I was trying to seduce him last night, I'll willingly admit that." At least, Caroline would admit that to a stable full of animals who couldn't reveal her secret.

"But only because I was hoping to make him want me as much as I want him. Instead, all of his damn restraint and chivalry are now only making me fall harder for him."

The horse gave a little whinny, throwing back her nearly white mane and stomping her forelegs, probably in a show of sisterly solidarity.

"You're wearing jeans." Craig's voice surprised her and she caught her toe on the lower rung as she hopped down from the stall. The sun was starting to rise outside and his gaze traveled over her in the dim light, making her shudder in excitement. "And boots."

"Thanks for the warning," she whispered into her new friend's fury neck before turning toward Craig. "C.C. loaned everything to me."

"Everything except for the jacket," he replied, using his chin to gesture at the coat made of faux red leather with faux fur lining.

Caroline pulled it closer around her torso, feeling like a complete faux herself. She wished she had brought suitable attire with her to the ranch so it didn't appear as though she was overplaying the roles of both fiancée *and* cowgirl.

"I saw it on the hook by the back door and assumed it was your sister's, as well."

"Nah, Meemaw just thinks she's of a similar age as you and C.C. and shops accordingly."

Caroline's steps faltered as she thought about the way Craig's body had stiffened beside her last night when his brother Rob had made the joke about him robbing the cradle. She'd never really given his age any thought, but it was interesting that she and his so-called "baby sister" were only a year apart.

Yet, as she approached him, Craig stared at her legs encased in the tight denim as though he wasn't thinking of either his sister or grandmother at that exact second. A jolt of hope surged in Caroline's veins and she asked, "Why are you looking at me like that?"

"I guess I'm not used to seeing you in anything but skirts and dresses and high heels," he replied, rubbing the scar along his neck. "You almost look like you could fit in here."

"Almost?" Seeing the dark circles under his eyes put a little more swagger into her walk. Not that she wanted to see him exhausted, but it was somewhat of a relief to know they were both on a level playing field as far as lust-filled sleep deprivation went.

"I mean, we'd have to get you on a horse to really be sure." He smiled and she wondered if he was hoping to avoid any conversations about how hot and heavy things had gotten between them last night.

Recklessness coursed through her and she rested a hand on a jutted-out hip. "Is that an invitation to ride?"

"You actually want to go for a ride? On a horse?"

"Show me where you keep the saddles."

Caroline followed Craig to the tack room and looked at the rows of reins and bits hanging from the walls. This ranch operation of theirs was definitely bigger than she'd first thought. If she wanted to get to know the man, then she really needed to get to know all aspects of him, including his land. A little thrill of excitement shot through her.

But it sputtered to a halt when he patted a leather horn. "This one should fit you okay."

"It's a Western saddle, though." She pulled her bottom lip between her teeth as she studied her choices. Sure, the one Craig had picked out was smaller than most of the others, but it was still huge. Maybe she'd gotten a little too cocky when she'd suggested going for a ride. "Do you have an English one by any chance?"

"Wait." Craig did a double take in her direction. "You know the difference?"

"My parents were at Oxford when I was eight and then again when I was fourteen. I took equestrian lessons both times."

Craig studied her before finally hefting the smaller saddle onto his shoulder. "Trust me. Since we're not doing any show vaults or playing polo today, you're gonna want the bigger one to distribute your weight."

"And do you have a horse in mind for me to ride?" Caroline asked as she picked up a plaid-patterned saddle blanket and followed him out of the tack room.

"I figured you'd want to take Marley out this morning. Looked like you two were pretty deep in conversation when I walked in."

Despite the low temperatures outside, heat filled Caroline's cheeks. *Lord, please tell me Craig was too far away to hear what I was saying to the mare.*

But the only answer was his boots crunching along the straw-covered concrete. With his arm lifted high to balance his load, the hem of his work jacket rose above the waistband of his worn jeans, exposing his well-muscled rear end.

That's it, she thought, racing across the stable floor to catch up with him. From now on, Caroline would have to always stay one step ahead of him. She was supposed to be the seducer, not the seducee. There was no way she was going to let this man and his perfectly shaped cowboy butt ride in front of her.

Craig tried not to watch the way Caroline's hips rocked in the saddle as she cantered along the trail in front of him. However, after a sleepless night with nothing but some unfulfilled fantasies to keep him company, he couldn't think of anything but his attraction to her.

Well, his attraction to her *and* her age. Rob's cradle-robbing comment from yesterday had been fleeting and made in jest, but Craig's doubt about their age difference still lingered.

Caroline was young and adventurous and had her whole life in front of her. And she was full of surprises. Every time Craig found out something new about her, he was taken aback. He shouldn't have been shocked since she'd grown up traveling all over the world and had experienced things most people could only dream about.

He was beginning to think that there was nothing she couldn't do. Last night, he'd learned that she could easily count cards and would hold on to a winning hand before folding so that his competitive grandparents didn't get so huffy at losing. And now, this morning, he was still in a state of wonder at how well she rode a horse.

But looking the part was easy. Real ranch work was tough, and if Craig were to ever change his mind and get married, it would have to be to someone mature, someone who could step up to that kind of responsibility.

"I don't think I've ever seen a more perfect sunrise," Caroline called over her shoulder as they approached the trailhead. A pinkish glow outlined the mountains off in the distance and when he turned to look in that direction, he was immediately reminded of the exact shade of her dusky nipples last night as he'd cupped her breasts in his hands.

Groaning, Craig shoved his Stetson lower on his forehead and asked, "Are you ready to head back now?"

"Back to the ranch? Sure." Caroline clicked her tongue at the mare, then pulled the reins around until Marley was nose to nose with his own mount. "Back to Rust Creek Falls? Not quite yet."

"You mean you want to stay here?" Craig felt the creases on his forehead push against his hat brim.

"I would love that." Her smile was bold and confident. "If I didn't have Josselyn and Drew's wedding to plan or that Presents for Patriots party we're hosting next week, I'd be all for staying right here with you."

"That's because it's the slow season now." Craig squeezed his knees against his stallion's sides to get moving. "Give it a day or two during calving season when we're busy from sunup to sundown rotating the herds, reseeding our grazing pastures, maintaining the equipment and then spending the entire night on birthing watch. You'll think the chores will never end."

"I don't mind hard work." Caroline shrugged.

"Well, working hard at planning parties and working hard at wrangling cattle during a muddy spring are two different things."

"Says who?" she asked, and he recognized that squared-off shape to her shoulders. "I've never worked on a ranch and I'm guessing that you've never pulled off a successful outdoor wedding for four hundred guests in the middle of a thunderstorm. Therefore, neither one of us would be qualified to make those kinds of comparisons about whose job is more difficult. But if you know someone who has done both, then I'd be glad to hear the results of their findings."

"Fair enough," Craig replied. "There's no way I could do what you do for a living."

"Is that why you were so quick to beat a hasty retreat every time you dropped me off at my office this week?"

"Pretty much." He nodded. "Discussing flower arrangements and table seatings and poofy white dresses surely has to be one of the most headache-inducing tasks on this earth. Just thinking about dealing with all those brides and their talk of having a perfect day makes me squirm."

"Says the man who works with bulls and artificial insemination," she replied.

"Exactly. I *still* wouldn't trade any of my duties on the ranch for any of the mind-boggling demands and events you have to wrestle with every day. Except for maybe cake tasting. I could probably handle that responsibility."

Caroline laughed. "I bet you could handle any responsibility where you're in charge."

"Are you calling me bossy?"

"I'm just saying that you really like to look out for other people."

Craig grunted, unsure whether that was supposed to be a compliment or not, then clicked his tongue at his stallion to move along. "Come on, Jake."

"Jake?" Caroline said, drawing on her own reins to slow down. "You've got to be kidding me."

"What's wrong?" he asked, appraising her startled expression for any sign of injury.

"Let me get this straight. Are we currently riding horses named after Ebenezer Scrooge's business partner—Jacob Marley?"

"Technically my horse's name is Jake, not Jacob. And C.C. named your horse after that book about the dog." Still, Craig couldn't deny the coincidences of so many references to *A Christmas Carol*. But he merely faked a casual shrug and urged his horse forward.

They trotted along silently for a few minutes and then she eased her mount closer to his as the trail narrowed. She really was accommodating nicely to this different style of saddle and it made Craig wonder if she could actually accommodate other parts of his life.

No. He shouldn't even be letting his mind wander in that direction.

"Did you always want to be a wedding planner?" he asked. Not that he would ever want a woman to give up her career to better facilitate his own. But it wouldn't hurt to confirm that there was no chance she was actually willing to relocate to Thunder Canyon and become a cattle hand. The confirmation would be another red flag to add to his list of warnings on why he shouldn't let their relationship go any further.

"No way." Caroline chuckled. "I didn't know a thing about the industry until Vivienne Shuster hired me."

"So then how did you end up in Rust Creek Falls?"

"I'll tell you if you promise not to laugh at me." Her face was solemn as she held up her palm, as if she was expecting him to repeat an oath. Craig humored her by crossing his finger over his heart. "It's a long story, so I won't go into the boring details, but when I was fifteen, my mom was doing a lecture series at the University of Montana about the history of overlooked female buffalo hunters. Anyway, I fell in love with the area and the campus, breaking my parents' hearts because they'd hoped I'd choose to attend an Ivy League school."

"Why would I laugh at that?" Craig sat up a little straighter as he surveyed the land. "I definitely can't blame you for loving Montana."

"That's not the odd part. So I visited Rust Creek Falls a couple of years ago before I graduated college. And I... Well, let's just say I had a premonition."

"A premonition?"

"You promised. No laughing." She narrowed her gaze at him until he forced the smirk from his face. Then she continued, "I have a degree in biology. Trust me, I understand science and reason and, therefore, realize exactly how crazy this must all sound. But the truth is, I've always known I had a destiny."

"And planning weddings in Rust Creek Falls is your destiny?" Craig was trying to make sense of it without appearing to sound doubtful.

"Ever since I was a little girl, I've dreamt of getting married. Not like in a creepy Miss-Havisham-pining-for-a-bridegroom sort of way, but just in an excited, purpose-driven way."

"A purpose-driven way?" he repeated. Like she'd been so determined to get married, her brain seized on the first potential groom it could find and then completely fabricated him as the lucky guy? But before he could go down that road, she continued on.

"When I was debating where to move after graduation, I saw an online ad for an assistant wedding planner and it just seemed logical that if I wanted to eventually get married, I should work around like-minded people."

"Like-minded people?"

"Why do you keep repeating everything I say?" she asked and he shrugged. He had no idea why he was having such difficulty wrapping his brain around her words. "Anyway, I saw the job opening as a way to reach my destiny."

"So your destiny is to get married? That's it?"

"Well, to get married to the right man, obviously."

"And how are you supposed to know if you find the right man?"

"I already have." Caroline smiled and Craig's stomach dropped.

"But *how*?"

"Like I said, I can't really explain it. I've always been of the mind-set that I'll know when I know. And finally, I know."

Craig hadn't noticed that his horse was completely standing still as he stared at Caroline. Surely she wasn't saying that she thought *he* was her destiny or that they were meant to be together in some mystical way. He'd promised not to laugh, but he couldn't prevent the sarcasm lacing his voice. "Sounds very scientific."

"Science can explain a lot of things, but it can't always explain emotions. Some intuitions are so powerful, they just feel right. Okay, let me try and break it down another way. Have you ever felt so connected to someone or something that you just knew it was part of your future?"

"This ranch," Craig admitted. "I always knew I was going to work the land and carry on my family's legacy."

He didn't admit that he'd originally planned to do so with Tina.

"So just out of curiosity," she asked as she tilted her head, "if ranching is such grueling work, why do you do it?"

"Because I couldn't imagine doing anything else."

"What about the rodeo?" she asked.

"Life is full of detours, I guess."

"Exactly. Some people might refer to those detours as fate. As though there's a driving force that brings you right to where you belong."

"If by *driving force* you mean a busted collarbone, then yeah, that's what brought me home."

"So that's how you got your scar?" She reached out toward him, but the horses kept them too far apart.

He touched the warm, jagged line along his neck. "Not exactly."

The silence hung between them, but as the wooden outbuildings appeared in the distance she asked, "Then was it another detour?"

Chapter Fifteen

"When I was twenty-one, I was coming home from
my engagement party of sorts in Kalispell," Craig
began. He continued talking but he'd used his boot
heels to urge Jake forward, so he was no longer making eye contact with her as he spoke, and all Caroline
could focus on were the three words he'd said. *My engagement party.*

He'd been engaged before. She gave her reins more
slack and Marley took the few steps to catch up when
she heard him say something about a crash.

"What kind of crash?" she asked, her pulse pounding. "What happened?"

"Tina didn't get to see her cousins very often, so
she wanted to go out to a bar with them after the party.
I was exhausted and needed to be back in Thunder

Canyon early the next morning to meet with the veterinarian about one of our prize heifers. Tina wasn't a drinker and told me that she was fine to drive home while I slept in the passenger seat."

Tina.

Caroline's heart was clawing for more information, needing to know more about the woman Craig had been in love with, but she pressed her lips into a tight line, letting him tell his story uninterrupted.

"The highway patrol officer who did the investigation said she probably didn't even see the stalled logging trailer when she took the turnoff too quickly."

Caroline's hand flew to her mouth. Oh, no. Craig's strange reaction to his parents' not wanting him to drive last night when he was tired suddenly made more sense. It was then that she recalled his tension during the first half of the drive here yesterday and she blurted out, "The cross!"

"What?" Craig's head pivoted toward her as though he'd just remembered she was still beside him, still listening.

"We passed a white wooden cross when we were on Highway 90," Caroline offered.

"That's where her Jeep went off the embankment. She'd swerved, but the left fender still swiped the back of the trailer. The initial collision woke me up, but by then we were already skidding off the road. It was her daddy's old ranch vehicle and the windshield was one of those fold-down types. The hinges had gotten rusty, so when we rolled, the impact caused the whole thing to go in the opposite direction toward us. I don't remember landing, but when I came to, the top corner of the windshield frame had me pinned against the roll bar."

By this time, the horses were standing still again, as though Jake and Marley were in equal stages of grief and couldn't move. Anguish covered Craig's face and Caroline wanted to climb down off the mare and drag him into her embrace. She wanted to hold him, to comfort him. "How long were you stuck like that?"

"The responding officer said it was only five minutes. The driver of the stalled rig had seen us go off the road and called 9-1-1."

"And Tina?" Caroline asked, already knowing the answer.

"We should've driven a safer vehicle, but I'd just sold my truck because we were saving money to build our own house on the property line between our parents' places. The Jeep was built well before anyone had even heard of airbags. Hell, it was so old, we only had lap belts. So there was no way to prevent the steering wheel from breaking her ribs and puncturing her lung."

Caroline bit down hard to force back the gasp rising in her throat, then looked up toward the sky to keep the tears from trickling out of the corners of her eyes.

"I couldn't get to her." Craig's voice was flat when he spoke again. Flat and so defeated. It made the tears Caroline had been holding back spill over. "I fought against the broken windshield but the struggle drove it in deeper. The only part of her I could reach was her hand. I was holding it when she took her last breath and all I could think was that it should have been me driving. I was supposed to protect her. She was looking at me, smiling at me, before she died. But I couldn't save her."

"I can't imagine how painful that must have been for you, Craig. I'm so sorry."

His only acknowledgment of her condolences was a brief nod. "We'd grown up together and had always planned to eventually join our families' cattle operations. But being here at the ranch was a constant reminder of that dream dying alongside her on the highway. I stayed long enough for her funeral, but left for Billings the next day. I had a friend doing the PBR circuit and, at the time, it seemed like traveling from town to town while simultaneously punishing my body in the arena would be the easiest escape."

"But then you came back." Caroline understood why he'd left, yet she also understood why he couldn't stay away. Not only was this land beautiful, but it also filled a person with a sense of peace. A sense of belonging.

"Yep. A few broken bones and one career-ending surgery later, I came home. I had nowhere else. She was gone, but I could still make the ranch live on."

"You must have really loved her," Caroline whispered. He possibly loved her still.

Craig was gazing at something in the horizon, seemingly lost in his own world, when he said, "Tina was the perfect woman for me."

"I think Tina would've loved her," Will said as he drove the all-terrain vehicle along the perimeter of his property the following day.

Craig kept his hat low and his face averted, studying his brother's fence line for any loose posts or fallen wires. "Loved who?"

"Caroline. You know? The woman you're engaged to?"

Clenching his back molars together as Will swerved to avoid a rut in the narrow dirt trail, Craig tried to remember why he'd agreed to come to Will's ranch today and help him do some minor repairs before the breeding season started. Oh, because he'd poured his heart out to Caroline yesterday morning in Thunder Canyon and then she'd barely said a word to him the entire drive home last night.

Her home, that was. Not *his* home. Craig didn't really know what to call the little rental house here in Rust Creek Falls. Although, he'd packed a second duffel bag and brought it with him as if he'd planned to move into the place with her.

It had been late when they'd finally pulled into her driveway, and while he'd been relieved that she didn't invite him to sleep in her bed with her again, Craig had spent the remainder of the night on the sofa wondering if he'd done something to hurt her feelings.

When an emergency call came in this morning from a bride demanding Caroline drive to some dress shop in Kalispell, Craig grabbed his keys off the hook by the kitchen. But Caroline insisted that she could drive herself and then proceeded to tell him in painful detail what it would be like when an elderly, no-nonsense seamstress told a very vain and very stubborn bride that she would need to lay off all the bridal shower cake and mimosas if she wanted to fit into her dress on her wedding day.

So instead of subjecting himself to that particular brand of misery—which was only slightly worse than worrying about Caroline driving herself—Craig had accepted Will's request for help on his ranch. Too bad they couldn't have taken a good old-fashioned work truck out to the fields instead of this four-wheel-drive Raptor.

"We're not engaged," Craig ground out as his stiff neck rocked side to side against the five-point harness. "Remember, I already told all of you about her head injury and the confabulation and how she thinks I'm her fiancé."

"So then why don't you just explain it to her like you did to all of us? She seems like a smart woman to me." Will looked in his review mirror, probably to make sure one of the shovels hadn't bounced out after that last bump.

"She's incredibly smart. But it doesn't have anything to do with intelligence. Drew said that it's her *brain* tricking her, not me. So no matter what I tell her, she's going to listen to her brain."

"Then what happens when her brain stops tricking her?"

"What do you mean?" Craig snatched his hat off his head because he was tired of adjusting it every time his skull banged into the headrest.

"Well, eventually, she's going to get her memory back. What are you going to do then?"

"I've been trying to figure that out. Jeez, Will, have you ever thought of getting a bulldozer out here and doing a little grading? Perhaps smoothing out a real road?"

"What's there to figure out?" Will asked. "From what I can tell, she's perfect for you. That's why I said that Tina would've loved her."

"Caroline? But she and Tina are nothing alike."

"Apparently, both of them wanted to marry you, which means they were born with the same misguided taste in guys." Before Craig could bark out a retort, Will purposely swerved the ATV to hit a bump in the road, making Craig's butt completely lift off the seat.

"If you keep driving like a maniac, I'm gonna walk back to the stable."

"Speaking of stables, I heard you took Caroline for a ride when you were at Thunder Canyon. Rob said she looked pretty good in the saddle."

"Rob needs to find a woman with her own saddle," Craig muttered.

"Jealous much?" his brother asked, then chuckled.

Craig only growled.

"My point," Will continued and Craig pinched the bridge of his nose since there was apparently no end to this conversation in sight, "is that Caroline seemed pretty comfortable on a horse. Hell, she seemed pretty comfortable in general out there on the ranch. I know that's what you're looking for in a wife."

"I'm not looking for a wife."

"She's also diplomatic and intuitive and has a good head on her shoulders," Will went on as though he hadn't heard Craig's objection. "Plus, I heard you've been eating all of your meals at her house, so I assume she's a decent cook."

"The best." Craig groaned, thinking of the Nutella-filled crepes she'd whipped up that morning. "But don't tell Meemaw."

"Pish," Will scoffed, then took his foot off the accelerator as they came to the end of the fence line. "As if I want her to think I'm taking Grandpac's side about anything right before she goes Christmas shopping."

A series of beeps chimed and Craig immediately reached for his cell phone, his chest filling with worry that something had happened to Caroline. But it wasn't his phone that had rung.

"That's probably Jordyn," Will said, idling the engine and pulling out his cell phone to read his wife's text. "Like everyone else in town, she's curious about what I've found out about you and Caroline."

Craig rolled his eyes.

"Nooooot muuuuuch." Will sounded out the words as he typed a response.

The phone pinged again.

"Jordyn thinks we might have better luck getting you to talk if you have a couple of beers in you."

"Well, you two would have firsthand experience at how alcohol can lower a person's inhibitions," Craig pointed out.

"I'm going to tell Jordyn that you're teasing us about the night we met." Will began typing and Craig tried to grab the phone from his brother when it vibrated again. "She's suggesting we go out tonight and celebrate your engagement."

"You mean my fake engagement?" Craig asked.

"Who cares if it's real or fake? At least you *got* an engagement, unlike me and Jordyn, who accidentally drank some of Homer Gilmore's spiked punch one night and woke up married."

Craig snorted. At least he hadn't gotten himself into a similar predicament. Although, things seemed to have worked out pretty well for Will and Jordyn.

"I'll tell her we should be done with the south pasture around four," his brother said. "We can hit the Ace in the Hole after that."

"Sorry, man," Craig said, not the least bit sorry. "Caroline has a meeting with the food and beverage director over at the Maverick Manor late this afternoon. So we'll have to take a pass on the celebration that's really an inquisition."

"No problem." Will tapped at his screen for several seconds, then looked up and smiled. "The Maverick Manor has that fancy bar inside the massive lobby. I just told Jordyn we can all head over there after Caroline's meeting."

Craig had texted her about the last-minute get-together with Will and Jordyn. However, Caroline certainly hadn't been expecting an impromptu engagement party of sorts until Jonathan and Dawn showed up, followed by two of the Clifton sisters with their spouses, along with several of the Stricklands.

When she finally realized what was going on, Caroline wanted to come clean then and there about her restored memory. It was one thing to let people be under a mistaken impression. It was quite another to celebrate it.

Unfortunately, before she could say anything, Ben Strickland raised his glass in a toast. Craig shot death looks at his childhood friend, but didn't correct the well-wishers or turn down any of their hearty congratulations.

Her original question, the one she'd pondered the night of that first intense kiss, returned with a cold force.

Why was Craig going along with this?

Now that she knew about Tina and how he'd tried to save her, Caroline could somewhat understand his desire to redeem himself by taking care of Caroline after her concussion. She could even understand how he might indulge an injured woman by allowing her to go on believing whatever she wanted. However, the thing she absolutely couldn't figure out was why Craig wasn't telling his closest friends and family the truth.

Why was he silently drinking to their toasts instead?

There must be a reason why he hadn't already put a stop to all of this—especially if Craig was still in love with another woman.

The only person who could help solve that riddle was Josselyn Weaver. She'd been there when Caroline had hit her head and then again when Caroline had woken up and thought Craig was her fiancé. But Josselyn wasn't here now, and Drew, who'd also been at the hospital part of the time, was never alone long enough for her to ask any meaningful questions.

Questions such as *What's in it for Craig?* and *How far is he willing to go to keep up this pretense?*

The champagne bubbled inside Caroline's tummy and it felt as if corks were popping inside her head. She needed to go somewhere quiet and think this through before people actually began expecting invitations to their wedding.

"Excuse me," she whispered to Craig, who had just clinked beer bottles with his brother Jonathan. "I need to use the ladies' room."

The tight line of his mouth softened with concern and he put the backs of his fingers to her forehead. "Are you feeling okay? Maybe you shouldn't be drinking so soon after your concussion. I told them you probably weren't up for a big night out like this."

"Did you know that everyone was going to be here?" she asked. "That it was going to be like…this?" She'd caught herself from referring to it as an engagement party, because the idea might fill her with too much hope.

"I had a feeling, but I also knew that when my family and friends get an idea in their heads, they're not going to be deterred. It was either this or risk having everyone show up at your office to offer us their congratulations." His arm was draped around her waist as he leaned down to speak in her ear. Suddenly the champagne bubbles weren't the only thing tingling inside her. "But I can take you home if it's too much."

"No, it's fine," she replied, taking another sip before setting down her glass on the polished mahogany bar inside the old log mansion. "I'll be right back."

A few minutes and two enthusiastic congratulatory hugs later, Caroline stared at her reflection in the mirror over the bathroom sink, telling herself it was too risky to keep this pretense up.

She couldn't very well seduce a man who was probably still in love with someone else. Although, during their quiet drive home last night, she'd wondered more than once if he was staying at her house because he genuinely cared for her.

Touching her lips, Caroline remembered the kiss they'd shared in his childhood bedroom. She might be young and inexperienced, but even she knew that wasn't the type of kiss a man gave a woman if he was only feeling protective. The bottom line was that she'd fallen in love with Craig and her underlying instinct that he was the one for her wasn't likely to go away. However, she needed to know that Craig was with her because he actually loved her, not because he was trying to save her.

Unfortunately, she didn't quite know how to do that without telling Craig that her memory had returned. And if she admitted as much, would he consider his hero duties fulfilled and leave her?

A toilet flushed and Caroline quickly turned on the faucet to pretend she was there to wash her hands and not to give herself a strategic pep talk.

"Just the woman I wanted to see," Cecelia Clifton Pritchett said as she came out of a stall. "You're coming to the Presents for Patriots dinner dance next week, right?"

"Oh, um, yes. Our company is actually sponsoring the event and planning it out at Sawmill Station."

"Good. That means Craig will finally be going to a social function. My big brother needs to get out more. I haven't seen him this happy in a long time."

"Really? Because I was just thinking he seemed pretty uncomfortable out there with everyone congratulating us on the *engagement*." Caroline emphasized the last word to gauge Craig's sister's reaction.

With the exception of his grandparents, nobody had mentioned their relationship status at Thanksgiving, let alone questioned it. Surely his family must be wondering what was actually going on.

"Nah." Cecelia dried her hands on a paper towel. "He just hates being the center of attention. And, because he carries the world on his shoulders, he probably thinks he should be feeling guilty."

"Guilty?" Caroline's fingers shot up to the V-shaped collar on her dress and toyed with the ruffled edges. "Why would he feel guilty?"

"For finally moving on and allowing himself to open up to someone a second time."

Cecelia stood beside her, applying lipstick while Caroline sucked in her cheeks, fighting the impulse to ask for some sort of proof that Craig really was in fact ready to fall in love again.

Chapter Sixteen

Yesterday, when Will had railroaded him into the party at the Maverick Manor, Craig had known he should level with all of his family and friends. But then the toasts had started and Caroline, who hadn't spoken to him much during their drive home from Thunder Canyon on Friday, had gotten all flushed and became even more subdued before rushing off to the bathroom. He'd been worried that the impromptu celebration was too much for her—especially on the heels of meeting all of his family at Thanksgiving—and he'd just wanted to get her home and comfortable and away from all the pretending.

Other than the accident investigators, Craig had never really spoken to anyone else about the night Tina had died, and maybe he'd been a little too open with

Caroline during their ride. But she'd been talking about all that destiny stuff and people knowing where they belong and he needed to make her see that his entire life was the ranch.

That was *his* destiny.

Tina had understood more than anyone else what sacrifices it would take for that lifestyle. But she was gone and Craig would be better off alone than forcing a young and vibrant woman like Caroline into a world that wasn't for her.

It would be one thing if she had her memory back and was able to make rational decisions based on full disclosure. However, he worried that she was just acting upon some childish fantasy of getting married and, as much as he desired her physically, there was no way Craig could be with any woman under false pretenses.

"Let's go get a tree today," Caroline had said that morning, taking a tray of homemade cinnamon rolls out of the oven. "It's going to be a crazy week at work for me and I don't know when I'll have another chance since I've got weddings and parties booked every weekend this month. Besides, Christmas is my absolute favorite holiday and I can't wait to decorate."

Apparently, neither could the rest of Rust Creek Falls, Craig thought grudgingly a couple of hours later when they arrived at the tree lot adjacent to the Masonic Lodge downtown. The town was already getting into the Christmas spirit with lights and garlands going up on Main Street and notices announcing collection locations for Presents for Patriots, as well as the upcoming holiday pageants at the local schools.

"Where are we going to put it?" Craig scratched the back of his neck as he studied the eight-foot-tall Douglas fir.

"If we move one of the bookshelves over to the left, we can put it in front of the living room window."

The word *we* was getting passed around in this conversation an awful lot. But Caroline's eyes were bright and the tip of her nose was turning pink as the first flurries of snowfall dusted the green branches around them. Her enthusiasm for the holidays was contagious, and since the moment she'd opened her eyes in that hospital emergency room, Craig really hadn't been able to deny her anything.

The Freemasons had partnered with the varsity football team to sell Christmas trees as a fund-raiser, and Craig tipped the defensive tackle who'd carried the freshly trimmed bundle to his truck for them.

"Thank you, sir," the teenager said before turning to Caroline, who, in her knit beanie and oversize red plaid scarf, appeared young enough to be the kid's homecoming date. "I'm also supposed to tell all the customers that if you're looking for homemade ornaments or decorations, they're having a craft fair right now inside the high school gym."

Caroline slapped her mitten-covered hands together and gave an excited bounce before turning those pleading, doe-shaped eyes at Craig. And that was how he ended up spending the rest of his Sunday afternoon picking out glass balls covered in glitter, rolling his eyes in camaraderie with the other men hiding out at the hot chocolate stand and tipping his hat at the ladies from the quilting club who offered to sell him a hand-sewn tote bag for all the purchases he was carrying as he walked behind his pretend fiancée.

Not wanting to be a complete Scrooge and begrudge her the excitement and wonder of the season, Craig followed along and whipped out his wallet to pay for her decorations. In fact, if was being honest with himself, he was kind of getting a kick out of her enthusiasm as she practically skipped along, gushing at the displays at each booth.

Later that night, as a cinnamon-scented candle filled the air, they were hanging their new ornaments on the tree that barely fitted inside her tiny house. Caroline reached into one of the paper bags and pulled out matching red velvet stockings with each of their names stitched along the tops.

Craig gulped and all the pleasure from his earlier indulgences faded away, leaving nothing but a guilty taste in his mouth. "When did you get those?"

"I saw them when you were at the caramel corn stand, getting us those popcorn balls. The Embroidery Club was selling them and offered free customizing while we shopped."

"Don't you think we're a little too old for stockings?" he asked. And where would she even hang the things? It wasn't like she had an actual fireplace in this dollhouse of hers.

"Says the man who ate an entire roll of cherry Life Savers on the drive home." She winked at him. "Didn't you have a stocking growing up?"

"Yeah, but as I got older, my parents put me in charge

of filling them for the younger ones. Same thing with hiding the Easter eggs."

"Well, I figured we could start our own family traditions." Her last two words hit him with a force, and panic clawed at the back of his throat.

Or maybe it was guilt. After all, if it wasn't for him going along with all of this imagined-fiancé business, she wouldn't be under the misguided impression that they had any family traditions to start.

Either way, he could feel a line of perspiration dampen his hairline as he studied their embroidered names. The only thing more permanent would've been a tattoo. Or a scar.

He swiped at the prickling skin along his neck.

How could he convince Caroline that she shouldn't allow herself to get too attached to him? That she shouldn't believe this fanciful notion of hers that he was the man for her. If he had permission from Dr. Robinson, he would gladly steer her in that direction right this second.

But since he couldn't risk stressing her out by saying what he wanted, Craig said the first thing he could think of. "There comes a certain point in everyone's life when they need to grow up and stop believing in Santa Claus."

Last night, Caroline had tried to pretend Craig's words hadn't hurt, pasting on her smile that she used when dealing with an overpriced vendor or a client's negative mother-in-law. They'd gotten the Christmas decorations up—minus the stockings, which she'd discreetly slipped back in the bag—and then she'd made creamy tomato basil soup and grilled cheese sandwiches for dinner because that wasn't quite as juvenile as chicken nuggets and tater tots, which were the only things she had in her freezer.

Despite going to bed early to escape the awkward tension, she'd been awake until midnight, tossing and turning and rethinking what he'd said about her believing in childish things. Thank goodness he didn't know about the psychic or he'd really think Caroline was naive and impressionable.

If she and Craig were meant to be together, then Caroline needed to prove to him once and for all how much of a woman she was.

Sitting at the conference table in her office that morning, Caroline stared absently at her blank notepad, trying to figure out how to do that. Cecelia had implied that Craig was willing to move on, so maybe it wouldn't be such a bad thing for Caroline to seduce him after all.

She tapped her pencil against her chin. The problem with that was she didn't know how to go about it. Especially since her past attempts at physical intimacy with Craig had been rather unsuccessful and only left her wanting more.

"I go away for two weeks and come back to find my favorite employee engaged."

At the sound of the familiar voice, Caroline looked up to see Vivienne entering the office.

Smiling widely and looking sun-kissed and refreshed

from her honeymoon in Fiji, she gushed, "I can't wait to hear all about it."

"Yeah, it kinda happened fast," Caroline said, then let out a deep breath and slouched against the chair's brightly upholstered fabric. "The engagement, that is. It took on a life of its own, if that makes any sense."

"You have no idea how much sense that makes to me." Vivienne gave a little chuckle. "Did I ever tell you how Cole made up an entire fiancée in order to have me plan his pretend wedding?"

"But Cole loves you," Caroline said, referring to Vivienne's new husband.

"He barely knew me when he came up with the plan."

"What plan?" Josselyn Weaver asked as she came into the office for her rescheduled consultation. Ever since their first meeting had ended in a hospital stay, Caroline had the feeling her client had been purposely avoiding her. Fortunately, the woman still had a wedding to plan, which meant Caroline could finally get some answers.

"We were just talking about my engagement." Caroline studied her for any signs of conspiracy. Josselyn gave a discreet cough and looked away, practically inviting the next question. "Did you know I wasn't engaged to Craig when I woke up in that hospital?"

Josselyn gasped before narrowing her eyes. "Wait. Did *you* know you weren't engaged to him?"

"Not at the time I didn't." Caroline sighed in frustration, sinking lower in her seat. "I really believed he was my fiancé when I first saw him."

"But now you know..." Josselyn made a circular

motion with her wrist, encouraging Caroline to fill in the blanks. "What exactly do you know?"

Caroline went on to tell the two women about everything, from Winona Cobbs to her late-night research on confabulation to how her memory had come back as soon as Craig kissed her.

"So you guys kissed?" Josselyn asked, settling down into one of the chairs at the conference table. "How was that?"

"Wonderful and confusing and then wonderful again when I met his family."

"Oh, boy, you already met his family?" Vivienne asked, joining them at the table.

"Yes. I went there for Thanksgiving. And then some of them and his friends had this impromptu engagement party for us at the Maverick Manor the other night and everyone was congratulating us, and I sat there, knowing the truth yet saying nothing."

"Well," Josselyn started, "if it's any consolation, Craig also knew you weren't really engaged."

"Exactly. Craig knew it and, for the life of me, I can't figure out why he would go along with a pretend engagement." Caroline placed her elbow on the table and braced her forehead in her hand. "Who else knows it isn't real?"

"Well, Drew and I knew since we were there at the hospital when you came to and made the surprising announcement. Sorry for not speaking up sooner about that, by the way. The doctor didn't want us saying anything that could give you any more anxiety. Plus, Drew promised me that you were in good hands with Craig."

"But what does his family think of your relationship?" Vivienne asked.

"I'm not sure what they think." Caroline looked over to Josselyn, who only smirked.

"So, I wasn't able to attend the party at the Maverick Manor, but I heard that his siblings nominated Cecelia to be the one to tell you that they approved of the engagement."

Her tummy flipped in excitement. Having the rest of the Clifton family's approval boosted her confidence. But just to be sure her feelings weren't completely one-sided, she asked, "You guys don't think all of this is totally nuts?"

"From what I understand, there have been crazier courtships in Rust Creek Falls," Vivienne offered. "If you want him, I say go after him."

"I definitely want him, but only if he wants me in return. What happens, though, when he realizes that I remember everything? Will he be relieved that he can finally walk away?" Caroline rested her head against the back of the chair and studied the ceiling. "How do I come clean and still keep my cowboy?"

"I don't know Craig as well as the rest of the Stricklands do." Josselyn leaned forward and wiggled her eyebrows. "But I've seen the way that man looks at you."

Hope blossomed in Caroline's chest and she sat up straighter. "How does he look at me?"

"Like he's in no hurry to walk away."

She sincerely hoped that Josselyn was right. But just to be sure, Caroline decided to take matters into her own hands.

Chapter Seventeen

"Your drink matches your outfit," Craig said over the strains of the band's rendition of Mariah Carey's "All I Want for Christmas."

"Huh?" Caroline's nerve endings were pulsating along with the tempo of the festive music.

He nodded at her rum-laced eggnog in a miniature Mason jar and repeated himself.

Caroline had carefully chosen an ivory cashmere sweater and paired it with a matching fitted skirt that flared into a short ruffle of chiffon above the knee. Despite the snow outside, she'd kept her legs bare and her feet festive in a pair of glittery gold pumps. "Well, that's a party planner's job. To work from behind the scenes and blend in with the surroundings."

"As if you could ever blend in anywhere," Craig said,

his unconcealed stare turning her pulsing nerves into a throbbing ache under her skin.

It was the night of the Presents for Patriots fund-raiser and they hadn't driven to the party together because, technically, Caroline was working. At least she had been the first half of the evening. But the caterers and the band and even the bartenders had worked previous events at Sawmill Station and didn't need much direction. So, after dinner and the silent auction, the only thing left for her to do was dance.

Of course, the sexy cowboy standing in front of her didn't seem all that eager to pull her onto the dance floor despite the fact that his warm hands kept sliding lower along her back each time he'd come over to check on how she was feeling.

In fact, judging by the way his palm was now resting along the upper curve of her bottom and threatening to dip lower, Caroline got the impression that he was much more eager to get her alone.

And truthfully, Caroline didn't want to wait any longer to make Craig hers.

They'd been living together for almost two weeks now and there was no way she was going to let him sleep on her sofa one more night. Maybe it was the intoxicating fragrance of all the swags of pine branches and mistletoe running along the white linen-covered farm tables. Or maybe it was the warm glow from the white twinkling lights hanging from the rustic wooden beams of the old freight house. Perhaps it was the spiced eggnog concoction warming her veins. More than likely, it was a combination of all three making her grow bolder and more confident by the minute.

It was either now or never.

"Are you ready to go home?" she asked, turning toward him and laying her hand on the lapel of his dark sport coat. "I want to give you your Christmas present early."

She saw the muscles of his neck contract as he tipped back his head and swallowed down the rest of his beer. Setting his empty bottle on the nearest table, his voice was low and rushed when he said, "Let's go."

Vivienne—who was standing with her husband beside the vintage red sleigh loaded with gifts donated for the Presents for Patriots charity—gave Caroline a thumbs-up as Craig guided her toward the exit.

The ten-minute ride back to her house was the same one he drove every day. But now it seemed as though it only took seconds before they were pulling into Caroline's driveway.

Maybe he knew what she had planned and he was just as eager for it. Snow was falling as they walked to her front door, yet her skin was on fire and anticipation raced through her. The sight of her spare key attached to his key ring gave her another jolt of confidence that Craig wasn't in a hurry to go anywhere. At least, not yet.

"Wait here," she said, pointing toward the sofa because it would've been too mortifying to suggest he wait on her bed. And trickier to explain without giving the surprise away. And she had a feeling that she was going to need the element of surprise.

Caroline went into her bathroom and carefully removed her sweater and skirt, then reached in the vanity to find the matching lace bra-and-pantie set she'd hidden there for this exact moment.

Her cheeks turned the same crimson shade as the lingerie and Caroline was glad she'd been smart enough not to wear such a sexy thing under her clothes earlier. She would've been entirely distracted throughout the party, constantly aware of what she had on underneath and thinking about who would see it later.

She was dying to splash some cold water on her face, but didn't want to ruin her carefully applied makeup. Instead, she settled for a gulp of water out of the faucet, then stared at her reflection wondering if there was anything she'd forgotten when she'd come up with this plan. *Don't think of it as a plan*, she told herself. *Try to act natural.*

Unfortunately, the longer she stood in this bathroom, the more she would second-guess herself. Steeling herself, she listened to that initial instinct—the one that had never steered her wrong before—and walked out into the living room.

Caroline heard Craig's sharp intake of breath, saw the heat fill his eyes, and it was all she could do not to smile in triumph. She was sure he could see her heart thumping behind her rib cage.

"I have to tell you something," Craig blurted out. His voice held a slight tremble and Caroline guessed that he was just as nervous as she. Another ounce of courage filled her and she straightened her back, causing her breasts to thrust forward.

"Don't you want to unwrap your gift first?" she asked.

His only response was his Adam's apple bobbing up and down. Normally, when he was uncomfortable or trying to avoid a question, he focused on some distant point while he spoke to her. Right now, though, his eyes were drilling into her, and Caroline's confidence soared.

He'd already discarded both his heavier outer coat and his sport coat and was now only wearing a white dress shirt. She walked toward him and slid her hands up his chest until her fingers landed on the first button-hole. "Or can I unwrap mine first?" she asked him as she opened his buttons.

"I'm not who you think I am," he said in a rush, and Caroline didn't quite feel like herself, either. Boldness had overcome her, and right now, if she allowed him to distract her with all his chivalrous excuses of why they couldn't be intimate, she would surely lose more than her memory. She might lose her mind.

Putting a finger up to his mouth to gently shush him, Caroline ended up tracing his lower lip. "But you're ex-actly who I want."

"How do you *know*, though? Your head—"

She cut off his words with a kiss. Caroline was tired of explaining that her concussion was perfectly healed. Her only option now was to show him. And she did so with her mouth, her hands, her entire body, distracting him from any argument about why they shouldn't fi-nally consummate their relationship.

There was a slight resistance when she tugged on his hand, trying to lead him toward her bedroom, and she could see all the conflicted emotions pass across his face. Cupping his cheek, she whispered, "Craig, trust me, I know what you want to tell me. But there isn't a single thing you can say that would stop me from wanting you. Unless it's that you don't want me."

"Nothing could be further from the truth," he replied, his voice deep and loaded with desire.

"Then prove it."

Craig groaned as he lifted her into his arms and carried her the rest of the way to the bed. His mouth claimed hers and as he set her down, she slipped her hands into his undone shirt and yanked it free just as his body followed hers onto the comforter.

There was more kissing, more touching, more moaning as her bra came loose and her panties slid from her hips. Caroline was pushing his jeans past the rounded muscles of his rear end when his body stilled.

"I need to go get some protection," he murmured against her temple, then began to push off her, but she wrapped her legs around his waist and pulled him back.

"Don't leave," Caroline said, thinking she would die of humiliation if he came to his senses and rejected her now.

"Honey, I'm just going to the living room to get them out of my duffel bag."

Pleasure engulfed her as she realized that he must have known in the back of his mind that they would eventually make love. He'd prepared just as she had.

"That's okay," she replied, leaning toward her bedside drawer to retrieve the package she'd brought home from work. "I was too embarrassed to go to the drugstore in town, so I found these in one of the favor bags we had left over from a bachelorette party last summer."

When he rolled the condom on, Caroline knew with a certainty that this was the man for her. This was her destiny. He entered her slowly and Caroline gasped as the hard tip filled her.

"Are you okay?" he asked and she could hear the tension in his tone, as it must've taken him an extreme amount of willpower to hold himself back.

"I've never been better," she sighed. "Please don't stop now."

"I never can tell you no," Craig said, then thrust deep inside her, only to freeze when she winced in pain. "You...you're a..."

"I'm yours," Caroline said, using her calves to wind around him and draw him in closer.

She'd been a virgin, Craig thought, trailing his fingers along her spine as she curved her body next to his afterward. There was no turning back now. Caroline had unwittingly given him a precious gift and all he'd given her in return was false hope.

Unless...

What would happen if Caroline never regained her memory and went on believing they were engaged? Could Craig actually go through with their marriage? The past couple of weeks, he hadn't faked his attraction for her or even how much he cared about her. In fact, the more he'd gotten to know her, the more he could see that she was well educated and determined to live her life the way she wanted.

And apparently, she wanted him.

Caroline sighed and hooked her left leg over his thigh. His own arm under her shoulders instinctively pulled her closer, as though he could never get enough of her. And deep down, he knew that would be the case. How could he possibly let her go now?

If she really wanted that life to be on the ranch in Thunder Canyon, there was no way he would be able to tell her no. Besides, Craig was tired of being the voice of reason.

The truth of the matter was that the night she'd pulled out those matching Christmas stockings, he'd been terrified at first. But as he'd battled sleep all night on her sofa, he'd come to the conclusion that he could no longer imagine his life without Caroline in it. All he could hope was that, if she remembered nothing else, she knew that he'd always tried to do the right thing.

Her left hand was absently caressing his chest and Craig knew that if she continued, he would want her on her back again. Or on top of him this time. As great as their first time had felt, he didn't want to make her sore—or at least sorer than he'd probably already made her. Using his palm, he cupped her hand in his, slowing her motion.

After a couple of seconds, he found himself stroking her left ring finger, the one that had remained bare throughout all of this supposed engagement. Craig froze at the realization, wondering how both of them had overlooked something so obvious.

"Are you okay?" Caroline propped her chin up on her right hand. Her brown hair was thoroughly disheveled and hanging in messy waves around her face and she had never looked more adorable or more loved.

Oh, God. He'd fallen in love with her.

The realization should have made him go cold and sink into the bed with fear of the unexpected. Instead, Craig basked in the warmth of Caroline's heated body as a feeling of weightlessness and euphoria settled into a cocoon around him.

"Actually," he said, unable to stop the smile that played on his lips as he began tracing her ring finger again, "I was just thinking we should go to a jeweler to pick something out soon."

Caroline gasped before scrambling up to her knees, not bothering to take the bedsheet with her as she beamed a smile at him. "You mean an engagement ring?"

"Of course," Craig said, then chuckled as she rained kisses down over his face.

"I—" she kissed his cheek "—love—" she kissed his forehead "—you—" she kissed his chin "—so—" she kissed his other cheek "—much." She kissed his lips. Then she held her face over his and he saw the depth of her happiness reflected in her eyes. "I was hoping that you'd propose by Christmas."

Hearing her say that she loved him gave Craig the strength to take over the world. Or at least to flip her over and take his time covering her with kisses.

But then he heard her last sentence.

"Propose?" He braced his hands against her shoulders, holding her in place and preventing her from distracting him anymore with her full, sensuous lips. "But we're already engaged."

"Not officially, though."

"What do you mean 'not officially'?"

"Craig." Caroline opened and closed her mouth several times. "Look, I know you were a good sport to go along with all those things I said after I bumped my head. I can't imagine how crazy you must've thought I was. But we can stop all the pretending now, can't we?"

"Hold on." Something clawed at his throat and it took several attempts to swallow the shock down. "You got your memory back?"

Chapter Eighteen

"Technically, I've always had my memory." Caroline's smile was less dreamy this time and a bit more sheepish, and the hair on the back of Craig's neck stood at attention. "I just also had one additional memory that wasn't quite real."

"When did you realize we weren't engaged?" He had a million questions he wanted to ask, but that sensation that had clawed at his neck earlier was now throbbing near his ears and he wasn't sure he wanted to hear the answers.

Caroline sat up much less playfully than she had earlier and slowly tucked the bedsheet under her arms. "The first night you kissed me. I knew there was no way I could've forgotten something like that. Everything came flooding back."

"You mean, you knew for almost two weeks and never told me the truth?"

"I thought…" Her voice trailed off and two little creases appeared above her nose.

"No. Don't give me that confused, hopeless, please-rescue-me face," Craig said and could see by her recoil that his words had hit their mark. He stood up and snatched his jeans off the floor before continuing, "I'm the one who should be confused. I'm the one who looks like the hopeless fool. I'm the one who got played."

He heard her indrawn breath before he'd scooped up his abandoned dress shirt, shoving his arms through the sleeves as he stomped out of the bedroom. In the living room, he fumbled with his boots, anger blinding him and frustration making his motions erratic. He needed to get out of this house. He needed to get away from Caroline, away from all the deception.

It felt good to slam the front door behind him, until he realized that he'd forgotten his keys in the pocket of his winter coat. The coat he'd left inside, along with his hat and his dignity.

But there was no way he'd go back inside to retrieve his belongings. At least not now. He stared at his truck covered with at least two inches of snow, shivering when he realized the crew cab doors were locked and he couldn't climb inside for warmth. All he had on was jeans, a thin dress shirt and boots, minus the socks. He wasn't sure where those had ended up earlier in the evening when he'd been in a blinded hurry to shed his clothes and feel Caroline's skin pressed against his.

Crunching the fresh powdery snow under his heels,

Craig strode toward the street, refusing to think about the cold or about Caroline's warm naked body. His heartbeat pounded in time to each angry step he took. He should call someone for a ride, but he'd been so stupid in his rage, he'd also forgotten his phone and his wallet.

Had he ever been this upset before?

With no destination in mind, he thought about continuing down to the boardinghouse to get a room for the night, but Melba and Gene Strickland were pretty old-fashioned when it came to relationships and the types of people they allowed to stay at their place. They likely preferred a guest who didn't show up and disturb them in the middle of the night after a reckless bout of lovemaking with a woman who'd been pretending to be his fiancée.

Instead, Craig made a left at the corner and found himself walking down Rust Creek Falls's picture-perfect Main Street. As a kid, he'd remembered a pay phone in front of Crawford's General Store, but when he arrived, he saw that it was long gone. Just like his youth. Just like his common sense.

Caroline probably didn't even know what a pay phone was, Craig thought as he kicked through the layer of snow on the sidewalk. He should've known better than to fall under the young woman's spell. His life had been exactly the way he'd wanted it before he walked into that wedding planner's office. Before he'd rushed to save a pretty stranger from knocking herself out. Before it was *his* world that got knocked off its axis.

The twinkling Christmas lights along Main Street

mocked him, each blink reminding Craig of the holiday he didn't know he'd been looking forward to. The holiday he'd been starting to think of as his and Caroline's.

They were going to do the Candlelight Walk together and he'd envisioned the two of them wrapping presents side by side at the community center next week for Presents for Patriots. He'd even planned to take her home to Thunder Canyon and hang their matching stockings over the family's huge fireplace on Christmas Eve. The stockings he'd made fun of.

The life he'd thought he no longer wanted.

Originally, he'd wanted a partner for the ranch. A helpmate. Now, though, all he wanted was her.

His brain told him that there could be no love if there wasn't trust. Yet, at the same time, his heart told him that there could be no love if he wasn't with Caroline.

Craig's steps slowed and, as his anger cooled, so did the rest of his body. Shoving his hands into his front pockets, he arched his back, bracing against the cold wind pummeling him from behind.

"Craig!"

He whipped around to see Caroline rushing toward him, balancing a bundle in front of her as she navigated the icy sidewalk in faded jeans and cowboy boots. Bright turquoise ones and, judging by the worn leather, not exactly new. So she *did* own a pair after all.

He tried to tell himself that it didn't mean anything. It didn't mean that she belonged on his ranch or in his world. But then he saw what she was carrying and his breath left his body, his ribs squeezing against his lungs.

"When I noticed that you didn't take your truck, I

was worried about you being outside in this weather without your coat." Caroline handed him the folded sheepskin coat with his Stetson hat on top, then, without saying another word, she turned around and walked back toward Cedar Street. She didn't apologize or make excuses or try to convince him to come back to her house to talk things out.

Was she really just going to let him go?

Craig slammed the hat onto his head and began walking after her, tempted to ask about his truck keys. As he was shrugging on his jacket, something fell to the ground. He reached down and came back up with a wool scarf. This wasn't his. When had he ever worn a scarf?

Yet the sight of the red plaid pattern stopped him in his tracks. Her scarf.

She'd chased after him. On foot and in the middle of the night with snow barreling down on her, Caroline had trekked along the frozen sidewalks just to bring him a damn scarf. She'd given him her trust. She'd given him her virginity. She'd given him her love.

And he didn't even have the decency to say thank you.

Now it was his turn to chase after her.

"Caroline, wait," Craig called out as he quickly caught up with her at the corner. She didn't turn around, but at least she stopped. "Thank you for bringing my coat."

He saw the back of her head nod and his stomach clenched. She took another step and Craig suddenly didn't want her to leave.

"How did you know where I would go?" he asked,

burying his hands in his fur-lined pockets and rocking back on his heels. His bare feet slipped inside his boots and he cursed himself for forgetting his socks.

Caroline turned around and, in the dim glow of the old-fashioned streetlamp, he could see the dark sadness in her usually bright eyes. "I followed the footprints. Apparently, you're the only fool running around downtown Rust Creek Falls in the middle of a snowstorm."

"I definitely feel like a fool," Craig admitted.

"And you don't think I felt like a fool, too?" Caroline's face tilted up and he could see that the normally happy and composed wedding planner was also willing to fight some battles.

Originally, Caroline was only going to make sure Craig wasn't wandering the streets of Rust Creek Falls without a coat, his stubbornness exposing him to the bone-chilling elements. She'd anticipated him being annoyed that she hadn't told him about her memory returning earlier and she didn't blame him for that. However, she wasn't the only person who'd done some misleading in this relationship. In fact, if anyone had been played the fool, it had been her.

"*I* was the one who looked like an idiot when I fell off a stupid chair in front of a stranger and hit my head on the ground," Caroline started, the stiffness in her spine having nothing to do with the snowfall or the chill in the air.

"Just for the record," he said, shrugging as if the weather wasn't bothering him at all, "you hit your head on the bookshelf. I caught you before you actually hit the ground."

"Like that makes it any less embarrassing?" Caroline rolled her eyes before continuing. "*I* was the one who woke up in the hospital thinking I was engaged to that same stranger. *I* was the one who insisted you were my fiancé to the doctor, to Josselyn, to everyone who came into my office later that week, despite the fact that I knew all of you were keeping a secret from me. My mother, a national icon for women's rights who doesn't believe in marriage? Yeah, *I* told her we were engaged, while you stood there looking all sexy and shirtless in my kitchen. *I* gushed about our relationship that *you* knew was completely fabricated."

"You thought I looked sexy when I was shirtless?" Craig dipped his chin, lowering his voice.

But Caroline would not be swayed by her body's traitorous reaction to him when she still had things to say. "Yes, I got my memory back that night you first kissed me and didn't tell you. It was selfish of me to keep quiet this past week. But I did it because I fell in love with you and wanted to keep you."

"You wanted to keep me?"

"Of course I did. Craig, I wanted you from that moment you carried the donut box into my office. I never would have believed that we were supposed to be together or said any of those things if I didn't already know in my heart that I meant it. I meant every word I ever said. My feelings for you were never a lie. So, now, tell me your excuse."

"My excuse?"

"Why didn't you tell me the truth from the beginning?"

"Because the doctors told us not to upset you. They said you would eventually remember things at your own pace."

"But you *stayed* at my house. You willingly jeopardized my reputation."

"Dr. Robinson said they couldn't release you from the hospital unless someone could watch out for you. And you were the one insisting I stay with you when Josselyn invited you to recuperate at Sunshine Farm."

"But Dr. Robinson didn't say you had to take me to Thanksgiving dinner with your family." Caroline put her hands on her hips. "Dr. Robinson didn't say you had to go along with that engagement party at the Maverick Manor."

"Fine. Dr. Robinson didn't say that I had to like being around you either, but guess what? I did. I liked the way you were always positive and happy and made these wonderful home-cooked meals without any vegetables. I liked that you were patient with my bickering grandparents and that you were kind to my grouchy cat and that you slipped a roll of cherry Life Savers into my shirt pocket every afternoon when I picked you up from work. I liked that you knew so many random things about so many subjects and could count cards to come up with the best hand, but were still humble enough to fold and let Meemaw and Grandpac win the game."

Caroline shivered, not from the cold, but from his words. Craig unfolded the red plaid scarf, which was still in his hands, and coiled it around her neck, using the ends to pull her closer to him. "I liked being your fiancé because I like you."

"Just 'like'?" she prompted, walking her fingers up the lapels of his coat as she arched one eyebrow.

"Maybe a little more." Craig groaned when she pulled her hands away from his shoulders. "Okay, a whole lot more. But it took me a full two weeks to fall in love with you. How did you know so soon that I was the one? Would any cowboy who had walked into your office that day have been the man you wanted?"

Caroline's heart fluttered at his words that he'd fallen in love with her. "Have you ever heard of Winona Cobbs?"

"The old psychic?"

Caroline nodded. "Well, she predicted I'd be engaged by Christmas and then she gave me a few clues as to who it would be. The second you walked into my office, I was sure it had to be you. It was my last thought before I hit my head."

"I'll admit, there was something about you in the beginning that made me want to take care of you. I don't know if I agree with all that premonition and destiny stuff, but it's hard to deny that I was in the right place at the right time."

"Or maybe *I* was in the right place at the right time?" Caroline offered. "Maybe *you* were the one who needed rescuing?"

"Only time will tell." Craig smiled, cupping her cheek.

"Then why don't we start over from the beginning and take things slowly?" Caroline stuck out her hand

and said, "Hi. My name is Caroline Ruth. It's nice to meet you."

"Hi, Caroline. I'm Craig Clifton and I am completely in love with you." He pulled her hand up to his lips and giddiness bubbled in the back of Caroline's throat. "That should be all the time we need."

As his mouth landed on hers, all either one of them could think was...

Engaged by Christmas.

Epilogue

On Christmas Eve, Craig shifted in his metal folding chair beside Caroline as they watched the elementary school's performance of *A Christmas Carol* at the community center in Thunder Canyon.

"What'd Bob Cratchit say?" Meemaw whispered loudly down their row. She'd had to lean across Grandpac to ask Caroline since Craig's grandfather had been the first to arrive this evening and had used name-badge stickers to save seats for the entire family.

"Dammit, woman," Grandpac whispered back. "Get your hearing aid fixed. And you can't just move your chair and sit wherever you want. You're blocking the aisle."

"Well, seeing as how you conveniently saved my seat on the opposite end of the auditorium, I didn't really have a choice."

"I should've saved a seat for you in the dang parking lot," his grandfather muttered loud enough to draw the attention of the fifth-grade usher.

Craig rolled his eyes, hoping his grandparents didn't completely ruin the surprise he had planned for Caroline. Or worse, get them kicked out of Caroline's favorite holiday play.

"Cratchit is basically telling his wife that it's Christmas and she needs to set a good example for the children by toasting his horrible boss, Mr. Scrooge," Dr. Ruth whispered as he turned around from the row in front of them. Caroline's dad, who'd flown in with Caroline's mom from India late last night, held up the bright screen of his electronic tablet. "I have both the book, as well as the adapted script for the play, loaded on my iPad if you want to follow along."

"Did you know that Charles Dickens never even gave Mrs. Cratchit a first name in the original version?" Dr. Rodriguez put her arm along the back of Caroline's father's seat as she spoke to the entire row behind her. "Because women apparently didn't deserve any sort of notability or recognition in Victorian England."

While Craig had been excited to meet Caroline's parents for the first time, he was also now questioning his own parents' offer to extend an invitation for everyone to come to Thunder Canyon for the holidays. He shifted in his seat again, wishing he had brought Caroline here tonight alone.

"If you ask me, Mrs. Cratchit should tell ol' Bob to shove his brownnosing toast to Scrooge up his—"

"Shhh, Meemaw." Craig pointed to something going on offstage. "The important part is coming up."

The boy who was playing the role of Tiny Tim limped off the stage, trying to hold on to a wrapped gift box that was meowing as the rest of the audience murmured and giggled.

Dr. Ruth held his tablet closer to his face. "I don't remember this happening in the original."

Craig caught the young actor's eye and was about to lift his arm behind Caroline's back to point her out. But Grandpac beat him to it. "She's right here, kiddo. Next to me."

When the little boy set the squirming box on Caroline's lap, he announced in a proud voice, "A Merry Christmas to us all. God bless us everyone!"

The crowd hushed as they swiveled to watch Caroline remove the lid to her gift. Tiny Tim, the feline version, was inside, squatting on his two good hind legs and proudly meowing his normally grouchy head off.

Caroline giggled and lifted the cat out and Rob spoke up from behind Craig's shoulder, "I can't believe you put your poor cat in a box, Craig."

"It was my idea," C.C. said from where she was now standing next to the young actor in the aisle. "And look, Tiny Tim is loving being the center of attention."

The animal was in fact now purring in Caroline's arms, his tail slowly swishing back and forth as if he was ready for his encore. Craig's father hovered behind them, his video camera zooming in.

"Sit down, dear." His mother pushed his father's arm. "I can't see."

"I'm in the middle of something here," Craig reminded everyone and Caroline gasped when she saw him drop to his knee.

"Caroline Ruth," he started, and Dr. Rodriguez gave a not-so-discreet cough. "I mean, Caroline Rodriguez Ruth, would you do me the honor of becoming my wife?"

Tiny Tim let out another meow as Craig untied the ribbon attached to his collar and pulled the diamond ring free. "As well as my spoiled cat's adopted mom?"

A tear trickled out of Caroline's eye as she eagerly bobbed her head up and down while Craig slid the ring onto her finger. When he pulled her and Tiny Tim into his arms, the entire community center erupted in applause.

Two months later, Craig was knee-deep in overseeing the cattle breeding season, while Caroline was busy establishing the Thunder Canyon location for her and Vivienne's newest wedding planning office.

But both of them always made time to meet with the architect and builder they'd hired to create their dream home on the Clifton family ranch. There would be a small guest cottage for when Caroline's parents came to town—or for when Grandpac needed a space to cool off after having a big fight with Meemaw during holiday dinners—and there would be plenty of bookshelves for their memories and pillows for Tiny Tim.

Caroline and Craig still hadn't set a wedding date, but now that they'd been engaged by Christmas, fulfilling their destiny was no longer as important as the rest of their journey.

* * * * *

COMING SOON!

MILLS & BOON

Coming next month

BEST MAN FOR THE WEDDING PLANNER
Donna Alward

They were just making their way to the lobby when Holly gave a squeal and picked up her pace.

'Dan!'

Adele was adjusting her purse strap, but when she finally looked up, her heart froze and her feet stopped moving. Holly skipped forward and hugged the man standing in a tan wool coat with one hand on the handle of his suitcase and a garment bag over his other arm.

Dan. Just saying his name in her head made her heart squeeze a little. Daniel Brimicombe. Of all the Dans in Toronto, he had to be the best man. It was too far-fetched to be even comical, but here he was, in the flesh, smiling widely for the bride. The man Adele had once planned to marry. The one who'd whispered plans in her ear in the dark.

The man whose heart she'd broken…and in the breaking of it, broken her own.

Best Man Dan.

Adele Hawthorne, wedding planner extraordinaire, solver of problems and manager of crises, stood rooted to the spot with her mouth dropped open and her hands hanging uselessly at her sides. This was one wrinkle that she hadn't seen coming.

Adele tried to unscramble the mess that was her brain. Dan hadn't noticed her yet, thankfully. She was still trying to recover, and it was difficult because he hadn't changed at all. Oh, sure, there was a slight maturity in his face but really…it was like it had been eight days rather than eight years since they'd seen each other. Dark, perfect hair, just a little stubble on his chin, and the way his coat fit on his shoulders…as if it had been specifically tailored for his build.

He'd always carried himself with that calm confidence. She'd envied it back then. Still did.

And then he adjusted his garment bag, turned around, and saw her.

His face paled. 'Delly?'

Her throat tightened. Damn. He'd used his old nickname for her, and that made it a hundred times worse. She wasn't Delly. Not anymore.

'You know Adele? Oh my God, that is so weird!' Holly seemed totally unaware of the shock rippling between Adele and Dan.

Dan recovered first, and the color came back in his cheeks as he smiled. The smile didn't quite reach his eyes. 'We knew each other in university. I haven't seen her in eight years.'

Eight years, seven months, and a couple of weeks, if they were going to be exact about it.

'Hi, Dan. It's good to see you.' It wasn't a lie. It was a huge mess, but it was good to see him.

Continue reading
MARRYING A MILLIONAIRE
Donna Alward

Available next month
www.millsandboon.co.uk